THE BLUE HOUR

ALSO BY JULIE TETEL ANDRESEN

And Heaven Too

Lord Laxton's Will

MacLaurin's Lady

My Lord Roland

Simon's Lady

Sweet Sarah Ross

Sweet Seduction

Sweet Sensations

Sweet Surrender

Sweet Suspicions

Tangled Dreams

The Temporary Bride

The Viking's Bride

AVAILABLE FROM MADEIRA BOOKS

Swept Away

THE BLUE HOUR

A NOVEL BY

JULIE TETEL ANDRESEN

MADEIRA
· BOOKS ·

A DIVISION OF WINDOWS ON HISTORY PRESS, INC.

Published by
MADEIRA BOOKS
604 Brookwood Drive
Durham, NC 27707
madeirabooks.com
theauthorsstudio.org

Book design and production by Running Feet Books,
    Morrisville, North Carolina.
Illustration montages by David Terry.

ISBN 0-9654499-1-2

Please come visit us at madeirabooks.com.
Madeira Books is a member
of The Authors Studio,
theauthorsstudio.org.

LC NUMBER 98-86468

10 9 8 7 6 5 4 3 2 1
First Edition

ACKNOWLEDGMENTS

I THANK THE many people who contributed to the writing of this book: Damaris Rowland for having encouraged me to tell this story; Nancy Hewitt and Melissa Malouf for having given me their expert advice in the early stages; Fred Kull of Glaxo Wellcome for helping me work through the details of the cancer diagnostic product I named Test Early, Feel Safe; Joanna Radwanska for serving as my Polish American informant in Chicago; Pat Saling of the Duke University Medical Center for offering me a richly informative day in her lab; Joe Subbiondo for kindly supplying me with information about the Art Institute of Chicago; Charm Amarasinghe, Joyce Andresen, Edna Andrews, Pille Bunnell, Robyn Carr, Trish Hagood, Lisa Crapo Hochrein, Lauri Langham, Renee Kennedy, Kristine Mahood, Marie Moulin, Alice Oglesby, Sarah Sheffield, Carol Sherman, Marianna Torgovnick, and Maria Tsiapera for reading complete drafts of various incarnations of the novel; and Nalini Milne for giving the story its final shape. Finally, I thank Marcel Tetel for his continuous moral support.

Too many sources have gone into the writing of this book to mention them all, so I will single out only one: *Henri Gervex 1852–1929*, published on the occasion of retrospective shows of his work in Bordeaux (1992), Paris (1993), and Nice (1993). In particular, I was inspired by the article by Hollis Clayson titled "A corset (horror!):

surrogate deviance in Henri Gervex' *Rolla*." The painting *Rolla* (1878), which hangs in Bordeaux, was perhaps the most scandalous painting of its time. To this day it is the highest-selling postcard in France in any museum outside of Paris.

THE BLUE HOUR

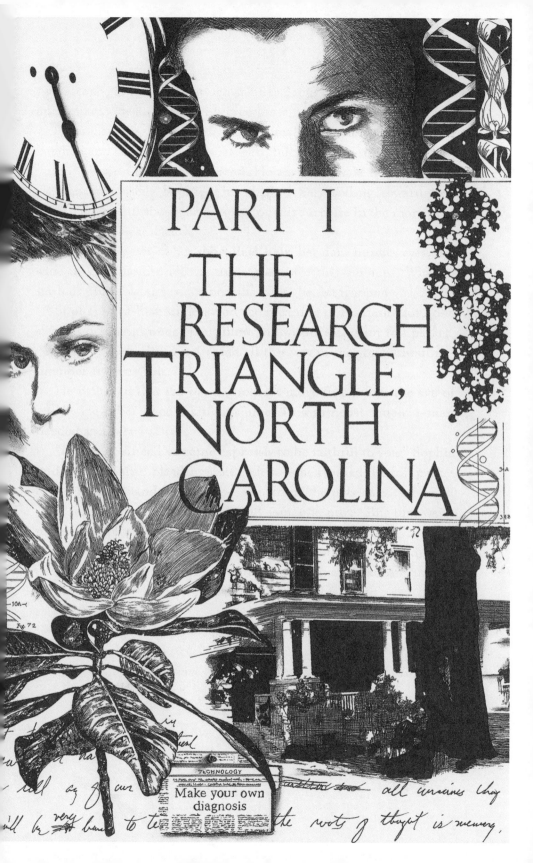

PART I

THE
RESEARCH
TRIANGLE,
NORTH
CAROLINA

ONE

DR. LAWRENCE ROSENBERG strode into his microbiology lab, letting the swinging door shudder behind him. He looked at his team of bench scientists and postdocs and clapped his hands for attention.

"All right, listen up! Our meeting is set for nine o'clock tomorrow morning. We have to be sharp and look sharp. Sandifer, you'll need to wear a tie other than that Daffy Duck piece of crap you wore at the last division party. McCarthy and Wu, your appearances will improve just by getting some sleep. No all-nighters in the lab tonight. And don't forget to shower and shave." At signs of indignant protest from these two lab rats, he held up a hand. "I'm leaving nothing to chance here." Turning to address the fourth member of his team, he continued, "Now, A.K., I know I can depend on you to—"

He broke off, then gestured toward the woman still bent over a microscope. "Is she with us today?"

Jack Sandifer, her lab partner, replied, "More or less."

Scotty McCarthy thought it was less rather than more. Hao Wu agreed with Scotty, citing as evidence the fact that she had been humming more than usual.

Dr. Larry nodded. In a normal tone of voice, he tried again, "A.K. Come in, A.K." When that got no response, he said louder, "Alexandra," then resorted to singing out in a rich baritone, "Oh, Miss Kaminski, would you please join us?"

At that the blond head came up to reveal what might be a very pretty young woman, although it was hard to tell at the moment since she resembled what Glinda the Good Witch would have looked like if she had gotten caught in Dorothy's tornado.

"We're discussing the nine o'clock meeting tomorrow at Seine-Lafitte," Dr. Larry informed her, "and just out of curiosity, I'm wondering whether you'll be able to get your hair to look somewhat normal before then."

Alexandra smiled sleepily, as if she had just woken up. "No problem. This happens all the time."

Dr. Larry looked skeptical. "Although your hairdo is the least of my concerns, we are meeting the top brass of a French pharmaceutical company, you know. I don't think they're expecting Parisian style from us, but I don't want to scare them either."

Alexandra laughed. "That bad, huh? But it's a good sign, really."

"Another vision?" Scotty asked.

She shook her head. "This must be a hallucination."

"I thought your visions *were* hallucinations," Hao said.

"No, all my visions are real. This is the first time I've had a hallucination."

Jack was a practical man. "Then how do you know it is one?"

Alexandra put her eye back to the microscope and was surprised all over again to see her minuscule world of acids and bases misbehave. For the past ten months she had been working with repeating sequences of DNA that elongated and slid under her microscope, but today something new was happening, and she was seeing thymine and guanine elongate and slide into a pallet of shimmering TTGGGGs spreading across a canvas.

She lifted her head and said, "Because I seem to be seeing telomerase in my yeast culture. *Telomerase.*" She blinked to restore proper vision and wondered how she could witness uninhibited cell division brought about by an enzyme that wasn't even there.

4

Jack, Scotty, and Hao concurred: hallucination. Telomerase wasn't in the DNA sequencing experiments on acids and bases they were running this week.

Before talk veered too far off into those experiments, Dr. Larry intervened. "Now that we've properly categorized A.K.'s perceptual eccentricities, let's run through our presentation for the meeting tomorrow. Then you can all get back to finding the cure for cancer—without any enzyme funny business. How about it, huh? Now, here's the deal . . ."

Alexandra rolled her stool away from her lab station, stood up, and stripped off her gloves. Shrugging off the effects of her hallucination, she patted her head to find the antique tortoiseshell combs—her good luck charms—that she had put on this morning for an extra bit of brain power. She dragged the combs through the mess, bringing both hair and thoughts to order, and replaced them at her temples. She joined the group just in time to add the points she intended to make at tomorrow's presentation.

As the discussion was winding down, Deb and Rosa, the lab technicians, returned from lunch. They had some autoradiogram film results to go over with Jack and Hao, and Dr. Larry took the opportunity to speak to Scotty of the norms that governed polite conversation in anticipation of tomorrow's meeting. Since Alexandra didn't need further exposure to Scotty's ever-active libido, she decided to go out for a bit of fresh air.

As she was leaving, Jack called out, "Where are you going?"

"For a walk. Maybe the gardens. It's a nice day."

"Want company?"

She declined the offer, then pushed through the swinging door and walked down the hallway connecting the lab to the main hospital corridor. She found the staircase and skipped two flights down. On impulse, she decided not to shock herself with the alien beauties of a North Carolina garden in glorious springtime. The city girl in her preferred crowds. So instead of leaving the building, she began to move through invisible hospital boundaries. Yellow zone. Red zone.

Purple. She threaded her way around patients parked in wheelchairs holding hands with relatives and orderlies in greens pushing gurneys with patients held in the grip of ambulatory IVs.

Feeling psyched, she jingled the loose change in her lab coat pocket and entered the most public spaces of the hospital. Here in the hallway bustle, she indulged her vivid imagination and let herself revisit the Chicago streets where she had grown up.

For the moment, she was once again a string-bean sophomore at Schurz High, walking with her girlfriends down Milwaukee Avenue through the neighborhood of Jackowo Polonia, with ice skates slung over her shoulder. She breathed in the soot of bus exhaust and the smells of kolaczki wafting from the bakeries. She heard the men from the old country on the steps of Saint Hyacinth, discussing the politics of the Fifth District and the latest from Rome and Papiez Jan Pawel II. She felt Chicago cold pink her cheeks when, on the ice rink at Edison Park, she told her girlfriends that she wanted to go to college, maybe even become a doctor. They crinkled their noses and said they would much rather marry a doctor than be one.

And now she was skating down the hallway of the Duke University Medical Center, a twenty-six-year-old biology postdoc on Dr. Larry's research team, smelling antiseptic and excitement.

By the time she arrived at the main thoroughfares of the hospital, the congestion was heavy with the late lunch flow of doctors and residents, medical students and staff. She moved through several long corridors, then stepped out of the line of traffic in order to scan the menu posted on the board at the entrance to the hospital restaurant. Her attention was soon diverted by calls of "Coach K! Coach K!"

Curious, she turned to look for the well-known head coach of the men's basketball team, just like everyone else within hearing. She didn't see anyone who resembled Mike Krzyzewski, but she did recognize Erica Monroe's bald head skimming toward her. Alexandra had befriended Erica the month before when Erica had sailed into Larry's lab and demanded to know why Alexandra, Jack, Scotty, and

6

Hao were sitting around drinking coffee when they were supposed to be finding a cure for the Big C, for God's sake.

Erica's age was obscured by her illness, but Alexandra knew it to be a heartbreaking nineteen. Her gender was violently proclaimed by a pair of earrings composed of clusters of miniature, stainless-steel surgical instruments. Alexandra had seen them on display at the Hospital Staff Auxiliary Services craft fair the week before on Kilgoe Quad. At the time she had wondered who would possibly wear such outrageous jewelry. She smiled now to see the answer walking toward her.

Erica separated herself from the stream and hailed again, "Coach K!" at which point Alexandra's smile reversed itself.

Erica stopped short in feigned alarm. "From the look on your face, you must have seen my chart!" She sighed theatrically. "Tell me the worst."

"I don't have access to your chart, as you know," Alexandra said, "and the worst I have to tell you at the moment is that you have no shame."

"Shame, yes. Fashion sense, no." Erica looked down at her ratty slippers and Sailor Moon superheroine bathrobe whose edges sprouted a hospital-issue gown. "You're referring, of course, to my outfit. It's scary to think how good I think I look in this."

"No, I'm referring to the fact that you called me Coach K. I hardly wish to steal the real Coach K's thunder."

Erica seemed surprised. "You prefer I should call you the Slavic Queen?"

"What's wrong with 'Doctor Kaminski'?"

"I wouldn't want you to think that I was pandering to your vanity."

"God forbid!" Alexandra murmured.

"And I hate to waste time when there are matters far more important to discuss than your vanity. Case in point. I'd like to know why you're cruising the main drag. It's not like you, Coach. I think you need to account for yourself here."

Alexandra pointed to the menu on the wall. "I'm thinking about the chicken Caesar."

7

"Me, I'd like . . ." She perused the menu, then jabbed a bony finger at the fettucine Alfredo. "Heart attack on a plate. Privilege of the sick." She batted her lashes. "How do I keep my girlish figure?" she mused songfully. "You know the food here sucks, so forget about it and tell me what you're really up to."

When they reentered the stream of traffic moving down the hallway, Alexandra replied, "I just finished an experiment and was so charged that I needed to work off some energy. I'm actually heading back now."

"Wish I could join you, but my soaps will be on soon. Then again, I've started this." Erica held up a paperback book. "So I don't know whether to make sure that Luke and Laura don't screw up more than is absolutely necessary or to meditate on my past lives."

Alexandra read out the title that spiraled inside an intricate mandala. "*Bardo Thodrol, or the Tibetan Book of the Dead*. Interpreted by Rob Breslin." She looked at Erica. "Is it good?"

Erica was enthusiastic. "It's amazing! It describes exactly what happens to you in the forty-nine days between your death and rebirth. It's very important to think the right thoughts at the moment of your death and to follow the path laid out by the bodhisattvas; otherwise you might come back as something noxious like a cockroach, a talk-show host, or Jesse Helms."

Alexandra chuckled. "Awful!"

Erica shuddered expressively, bringing the teeny scalpels dangling from her earrings into savage play against her jawbone. "No joke, and it makes me wonder what I did last time around to have been born in Shelby, North Carolina. Talk about your bad karma."

Better to wonder that, Alexandra reflected, than to wonder what she had done to contract lymphoma. "Do you think you're going to find out what you did last time around?"

"Sure, because I'm about to begin the chapter that describes the techniques for recovering past lives. So you see I'm kinda torn what to do for the next hour."

"I take it you buy this idea of reincarnation?"

"Nah, I'm only renting it."

Alexandra laughed.

Erica nodded. "That's right, Coach. I make you laugh. You make me well. That's the deal."

Alexandra gave Erica an affectionate hug. "That's the deal."

They turned down another hallway. On the right was the exit to the restaurant. On the left was the entrance to the cafeteria. Standing under the green awning of that entrance, Alexandra caught sight of Ron Galway, director of Research and Corporate Sponsorship, speaking to a man in a business suit. Remembering the director's hand on her tush at the Christmas party three months earlier, she avoided eye contact with him and kept on walking.

At that point Erica peeled off saying, "Wait here," and added something that sounded oddly like, "I've just clued into one of your lovers from a past life. Maybe I can fix you up."

Alexandra stopped and watched in disbelief as Erica made straight for Dr. Galway. Alexandra knew that Erica was weird, but she had never thought her malicious. Erica couldn't be, no, she couldn't be trying to fix her up with a married man who had the worst rep in the hospital and the power to get away with it. But there she was, speaking to the director, her bald head bobbing atop her skeletal body, her earrings out for blood.

Erica turned to speak to the business suit. Gray pinstripe. Good cut. Elegant. A moment later the suit looked across the hall and focused on Alexandra.

Fine gray eyes assessed her.

Her visual field cracked wide open, and she was once again in high school, once again at Edison Park. This time it was a spring day of her junior year, and she was alone. Taking a shortcut through the bushes, she had run across the path of handsome Bobby Dembrowski, a senior and a football idol. Bobby had noticed what every other boy in school had noticed, namely that scrawny Alexandra Kaminski had blossomed into the stuff of wet dreams.

She blinked, but the vision didn't go away. Instead, an incident long buried sprang to life, and she remembered how Bobby's hands had been all over her. She remembered her nerves leaping in surprise. Her struggles. The derisive tone in his voice when he said, "Hey, dziwko, think you're too good for me?" Her taunt of "Polack lowlife." His swift retaliation. Her back thudding against the soft, wet ground. Branches scraping. His weight. His anger. Her panic. Her blouse ripped. Hot hands to breast and thigh. Blood burning behind her eyes. Being pinned. Thrashing. Bony knee to busy groin. A half-second's release. Scrambling to all fours, then to her feet. Running. But not getting away fast enough to avoid hearing him curse, "Just wait, kurvo, to see what you'll get from any man who isn't a Polack, and it won't be respect!"

She had run all the way to her apartment, where her grandmother informed her that her guidance counselor had called to say that Northwestern University was offering scholarships to low-income women from the city to study molecular biology. She had never heard of molecular biology, but it sounded wonderful.

Fine gray eyes dismissed her.

She had no idea why that humiliating high school incident should come to mind now. The elegant suit across the hall had nothing in common with the thick-muscled boy from the old neighborhood, and his once-over was plainly disinterested. All for the good, of course, since she definitely didn't like his type.

Her lab visions were one thing, but this Bobby D replay was another thing entirely. She adjusted the combs at her temples, thinking that maybe she had pushed them in too tight.

TWO

ERICA TURNED AWAY from Old Goat Galway and Lover Boy, thinking, Jesus, Monroe, you probably just stepped in a shitload of cosmic crap, and all you were trying to do was class up Kaminski's half-ass dating act. Don't you know what the road to Hell is paved with? Don't you know that you can't afford to let them hellfires get within scorching distance? And don't you just have a habit of forgetting that the very thought of the Eternal Hickory-Smoked Pig Pickin' Starring Erica the Pig is itself carcinogenic? So instead of fretting over excess karmic baggage, maybe you should write your little ol' bad feelings down to the possibility that your white cell count has just taken a swan dive.

Oh, yeah, *much* better.

Either way, bad vibes is bad vibes, and Lover Boy was bad news.

Erica made her way back to Alexandra, and they resumed their walk down the hallway. "I overheard Old Goat call him Val," she said, taking first things first. "What kind of name is that? Val? Yuck!"

"Erica!"

"Now, our man Val might have had an accent, but he didn't say much, so I couldn't tell. I'm thinking he's the silent type. Maybe not the strong, silent type—he's not beefy enough for that—but he has a good sinewy build, and I liked the lean lines of his face. Only at first, however."

"Erica!"

"He must be with some drug company, since Old Goat is using the private sector to bankroll his operation these days." She considered. "Glaxo Wellcome, perhaps?"

"Erica!" This, sharply.

Erica swirled her head around, bringing her earrings into motion. She liked the feel of the itty-bitty knives and probes grazing her neck. "What?"

They had turned the corner to the adjoining hallway, the one with the Wachovia Bank branch and the public phones. They came to a stop in front of the blue-lit shelter of the ATM.

The Slavic Queen's big brown eyes flashed with annoyance. "I want to know what you thought you were doing!"

"I gave Lover Boy your name, telephone number, pager number, social security number, bra size, date of birth, and told him to get in touch with you."

The Slavic Queen wasn't biting. "No way."

"You're right. I don't know your social security number."

"Get serious, Erica. I mean it!"

"All right, all right! When I first saw him, I thought he was much better than the usual bozos you hang around with, but when I started speaking to him I changed my mind." She didn't mention how a wave of some feeling, almost like fear, had flashed over her skin when she had come next to him. Instead, she smiled brightly and asked, "So, what did you notice first about him?"

"Nothing."

"Try again."

"Okay. His briefcase."

"Me, I noticed his shirt," Erica said. "That was my tip-off." Her persistent bad feelings prompted her to add, "I gotta tell you, Coach, and listen to me now. Don't mess with this guy. Remember that."

The Slavic Queen wasn't in the mood for good advice. "Look, you just can't walk up to some strange man and give him my phone number—not that you did, but even the intention is bad. How do you know he's not an ax murderer?"

"He's not."

"And Dr. Galway? What could he possibly think of what you did?"

"It doesn't matter."

"Dr. Larry is about to secure corporate funding, and he needs Dr. Galway's support. This is my job, after all!"

Erica felt smug. "Not to worry."

"But you just can't *do* that!" Alexandra insisted.

"Yes, I can. Another privilege of the sick, aged, or infirm. I'm like Sophia on the *Golden Girls*."

"Who?"

"Estelle Getty."

"Who?"

"Sophia was really old and, by virtue of her stroke, could say anything she wanted." Erica looked at Alexandra with indulgent amusement. "You really did spend the eighties with your nose in a schoolbook, didn't you? I sometimes forget that you're from the Cultural Void."

"I know who Coach K is, and that it's ACC tournament time."

"Which is only to say that you have a pulse. By the way, it's a Mark Cross."

"What's a Mark Cross?"

"His briefcase."

"You could tell that?"

Erica put a hand on her hip and poured on a drawl thick as barbecue sauce. "Aaah'm from Shelby, so that makes me stu-u-upid."

Alexandra laughed. "I want to be angry at you, Erica. No, I *am* angry at you."

"If you stay angry at me, I'll make you the butt of all the jokes in the sitcom I'm writing." Erica smiled with satisfaction. "That's a threat."

The Slavic Queen threw up her hands. "Oh, Lord, what next?"

"It's about a Chinese American family that moves into the town of Memory, North Carolina," Erica explained, "and winds up in a redneck neighborhood. High jinks ensue." She added knowledgeably, "That was a key industry phrase in the seventies, you know, 'high jinks ensue.' In the nineties, situationers are mostly friends sittin' around—*not* funny!—so I figure it'll soon be time for a high jinks revival. Anyway, I'm thinking of calling it *A Wok down Memory Lane*, y'know, w-o-k." She pulled a face. "Or maybe *Y'all, Honey Chile, Magnolia Blossom, and Dim Sum* just to get in all the stereotypes at once. What do you think?"

Slavic Queen had the answer to that. "That I'm already the butt of all your jokes."

"Good one, Coach! But as a point of information, one title is too corny and the other is too long. Sponsors wouldn't get behind either."

"You're serious, aren't you?"

"Listen, Coach, the day you control these cells in my body, I'm heading for Hollywood."

Erica would have elaborated on this interesting theme, except for the fact that Alexandra Kaminski suddenly looked a whole lot less like a Slavic Queen and a whole lot more like Fred MacMurray as the absentminded professor. Total zone out.

Erica waved a hand. "Hello, hello! I'm looking for signs of life!"

At mention of Hollywood, Alexandra saw an enticing chorus line of TTGGGGs dance into her head for the second time within the hour, and she began to entertain some curious thoughts about cell life and death. She wondered if it mattered whether she had really seen telomerase in her last experiment or just imagined it. In either case, the possibilities were intriguing. Maybe she should find a way to inject the enzyme into the cellular process at various points and see what would happen. The experiment would be tricky, but if telomerase were present at the right time—that is, the wrong time—it might be responsible for causing a cell to exceed the limits of healthy growth.

Then Erica's hand was waving before her eyes, and Alexandra's concentration broke.

"Hello, hello!" Erica said. "I'm looking for signs of life!" She stopped waving when she had Alexandra's attention again. "Well, it's getting late, but what to do? Book. Soaps. Book. Soaps." She chanted her alternatives, shaking her hands as if she were holding maracas instead of nothing and a book. "I'm a busy woman, even if you're not. I just may succumb to the book and my past lives. Well, gotta go!"

As Erica began to walk away, Alexandra said, "I should have taken my walk in the gardens."

Erica turned and flashed a wide grin. "Too late!"

"I hope not."

Erica held up a hand, trilled her fingers in parting, and continued to scuff down the hallway in her ratty slippers.

Watching Erica depart, Alexandra suddenly felt mighty inspired. On a whim, she went to the Blue Devil Trading Post, bought a Snickers, and devoured it.

Back at the lab, she was determined to see her DNA sequencing experiment anew. She had plenty of yeast culture left but no luck. Her eyes conspired against her. Her thumbs conspired against her. The Lurking Lab Gnomes scurried out of their cracks and did what they could to muddle every chemical compound known to man and yeast. For some ridiculous reason, she snapped at Jack. He got up and left. Hao was gone for the day, having come in hours before at midnight. Scotty was still hanging around the hospital, trying to chat up nurses, no doubt. Rosa and Deb must have been on break, because she was suddenly aware of being alone in the lab.

She inadvertently knocked over her flask, cracking it and spreading goo across the counter where she was working. In trying to clean it up, she made a worse mess, so she reached for the nearest bottle of cleaning fluid and got into an argument with a too-tight cap. Disgusted, distracted, still fighting with the cap, she glanced at the clock. The cap lost the battle but won the war by springing off, causing the bottle to tip and to stream fluid and foul fumes across her breasts.

Before she looked down to mop up the mess, her eyes fixed on the evil face of the clock. It frowned down on her at twenty minutes to four and jeered, "I can make time slip inside out. Have a bad day."

She stood up abruptly. She felt dizzy. She had a vague notion that she shouldn't have eaten that Snickers. She was sure her combs were in too tight, causing her temples to throb. The glare of the fluorescent lights fuzzed, melting the clutter on the counters and cabinets and discomposing the white light into drips and drabs of color. She strained to focus. She thought she saw the lab door swing open, then shudder rhythmically, hypnotically, as if someone had entered. Or was it that she was leaving? She felt herself walking, no, floating, toward the door.

WHEN SHE CAME to the door she felt better. Or, rather, she had no notion that she had previously felt bad. The late-winter-afternoon sun cheered her, and its rays ſtretched in when she pushed open the louvered swinging doors from the ſtreet and entered the hall. She let the doors flap carelessly behind her. Their wobbling announced her arrival and chopped the slanting sunlight into crazy bits behind her.

She ſtrode across the darkened hall, footſteps echoing. She undid the breaſt-high buttons on her jacket, slid the half-coat off, and caught it in the crooks of the fingers of one hand. With the other hand, she fiddled with the lace on her bodice. She was aware of the skirts brushing around her ankles but, of course, she was always aware of her feet and her ankles and her legs. With a practiced flick of the wriſt, she lifted her skirts—not silk, but maybe someday—to reveal plain petticoats. She ſtretched a leg, pointed her toes, and circled her supple ankle encased in a high-button shoe. She dropped her skirts without missing a ſtep.

She headed for the back room behind the ſtage. For no reason whatsoever, the magic words *Au printemps* darted into her head, then darted out again.

"You're late, Jeanne!" a voice intoned from shadows. It had come from the wall along which ran the bar.

She changed course and moved toward the voice. Her reply was smug. "It's not yet four o'clock, Maurice." When the voice did not respond, she added saucily, "You perceive the dangers of a poor working girl learning to tell time."

Maurice grunted his disapproval. "Telling time now? What next?"

"Learning to read," she informed him, "but that is going more slowly."

Maurice muttered something about the decline of civilization and blamed the cursed republicans for all of it—and never mind the fact that he had voted for them.

By the time she arrived at the bar, her eyes had adjusted to the dimness. She was already long accustomed to the inconsistency of Maurice's politics. She tossed her jacket atop the marble counter and placed her hands as if she were standing at a ballet barre. With her back perfectly straight, she lifted her leg out at a right angle. As she moved it in a slow quarter circle, side to back, she said, "And if you think that I need to arrive at four o'clock in order to begin warming up, then you know nothing of me and my art. I have been dancing already all day."

Maurice was not appeased. "You have other work to do besides warming up," he scolded, "and if you've been dancing all day, you'll be tired for tonight's chahut."

"When have you ever known my dancing to be tired?" she replied. "And when has anyone ever frequented Le Chat Noir because I served them a drink?"

"As to that, Jeanne . . .," Maurice began. He did not finish the thought, which needed no finishing.

"Your business has not been hurt a day since I came here to dance —only to dance," she said confidently. "In fact, it has improved."

"That's right, Maurice. Leave Jeanne alone," a voice rasped. It belonged to a woman who came from behind and slipped her arm through Jeanne's. "We'd lose business," the woman joked, "if you began to sell Jeanne's favors. Why, the men would be killing each other over her."

She turned to smile at Charlotte, Maurice's wife, and hailed her friend, "My kind protectress!"

Charlotte gave her arm a conspiratorial squeeze. Maurice grunted again, this time disapprovingly, but he did not argue with either of the women.

Elbow linked with Charlotte's, she observed her crabby friend, fat and balding, as he methodically wiped the legion of glasses that would be dirty by evening's end. His head was bent to his task. His girth was swathed in a wide linen apron. His back was reflected in the mirror behind him, in which she could also see the smudged contours of her own face and Charlotte's. Two windows high above the mirror let in light that seemed to drift down like snowflakes to dust with luminescence the contours of the bottles shelved around the mirror. She liked this moment in the day, when the music hall slumbered, when the tables and chairs were stacked around the walls, when she felt both protected and freed by the empty spaces around her.

Before she knew it, the hall was brightly lit, the space was filled with animated patrons, and the air was thick and sweet with the fumes of beer and spirits and tobacco smoke. She was still standing at the bar. She was no longer wearing her street clothes but rather her stage dress, a pink-lined black silk—laced bodice, puffy pink taffeta skirts gathered in front to her knees and dropping like a swallow's tail in back, and black silk stockings. A soft challis shawl kissed her bare skin, warming her shoulders and arms. Her calves felt stretched and relaxed. She had already danced.

She drifted away from the bar to listen to the singer on stage. She stopped at the first table that was of the height for standing and bent an elbow idly on top so that she could prop her head in her hand. She felt haloed by her surroundings, and the glowing gas globes made everything shimmer as if in a pool of water: the ugly, life-sized paintings that hung on the walls, the old weapons and wooden statues that filled the corners of the hall, the enormous stuffed carp that hung from the ceiling. Maurice was serving drinks behind the bar, doing his job. Charlotte was trading quips with the customers, doing her job. The evening was pleasant. She didn't have a care in the world.

At one point, a drift of cigarette smoke enveloped her and Charlotte's raspy voice whispered into her ear, "A guest wishes to buy you a drink, Jeanne."

She imagined that Charlotte was joking. Turning toward her friend, she said, "You know my policies about accepting drinks from guests." She took the cigarette out of Charlotte's mouth and crushed it underfoot.

"What are you doing?" Charlotte demanded indignantly.

"You look out for me, and I look out for you," she replied. "Those things are no good for you, as I've told you before."

Charlotte's protest was smothered in a fit of coughing. When she recovered, she said, "This guest is new, Jeanne."

She had already sized up the crowd. She had picked out the regulars and identified the new faces. Among the new were several English gentlemen in evening dress and a group of boisterous military men. Although she could not yet read every word on a page, she could read uniforms down to the last medal and loop of gold braid. She knew the military men to be Austrian officers.

She had noticed another man too, who had come in alone, sometime before she had danced. She had known from a glance at the cut of his overcoat that he had come to slum—*s'encanailler,* as the saying went—and she had made a mental note to steer clear of him. She hoped it was not the well-dressed man who wished to buy her a drink.

She searched Charlotte's normally lively expression for a hint that her friend was joking, but found none.

Charlotte added, "This one is different, Jeanne. The request comes from the man in the overcoat. You know which one I mean."

She did. Maurice must be serious about her accepting a drink from the high-class man who had come in alone; otherwise he would not have sent Charlotte as his messenger.

She felt suddenly vulnerable in a way she hadn't felt since she left her village, since she found a job and a kind of home with Maurice and Charlotte. She looked at Charlotte in a way that suggested betrayal. "Are you saying I have no choice?"

Charlotte's expression turned sad. "No choice, no." She coughed again. "Not this time."

She said coolly, "Then you may bring me my usual."

"Not your usual, Jeanne," Charlotte protested. "You will offend him."

"My usual," Jeanne said implacably, "or nothing."

Charlotte moved away. Out of the corner of her eye, Jeanne saw the man approach. He had shed his overcoat. Although she did not look at him directly, she guessed well enough to which exalted ring of the social order he must belong. She kept her eyes trained on the stage, but she could no longer hear the music. She felt his eyes on her. She felt anger, then defiance.

He stepped up to her side.

Charlotte returned with a tray on which were balanced a cognac for him and a glass of water for her.

THREE

JACK RETURNED TO the lab, took one look at
the vacant look on Alexandra's face, and for one
heart-stopping second feared she was in cardiac
arrest and would keel over and expire on the spot.

He quickly took in the details of the scene. He flew to her side.
Boy Scout time. His hands clawed off her deadly lab coat. Ancient
chivalry gene activated. Stray thought to the effect that he had been
fifteen years old before he had finally realized that the phrase *damsel
in distress* wasn't, in fact, *damsel in this dress.*

Then she was in his arms. Where she had never been before.
Where she belonged. His damsel. In distress.

Jack Sandifer, knight in shining armor, to the rescue.

"A.K.! A.K.!"

No response.

"Alexandra!"

Her eyes fluttered open, struggled to focus. They fixed on him
without recognition. Her pupils were dilated. She was still in the
danger zone. He shifted all her weight onto the arm he had placed
behind her neck. He knew just what to do, had seen all the right
movies. Good thing they were near the sink.

His free arm reached out for cup, faucet handle, tap. He filled
the cup, put it to her lips.

She turned her head, refusing it. "Water," she murmured. "You know I only drink water, and I don't even want that."

"This is water," he confirmed. "Drink!" He forced her to take a sip.

She swallowed, then opened her eyes. Lovely brown pools, fuzzy at first, clarified with the return of consciousness. They registered his presence and in one magical moment gave him all he had ever yearned to receive from her. Recognition. Warmth. Acknowledgment of the comfort and security of his presence. The gentle surprise of happiness to be with him.

He felt strong, protective, needed. He strengthened his hold on her and indulged the possibility that this was a lover's embrace.

She rolled her head against his arm and looked around her. Then she drew a deep breath and uttered a heartfelt "Thank God I'm in the lab!"

"Where did you think you were?"

A practical question, thoughtlessly asked. It made her frown and push away from him. If he had said, "Of course, you're in the lab, and you're here with me, Jack," he would still be holding her. Instead, he had missed his cue, and she was standing on her own two feet, rubbing her temples. His arms fell to his sides.

Her eyes widened in shock. She clutched his arm and said seriously, "French was always my worst subject in high school."

Scotty McCarthy had just returned to the lab. His gaze moved from the bottle on the counter, to the lab coat on the floor, to an an obviously groggy Alexandra. Jack was annoyed by the interruption, but since his Perfect Moment was long gone anyway, McCarthy might as well be good for a second opinion.

Jack asked, "Should we have her checked for poisoning?"

McCarthy gave Alexandra a professional once-over. "It looks like you got her lab coat off before any real damage could be done, but since you weren't interested in taking any more of her clothes off, I gotta ask, hey, what's going on here?"

Jack answered the question by saying to Alexandra half-playfully, half-sternly, "Next time you want to play with chloroform, I suggest you keep your head under the fume hood. You're lucky that the fluid fell mostly on your ID tag so it didn't burn you."

Alexandra was evidently sobering to her surroundings. At his comment she turned her attention to the lab table where stood an empty bottle marked with a bold $CHCl_3$. "Well, no wonder I was knocked for a loop," she began, then got all fuzzy again. "Loop, loops . . . that reminds me of something . . ."

When she was unable to finish the thought, Jack said, "I've a mind to run you down to Detox, just to make sure."

Alexandra shook her head, as if to clear it of its chloroformed fancies. "No, no, I'm all right. Really. I was trying to clean up the mess I made and must have grabbed the wrong bottle." She glared at the bottle. "What an odd mistake to make."

"Very," Jack agreed.

"I remember looking at the clock." She glanced at the wall and seemed surprised to see that it was a quarter to four. She shook her head once more, this time decisively. "Good heavens, those five minutes felt like five hours, and now I really do have to get out of here." Her voice had returned to normal. "Forget taking another walk. What I need is an aerobics workout."

Jack seconded the idea and shooed her out of the lab, wishing she had asked to have the strength and protection of his company for the evening. He settled for the thinner satisfaction of having been there when she needed him most. At least he had her gratitude.

With the door still flapping behind her, McCarthy said, "God, she's hot. I'd go after herself myself, except that you'd want to punch my lights out—not that you could—and then we'd never get any work done around here. But, man, what are you *waiting* for?"

Jack could have punched McCarthy's lights out with great pleasure. "She's not like that, McCarthy, so just shut up."

. . .

AN HOUR LATER at Metrosport, Alexandra had worked up to a fine sweat and her optimal heart rate. She decided that she wasn't upset by the fact that she had drenched herself in chloroform but rather by the eerie specifics of the anesthetic-induced experience. The chloroform should have made her fall asleep. Instead she felt as if she had stepped into an Impressionist painting of a Paris music hall, and it had come to life around her.

That realization made everything fall into place.

Of course she didn't know French. Of course she hadn't had a past-life experience. Of course a man with a gray suit and gray eyes had had nothing to do with her strange experiences in the lab. Rather, her drugged brain had taken that absurd conversation about reincarnation she'd had with Erica, jumbled it with her sugar high from that candy bar, and folded it into her memories of the hours she had spent with her grandmother at the Art Institute of Chicago looking at the paintings of Manet, Renoir, Degas, Toulouse-Lautrec.

The scientist in her was satisfied by this perfectly rational explanation.

FOUR

 VAL DORSAINVILLE DELAYED his departure
from his home in Cary to avoid the thick of the
morning rush-hour traffic on I-40. He made
up for whatever time he had deliberately lost by
taking unfair advantage of American driving habits, which were far
more polite than his. He hit the Durham Freeway having shaved two
minutes off his usual driving time, but that didn't mean that he felt
any obligation to slow down once he exited the freeway and entered
the Research Triangle Park.

He skimmed along Alexander Drive and the sculpted stands of
pine that scalloped a cerulean sky. He whizzed past the secluded research facilities of such global giants as IBM and Rockwell. He
turned into the driveway of Seine-Lafitte Pharmaceuticals, hardly
noticing its manicured median planted with a double row of silver-
bells hinting already of green in March. He stopped at the security
booth, whirred the window down.

The guard stepped out, slid admiring eyes from hood to trunk,
and offered his one-word opinion. "Sweet."

"Good morning, Raeford."

Raeford looked at the driver and exclaimed, "Mr. D! When you
left last week you were driving a Lincoln Town Car. I didn't recognize
you in the Eldorado touring coupe."

"That's the advantage of being in the States for only a few months at a time. I rent whatever strikes my fancy."

"Then let it strike a Ford F-150. It'd look good on you."

Val's smile was wry. "I didn't see such a model available at Hertz."

"You gotta go to Dixie Rents Pick-Ups in Pittsboro for the really fi-i-ine vehicles. Tell 'em Raeford sent you."

"In the meantime, you'll let me pass, even if I'm not driving a Ford truck?"

Raeford waved him on by raising his fist and reciting congenially, "No taxes on tobacco."

Val drove on toward the wide sweeps of concrete and glass trimmed in swimming-pool blue. He took the curve to a parking lot hidden behind a low berm and nosed into his reserved parking place. He reached for his briefcase and suit coat slung across the passenger seat in the same way he used to pick up his tennis duffle and warm-up jacket before a big tournament. In fact, as he shrugged into his coat and crossed the parking lot, he felt as good as he had when he had been at the top of his game. His boldest, most brilliant project was going well, and the work he had done this past week at Abbey Labs in Chicago could not have gone better. Although all the international patents for Test Early, Feel Safe were not yet approved, he was confident about the results and looking forward to updating Yves.

He pushed through thick, smoked-glass doors and approached the reception island in the lobby from the back side. The receptionist must have had good radar, for she turned and gave him a brilliant smile. He greeted her with an automatic "Ma Donna, bonjour" in a way he knew she liked.

"Mr. D," Donna returned, gushing a little, "did you just get in?"

"Yesterday morning. I spent the afternoon at Duke."

"Did you have a good trip?"

He assured her he had, but didn't elaborate. Instead, he leaned over the counter to scan the appointment book open on the receptionist's desk. "Is Yves in yet?"

Donna nodded. "Mr. DuBois is getting ready for a meeting," she said, glancing down at her book, "with Dr. Lawrence Rosenberg and his research team."

"That's right. We're working up an R-and-D contract with them, aren't we? Last week before I left, Bob told me something about a team-building seminar. The first meeting must be scheduled for this morning. Good. That means I'll be seeing Bob."

"Mr. Sutherland is spending the day in Raleigh."

Val's brows rose. "I thought he was in charge of the Rosenberg venture."

"Not according to Mr. Chevalier."

Val's brows rose higher. "Jean-Philippe? What does Jean-Philippe have to do with this?"

Donna held up empty hands. "You'll have to ask him."

"I'll make a point of calling him this afternoon, then."

"You can ask him this morning in person. He's here to attend the Rosenberg meeting."

This news came as a surprise, a vaguely unpleasant one. Val had been in touch with the Paris office just two days before, and as of Monday Jean-Philippe had been in Paris with no plans to come to the States.

He smiled easily. "Well, that simplifies things, doesn't it?" He paused to reflect. "I wonder if there's anything else I need to know at the moment?"

Donna flashed him a smile he knew just how to read. "Only that I have two tickets to the ACC tournament in Charlotte tomorrow afternoon." Her tone was inviting. "The tip-off for the State-Carolina game is at four-thirty."

He smiled and said with just the right blend of regret and reprimand, "You are teasing me, ma Donna, when you know that I will be tied up with Legal all day and tomorrow finalizing the Abbey Labs patents."

Donna's face fell enough to suggest that she hadn't known that Val planned to be tied up with Legal for the next few days.

He tapped a finger against the molded reception module and

said, "I'll try to catch Yves before or after the Rosenberg meeting, then, and if I don't see you before Monday, you can tell me all about the games I missed."

He gave Donna a smile that took the sting out of his rejection, crossed the lobby, and turned left down a long corridor. He glanced out the floor-to-ceiling glass membranes on his right that separated interior world from exterior environment. The panes caught and discomposed the light of a cloudless blue sky and gave him back his own image in fractured patches. By chain of association, Donna's not-so-subtle invitation reminded him of the encounter he had had the day before at Duke Medical Center when he had been standing in the hall with Ron Galway. Images came to mind of a bald woman with earrings that could kill and of a blonde in a white lab coat.

A man long accustomed to approaches from women, he had found the bald woman's role of carnival psychic rather original, even effective in the way she announced that she had "flashed on his past." However, the readings in her crystal ball seemed to have borrowed much from the newspaper astrology column, and it was pretty predictable that she would say that he was at a crisis point in his life. That his present circumstances were a result of past mistakes. That all his problems mysteriously involved the woman standing across the hallway—one he was sure he had never seen before. Then, not so predictably, the bald woman had left him without dropping her friend's name or slipping her phone number into his suit-coat pocket.

At the time he had dismissed the incident as a diverting absurdity. Just now it struck him as oddly ominous. Or perhaps he was confusing his response to yesterday's incident with his reaction to the news of Jean-Philippe's presence on this side of the Atlantic. Now, why that news should strike him as ominous he could not say. He decided that he was suffering from pre—championship match jitters and figured his nerves would settle down once he had all the patent approvals for TEFS. He shook off the bad feeling as he would the noise from distracting spectators in the stands, picked up his mental ball again, and put it in play. He continued down the hallway, reviewing the points he needed to discuss with Seine-Lafitte's product lawyers.

He had not gone far when elevator doors opened and out stepped Yves DuBois, Seine-Lafitte's president and chief executive officer. He was a compact and energetic CEO who managed to divide his time between Paris and the Research Triangle Park in a style that convinced everyone he was able to be in two places at once. This strategic illusion was maintained Stateside by his administrative assistant, Florence Washington, a sharp, handsome black woman who towered beautifully beside DuBois as he exited the elevator, an African Josephine to his Napoléon.

DuBois was also flanked by Jean-Philippe Chevalier, Seine-Lafitte's newly named general manager. Chevalier was trim, silver templed, and pushing sixty. He was battle trained but not battle hardened, at least not on the outside, and Val knew him to be as smooth and complex as a '58 Nuits-Saint-Georges burgundy.

Val first greeted Florence, then mentioned to Yves that he had encouraging news to discuss with him later. After that he extended his hand to Chevalier. "Jean-Philippe, it's good to see you."

Jean-Philippe accepted Val's clasp and made it hearty. "Yes, very good, Valéry."

They tended to speak English to one another, as a courtesy, when in the presence of American coworkers.

"And it's a surprise to see you," Val said pleasantly, releasing his superior's hand. "I thought you were immersed in the details of the Barcelona project."

"I've taken a small break from it in order to come here. I arrived yesterday evening."

"Your decision to come to the States was sudden, no? Last I heard, you were in Paris and planning to stay there through the next month, at least."

"Yes, such were my original plans, but then a few days ago I had a remarkable conversation with Florence," Jean-Philippe explained, rolling a lovely r in Florence, "about today's team-building seminar.

After hearing her description of it—the catch phrase is 'directed brainstorming,' I believe—I played with the idea of coming to experience myself this latest dada!" He smiled. "I am always interested to stay current with American business fads."

"And for this new experience of directed brainstorming you dropped everything in Paris and came here?" Val inquired cordially. "I'm impressed!"

"But allow me to explain further. Florence only whetted my appetite for this event. It was Sophie who pushed me over the edge."

"Sophie?"

"Yes, I ran into Sophie Monday evening, and she too was telling me about this curious new American custom of team-building seminars with their ideation sessions, wish lists, and the like. Well! I decided that I couldn't resist, and voilà, it is Thursday, and here I am!"

Val considered the possibility that Jean-Philippe was less interested in American business practices and more interested in company intrigue. Perhaps he had stumbled across news of Val's relationship with the firecracker Sophie DuBois who was as energetic in the bedroom as her father was in the boardroom. Val wasn't advertising his relationship with Sophie just yet, but if Jean-Philippe had caught wind of it, he might have decided to cross the Atlantic in order to keep a watchful eye on his junior colleague—and to keep him from rising too far too fast.

"I don't understand why Bob isn't part of the meetings today and tomorrow," Val said, "since I thought he was in charge of this research project."

"He still is," Jean-Philippe replied. "However, the rule for the team-building seminar allows only five members each from Seine-Lafitte and Duke, and I am afraid that I pulled rank, as the Americans say."

Val kept it light. "In any case, your involvement in this research project at all levels can only be for the good. Bob has banked a lot on this particular team, and his hopes are high."

"Ah, yes, hopes are a fine thing, but as the general manager, I must think of the risks. I must think of the risks!"

Jean-Philippe didn't have to tell Val that the world of pharmaceutical research and development was more volatile than the stock market on a bad day and more competitive than the Grand Slam tournaments. However, since Val was feeling so confident about the profits he expected from the diagnostic branch of Seine-Lafitte, he considered any new R-and-D venture ludicrously unrisky at the moment, and he was happy to have the opportunity to tell Jean-Philippe about the successes he had experienced from his Chicago project.

Jean-Philippe listened with interest and asked only, "But you do not yet have all the international patents, is that right?"

"Not all of them," Val conceded. "Not yet. But soon."

"I am delighted to hear it. Well! I am only sorry that you, cher collègue, will be unable to join us in the team-building meetings."

Val too expressed his sorrow and explained that he would be with Legal all day anyway, working on the patents.

Jean-Philippe nodded serenely and turned to speak with Yves.

When Val struck up a conversation with Florence, he was disgusted to feel a psychosomatic burn of tendinitis in his right elbow, and he hoped he wouldn't also have a psychosomatic bout of the back injury that had ended his professional tennis career ten years before at age twenty-three. He was decidedly miffed that Jean-Philippe's simple question about the international patents could so easily throw him off his game. Jitters, he told himself again and was glad when Larry Rosenberg's team appeared at the lobby end of the hall.

A company like Seine-Lafitte was always on the lookout for talented research teams to fund in a kind of high-stakes gambling to come up with breakthrough cancer cures. Since the scope of such searches was global, Val assumed that it was more coincidence than convenience that Bob Sutherland had chosen a team that happened to work in Seine-Lafitte's backyard. He was glad of that coincidence because it meant he already knew Larry Rosenberg through his dealings at Duke where he had run tests on his cancer diagnostic product TEFS.

As the two groups approached one another, Val acknowledged Larry with a nod and smile. He cast an assessing eye over the four bench scientists and postdocs on whom this risk was principally riding. He saw a cocky-looking redhead, a scraggly-bearded science jock in baggy corduroys, an Asian American, and a young woman.

Val's overall impression of the woman was of a ripe wheat field with a hint of green that flattered a woman of her coloring. The sun filtered in and glanced off her thick blond hair that was caught back from her temples and clouded around her shoulders. She had a supermodel figure that spoke to the taste of another era. She looked like a dressed up version of the blond woman in the lab coat he had seen the day before at the med center. But, no, this *was* the woman he had seen the day before . . .

Something peculiar was going on here, but he didn't know what, and he didn't have time to think about it. The two groups were meeting midhallway, and introductions all around had to be made. When it came time to shake hands with the woman, a pair of brown eyes rose to meet his, steadily but briefly.

The bald woman's warning, *If you're wise, you'll find out who she is,* crossed his mind uneasily. He looked down at her name tag: Alexandra J. Kaminski. The name meant nothing to him.

He greeted her conventionally. She responded in kind and withdrew her hand. They didn't get much beyond the usual niceties before Jean-Philippe whisked her away with a courtly elbow and a few slick words. Upon seeing her walk away with Jean-Philippe, Val remembered that the bald woman had added, *And, then, you'll stay away from her, or you'll live to regret it.*

FIVE

ALEXANDRA'S INITIAL EMBARRASSMENT at meeting the gray suit face to face wore off in Jean-Philippe Chevalier's charming company, and her desire to wring Erica's neck faded as the day at Seine-Lafitte progressed. The team-building seminar turned out to be a perfectly normal, even productive occasion during which she experienced no visions, disturbing or otherwise. Still, she wasn't sorry that Mr. Val Gray Suit—she hadn't quite caught his last name or his position—was not part of the two-day seminar.

During the midafternoon break, she sought the ladies' room, and because she needed to stretch her legs, she took a walk down the long hallway that adjoined the main corridor. There she found the rest rooms in an alcove. The men's room was on the left, the ladies' on the right, and a water fountain in the middle.

A few minutes later, she was washing her hands and straightening her hair. She took a moment to critically survey herself and decided that she looked pretty good in the camel wool suit and olive silk blouse she had bought at Loehmann's during the after-Christmas sales. Feeling confident, she left the ladies' room by thrusting open the door—which collided with the body of a man, to judge from the deep groan of pain she heard on the other side.

She rushed on through the doorway, thinking fatally, No, it can't be. It just can't be!

But it was.

She had smacked Mr. Val as he was rising from taking a drink of water, the edge of the door clipping him all the way up his back to his head. Stunned from the impact, he was momentarily robbed of speech, but the expression on his face was eloquent enough.

She put her hand over her heart and exclaimed, "I'm so sorry! Really I am! Good heavens, I've been having a lot of trouble with swinging doors lately!"

He swallowed hard, closed his eyes, and when he opened them again the focused gray of his gaze caused her to take a step back, as if he were another Bobby Dembrowski, which he wasn't. Then she perceived that his head was cocked to one side, his expression quizzical. He was daring her to speak.

She rose to the occasion and said the most pertinent thing that came to mind. "Erica has lymphoma."

Apparently the knock on his head had not deranged his senses enough to require explanation of that statement. He said, "She did inform us yesterday, in reference to her hair, that she shaved her head because she wanted either to try out for the NBA or become a Buddhist monk. Since we were standing in a hospital, I guessed that she had some form of cancer."

Alexandra chuckled. "Since beginning radiation, Erica has been proud to associate herself with Michael Jordan and Charles Barkley. Her Buddhist kick is new, though.

"Her opening lines were pretty funny," he acknowledged, then added, "and so were her exit lines."

She could not prevent herself from asking, "How about what came in between?"

His voice was lazy. "Do you really want to know?"

She wondered for one horrible moment whether Erica really had given him her bra size but then decided that he was merely teasing her. She shook her head. "If you put it that way, I don't think I do.

Please assure me, however, that Dr. Galway won't throw me off Larry's team. If I had known that you represented Seine-Lafitte, I might have been able to stop her from embarrassing me in front of him!"

His smile shaped the lean lines of his face into a nearly irresistible formation. "I can definitely assure you that your place on Larry's team is secure," he said. "For her parting shot, she told Ron in reference to you, and I quote: 'If you touch a hair on her head, slap a hand on her butt, or alter a penny of her funding, I'll let everyone know that you're screwing . . . someone—I forget who she said—on Tuesday and Thursday afternoons in your office.'"

Alexandra knit her brows. "Janice Turner, perhaps?"

"That's the one."

Alexandra was aghast. "Erica had the nerve to say that to Dr. Galway?"

"In fact, she had the nerve to say that everyone already knew about Turner. What she had in mind was distributing the pictures."

Her mouth fell open. She clapped a hand over it. She tried not to laugh, but couldn't help herself.

"Friend of yours?" he asked.

Her eyes met his. Nothing extraordinary happened to her vision, but she was suddenly aware of the fine fabric of his shirt, of his tie, and the precise shade of charcoal blue of his suit. What was it Erica had said yesterday about his shirt? She couldn't remember, but she was beginning to perceive the attractive power of clothing. Or maybe she had been hanging around white lab coats for too long.

She stepped out of the alcove, and Mr. Val followed. "Yes, Erica's a friend. She reminds me of someone I know, but I can't quite put my finger on who it is. Anyway, she makes me laugh."

"Have you known her long?"

"She breezed into our lab about six weeks ago. She was on her 'grand rounds,' so she announced. We took to one another."

"She must be an interesting friend to have."

"And an inconvenient one, at times!" she admitted. "When I saw you this morning, I was sorry about her antics yesterday, but now—

well!—Galway's the worst and I shouldn't be laughing, but *pictures!* Poor Janice!" She swallowed a last laugh, then said primly, "I suppose I should apologize to you for my good friend Erica's behavior."

"It was worth it," he said, "from several points of view."

Was he trying to tantalize her by making her guess what those points might be, beyond the obvious one that he had been entertained at Ron Galway's expense? She looked up at him again and saw that he was attractive, even dangerously attractive, with his gray eyes and easy stance in a well-cut suit. She might have been hanging around white lab coats too long, but she wasn't about to fall for the first charcoal-blue suit to come along.

"It will have been worth it," she said, "if we can find a way to arrest Erica's lymphoma."

"That's the business we're both in. Think you're destined to find the cure?"

She shrugged modestly. "If I live long enough."

She glanced down the hallway and saw the seminar participants returning to the conference room at the far end. She began to walk in that direction, and he accompanied her for the first few steps.

"Then I wish you a long life," he said and stopped at the open door to an office. His voice was lazy and teasing again when he asked, "So, are you going to tell me about the trouble you've been having with swinging doors?"

She felt the hairs on her neck rise. In pleasure? In warning? She couldn't tell and didn't want to know. She smiled politely and said, "Just don't get too close to one when you know that I'm in the neighborhood."

She moved on down the hallway but not before she read the plaque outside his door:

VALÉRY DORSAINVILLE

VICE PRESIDENT, DIAGNOSTICS

SEINE-LAFITTE PHARMACEUTICALS

Underneath his name and title was a stylized *S* and *L* ingeniously linked to form a chemist's flask. She had learned earlier in the day that this logo symbolized the company's origins.

A few moments later she reentered the conference room. If her meeting with Val had unsettled her, the uneasy feeling didn't last. Soon enough, she was back in Jean-Philippe's unalarming company and responding to his avuncular flirtation.

SIX

 ON SUNDAY AFTERNOON Alexandra was stand-
ing barefoot in her backyard, wearing well-
washed gray sweatpants with *Northwestern* written
in faded purple letters down the right leg and a
gray sweatshirt from the University of Chicago whose neckline had
lost its shape several years before. She was visiting over the back fence
with her next-door neighbor, Lauri Hopper, whose two boys were
running around outside after church, getting their good clothes
dirty. The armpit-high fence between their backyards was perfect for
lounging elbows for a good heart-to-heart. She and Lauri were having one this morning.

When Alexandra had first come to Durham the previous June,
she knew the moment she wandered into the neighborhood known as
Trinity Park that she had to live there. The streets were lined with
towering southern oaks that came to leafy vaults high overhead. The
lots were narrow, and the houses were either sprawling Victorians or
cozy bungalows. They were all old and dignified, and most had been
gentrified in the past fifteen years, although every now and then a
coveted fixer-upper might still come on the market. Trinity Park radiated gracefully out from two sides of Duke's East Campus and was
as close to downtown's good eating as it was to Durham's version of a
New Age shopping strip called Ninth Street. Inhabited by families,

empty-nesters, and "dinks" alike, it had a black Baptist church, a white Presbyterian church, a conservative synagogue, and a big old brick elementary school.

Alexandra had chosen to rent rooms in one of the three-story houses on Monmouth Avenue on the left-hand side of the first floor, which was divided in two. The space, the interior light, and the price were right, but Alexandra had been drawn to the house because the pattern of the cracks in the sidewalk caused by the thick tree roots reminded her of the ones outside her grandmother's apartment above Kolatek's Bakery. It was a decided plus to have a neighbor like Lauri.

The two of them swapped stories, including Erica's encounter with Dr. Galway on Wednesday, complete with her threat of distributing the pictures of him in amorous congress with Janice Turner if he touched a penny of Alexandra's funding. When they had finished laughing over the incident, Lauri said, "Speaking of pictures, I've got some to show you of my newest niece. I'll go in and get them in a minute."

The mention of baby pictures filled Alexandra with a sudden longing to see her own family album, and she made a mental note to ask her grandmother to send it to her.

Talk turned to the team-building seminar, Alexandra's experiences with the high-toned Seine-Lafitte brass, and the positive outcome of the meetings.

"We're going to get the contract," Alexandra announced. "It'll be FedExed to the lab tomorrow, in fact. However, because Larry left town yesterday and because he thinks Scotty, Jack, and Hao are too flaky to manage anything approaching serious money, I'm the one who gets to sign it! And that means I'm going to be the one to hand it over to none other than Dr. Galway."

Lauri had another good laugh about that, then asked, "So, tell me, is the Seine-Lafitte deal going to make you rich?"

"Rich? Never! But a little closer to my goal." Which, she had already told Lauri, was to put a down payment on a house for her grandmother.

Dreaming of getting Marie-Thérèse out of the city and into the suburbs, Alexandra rested her cheek on the forearm that was riding the fence. She had braided her hair into one thick plait this morning, and she was rocking back and forth on her feet, letting the tail of her braid brush between her shoulder blades.

Alexandra's face was turned toward the street. The narrow edges of the lot on either side of the house facing the street were also fenced, marking front yard from back. When she saw a man come into view above the street-side fence, she felt her eyesight go screwy. She raised her head, cautiously, to get a better look at this vision of Val Dorsainville. The vision was holding up a substantial envelope, apparently containing some papers.

"Hello. Alexandra Kaminski, right?"

"Oh!" she said, blinking. The deep voice sounded remarkably like the gray suit's. She snapped out of her reverie and stood up straight. "Mr. Dorsainville?"

"I'm sorry to bother you at home on your day off and to have come unannounced," he said, "but I've been calling you for the past several hours with no answer, so I decided to run this package by your house and leave it at your door. When I saw your front door open, I figured you were around here somewhere."

"I've been home all day," she said, puzzled. "I don't know why I didn't hear the phone." She eyed the thick envelope and discarded the idea that this was a social call. "Is that the research contract?"

He confirmed that it was. "However, Yves decided last night that a rep from S-L should run through it with someone from Larry's team, and you're apparently the one in charge at the moment. Yves made me the designated hitter on our end, so I wrote up two pages of questions and comments for you and gave you the numbers where you could reach me this evening. But it would be a lot easier if we could go over this now." He added apologetically, "If you don't mind."

"I don't mind." It was taking her some time to adjust, but she finally got herself in gear. "Go back around to the front. I've latched the screen door, but I'll go in this way," she said, pointing to her back door, "to let you in. I'll meet you inside."

The all-too-real vision nodded and disappeared.

Lauri's eyes were wide. "Who is that?" she asked, low and meaningfully.

"He's from Seine-Lafitte," Alexandra admitted uneasily.

"I gathered that. But," she enunciated on a meaningful whisper, "you mean I've been talking to you for fully one hour about Seine-Lafitte, and you didn't mention that you were dealing with a guy like *that?*"

"He wasn't part of the team-building seminar."

"So what? Who is he?"

"He's in Diagnostics," she said, distracted, "and he was a world-class tennis player at some point, oh, about ten years ago maybe."

"Really?"

"Scotty and Hao told me. They actually recognized his name. Anyway, that's about all I know."

Lauri clucked her tongue. "I've heard your postfeminist theory that women, once again, have to choose between love and career." She took Alexandra by the shoulders and turned her in the direction of the back door. "But if you're going to feed me that trash now, when the guy is actually *in* your career, then you really do deserve to die unloved." She gave her a friendly little push.

Alexandra hurried up the steps to her back porch, entered through her laundry room, looked down at her feet. She didn't have a pair of shoes to slip on, so she would have to go barefoot. It made sense. If she was wearing baggy sweats and no makeup, she shouldn't be wearing shoes. No problem. Really, no problem.

She light-footed it through her kitchen, which was a jumble of dirty pots and pans, and down the hallway. She had a straight shot through the front room that her landlady called the parlor but hesitated, fighting the irrational thought that she didn't want this man at her house, inside her personal space. As if the space wouldn't belong to her anymore. As if something bad would happen. As if she might die unloved, perhaps?

Not an ax murderer, Erica had assured her, and Erica knew everything. Even had pictures of most of it!

She peeked out the front window, saw a sleek, new-model sports car parked there. She caught a glimpse of Mr. Dorsainville standing on the porch at the screen door and thought that ax murderers didn't usually look so casually elegant in khakis, a light-knit natural pullover, and a black jacket straight out of *GQ.* Or did they?

The absurd question made her realize that her problem was far from a life-and-death crisis. It was rather that she felt Jackowo Polonia shabby to have him see her at her worst and among her flea-market furniture. She had no wand to wave to make herself and her apartment magazine perfect, but even if she didn't look like a high-powered professional at the moment, she could at least act like one.

She went to the screen door. She summoned a smile as she unhooked the latch and let him in.

SEVEN

VAL HAD DRIVEN over to Durham cursing the waste of his Sunday afternoon, but the moment he crossed Alexandra Kaminski's threshold he felt insensibly better. "Ah, so this is where the good smells are coming from," he said. "Out on the porch, I wasn't sure."

"I've been baking," she replied. "We can go over the contract in the kitchen and have cake." She motioned him through the front room. "Coffee or tea?"

"Whichever you prefer," he answered, following her.

Val moved through the play of lights and shadows in the room created by two windowed oblongs of sun slanting across the furniture and polished floorboards. He had a general impression of plump cushions, shawls fringing sofa and chairs, and leafy plants everywhere, ones with skinny spikes, ones with waxy spatulas, ones with spreading fans. He glimpsed elegant crown molding, a gracious fireplace framed by the two main windows, and faded wallpaper clouded with pouting roses.

"Tea, then," she said, leading him down the hallway, "which makes the next question: cup or pot?" She looked at him over her shoulder. "Or maybe I should ask, how long will this take?"

He met her glance. "Pot. Which is to say that if we focus, we can go through this in under two hours."

He caught the expression that flashed across her face before she quickly turned back around. Surprise was there. Displeasure too. He experienced similar emotions, differently mixed. He was surprised by her displeasure, but not entirely displeased by it.

He passed a room on the left, a whirlwind of paper swirling around a desk atop which sat a computer, the screensaver blinking its rhythmic ballet. He looked through the next half-open door and saw her bedroom. Again, an impression of pillows and fringe, cozy curtains, soft light. Room clean. Bed neatly made. Chaste. He sensed unseen forces begin to swirl, as if the mental tornado of her study might move into her bedroom and begin to funnel around her body. He didn't dwell on the stray thought.

Instead he tangled his gaze in her braid and laced it down her neck to the tip. He let his eyes travel farther down her back. He had rarely seen a woman look this good in sweatpants. Her luxurious curves weren't lost in the fabric. Instead they molded and defined it. He was content to walk behind her, swallowed by the shadows, tempted forward by the curled tip of her braid and by the aromatic fingers of fresh-baked cake streaming from the kitchen.

"Two hours, huh?" she replied lightly, but he heard the uncertain note in her voice.

"For the first go-around, at any rate."

She swerved her head around again, Slavic-tilted brown eyes narrowed. "First go-around?"

Her displeasure had grown. So had her apprehension, enough for him to be able to name it. "We'll see how much we can get done this afternoon," he said, teasing her because it was so easy.

"Oh, I see," she said, as if she didn't see anything at all.

They entered the kitchen. It was light and airy and lived in. More plants, flowering things, crowded nooks and sills. The Sunday newspaper was strewn across several surfaces. Used pots and pans were stacked in the sink and on the stove. A large rectangular tin of cake was cooling on a rack set on the long counter next to the sink.

She surveyed the landscape. "It's a mess, but that's the advantage,

I suppose, of not knowing company is coming." She began gathering up the newspaper. "No need to find an excuse for not having cleaned up."

"Your kitchen is no worse than your lab, I'm guessing, to hear Larry tell of it," he commented, "and a sure sign of creativity at work."

She laughed and tossed the newspapers in a recycling bin by the refrigerator. "So we tell ourselves, and it will do no good, now that you see this mess, to insist that Scotty, Hao, and Jack are the slobs."

"I hear that creative disorder is a sign of a good cook too."

She arched a brow, skeptical of his compliment. "Well, we'll see, won't we?"

He gave her a slight bow. He had never thought himself irresistible to women, but he had had enough success over the years to be charmed at having to exert himself to make him agreeable to a woman who wasn't really his type and who wasn't really glad to see him.

She filled the kettle, put it on the stove to heat, and gestured him toward the table, an oak island in a pool of sun overlooking a tiny and tidy backyard. Through the screened back door, he could hear the sounds of neighbor kids fussing about having to go in and change their clothes. He tossed the envelope on the table and pulled out a chair, ducking an extravagant pink lily that bowed down from the window sill. He took off his jacket and slung it around the back of the chair.

Before sitting down, he asked, "Are you from Chicago, by any chance?"

"Yes, from Warsaw on Lake Michigan, speaking from the Polish American perspective. Did you guess from my Midwestern accent?"

He shook his head. "I read your sweats."

She looked down at herself and smiled wryly. "Northwestern B.S. and Chicago Ph.D." Her voice held a hint of challenge. "Anything else you want to know about me?"

"What's the J for?"

"The J?"

"Alexandra J. Kaminski. What's the J for?"

"Janina."

She reached into the cabinet and gave him a choice of Darjeeling or decaf peach. He chose Darjeeling. She took down the teapot and a canister and put them on the counter next to the telephone at which point she uttered a dramatic "Aha!" and held up a dangling telephone cord. "No wonder you couldn't get hold of me this morning. I unplugged the phone the other day and forgot to plug it back in. Sorry about making you drive over."

"I would have had to drive over anyway," he said. "Do you often unplug your phone?"

She peered at the cord, as if looking for the answer to his question. "I can't remember why I would have . . . oh, I unplugged it Wednesday evening after—"

She broke off. Seeing her standing there, holding a limp phone cord and shifting her weight on bare feet, he felt the interior garden she had created come alive around him, luxurious and exotic. A fine strength surged through him, which he recognized as desire. He found it odd that the attraction should sneak up on him and after several encounters with her too. He usually felt these things up front, but this was different.

"—after I had a bad day at the lab," she finished, then frowned. "Or am I not supposed to admit that I have bad days at the lab?"

"I think," he said, "that a woman living alone is not supposed to unplug her phone, no matter how much she doesn't want to be hassled by some guy. Is that your only one?"

She nodded.

"Then we'll write into the contract a cellular phone for you." He slid the papers out of the envelope. "I'm on my way to Dallas tomorrow but began working on the list of contract points last night when Yves decided we needed a point-by-point elaboration. When I drove over just now, I had no hope of finding you here, so I didn't bring a duplicate of the document. We'll have to share this one."

She cut up the cake, arranged it on a platter, and placed it on the table along with platter, plates, cups, saucers, spoons, napkins, a creamer, and sugar bowl. When she sat down, she asked, "I know you're in Diagnostics, but are you on the legal side of things in that department?"

"No, product development."

"Oh. Then shouldn't someone else have done this work today?"

"Who did you have in mind?"

"Jean-Philippe, for instance?"

"He's winging his way back to Paris."

"Already?"

"Don't worry, he'll be back."

"I'm not worried. I was thinking only that since you're not in R and D, this is out of your field."

"This job fell to me by default. Everyone else who could do this work is out of town for the weekend."

She accepted the explanation and passed him a plate. "This is what my family calls babka. It's a plum cake."

"Thanks," he said. He picked up the piece of cake, bit into it, and stopped. Mouth full, he said, "Gâteau aux pruneaux." He swallowed. "It tastes just like my grandmother's plum cake. I thought the smell was familiar."

"It's my great-grandmother's recipe," she explained, "and I bake a couple times a week just to relax. I usually take it to the lab or give it to my neighbor's boys."

He took another bite, and his teeth made contact with a thumb of plum meat. He had a vivid memory of himself as a ten-year-old boy, scrambling over the locked gates of the estate in Bergerac once owned by his Great-Uncle Victor and snitching ripe plums from a beautiful orchard. He took a third bite and recalled how he had gazed at the graceful chateau, sold by his profligate grandfather to the Lafitte family, and how he had vowed to own it someday. He polished off the cake, his mouth watering anew for all that his family had lost and all that he intended to regain. He savored the taste as he would forbidden fruit.

He reached for another piece of his grandmother's plum cake and realized that the plums were not only forbidden fruit but also forgotten fruit. For a man not given to wallowing in past family glories, he remembered now the stories of Great-Uncle Victor who died without issue. Not so much a direct uncle, more of a cousin several times removed. Idle. Aristocratic. *Richissime,* it was said of Victor Louis Dorsainville, the Count d'Albret. The man who, at the turn of the century and on a whim, according to family folklore, invested in a small chemical company known as Seine et Companie. The man who, Val suddenly guessed, knew better than any Dorsainville in the past century how to spend his strength and how to save it.

When he had finished the second piece, his hostess pushed the platter of cut cake in front of him and said, "Help yourself."

He remembered again the bald woman's warning to stay away from the woman whose kitchen he was in, who didn't want him there, and who suddenly looked as pretty and ripe as the most tempting forbidden fruit.

Alexandra smiled inwardly when her guest wolfed down the first piece, the second, then the third.

The kettle shrilled a high note, so she got up, wondering why she had thought anything would go wrong. Sure, the air felt different, denser, more vibrant, but she was aware of it only because she entertained so few visitors. So few male visitors, that is. This one was here for a perfectly good business reason, and his manners were easy, even graceful. But how had he known that she'd unplugged her phone so that Jack wouldn't call her up a dozen times to make sure she was okay?

She dropped the tea ball into the pot, returned to the table with it, and set it on a hot plate to steep.

He moved a paper-clipped stack of papers toward her, then took two pens out of his inside jacket pocket. He handed one to her, a silver Waterman, and unscrewed the gold cap of his own. He moved his chair closer to hers, saying, "If we go article by article, it will go faster, even though the first few pages aren't problematic."

She looked down on page one of thirteen of the document titled simply Contract Agreement, but got distracted by his arm which was propped on the table next to her, by the fine fabric draped over muscle extending to a strong hand with long fingers. She became aware of his leg beneath the table. Why had she not noticed before how muscular he was?

She shook her head clear. Focus, girl, focus. Pretend this is your GREs or your prelims or your thesis defense. Pour out some tea. That's better. This contract business might be a bore, but you can get through it. Only thirteen pages.

She did get through them, the first eight pages of general procedures at any rate, and then the trouble began. Or maybe the trouble was simply continuing from the moment she had been fondling the fence and this man had surfaced in the line of her vision. In any case, she became distinctly aware of the trouble on page eight of thirteen, Article Twelve, or was that XII a twelve or not?

"Where are we, then?" she asked.

"Article Twelve. Delivery of semiannual reports of experimental results. Read through it, and mark it with a check if there's nothing you want to add or take out."

She glanced at the line where his pen was poised and saw the XII. She was looking down at the words on the page. She recognized all the letters but couldn't read one word. She had sipped a little tea and eaten a little cake, not inhaled chloroform, so there was no reason why the words should look so . . . so foreign to her. Like a language she didn't know. But that wasn't it. She recognized the words as he was reading them out to her. It was more as if she didn't know how to read.

She was in the absurd position of having to mark the paragraph with a check without having the faintest idea what it said.

Was this what lust did, then? Make a woman's brains go to mush in the presence of an attractive man, one with a long and lean body, keen gray eyes, and crisp, dark hair? It wasn't that he was conventionally handsome. No, it was something else about him. As if she could see the strength that lay just under his pullover and khakis. Just plain see it. Not to mention feel it.

She'd never gone stupid like this before. She felt as if everything she had ever learned was leaking out of her neurons and pooling into parts of her body she usually ignored. She had foolishly relaxed her guard in his presence and felt now as if all her thoughts and feelings were trapped below her neck.

"On to lab equipment," he said. He hadn't changed the level or tone of his voice, but suddenly it took on a haunting quality and shivered along her nerves. "Listed here are a new inverted microscope, thermocycler, and cryogenic preservation system . . ."

He mentioned five or six additional items that sounded vaguely familiar to her, but she had no idea what the equipment was, nor could she pick out the words on the page. This was getting scary. Not only could she not read, she discovered she couldn't write. As he went through the articles, she looked at the places he was marking with his pen and placed awkward checks.

Swarming into the spaces vacated by English, Polish words started buzzing in her head. She swatted them away like annoying flies. The effort to keep up was tiring, and by the end she was mentally panting with the effort. Last line last page, he lifted his head and aimed his sexy gray eyes at her. She raised her eyes to his, and her heart beat once spasmodically between desire and fear.

"Here are my phone numbers and fax numbers this week listed by day and time of day," he said, referring to his scribbles at the bottom of the last page. "You can call me in Dallas when you have shown this to your lab partners and spoken with Larry. I'm sure you'll want to run it by Ron Galway, as well."

She looked up at him and blanked. His eyes were steady upon her, stunning her with their intensity. She was supposed to say something, but she didn't know what.

Then she understood. She felt like Mickey Mouse playing the sorcerer's apprentice, peeking into a book she didn't know how to read, brooms marching out of control, about to be overpowered. She knew she had to protect herself against this man and his power, and she needed a magic charm. Not the kind she would find in a book, but the kind she would have to cultivate. That was it, then. Stupid women cultivated charm. No, not stupid women. *Uneducated* women. Uneducated women who cultivated magic charm weren't slutty. They weren't trying to draw men to them. They were trying to keep the men away, since they had nothing but their charm to protect them. It was a revelation.

She glanced at the clock on the stove and was proud of herself that she could tell the time. They had been at this for one hour and forty-five minutes. She glanced back at him and saw that he was still waiting for her to speak—or was he waiting to pounce?

She flipped the pages of the contract back to page one of thirteen. "I'll call you in Dallas, hopefully by Tuesday, with all the answers." She returned his pen, leaned back in her chair, and took control of the conversation that she had lost when he had stepped across her threshold. "Your English is pretty good."

"So is yours."

"But I'm American."

"You mean, you were born here."

"I mean, I was one year old when I came."

"Ah."

"Ah?" she repeated. "What's that supposed to mean?"

"That English isn't your first language anymore than it's mine."

"Yeah, but I don't have an accent," she argued. "Okay, yours is very light, but it's still an accent."

"You insult me."

"No, I'm requesting information."

"I've traveled in English-speaking circles for over twenty years," he offered.

"Tennis circuit?" she asked. "Scotty told me you played."

"Before that even, since I didn't turn pro until I was nineteen."

"What English-speaking circles, then?"

He relented. "The ones on the Riviera. My father fancied himself a man of leisure and liked to associate with the English crowd."

"But you're French, right?"

"Of course," he said. "I'd never crack the upper echelons of Seine-Lafitte without the correct nationality. We're not equal opportunity. In fact, the very notion is un-French."

"How long have you been with Seine-Lafitte?"

"Four years."

She was surprised. "And you've made it so far in so short a time?"

"Family connections," he said, "of a sort."

She resisted asking him what sort. "Nevertheless, it's quite a transition, from the tennis circuit to biotechnology, isn't it?"

He did not immediately reply.

"You know where I'm from, where I got my degrees, and what my current research project is, not to mention my income and tax status," she reminded him, "and I am simply asking of you what you know of me."

He rattled off his educational history, and when he came to his M.B.A., she couldn't help but interject, "You received an American business degree and had no background for it. None at all in business, in fact."

He smiled. "I had a better backhand than the director of Admissions at Wharton."

She was disgusted to think that she had to work her way into her degree program because her best shot was with a bowling ball, but such was life in this unequal world. On a flash of intuition, she asked, "Did you learn tennis from the English crowd your father hung out with?"

"I learned on grass courts on the Riviera, yes. Since I'm French, I also had to master clay. Par civisme, you understand."

She did, a little. "Did you do well on the circuit?"

"In my final season I was ranked twelfth."

"Twelfth what?" she wondered aloud. Then it dawned on her. "In the world?"

He nodded.

Impressive. More so than she had guessed. "So when did you leave the game and why?"

"I left at age twenty-three because of my back, which bothers me," he said in a way that brought the blood to her cheeks, "only when I serve at tournament level speed." He added, "And I still have the knees of a nineteen-year-old."

He was determined to turn the conversation one way. She was determined not to let him. She rose from her chair. He rose too, making no move to prolong the encounter, simply following her lead, but something told her that he'd stay if she gave him the least encouragement.

"Before you leave, I want to give you something," she said, by way of telling him where this encounter would go, which was nowhere. "In honor of your nationality."

She went to the counter, got down on hands and knees, and began to rummage in the lower cabinets through the array of biscuit tins that she had been collecting since high school. When he came to stand over her, she realized that the stretched-out neck of her sweat-shirt was gaping forward, giving him a perfect view down her front. She wasn't wearing the most transparent of her 36C support bras, but it was revealing enough. Given her position, he could apparently see enough for her to feel his eyes streaking along her skin, scorching her nerves.

She decided not to clutch at her neckline to close off his view. Weak and trembling modesty would not be an effective defense against the forces she felt swirling down from him, invisible yet strong, two strands wrapping around each other, surrounding her, like a double helix. She didn't panic, but let the forces settle around her. She sat back on her heels. Ran her gaze up the length of him. Tilted her head. Took hold of the cabinet door and swung it gently back and forth, brushing the leg of his khakis.

She said, "Remember what I told you about me and doors?"

His gray eyes were pinned on her. He didn't misunderstand. He had slipped his jacket on and its front panels were pushed behind him by his hands which were thrust deep in his trouser pockets. He didn't flinch. "The door's light. There's only so much damage it could do me."

"A very battered shin," she said with a sweet smile.

"I'll risk it."

"Well, it's your leg."

"And you think I wouldn't retaliate?"

On her knees before him, she dropped her eyes and was looking straight at his thigh. She felt her disadvantage but knew how to play it for what it was worth. "Retaliate?" she echoed. "On a defenseless woman living alone without her phone plugged in?"

"Try me."

She could play this game too. "Don't tempt me," she replied, swinging the door again, aiming for his shin.

"That's what you wanted to give me before I leave?" he queried. "A bruise?"

"Fair warning, that's all," she said, lightly. She bent back down to her task, her sweatshirt gaping forward again, daring to tease him, daring to enjoy his gaze upon her. The clinging strands of his attention intensified. The helix surrounding her turned hot and viscous. She continued to resist panic but was happy when she unearthed what she was looking for.

It was an antique biscuit tin box whose lid was painted with what must have been the bill of fare from a Paris music hall. A well-fed young woman wearing a flowered bonnet and a flowered corsage leaned invitingly against an oversized menu listing drink prices.

She rose. The blood rushed out of her face, then flooded it again, when she saw the look in his eye. "Let me fill this with babka, and you can take it home with you," she said. She turned to her task and pulled herself together. With her back to him, she continued, "I've always loved poking through junk shops. My guess is that this tin is from the eighteen eighties or so."

She turned back to him and handed him the box of plum cake topped with a pretty girl. He accepted it with a look that assessed and demanded. It frightened her too, but she was prepared and managed a cool, dismissive smile in response. Then she led him back through the hallway to the parlor.

They spoke of this and that, but they were really talking about something else entirely. She didn't think she could get him out her front door fast enough.

"Call me on Tuesday, Alexandra."

"I'll do that, Val."

He strode across her porch, paused at the steps to the walkway, looked back at her through the screen. He filled her, neck down, with a gray gaze. "Then we'll be ready for the next go-around." He wasn't teasing her this time. He was telling her.

She closed the front door and hurried back to the kitchen. She picked up the contract and tried to read it. Nothing doing. She put the papers down.

SEVERAL HOURS LATER, Lauri found Alexandra seated at her kitchen table in the dark. "I thought you'd come over after he left and tell me all about it," Lauri said, surprised and a little puzzled.

Alexandra raised her head and said, "I can't read anymore."

"Huh?"

"I've lost my ability to read. I can make out a few one-syllable words here and there, but the others . . ." She shrugged. "I'm not sure I'll be able to work in the lab tomorrow. Or do science again—ever."

Lauri laughed. "I've heard of guys having strong effects before, but this is too much! Quick, tell me what DNA stands for."

Alexandra answered automatically, "Deoxyribonucleic acid."

"That's at least eight or ten syllables."

Alexandra perked up a bit. "Try another one."

"I don't really know another one. All right, how about RNA?"

"No, I mean give me something difficult."

Lauri smiled. "If that's too easy, my dear, you're fine. Get a good night's sleep, and you'll be good as new in the morning."

"You're right. I'm exhausted."

"I'll lock up for you."

While Lauri checked windows and doors, Alexandra went to her bedroom. Not bothering with brushing her teeth or her hair, not even bothering with pajamas, she stripped to nothing, pulled back the covers, and fell into bed. She was asleep the moment her head hit the pillows.

EIGHT

 "SAY WHAT?" WALTER demanded, his deep, Southern voice an octave higher than normal. Then he slammed the ball.

Val grunted and returned the shot against the front wall. "Jean-Philippe planted her."

Walter puffed. "That's what I thought you said." He whirled and smashed the ball. "He's good, but he ain't that good."

On the squash court, their shoes squeaked musically, mirrored in the inch of polyurethane covering the hardwood.

"There's no other explanation," Val said, keeping his eye on the ball whizzing around the walls and placing his shot.

"How much sense does it make," Walter demanded, pumping over to the corner, "that our man Slick could just happen to get his woman on the research team that Bob Sutherland chose?"

"There's no other explanation," Val insisted.

"How about that she's a fox?"

"Try cat."

"Okay, cat. And this one I gotta see."

"I know it's a long shot."

"Miles and miles long."

The volley had been good, but Val finally missed, thereby ending it. He caught the ball and tossed it to Walter. "Jean-Philippe is capable of anything."

Walter stepped into the service box. "What evidence do you have that your cat is linked to Slick?" He rebounded the ball off the side wall, then the front wall.

Val swatted and hit. "She gave me an antique biscuit tin. It's French." His aim was off, and he gave Walter the gift of a no-miss shot.

Walter accepted the gift and sent the ball reverberating around the court, untouched. "Oh, man! You're losin' it! Your mind and this game! It's mine at fourteen, by the way." Walter scooped up the ball, went to fetch his towel. "That's four in a row, and I'm through."

Val bent over and put his hands on his knees. His towel was tossed in the corner, but he didn't bother with it. He liked letting the sweat run down the sides of his chin and neck and drop on the floor.

He felt good—at least better than at any time in the past two hours since he'd driven back from Durham to Cary in a record twenty-five minutes flat, avoiding two speed traps, running three red lights, steering clear of four possible collisions, and pulling up to his colonial brick two-story in an ugly, ugly mood. After an hour of grunting and sweating on the squash court, he was coming back to himself. So what if he had the back of a forty-year-old? He still had the knees of a nineteen-year-old. And his muscles were singing, feeling ageless.

"I can't figure why you didn't want to play me in tennis," Walter said into his towel.

Still bent over, Val turned his head. "I wanted a game, not a win. There would've been no glory in beating you at tennis."

Walter grinned. "No deal. You were dying for a win. But since it's Slick's face you want to whup, I think you oughta go find him and whup *his* bad-ass face, not mine."

"Jean-Philippe is already back in Paris, and I'm just looking for satisfaction."

"You ain't gonna find it with me. Not the kind you want. Tell me again what happened at your woman's house beyond the fact that she gave you a freakin' biscuit tin?"

"We went over the research contract, article by article."

They left the court together and headed for the locker room.

"Do I look stupid? Are you tellin' me that *nothing* happened beyond that?"

Nothing beyond the fact that Alexandra J. Kaminski had gotten right in under his skin. "That's right."

"Was she wearing edible underwear, or what?"

"Sweatpants and a sweatshirt."

"Damn. You French just don't know what looks good on a woman. You need a shower, my man. Make it long and cold."

In the shower, short and hot, Val realized the absurdity of the notion that Jean-Philippe had planted Alexandra on the research team Bob Sutherland had chosen for the sole purpose of—

Of what?

Val didn't have the answer to that. Nevertheless, the idea remained that Alexandra was, somehow, connected to Jean-Philippe and that their relationship spelled trouble for him. His only concrete reason for imagining the improbable link between Alexandra and Jean-Philippe—beyond the fact that Jean-Philippe had appeared out of the blue and had probably taken a liking to Alexandra—was the kitschy Parisian biscuit tin she had given him. Val had seen the original poster on the wall of that Montmartre music hall which was now an art gallery. But Jean-Philippe couldn't have known that, nor could he have given Alexandra an antique tin to stash in her kitchen cabinet to have on hand. And what did it matter, anyway? Such an object had nothing whatsoever to do with cancer research or international patents.

Still, by the time he was tearing away from Alexandra's house, he felt as if he'd had his head screwed around and put back on sideways. Maybe it wasn't the biscuit tin itself, but the plum cake inside. Maybe it was her brown eyes. Or the curl at the end of her braid. Whatever it was, an appetite was born in him that was more interesting than mere desire. It was a hunger to dominate. Not the kind that came with a one-hundred-ninety-kilometer-per-hour serve, but the ownership kind. The down-on-her-knees-before-him kind. He relished the image, knew what was wrong with it and didn't care.

He dressed and met Walter outside the locker room. On their way to the parking lot, Walter asked, "What's with you and Slick, anyway? Do you two go way back or something?"

Val laughed and shook his head. "Call it instant antipathy."

"Then how did you get your job at S-L?"

"After being turned down numerous times, I finally finagled my interview with Yves when Jean-Philippe, it so happened, was in Bangkok on an extended trip. Lucky for me. Upon his return, he took one look at me, smiled, and said that he had long admired my tennis career, especially my serve. I felt an itch between my shoulder blades and knew that I had better watch my back."

Walter Fearrington had worked at Seine-Lafitte before being picked off by a headhunter at Glaxo Wellcome, and he had enough of an idea of how Jean-Philippe operated to have given him the street name Slick. "And that was the first time you met him?"

Val nodded.

"Has he been on your case before now?"

"No," Val replied. "I've always watched my back, and he's kept his distance. He was recently promoted to GM, and now I'm feeling crowded."

"Do you know why he attended the seminar?"

Val shrugged. "I have a hunch or two."

"Find out for sure," Walter recommended.

Val walked across the parking lot to his two-seater Cadillac and drove away from the Raleigh Sports Club in considerably better shape than when he had arrived. He had filed enough of his rough edges to be able to think through all that had happened since meeting both Jean-Philippe and Alexandra Kaminski in the S-L hallway last Thursday morning.

He zipped around the Raleigh Beltline, almost empty on a Sunday night, resisting the trend of his thoughts, which were dragging him back into his past. He was even resentful of their backward tug, for what he liked most about America, apart from its telecommunications systems, was its extravagant denial of history, the way that not having a history was an integral part of its history. Where only the future counted, not the past.

He cruised into Cary, finally unable to resist the pull of his thoughts, whose direction had been established, classically, with a cup of tea and the taste of plum cake. He winced away from memories of his beautiful mother's alcoholic dissolution and his less beautiful and infinitely more dear sister's death from leukemia. He skipped over stories of his grandfather's financial stupidity and his father's threadbare though remarkably successful pretensions. His thoughts fixed, finally, on the day his tennis career had ended, and he saw with clarity the way the sunlight had flooded the red-ochered clay courts at Roland Garros and the French Open.

He had been having his best season. He was at the height of his serve. He was positioned to break into the big time. He was in the second round, breezing into the third. He'd been having trouble with his back some months before, but the pain had been completely absent during the tournament. He felt no trace of cramp or strain when he threw the ball up in the air, serving for game, set, and match point, but when his racket whooshed down, he was suddenly engulfed in a haze of pain that burned in every muscle and screamed in every fiber of his lower right back. Miraculously, he put away a down-the-line return and won the point, but he had to be helped off the court. "The Graceful Frenchman," "France's Next Grand Slam Hope," "The Athletic Aristocrat"—as the press loved to call him—never played another tournament.

He remembered the pain, of course. That was unforgettable. He remembered, as well, the despair he felt when he realized, upon reading his trainer's face, that he would never fulfill his vow to honor his beloved sister's memory with a big win. The pain and the despair were alive, but the most vivid facet in this fractured crystal of selective memory was his fear and loathing of the first words to come out of his trainer's mouth.

"Eh bien, Valéry," Stephanos had said. "You're fortunate to have your grace and good breeding to fall back on."

Meaning that he could lounge on the Côte d'Azur as the gigolo of some wealthy woman for the rest of his life. Or marry her. Or marry a succession of such women. Meaning that he had no skills other than his ability to hit a fuzzy ball with force and accuracy. Meaning that he had distinguished himself at his lycée precisely by the amount of work he never did. Meaning that he never went to university, had no discipline for anything but his sport, and, now broken, was pretty much good for nothing.

During the next year, he orgied. Then one day he woke up, addressed himself to the Ecole des Hautes Etudes Commerciales, and talked his way into the program on the strength of his grace and name and ruined back. A month later he found his way inexplicably blocked. He was never allowed to matriculate, and no one could tell him why. He left immediately for the States, not to return until he had a business degree in hand from the best. He had made it through a rigorous M.B.A. program with no preparation beyond his training in competition at the highest levels and a fear of living his father's lizard life on the Riviera.

As he pulled into his driveway in Cary, he had yet to determine what any of these recollections had to do with Alexandra Kaminski, and he decided that she had inspired in him nothing more than a touch of retrospection now that he was so close to accomplishing a goal he'd had in mind almost since the day his sister had died. He didn't bother parking his car in the garage and instead got out right at his front walk. Night had fallen, and the inside and outside lights, both on timers, came on, illuminating his way. He pushed the numbers of his security code on the pad to the left of his front door and walked into a house he had bought just before the housing price boom in Cary.

It was new construction, traditional on the outside with Palladian windows at the entry and a game room wing, which was one of his housing musts, for his pool table. The inside was contemporary Italian and had a second story with four bedrooms. Val occupied the master bedroom suite on the first floor which consisted of bed, bath, and paneled study. Upon returning home from Durham he had entered that last room where he'd aggressively punched out Walter's telephone number on his desk phone.

On this second return home, he went straight to the kitchen. He flipped on CNN, found the dinner his Moroccan housekeeper had left him in the fridge, and nuked the lamb couscous. He ate it standing up, swilling mineral water straight from the bottle. He kept his attention focused on the blue screen and the parade of the post-colonial, postcommunist, new multicultural world disorder that was dragging everyone into the twenty-first century by way of age-old ethnic antagonisms. He avoided eye contact with the biscuit tin he had earlier dropped on the kitchen table and on whose lid flirted a saucy little demimondaine, dimpled apple cheeks, sweet enough to eat.

He didn't bother washing up after himself. Flipping off the TV, he went to shoot several indifferent games of pool. When he felt himself tired enough for bed—the workout with Walter only shaving his edge off, not exhausting him—he performed his evening toilette. His American bedtime rituals were abbreviated. Fewer *petites habitudes*. He put away his clothing, slipped into black patterned silk boxers, and went to sleep with his shades open and his curtains undrawn against the North Carolina night sky.

He half-woke to darkness and the feel of hands on his back. Feminine hands, rubbing him sensuously, almost but not quite finding that spot on his lower right, that knot of stripped, striated muscles, long healed but always aching for a massage. The hands rubbed and kneaded, probed and soothed. He wasn't ready to be fully awake yet. He guessed the hands didn't want to fully awaken him either. They would let him know, he figured, when they were ready. The feminine hands were presumably attached to a feminine body. He supposed he would find that out in good time too.

In his semiconscious state, he was pretty sure the flirty tart from the biscuit tin had drifted into his imagination. Then the sensations became too real for those of a semiconscious dream, and he discovered that the feminine hands were attached to a very real feminine body that was naked and pressed along his backside.

A feminine voice spoke. "Don't you want to know how I got past the security code?" she asked.

It was Alexandra. He was sure of it.

"Tell me."

"Because I'm clever," she whispered into his ear, slipping her hands under black silk.

"I know," he answered, then realized, dimly, that she was speaking French. He hadn't known she could speak French. Clever Alexandra.

"You hadn't expected to see me so soon, had you? Glad I came?"

He was surprised she had come and perhaps, in a confused way, disappointed too, for he had not expected her to come so soon, or ever, or to play it this way. During that scene by the cabinet in the kitchen, he had come as close as he ever had to putting a fine polish on a woman's kitchen floor, and its effects had been roaming restlessly in his body the evening long and were coming into sharp focus now. So he was ready, even willing, to accommodate her, but he wasn't going to be her man for the long run. Maybe no one's man for the long run.

"Yes, I'm glad."

"I'm glad you're glad, given how far I've come and what I had to do to get here."

"And given that I'm leaving in the morning for Dallas."

"I'm coming with you."

Clever Alexandra. Aggressive Alexandra. She had taken the initiative, but he wasn't going to let her get away with that any more. He would take her just the way he wanted her to satisfy himself, then pleasure her later, at his leisure. He grasped her two hands in one of his and trapped them at his chest. Then without turning around, he stretched his other hand behind him and clamped it on her buttocks to stop her sensual wriggling. He paused at length, registering the significance of grasping a much smaller handful of flesh than he had anticipated. He almost lost his erection.

"You have to be surprised that I'm here, Valéry," the woman laughed and nibbled his ear. "At least, tell me you're surprised."

His pleasant dream evaporated. He was fully awake now.

"I'm surprised, Sophie," he obliged her, rolling toward her. "You'll tell me all about the reasons for this surprise in the morning."

"On our way to Dallas."

He looked down at her short dark hair, her dark hungry eyes, her wide smiling mouth. He was unprepared for this moment. With no stash of prophylactics in his bedside table, he felt trapped.

Sophie must have understood the meaning of his hesitation. She slipped one hand under the pillow and withdrew a slim foil packet. "You see, Valéry, I did not come all this way to see you without remembering your rules."

He reflected that sex was a whole lot more fun before the age of AIDS. He never liked taking a shower in a raincoat, but if a man needed a shower . . .

"However, since I've come expressly to be faithful to you," Sophie said on a hopeful, pleading note, "this"—she rubbed the foil packet between thumb and forefinger—"should not be necessary."

It would not be, if he could find someone pure. But that was a project for another day.

Impure Sophie, correctly interpreting his silence, nipped open the foil packet with her teeth. The demimondaine, beckoning to him from the lid of the biscuit tin, floated into his mind's eye again. Blended with Sophie. Apple cheeks, top and bottom. Crisp, tart, firm. He willingly sank his teeth into the delectable apple being offered him, but he desired—across his shoulders, down his spine, through his groin muscles—the watering taste of juicy plums. His forbidden fruit, but no longer forgotten.

NINE

 SHE AWOKE REFRESHED. Dressed while danc-
ing. Danced while dressing. Once dressed,
danced down the four flights of ſtairs to the
cobbled inner courtyard. Went to the portal,
unlatched the complicated bolt of brass by touch in the shadows, and
pushed open the heavy green door. Let it close behind her, its precise
clicking and locking shutting her out, giving her the world.

Smell of roaſted coffee, harsh cigarette smoke, fresh air. The hum
of the city, early-spring birds, the neigh of a nearby nag. Sparkling
rivulets of water rinsing the gutters, bright sky above ſtriped by tines
of white clouds. Yellow, benevolent sun. Early-morning pleasures
she did not usually know. A late-night working girl who cuſtomarily
rose at noon. Today was different.

She lifted her skirts and ſtepped over the running gutters, giving
berth to the ſtreet sweeper with his briar broom. A tiny square conjured from the haphazard interseſtion of three ſtreets, a planer tree
in its center circled by an iron railing that resembled a ſtanding rib
of pork. Angled toward the corner café. Wonderful familiarity of an
interior. Cracked marble floor. Pretty embroidered purse tied inside
her jacket. Clink of sous againſt the *zinc*. Coffee and croissants.
Smiles for the owner, Pierre, ſtrong and aproned, her good friend.
Smiles for all her good friends today.

She stood at the *zinc*, spoke with the regulars. Pierre stood behind the *zinc*, doing his job. He had folded the newspaper by his right elbow. She leaned over and peered at it. "*Le Figaro*," she said, causing Pierre to smile and to shove toward her the cheap, precious pages crabbed with black ink. She unfolded the newspaper and made an exaggerated little display of reading. She was able to make out several of the headlines.

Pierre reached down for something under the counter, withdrew another newspaper, and handed it to her ceremoniously.

She accepted it, a crease between her brows, fearing a test she would fail, but when she opened the paper, she blinked and read aloud, pridefully, "*Le Courrier français*."

"For you, Jeanne," Pierre said.

She didn't have to struggle very much with the date. "Last week's, even. You're a dream, Pierre." She rose on tiptoe, kissed his cheek, to the approval of the regulars.

"Tell us what's in it," a woman encouraged.

"I'll read it cover to cover and let you know." She smiled and tucked the paper under her arm. "Even if it takes me all day." Without embarrassment, "And it probably will! I'm dying for an article about the Opéra."

"You're going tonight," Pierre said. It was a statement.

Jeanne nodded. "Maurice and Charlotte are taking me."

"And on the fashionable night too," the woman commented.

"Not standing up," Jeanne added. She sketched the strut of a grande dame. "Four-franc seats." She struck an attitude. "It's Delibes's *Lakmé*." She twirled her foot. "There will be dancing."

She was to pay for those four-franc seats the same way she paid for reading lessons. By working in a laundry on her days off, washing, ironing, folding. By saving her sous and centimes. She could work all day and still not be tired for an evening at the opera. Maurice had agreed to accompany her, no doubt to atone for having made her accept that drink from a customer. Nothing had come of it, but she had been angry with Maurice. Charlotte had been too and did her part to make Maurice suffer. But harmony and friendship had been restored, and the three of them were going to the opera. Where she would see dancing.

Twilight. Twinkling lights. Glitter dust cast across the city. View of all from above. Descent by carriage to the Opéra. Clip and clop of hooves. Fresh air with a center strip of warmth and promise, as thin and perfect as the "white thread" in a soft brie. Shawl for fashion, not warmth. She had never been *frileuse*.

Then, lights. Everywhere. On the square, gas lamps ablaze. The edifice with curls at every scale, whorls to catch the eye. Pillars. Columns. Garlands. Wreaths. Statues. Archways. All of stone. Inside, more light, mellow light, more magical. The *grand foyer*. Double row of chandeliers. Thousands of candles. Winking off polished glass and burnished gold. Tiaras, necklaces, cravat pins. Fashionable throng. Hushed burble of voices. Exotic perfumes, expensive tobacco smoke. Gilded pillars, man-sized pedestals. Ceiling beyond imagination. Like Versailles, Maurice said. Like a Turkish bath, Charlotte joked, then coughed.

Rapt attention. Edge of seat. Intrigued by the curious shoes, *en pointe*, making foot and leg line long and beautiful. Enamored of the Italian prima ballerina, pretty in her white satin *basquine* flounced with lace. Pleasure in the music, in the dancers, in new moves and combinations. Pleasure in the critique as well. A move, a line, a sequence rechoreographed in her head. Not perfect, but nearly so. Pleasure in the perfection. Pleasure in the flaws.

Sweeping down the staircase, leaving for the working quarter. Sweet-sad knowledge that others were off to fashionable restaurants for supper. Gatherings. Sleeping in the next day. On the *rez-de-chaussée*, she noticed she had dropped a glove.

While Maurice and Charlotte waited for her, Jeanne returned to the curved staircase, lifting her skirts to climb back up, eyes scanning the steps above her, swimming upstream, crowd flowing around her. She spied her glove near the top. Before she got to it, a man bent down and picked it up.

THE BLUE HOUR

She took more steps up. He took one step down. Into her view came beautiful black shoes, black trousers, black overcoat unbuttoned, snow-white shirt above the sober vest. Cravat. Needle lace. Silk scarf tucked under well-tailored lapels. She looked up and into gray eyes and a face wearing an expression that was canny and amused. Suppressing triumph, but not quite hiding it. A face that was not blandly handsome but angled for interest, dimensioned with humor, mastery, the willingness to take a risk.

She dropped her eyes. She schooled her own features to blankness. Her heart shrank from the encounter. Her feet advanced another step, so that she was one down from him, so that she would not be at an impossible disadvantage. He did not take the next step down to meet her on her own terms. The crowd kept flowing around them. Too intimate, this private, public space.

"Mademoiselle."

"Monsieur."

"You have lost your glove."

"Yes, monsieur."

"Is this, perhaps, your glove?" The poor, lost thing was lost again in the hand he held out to her.

"Yes, it is, monsieur."

"I would like to return it to you." But he did not extend his hand, as if he were not yet willing to relinquish the lost item.

"I would like that."

"When shall I return it to you?"

This was all in the grand manner. It would have been exciting if she had not been born a peasant girl in the country and become a working girl in Paris. If she had been wearing silk and satin, not cambric and challis. If he had not been who he was, whoever he was. A monarchist, at the very least. As it was, the encounter was not exciting, but more like a game of cat and mouse, and she would not play it. The night she had met him at the music hall, she accepted no more than a glass of water from him, and that under duress.

She glanced up at him. Dropped her eyes again. "Now, if you

69

please, monsieur." She held out her hand. Hint of anger. Hint of steel and dignity.

He returned her glove with a bow, stylized but also stylish. He did not click his heels so much as kiss them together. It was well done, perfectly restrained, graceful. She knew an effective gesture when she saw one.

She also knew how to respond. She accepted the glove, dropped him a fluid curtsy. Proper bend to her swan's neck. Eyes downcast. A gesture with her right, gloveless hand, as if she were holding a delicate fan whose exorbitant value was of no moment to her. To a muscle she knew how to infuse her movements with irony, even with contempt. Strong message to stay away, since he knew where she worked.

She rose, keeping her gaze level so that when she turned her vision snagged on the sparkle of diamond shirt studs. "Thank you, monsieur."

"You are welcome, mademoiselle." He said it to her back.

She descended the staircase, straining every nerve not to hurry, feeling his eyes on her. She had been impudent, but he had deserved it. Shadow across her pleasure. Sanctuary in the company, once again, of Maurice and Charlotte.

Days later, the delicate bridge between late afternoon and early evening. In the back room of Le Chat Noir. High ceilings. Large, high-placed windows, cracked for ventilation, spreading light generously, shafts of blue, churchlike in their angles and effects. One wall of mirrors. Ballet barres. Her ideas. Standing at a barre with her fellow dancers. Accepting of their decisions to pursue profitable sidelines after-hours. Trying new steps. Importing opera dance to the music hall. Translating it. Thinking the opera would benefit from exports.

Her favorite hour of the day. Her favorite place in the world. Beyond the connecting door, the music hall shadowed and slumbering. Her hair braided around her head. Peasant blouse, brilliantly embroidered. A present from Pierre's Polish mother's hands. Woolen stockings, tied with garters above her knees, bunched around her ankles. Bare feet. Flutters of fabric at her waiſt, drifting around her knees, her calves. Her warm-up skirt. Bending. Swaying. Swaying. Bending. Kick. Stretch. Melting into the movement. Living inside the movement.

Chérie, Nina, and Louise giggling and leaving the room. Leaving, no doubt, to drink or pee or freshen makeup. Silly girls. Hands lightly grasping the barre. Facing the brick wall. Mirrored wall to her right. Pausing to imagine a new sequence. Letting her head rotate slowly. Lulled. Content.

She felt a new presence in the room. Someone had come to ſtand behind her. She knew that the girls had not left the room on their own but had been dismissed. She did not turn around. She knew who it was by the dark shadow that crossed her pleasure. No, that was not quite right. She knew who it was by the change in her pleasure, the dark shadowing of it; but her feelings had not soured to displeasure. She was ſtartled by her breathlessness. His timing was exquisite. He had waited juſt long enough to impress and reassure her with his deliberateness, and he had produced in her a textured anticipation of which she had not previously been aware.

She wished she felt more disguſted and less intrigued by this invasion of her privacy. She gathered herself, ſtood ſtraight. The air had changed with his presence, and was charged. She wondered if, in his deliberateness, he had known to choose this moment and this place to come to her, to insert himself at the interſection of her passions, when and where she lived moſt honeſtly in her feelings, in her body, in her equilibrium, in her responsiveness.

"I have come to speak to you," he said.

She knew his voice by now. She did not turn around, but neither could she resiſt glancing into the mirror at her right. He did not meet her gaze in the glass. He was ſtanding a breath behind her, his head bent toward her, his fine ſtraight nose near the crown of her hair. He was looking over her shoulder, down her blouse under which she wore an old-fashioned camisole. No corset. She regretted its absence, her exposure. In the mirror, she could see that not a thread of his clothing or part of his body touched her. His hands were clasped behind his back. Yet she felt him all over her, around her.

She looked ſtraight ahead again, at the brick wall. She gripped the barre tighter so that she would not shudder. She wished to betray neither fear nor acceptance of his nearness.

"What have you come to speak to me about, monsieur?"

"The opera," he said, "among other things."

"I will gladly speak of the opera, monsieur." She would not gladly speak of "other things."

"Very well."

"Is it my opinion of the dancing you wish, perhaps, monsieur?"

He shook his head. She could feel it in the minimal movement of air behind her. "I wish to ſtraighten things out between us."

There was nothing to ſtraighten out. A denial, however, was not what the situation called for. She preserved a cautious silence.

He said, "When you see me in public, you are to acknowledge me as someone you know."

"I see."

"I am not sure that you do. Laſt week at the opera, you were un-civil."

"It's a lesson in manners, then, that you have come to give me, monsieur."

"Yes."

Her manners, she knew, had not been at fault. Her curtsy, how-ever, had provoked him. But he had given her no choice. She re-mained silent, knowing that was provoking him too, knowing that anything she said or did at this moment would provoke him. Not un-happy about it, for the provocation was her protećtion. Perhaps only temporary. Only keeping him at bay.

"You saw me several weeks ago, as well," he said, "you will recall."

She did recall it, and was surprised because she had not thought he'd seen her, had done everything at the time to avoid him. It was on the tip of her tongue to deny having seen him.

Before she perjured herself, he said, "At an exhibition of painting I saw you, and I recognized the artists you were with."

"It is our custom to go as a group to such exhibitions, monsieur, and my artist friends tell me which paintings I should admire and which I should scorn."

"You have no opinions yourself, then?"

"My taste, it seems, is as bad as my manners." She said this to provoke him further, since she had no other mode in which she could behave with him. "My friends laugh at what I like."

"The next time you see me at an exhibition, then, and I approach you, you shall not hide from me. Instead, you will greet me, introduce me to your friends, and explain what you like and what you have learned about why you should not like it."

"Yes, monsieur."

"I am not a 'monsieur.'"

At that, she turned her head, swept her eyes up his face, and over her shoulder gave him a glance of sultry irony whose effect far exceeded her intentions. Her lips curved up in a small, derisive smile to suggest that no, he wasn't a monsieur, he was a creature of a far less distinguished sort. She knew, of course, that he meant he was titled, and so with every passing second she felt herself sinking deeper into something that she should have been more strenuously resisting, torn between the knowledge that it was her very defiance that drew him and that if she didn't defy him, she would be beyond saving.

He held her eyes with a look that acknowledged her irony. That demanded obedience. That predicted his success. That scorched. "You shall greet me," he continued, "by name. It is Victor."

She turned back to stare at the brick wall. She nodded.

"Say it."

"Victor," she obeyed.

"Now you will tell me your name."

"It is not Olympia," she said, referring to the pseudonym favored by Chérie, Nina, and Louise when prostituting themselves, and added defiantly, "monsieur."

"I know it is not Olympia. That is why I have come to speak to you about your manners."

She drew a breath. "Surely you do not mean to degrade my manners, only to improve them," she said, this time without daring the derisive "monsieur."

"We are agreed that your name is not Olympia."

She said in a rush, "It is Jeanne."

"Jeanne what?"

"Lacombe."

"Where were you born?"

She paused. "A little village on the Dordogne. Sainte-Foy-la-Grande. You will not know it."

"Bergerac. I know it."

He hadn't touched her, she was sure of it, but he might as well have put his hands at her neck and pressed them down, over her breasts to her stomach, around her hips, her thighs, her calves, then brought them back up again. Her skin rose in goose bumps. Everywhere.

She needed to say something, anything. "So you have come to teach me a lesson in manners. I am to greet you by name, introduce you to my friends, and tell you how I see what I see and how I should see it differently. What else?"

"You are not to be impertinent."

"That will be difficult," she said demurely.

He made no response. She did not need to glance at the mirrored wall to her right to see that his expression was one of calm belief that he would bring her to heel. He stood behind her a moment longer, his hands still clasped behind his back, then turned and strode out of the room. She heard his footsteps echo and fade.

Later she learned the startling news from Charlotte that the Count d'Albret—the man she knew as Victor—had bought Le Chat Noir. That night, Maurice's eyes followed her everywhere, his expression improbably blending apology, remorse, a curious kind of parental surprise and pride, and a happiness that came when a man knows his future is secure. Victor chose not to return to his newly purchased establishment for some time.

ALEXANDRA AWOKE TO the pitch of night and sat bolt upright. Her bedside clock glowed an unmistakable orange three o'clock. She was sweating, heart pounding, temples throbbing. She looked down at herself, was shocked to see she was naked, and felt as if she was sweating in the wrong places. She must have been having a nightmare but couldn't remember what it was. Only half-awake, she groped for the robe at the end of the bed, slipped it on, pulled her braid out, flopped it over the collar.

She got up and padded barefoot to the kitchen. She called out, "Erica? Is that you?" She switched on the kitchen light which lanced her pupils, bringing her fully awake. She massaged her temples and shook her head clear of the feeling that Erica's spirit had slipped outside her body and had wandered over to tell Alexandra something important.

TEN

WORKING OFF A hot tip that Dr. Larry was out of town for the week, Erica decided to keep an eye on the Mod Squad, so she breezed into the lab midafternoon to find it half-empty. In one corner was a lab-coated back hunched over a microscope with the top of a red head just visible above the shoulder line. Near the sink was an absurd gizmo that was shaking like a washing machine with a lopsided load in the spin cycle. The Slavic Queen was standing next to it.

The sight of her stopped Erica dead in her tracks. "Yech! Coach, your aura's out of whack!"

Alexandra looked up from the machine. "Look who's talking."

"What's not to like about my outfit today? I've got on normal street clothes."

"Normal, huh?"

"This is a Bette Davis dress, I'll have you know, and the green plaid high-tops were a real find."

"I think the fashion problem is with your earrings—that is, if the miniature rubber chicken in one ear and the oversized safety pin in the other qualify as earrings."

"Retro punk," Erica commented, "but enough about me. Let's get back to your aura. It's a mess."

"Yours would be too if you spent the night I did. Not much sleep."

"Well, you do look like something the cat dragged in."

"Don't talk to me about cats."

Ooh, so Coach was cranky today. "Mad at me about Val?"

Kaminski glanced at Hot Stuff, a.k.a. Scotty McCarthy, and glanced back when she saw that he was still making love to his microscope. "No."

"Good," Erica said. "I just came from scoping the main drag and didn't see our man Val, so you don't have to worry about running into him today or anything."

"I know," Alexandra said. "He's in Dallas."

Erica wasn't quite ready to swallow the bait. "Dallas, huh?"

"Yes, Dallas. At least, that's what he told me yesterday."

Erica felt a distinctly unpleasant turn in every cell of her diseased body. She opened her mouth to say something, changed her mind, then settled on one word. "Spill."

"Val Dorsainville is a vice president at Seine-Lafitte. Although he has nothing to do with our research grant, he was chosen to be the one to go over the final version of the contract agreement with me. We did it yesterday at my house."

"At your house?" Erica's bad feeling got worse. "What kind of clothes was he wearing?"

Coach rolled her big brown eyes. "What kind of question is that?"

"A good one. Tell me about his clothes."

"Knit pullover shirt. Khaki trousers. Black jacket. Does it make a difference?"

Erica thought so, but couldn't say why. "Damn," she said more to herself than Alexandra. "I didn't know my powers were so strong."

"You know, Erica—just a sec while I turn the centrifuge off." Kaminski flipped a switch, opened the lid. "I'm in the middle of some very important experiments, and instead of concentrating of them, I'm having to worry not about your so-called powers but about your judgment. What exactly did you say to Mr. Dorsainville last week?"

"That's the spirit, Coach!" Erica approved. "Don't take this lying down. But to answer your question, when I first saw our man Val I thought 'Wow!' but by the time I was next to him, I sensed trouble. So I warned him away from you."

"Well, he didn't have a choice in the matter, since he was required to work with me on the contract agreement."

"Yeah, and there goes my good mood."

Coach looked ridiculously hopeful. "Did your lab results improve?"

"Nah. My blood count is still in the toilet, but my team won in Charlotte over the weekend. The problem is"—Erica took a deep breath—"the problem is that I've been following the techniques suggested in the *Tibetan Book of the Dead,* and I've discovered that my karmic problems result from giving bad advice. Or, at least from messing up my friends' lives."

Coach's crankiness evaporated. She laughed. "No, Erica! Don't tell me that you believe that!"

"And last time around, I had a bad case of TB."

"Well, you don't have tuberculosis now, and if you think you've messed up my life, you can forget it. No harm done."

Erica needed to get to the heart of the matter, so she asked half-jokingly, half-seriously, "Is it possible you didn't get enough sleep last night because you were enjoying a night of fabulous sex with our man Val?"

Coach's crankiness returned. Industrial strength. "Good heavens, no, Erica!"

Phew. Erica would have pressed the issue if Hot Stuff hadn't entered the conversation.

Without looking up from his microscope, he said, "You're such a liar, A.K. As if I didn't hear you say a minute ago, 'We did it yesterday at my house.' Direct quote. 'We did *it.*'"

"Is sex all you ever think about, McCarthy?"

"Pretty much, yeah. Speaking of which, if you want a reading on your aura from the male perspective, you don't look anything like something the cat dragged in. In fact, I think you've never looked hotter than you do today. Sizzlin', I'd say."

"You can keep your comments to yourself, McCarthy."

"Hey, it was a compliment."

"I think I know a compliment when I hear one."

He still didn't look up. "I'm not so sure about that."

"Have the courtesy at least to look at me when you talk to me, Mr. Scott McCarthy. How about some manners around here?"

Mr. Scott McCarthy was not persuaded to look up. "Who died and made you principal investigator?"

"You were there when Larry appointed me his proxy for this week."

"Only for administrative matters regarding the contract."

"He wouldn't object to seeing me clean up your act."

Erica bellowed for time out. "Hot Stuff! Coach! Cool it! You know, I figured something like this would happen. It's exactly like that episode in the Smurfs when Papa Smurf has an explosion in his lab and goes away to find the ingredient he needs, and all the Smurfs fall to squabbling among themselves."

Coach was not amused. "Thank you, Erica, for the cultural high note."

"What episode is that?" McCarthy wanted to know.

"The one where Smurf decides to run for head Smurf," Erica explained, "and launches a campaign getting everyone to vote for him, and when he's elected, he turns into a dictator. Sort of a Napoleon figure. Then there's a civil war. Of course, Papa Smurf returns and restores order."

At last the red head came around. "I never saw that one."

"You couldn't have," Erica informed him, "because I'm pretty sure it was banned in this country. Did you know that the Smurfs are Belgian?"

"No shit."

"Yeah, and I think that episode was never imported here because it's basically about the corrupt basis of the electoral process, namely self-interest." Erica then launched into a Marxist analysis of smurfiness, positing Papa Smurf as a benevolent Louis XIV figure, and was interrupted only by the arrival of an express delivery man who entered the lab and asked for Dr. Kaminski.

Coach signed for the package, opened the box, and when she read a short note, a strange expression came over her face. She held up a cellular phone. "It's from my grandmother."

McCarthy was idiot enough to ask, "A cellular phone from your Polish grandmother who still has a rotary baby, so you tell me, and can barely work that?" He squinted at the phone. "The latest model, no less."

"I guess she's moved into the nineties."

As far as Erica was concerned, Kaminski was lame, lame, lame. "What does the note say?" Erica asked.

Kaminski huddled the package. "It's in Polish, so you wouldn't be able to read it."

McCarthy might not know the difference between a lie and the truth, but Erica did. "I don't believe you."

Kaminski got crafty. "Since you're the psychic around here, you tell me who the phone's from."

Erica cackled with delight. She put her fingers to her temples as if receiving signals from another dimension. "I'll work on it," she said, "and get back to you. But seriously, folks, what you need—all of you, including Jack, Hao, Deb, Rosa—is a night on the town together so that you can all be friends again."

When she got no response, she added, "It's a matter of life and death."

McCarthy's laugh was derisive. "Whose?"

"Mine," Erica was happy to tell him. "If you swell guys and gals can't get along at the beginning of the week without Papa Smurf, think how bad you'll be by the end. And if you can't get along, then you can't work together. And if you can't work together, then you won't find a cure for cancer. And I'll die."

The two Smurfs looked contrite.

"So do it for me. Dinner, dancing, whatever. Make it Friday night, and let me suggest the Alhambra for atmosphere."

Erica left the lab with sincere assurances that the whole gang would go out together on Friday night. She smiled smugly. *Tell 'em you're gonna die, and they'll do anything for you!*

ALEXANDRA GOT HOME about six. She was sitting peacefully on her parlor sofa, reading her mail, when her briefcase began to buzz on the coffee table in front of her. She stared at it as if it might bite. Then, realizing what was up, she fished out the cellular phone, pulled up the antenna, and pushed Talk.

A pralines-and-cream voice greeted her. "Dr. Kaminski?"

"Speaking."

"Dr. Kaminski, this is Marie Biddle, Mr. Dorsainville's assistant?" Marie spoke only in rising intonations. "He asked me to call you to confirm that you received your cellular phone?"

"Yes, well, you know, I'm speaking on it now."

"I know that, Dr. Kaminski?" Marie sounded adorable. "I'm calling to make sure you've got it turned on and to confirm your telephone appointment with Mr. Dorsainville tomorrow afternoon?"

The conversation ended with Marie's expressed intention of calling her boss in Dallas to assure him all was in working order with the phone. Alexandra punched Off, feeling as if Val had just checked up on her. She didn't like the thought of being connected to him by a delicate lattice of plus and minus charges in the electromagnetic spectrum, like a cyberspine joining two nervous systems.

However, if she was connected to him, she figured she was connected to the rest of the world as well and acted on a whim to speak to her grandmother. When the much-loved voice crackled across the line, she said, "Babciu, hello."

"Alexandra Janina? Ah, my child! It is always good to hear from you. Is everything all right?"

Alexandra felt a sudden sense of safety to be speaking Polish. She assured her grandmother that everything was just fine and said that she was calling for a favor.

"Anything, my child."

The longing Alexandra had felt on Sunday to have the family album in her hands had become an inexplicably urgent yearning. "Babciu, I want you to send me the family album. The one with the pictures of Piotr Wojinski. Yes, of course, the one who lived in Paris. I want to see the pictures of him and his daughter, Lisette. Yes, yes, babciu, I know Lisette was your mother. Why do I want to see them? I don't know. It would make me happy to have the album here. That's all. Yes, thank you."

They chatted of this and that, and when Alexandra had heard the latest gossip from the old neighborhood, they ended the conversation.

Hardly had Alexandra pushed the antenna down when the phone began to ring again. She braced herself, expecting it to be Val.

Instead, through thin air came an unmistakably smooth French accent. "Miss Kaminski? Alexandra?"

She relaxed, put her feet up on the coffee table.

"Yes, sir, Jean-Philippe," she replied. "You're in Paris, aren't you? This is a remarkably good connection."

"A remarkably good telephone, as well. Seine-Lafitte buys only the best, Alexandra, and I believe I am speaking to you on one of our cellular phones."

"It was added to the contract yesterday, and I received it today."

"And how did the contract review go, my dear? Any problems?"

Beyond the fact that she had temporarily lost her ability to read? "No, no problems. It was a piece of cake, you could say."

"Good. I am sorry only that Yves decided on the review at the last minute. If I had known he wanted it, I would have delayed my return to Paris in order to go over it with you myself."

"That would have been nice."

"Yes. I would have been more comfortable, in fact, if that had been the case, since I am more familiar with the R-and-D particulars than is someone from Diagnostics."

"Well, I'm sure that Yves has confidence in Val."

An infinitesimal pause. "Yes, I am sure he does." Jean-Philippe went on to discuss various items in the contract, explaining that he was merely checking to see whether all was in order. "To assure myself, my dear, that Mr. Dorsainville dotted the i's and crossed the t's, as you say in English, and highlighted what was important. I wouldn't want anything to jeopardize this research project that promises such success."

Jean-Philippe detailed a number of items he apparently thought worth emphasizing. She had to fake her responses to most of his questions, because she had been so fuzzy by the end of the contract review with Val. However, she could hardly explain that to Jean-Philippe or imply that Val had not properly done his job.

Jean-Philippe soon shifted to lighter topics of talk, wound the conversation down, and brought it to a natural conclusion.

She was smiling when she said good-bye and turned the phone off. She stretched out against her sofa, glad for Jean-Philippe's phone call. As she ran through the points he had brought up, she focused particularly on his mention of the clause that the Rosenberg research funds would stop if Seine-Lafitte experienced a two-quarter downturn in profit this fiscal year. She didn't recall any point remotely similar to that from Sunday, but she knew it was worth remembering and discussing with Larry. It was reassuring to her that Jean-Philippe was such a dedicated administrator, for here he was still working on this contract even though it was probably midnight Paris time.

ELEVEN

 VAL HAD ALWAYS liked the uncluttered file drawers in his office at Seine-Lafitte RTP, North Carolina. Their relative emptiness seemed hopeful, a setting aside of space to be filled in the future. He was planning to put the final international patent approvals for Test Early, Feel Safe in there before too much longer, alongside the files labeled Diagnostic Research Results/Abbey Labs; Federal Drug Administration Approvals; Polymerase Chain Reaction Process License/Hoffmann-La Roche; and Endorsements/American Cancer Society, World Health Organization.

He didn't normally spend time with files, but today he was familiarizing himself with the past year of legal correspondence. He had already read what was in the first, second, and third drawers. He hitched his trouser legs and squatted, balancing himself comfortably on his heels, and opened the bottom drawer.

As he ran through the last file, a memory flitted into his head that would come to him at odd times. It was of the ungainly ball-pitch contraption his father had rigged when Val was about six or seven years old so that Val could improve his swing. The contraption could spit out up to three hundred tennis balls an hour, and Val remembered swatting at over a thousand balls a day. Sometimes ten thousand balls a week. Click, pock, whiz. He recalled the sight of the balls coming at him, second after second, hour after hour, in an unusual form of paternal cruelty.

He could almost smell the hot wax melting inside the contraption that activated a kind of hook scoop that shot the balls at him. He could hear the clumsy crank of the rusted ratchet that wheezed as it turned. And behind the contraption always hovered his half-crazed grandfather, replacing the wax, tending the fire that melted it, blathering about all the Dorsainvilles had lost.

Half-crazed grandfather. Completely crazy contraption. But since its unlikely mechanism was at the basis of his TEFS patent, it was going to give to Val—not to mention Seine-Lafitte's bottom line—all the Dorsainvilles had lost, and more.

"Would you like to see the fax that has just come in from Abbey Labs, Mr. D?" came a sweet voice behind him. "Do you think I should start planning your return trip to Chicago?"

Val rose to his feet on knees that never failed him. He turned toward Marie who was holding a curling piece of paper.

"Return trip?" he asked, frowning as he accepted the fax.

Marie explained how Mr. DuBois happened to be in Val's front office when the fax came in. He was of the opinion that Val should return to Chicago and straighten out the problems in person.

Val read with disbelief that the European Community Patent Commission had turned him down flat. Europe, of all places. Obviously Yves thought the problem was not in Europe but with the patent attorneys at Abbey Labs, and he was probably right.

"Does Yves think the trip can wait until after Easter?" he asked, returning the fax to Marie.

Marie didn't have the answer to that, but Yves's daughter did.

Sophie DuBois dismissed Marie and walked into the office. She strutted up to him, slid an arm around his waist, and kissed his neck. In French she said, "I crossed Yves in the hallway, and he wants this patent business settled. He's aiming to have your project and Seine-Lafitte on the front page of the *Wall Street Journal,* the *Frankfurter Allgemeine,* and the *Tokyo Shimbun* by the end of the year. He'd go with you to Chicago, except that he has to be in Paris at the end of next week."

"Those were my plans," Val replied lightly.

"Mine too. I'd go with you myself, but I've already got my flight back to France booked with Yves." She kissed him again. "That's why I'm glad we had our three days in Dallas."

Sophie had been to the States many times, but her English was not good, deliberately so, since she always traveled the francophone circuit. She knew everyone there was to know in Dallas and had entertained herself during the day while he had turned a profit. She had made sure his evenings were equally profitable by increasing his social contacts with soirees in Texas society. She made sure to entertain him at night too, actively and athletically.

Val had been with Sophie for about six months, more or less, since her return to Paris from several tours around the world. These trips involved spending money and doing for Seine-Lafitte whatever it was she did for the company, which was on the order of what she had done in Dallas. She was slim, sophisticated, and stylish from the tips of the upturned collars of her Lagerfeld suit to the points of her Charles Jourdain shoes. Her black hair was sleek and attractively cut. Her dark eyes had seen all there was to see. She surveyed the world from the top. Nice view.

"What you're not admitting," Val replied, "is that you don't know as many people in Chicago as you do in Dallas."

"That's true."

"And that you don't want to wait for me in the Research Triangle because it bores you."

"That's true too. But what I'm really not admitting is that I dropped everything last week in Paris to come to you and am putting it all on hold this next week too." Her smile was suggestive. Her embrace became seductive. "I can only put so much on hold for so long."

His smile was knowing, and he increased the pressure of her embrace. "You mean, you're worried that the man you left to come here to be faithful to me might stray."

She pushed away from him. "Wretch! How dare you accuse me of cheating on you? And such a suspicion is the surest sign that you're cheating on me! But if you must know, my most pressing business at the moment is offering moral support to Lucie."

"Oh? Does that mean that she and Jean-Philippe are going through with the divorce?"

Sophie made a moue. "They've agreed to stay together."

"It's true love, then, even after thirty years."

Sophie lifted one carefully tweezed brow. "It's stock options."

"I can see why Jean-Philippe wouldn't want to lose control of the Lafitte shares. Especially not now."

"But, no, Jean-Philippe wouldn't lose what's his, since his mother was the sister of the Lafitte who bought out D'Albret all those years ago. I was speaking of Lucie's interests in staying together. She has agreed to overlook Jean-Philippe's philandering." She cocked her head and measured Val with her eyes. "I'm not sure I approve."

"No?"

"*I* would certainly never overlook *your* philandering," she replied, wrapping herself around him again. "But how odd that you didn't know that Jean-Philippe was the Lafitte."

Indeed, Val found it strange to discover that he had misunderstood Jean-Philippe's relationship to the company. He had somehow always assumed that Jean-Philippe had married into the Lafitte family rather than being a descendent of it. His knowledge of Seine-Lafitte history was admittedly sketchy, and he had learned only what he had thought necessary: his grandfather's loss of controlling interest in the twenties and the Lafitte buyout with the collapse of the Dorsainville fortune in the thirties. Yves took over four decades later after the direct Lafitte male line died out.

Val shrugged. "I had it backwards. I thought Lucie was the Lafitte. No matter."

"Lucie is a Gervais," Sophie informed him. "Excellent family. Her uncle was the director of the Ecole des Hautes Etudes Commerciales for many years—but you probably already knew that."

Val was surprised for the second time in as many minutes. He had not known that Jean-Philippe had any connection to this distinguished business school, and he now reconsidered the fact of his mysterious rejection ten years earlier. He added two plus two, but he was not sure the sum equaled a straightforward four.

"Well," was all he said.

Sophie twirled her tongue around his ear. "That's what I love best about you—your careless disregard for who's who."

Val grasped her hand and brought it to his lips without quite kissing it. "I thought what you loved best about me was the diagnostic product I'm about to put on the market that will rake in millions for Seine-Lafitte."

Sophie's laugh was throaty. "Settle the international patents for TEFS, and I'm yours forever."

"I'll do my best, chère Sophie, but speaking of Jean-Philippe, did you happen to see him in Paris before you came and share with him your clever plan to surprise me here?"

Sophie tugged at his tie. "Maybe I did, and maybe I didn't, but maybe I did see him at a party one evening. You and I haven't gone public yet as an item, but we're not a secret either."

So, Sophie had tipped her hand to Jean-Philippe, and Jean-Philippe had flown to the States on the flimsy pretext of attending the team-building seminar. Although it was good to know where Jean-Philippe stood—which was so close at Val's back that he could feel the older man breathing down his neck—what he didn't know was why Jean-Philippe was standing there. He began to wonder if his careless disregard for who's who was in his best interest, after all.

"Yes, I saw Jean-Philippe at a party," Sophie said, "and that gives me an idea. Let's throw one next weekend, say Saturday night, because Yves and I are leaving the next day. It will be a kind of going away party for me and Yves and a success-in-Chicago party for you."

Val could think of better ways to spend the next weekend.

"We'll invite everyone, and we'll have it at your house. Why, what a delightful idea! Yes! I'll contact the caterers, and Marie can send out the invitations."

When Val did not respond, Sophie looked up at him, pouting prettily. "Do you deny me?"

Val hesitated.

"Remember, I'm the boss's daughter."

Val felt thwarted by the international patents and crowded by Jean-Philippe, but he was holding the boss's daughter, and she could buy him time, if he needed it.

He kissed her neck and lips. "I don't deny you."

TWELVE

 ON FRIDAY EVENING Val was standing outside the Alhambra with Walter and two guys named Stan and Phil. The four had come in two separate cars from a dinner party in Raleigh, and they had come stag. Stan and Phil were single and always on the prowl. Walter's wife had declined to come, and so had Sophie, largely because Walter had described the Durham café-cabaret as a dump. But Walter knew several members of the jazz quintet who were playing and had talked Val into hearing the group.

Val walked through the door of the Alhambra to the smells of African cuisine, a crowd mixed along every census category, and live jazz. His eyes were drawn immediately to a table where sat Seine-Lafitte's newest cancer research team, which included the Asian American, the cocky redhead, the scraggly-bearded science jock, two women he had never seen before, and one Alexandra J. Kaminski.

"There's a free spot," Walter said, moving forward.

Val didn't follow. "No hurry to sit down, is there?"

Walter shrugged and waited against the wall. Stan and Phil headed toward the bar which was adjacent to the entrance. Val studied his forbidden fruit.

Alexandra's thick hair was caught back from her face and was floating about her shoulders. The shifting colors of light danced across the blond mass, turning it now chlorine green, now bubble-gum, now citron. She had on a blouse so white it was blue in the light. It had a stand-up collar and an off-center closure, both collar and closure embroidered in a way that made him think she was wearing a Sunday-best Polish peasant blouse.

Stan and Phil returned with four bottles of beer, and Val said, "I've found our table, and I'll introduce you to S-L's newest hires."

Walter perked up. "I'm going to meet the cat, after all. Do I have to guess which one she is?" He scanned the table toward which they were headed. "Don't think I do." His deep chuckle rumbled. "Man, you're in some deep shit."

It didn't feel that way to Val. He thought rather that he had entered a smoky plum orchard whose air was incongruously spiced with *piment,* the English name of which escaped him at the moment, and interwoven with the music of a husky-voiced, husky-figured jazz singer. He liked the coincidence of meeting Alexandra here. He liked the way she looked at him, soft and vulnerable. He liked the way she looked away from him, strong and dismissive. He knew just how to play this one.

When the introductions had been made, and the invitation to join the table accepted, Stan and Phil swung chairs around and into action down at Alexandra's end. Val motioned Walter to stay with him at McCarthy's end.

Brief allusions to his few days in Dallas. Recap of last weekend's ACC tournament. Predictions for the upcoming NCAA tournament. This was a crowd that knew basketball. All the while, he was judging the music so that he could judge his moment. When he had finished ignoring her to a more refined degree than she was ignoring him, Val stood and walked over to Alexandra. She turned her head and looked up at him.

He extended his hand and nodded to the space in front of the musicians where other couples were moving to a lazy, moody melody.

She hesitated, surprised.

"Our shoptalk will bore everyone else at the table," he said.

She looked justifiably skeptical. "Shoptalk?"

"I thought we could dance and take care of business at the same time."

"We took care of business on Tuesday."

"And now it's Friday."

She must have figured he wouldn't let her refuse him, and since any more of this would make a scene worth analyzing, she smiled politely and rose from her chair, but didn't take his hand.

He ushered her away from the table without touching her. He appreciated the jeans she was wearing, which she filled even better than her sweatpants. Out of the corner of his eye, he caught Jack Sandifer's reaction to his move and didn't miss the fact that Sandifer would have gladly strangled him.

Val found them a place on the floor. He put his right hand at Alexandra's waist, and she put her left hand on his shoulder. He let her outmaneuver him for the placement of their other hands and settled for a light clasp. He would have preferred to have his other hand at her waist too, but figured it wouldn't hurt to let her win one in order to lower her resistance to him. He looked down and thought that the strength he felt coming from her was as delicate and durable as the antique tortoiseshell combs that tamed her hair at each temple.

"Shoptalk," she said.

He heard her statement as a demand to keep the encounter on a professional level. He said easily, "First, I assume that you filed the papers with Ron Galway on Wednesday after we agreed on all the points Tuesday afternoon."

"That's right. I told you I would call you back if there was a problem and that no news meant good news."

He heard that as a challenge to justify this dance. "And, second, I suppose you heard that Galway is having his office rewallpapered."

Her lashes swept up. She looked at him with reluctant laughter in her Slavic brown eyes, and he saw her lose her internal struggle to resist him and her amusement. She chuckled. "Yes, in fact, Erica told me about it the other day. How did you hear?"

"Grapevine."

She frowned. "A grapevine that extends to Texas?"

"Why not?"

Her frown deepened. "Are you in contact with Erica?"

"No."

Her expression cleared. "Oh, for a moment I thought . . . but, never mind! Anyway, Erica was crowing with triumph over that item of hospital gossip."

"It was conveyed to me only as an oddity, that Galway would redo his offices after having remodeled them as recently as last year."

"But we know better," she said. "Erica is convinced that Galway was looking for hidden cameras. She had every reason, I suppose, to imagine she had scored big on that one."

Alexandra realized that if she wanted to keep the discussion impersonal, she would have to take control of it, which was not easy given that she was encircled by Val, moving against him and with him. She accepted the coincidence of meeting him this evening with a touch of fugitive humor, thinking only that Erica had an uncanny knack for bringing them together. And this time, she's thrown me into his arms!

To gather her wits, she let her gaze skim across the shoulder of his jacket. It fell on the table where sat a man and a woman Scotty had identified earlier as a pimp and a prostitute. She saw that another man —a customer, no doubt—had joined them. She looked away from the table, up at Val, and met his gray eyes. She was aware of the places their bodies were laced. Breasts, hips, knees, elbows, braided fingers.

"Oh! I've just this instant remembered to ask you about those clauses in the contract," she said, "that refer to the funding of the research project based on Seine-Lafitte's quarterly profits."

"There are no such clauses in the contract."

She was struggling to remember her conversation with Jean-

Philippe. "You mean, our cancer research will be funded even if Seine-Lafitte experiences a two-quarter downturn this year?"

"Yes, of course, and in any case Seine-Lafitte will not be experiencing any downturns this year. What brings this up?"

Her eyes had gone screwy on Sunday and caused a reading lapse, so perhaps her ears had gone screwy during the phone conversation with Jean-Philippe on Monday and she had misheard him. She had no intention of explaining any of this to Val, so she said, "Nothing. So. Tell me about your business in Dallas."

"Business was good."

"What was your business?"

The smile in the back of his eyes melted her. "The usual."

"What was the most interesting part of the usual?"

The smile in his eyes deepened, and she was almost sorry she had asked that question, but his answer surprised her. "I bought a painting."

"You did? What kind of painting?"

"It's futuristic. Hard to describe. Large canvas. Perhaps I should show it to you when it's delivered, and you can help me decide the best placement on the wall I have in mind for it."

"In your office?"

He shook his head.

She had a sinking feeling that he would say "in my bedroom."

"In my house," he said, insinuating nothing.

She relaxed. He wasn't a jerk. She didn't immediately respond, for her attention was momentarily distracted by a commotion at the table where sat the pimp, the prostitute, and her client. Tremors of angry voices beneath the music. She turned her attention back to Val.

"Do you do that often, buy paintings on business trips?"

"No. This was the first time. I was at a gallery opening one evening. I saw it and decided to buy it. Now I don't know where I'm going to hang it."

"High-class problem," Alexandra commented. "Are you always so impulsive in making what I suspect are major purchases?"

94

"Depends on the item in question and my desire to own it."

The smile in his eyes slipped onto his lips. She was sure but, then again, not so sure what they were talking about. She had to look away to recover her composure. She saw that the pimp, the prostitute, and her client had risen from their chairs. The men were glaring at one another and stanced for threat.

"It doesn't depend on the item's price tag?" she asked.

"Well, now, sometimes the desire to own an item increases proportionally to the cost," he said, then changed the subject by observing, "You like to dance."

She affirmed that she did. She would have pursued this tantalizing discussion of ownership but was distracted by the pushing and shoving of bodies and tables that erupted behind Val.

Out of the corner of her eye, she caught the flash of a silver arc hurtling their way, but she was unable to move quickly enough to prevent the frame of an aluminum chair from clipping Val in his lower right back. He staggered backward, bringing her with him, until the backs of his thighs slammed against the nearest table. From the spasm of pain that crossed his face, she knew that the chair had hit a sore spot. The table hadn't done his legs any good either, although the table was the only object now supporting them.

In that instant, her hands fell to his waist, fingers splayed. An instant later, a brawling body sprawled their way, flattened her momentarily against Val. The shock of full-body contact was like the kind of silent explosion she might see under a microscope, when two cells met and merged to synthesize protein. Or maybe the two cells were involved in a less benign process, one that might be difficult, once started, to get under control. As if, when combined, the two cells activated telomerase, the enzyme that might cause uninhibited cell division.

But how could something that felt this rich, this good, be dangerous? It was a luxury to feel him against her, her nose pressed to his neck, her legs stumbled against his, her hands grasping him so tightly she could feel the ribs in his lower back.

In that first flash of a half second, she realized that her grasp was not so tight. It was more that the tips of her fingers, princess-and-pea-like, were sensitive to his body beneath several layers of clothing, so that she could feel the writhe of his back muscles as they quivered from the impact of the chair. All she had to do was to apply the lightest, most precise pressure with her fingertips to calm those poor, bruised muscles. She yielded to temptation.

In the flash of the next half second, Val brought her chin up, and when she looked into his eyes, she saw their black points focus from soft seduction to sharp demand. She was aware that her touch was too intimate, had caused cells of desire to proliferate wildly. She was aware that the music had stopped and that the plainclothes security had moved in.

She attempted to explain herself, "You were hurt."

"Not badly."

She withdrew her hands from his waist, but the thick effect of cell growth out of control did not diminish. She managed, "Is your back better?"

"Yes."

Val shoved himself away from the table, steadied her with his hands poised lightly on her shoulders. Elusive, invisible forces seemed to swamp them whenever they were together. Before he could say anything more, they were surrounded by other elements. Walter, Stan, Phil. Jack, Scotty, Hao. Separating them. Using space to dilute the forces. Reversing the chemistry. Restoring them to their respective groups.

The fight had been subdued, the fighters cuffed and already out in the street, to be booked along with the prostitute. The music started up again. Couples moved back out onto the floor and began to dance, thereby mending the rent in the fabric of the evening. It was as if nothing out of the ordinary had occurred, and for the Alhambra nothing had, but for Alexandra and Val the party was over.

. . .

JACK HAD BEEN in a funk all evening. He'd gone along with the idea that the gang should go out on Friday night in order to get their act together for the return of "Papa Smurf," but the evening had not gone the way it should have. Alexandra had been treating him like her best friend, and every man on the planet knew what it meant when a woman thought of a man as a goddamned *friend*. Then Val Dorsainville had shown up, and Jack had felt murderous. Wished *he*'d been the one to throw the chair.

In the car on the way home, he was perversely happy to have a solid case against the half-assed tennis player turned half-assed businessman, and he freely aired his opinion of the way the goddamned half-ass had exposed Alexandra to danger and violence.

And Alexandra, goddamn her, defended him. "It was hardly his fault, Jack."

"He shouldn't have asked you to dance."

"You mean, because he should have known that a fight would break out and that he would get hit by a chair?"

"Watch out for this guy, A.K. Just watch out for him."

Alexandra's response angered him beyond reason. "We've been friends for a long time, Jack, and I value your opinion, but this time I've got to say that I don't know what you're talking about."

THIRTEEN

 BY THE END of the following week, Alexandra knew exactly why she should watch out for Val, but by then it was too late. In the meantime, her thoughts had been given a new direction by the arrival of the family photo album.

One weekday evening, comfy in her sweats, she plopped on her parlor sofa and opened the album at the back, starting with the most recent photos. She looked first at her parents' wedding in the late fifties. Her pretty mother, Janina, holding hands with her new husband, Lech. Both of them smiling, imagining the future that would never be theirs. Waiting almost ten years for a pregnancy that could be carried to term. Lech's accident one month before Alexandra's birth. Poor, fatherless baby. The decision to leave one complete and consistent universe in Warszawa, Polska, beloved but inhospitable. The need to embrace another one, alien and contradictory, in Jackowo, Illinois, Land of Lincoln and One Million Poles. Janina's weak heart.

Alexandra leafed slowly backward through the stiff pages. With each page she turned, she sank farther back into time and across the scars of Polish history, the faces not always smiling, but always poised and conscious of the camera. She was moving in space too, from Warszawa to Lodz to Paris. There were pictures of the baby Janina in the arms of her mother, Marie-Thérèse. Baby pictures of Marie-Thérèse in the arms of her mother, Lisette. Fewer pictures of Lisette, of course, born in the last century, and none of her as a baby in the arms of her mother. None at all, in fact, of Lisette's mother.

Alexandra savored these pages. Lisette and her handsome husband who didn't make it through World War I. Lisette, an elegant young ballerina about twenty years old, performing in Warsaw. Lisette at fifteen, dropping a graceful curtsy after a dance recital in Lodz. Lisette at ten, already confident on toe shoes. Lisette at five, striking a pose before a metro station under construction in Paris. A man—Piotr Wojinski?—holding her hand, only half his torso and one leg visible.

Alexandra turned back another page. Lisette as a toddler, with masses of light brown hair, looking up at what must have been the Eiffel Tower. In this photograph Piotr Wojinski was completely visible. He was holding Lisette on his hip, standing straight before the camera, his expression both proud and profoundly sad. His stocky body was framed in the arch of one foot of the graceful wrought-iron Godzilla behind him whose easily recognized silhouette was cropped by the camera lens. Lisette's exquisite little profile conveyed her awe of what she beheld. No poses for the camera. No awareness yet of how lucky she was not to have inherited either her father's face or body type. No awareness either, perhaps, of what she had lost with the death of her mother.

Lisette's father knew it, though, and he wore that knowledge in his eyes. A perfect Polak was Piotr Wojinski. Hard working. Owned a café in Montmartre. Tried to do right by his motherless daughter. Raised her in Paris, heroically alone, for a few years, then packed up and returned to Poland, to the town where he had been born. Surrounded by family, he mourned his wife the rest of his life. Never remarried.

What was her name, that beloved wife, Lisette's mother? Unable to recall it, she closed the album and placed it on the coffee table next to the dratted cell phone.

On Saturday, Alexandra had to get serious about the most immediate of her problems. Invitations addressed to each person on Larry's research team had arrived at the lab early in the week, and they had announced a Seine-Lafitte reception at Val's house. During the week Alexandra had gone to her closet several times, hoping to find a drop-dead dress hanging there, but since one still hadn't materialized by the time she had showered for the occasion, she settled on a far-from-flashy navy knit ensemble to which she added a single strand of pearls. A touch of makeup, her tortoiseshell combs, and she was as glamorous as she was going to get.

She went to the parlor to wait for Jack. To pass the time, she decided to have another look at Piotr Wojinski, but this time when she opened the photo album, a picture fluttered out from under the inside front backing sheet.

She retrieved the photograph from the floor. It was very old, one she had never seen before. Her heart leapt to behold a close-up of the side of a woman's face upturned, ready to receive the kiss of a man. The main subject of the composition was the lovely line of the woman's stark white neck, chin, cheek, and brow. At the very center of the picture were her lips, parted breathlessly, slightly smiling. Her eyes were closed. Her lashes were long and curled against a cheek that bore a tiny scar. The man's head was bending down to hers, only the cut of his jaw, a fine nose, and the half slash of his desirous mouth visible behind her face. His eyes, which occupied the top of the photograph, just above the woman's head, were downcast. His gaze rested on the woman's lips. His features were in soft focus and shadowed. The photograph had captured a moment that held promise and passion and crackled with tension.

Imagining this picture to be that of some long-forgotten relative, Alexandra turned the photo eagerly for an inscription and was disappointed to discover that it was a blank postcard. No message and no address inscribed. The only writing on the card was the title of the photograph, printed in the upper-left-hand corner, *Le Baiser*. The Kiss. That much French she knew, or could guess.

Since the postcard was apparently a memento whose significance was lost on her, she put it aside so she could study the photo of Piotr Wojinski on the first page. She let her thoughts float back to when she was ten and the one time she had visited Poland with her grandmother. She remembered an afternoon in some cousin's shadowy apartment crammed with ungainly furniture similar to that in her apartment above Kolatek's Bakery. The old ladies had been discussing Lisette Wojinski, of pre—World War I ballet stardom, and the talk had turned to Lisette's mysterious mother.

The question was raised, since Lisette had been born in Paris, whether the mother was Polish or whether she was French. Bits and pieces of half-truths were patched together. The matter was open for discussion. It was known that she had been as industrious as salt-of-the-earth Piotr, but it was rumored that she had been a laundress, as well. A laundress? Hah! Alexandra could hear the old ladies laugh. That meant washer woman, no? The case was decided. She must have been Polish.

But what was her name?

Alexandra still couldn't remember. She looked at the man smiling sadly, holding his daughter, in the shadow of the Eiffel Tower. She had always had a fondness for Piotr Wojinski, so solid, so dependable. He seemed to her to be the only man with a definite presence in this family album of women. He was the only man in her maternal line who had ever outlived his wife.

She heard footsteps on the porch and closed the album. Jack had come right on time to take her to Cary. She felt a happy lift in her heart to see how he had tried to spruce himself up by trimming his beard and pressing his clothes. The results weren't spectacular, but she appreciated his effort. In fact, she appreciated the effort he'd been making all week to atone for whatever had ailed him last Friday night and caused him to vent his foul mood on her. This evening they puttered over to Cary in his Toyota, comfortable together, and Alexandra was happy that Jack was once again his good old dependable self.

They arrived at Val's at a moment when the party was well under way. The first person they met in the foyer was not their host, but rather Bob Sutherland, who had decided for some strange reason not to attend the team-building seminar two weeks before. Although he didn't explain his absence, he did show great interest in their research.

She and Jack were happy to tell him all about it as the three of them moved through the living room to the dining room whose floor-to-ceiling sliding glass doors were open. The thick of the throng was gathered on the deck beyond the doors. Alexandra cast quick glances around, assessing Val's furnishings. Although they were out of her league, she was reassured that they were normal. Yes, normal. She had half-feared that upon entering his house, she might fall through the looking glass and follow Alice down the rabbit hole into some strange dream world.

She accepted a glass of champagne from a tray being circulated, took a sip, and decided that her feet-on-the-ground Polish common sense had been restored by means of a simple family photo album. She walked out onto the deck and into a fine late-March evening.

FOURTEEN

 VAL KNEW THE moment Alexandra arrived. He had been in the kitchen with the caterers discussing how best to maintain the temperature of the ginger peanut sauce for the satay. Yet he knew when she was in his house by the strength that ran through his veins, making him feel sinewy and giving him a fine edge.

He left the kitchen and deftly wove his way through the crowd. Reflecting that it wasn't all bad to have learned from his father the easy ways of the social lizard, he worked the room and left behind him a finely etched trail of appropriate comments like that of a reptile's tail in the sand. He didn't reject the self-image of the lizard. Rather, he indulged it, almost nostalgically, accepting a part of himself he hadn't acknowledged for years. He even liked this sense of evolution in reverse.

He spotted Alexandra on the deck. Her air was quiet and subdued. Her dress, with its smile of pearls at the neck, blended with the evening sky. Only the halo of her hair called attention to itself. He wouldn't have picked her out in this crowd if he hadn't already met her, held her, and mentally undressed her more than once. He mentally undressed her now and felt himself mutate, in under a minute, from reptile to wolf.

With no problem, no effort, and no notice from Sophie, who always pursued her own agenda at these affairs, he got Alexandra alone at one end of the deck.

"Sorry I wasn't at the door to greet you when you arrived," he said.

Her expression was pleasant but guarded. "That's all right. It was good to have run into Bob."

"Did you come as a group?"

"I came with Jack." She nodded to where Sandifer was standing with Sutherland along with Larry and his wife who had just arrived. "Hao came with the Rosenbergs, and I can guess he's well occupied at the buffet table, since I don't see him out here. Nice spread, by the way."

"Thank you. And McCarthy?"

Alexandra shook her head in mock disgust. "He had something very pressing to do on his way over tonight, which supposedly required him to drive here alone. But we all know he wanted to be on his own, just in case he got lucky."

"Has he never hit on you?"

Alexandra took a sip from her glass and chuckled. "I don't think I'm his type."

"Is he so choosy to have a type?"

She laughed again. "Yes, and it falls in the general category of 'easy.'" She cocked her head and looked at him, as if she regretted this turn in conversation, then added in a neutral tone, "I've met several of his girlfriends, though, and I must say that for the most part they're very nice."

That subject was firmly closed. Before a small silence fell, he asked, "Aren't you going to ask about my back?"

She put her half-empty glass down on the wide deck railing and replied, "Not unless you tell me that you were in a tournament this week and had to serve at high speed, which is the only time you said that your back bothers you."

"What, no sympathy for my injury in the barroom brawl?"

She shook her head. "You told me at the time that you weren't hurt badly."

That subject seemed to be closed too. Maneuvering her off the deck, he recommended several delicacies from the buffet and managed to produce another glass of champagne for her, which she declined. Without thinking twice, he commanded the waiter to fetch a glass of sparkling water for her and a whiskey neat for himself. He led her through the dining room and paused by the door to the kitchen where the caterers were bustling behind the scenes.

"I'd give you a tour of the house," he said, "but we'd be in the way. So, I'll just tell you that beyond the kitchen is the family room, which I prefer to call the media room. My friends—some of whom you met last Friday at the Alhambra—think it's a good place to park themselves for the Superbowl and other such events, even when I'm not in town."

"Were you in town for the Superbowl this year?"

"Paris," he said. "About twenty people congregated here anyway. I heard that I missed a great party."

"Are you gone for long stretches at a time? I haven't really grasped how you divide your time between two continents."

"I'm usually three months here and three months there. Not so much by design but that's how it works out. I'm planning a quick trip to Paris soon, but I intend to come right back."

"Since you're away so much, do you give your friends keys to the house so it looks lived in?"

"I have house sitters," he answered her. "They're in France at the moment on an extended spring holiday."

He bent toward her and pointed through the kitchen beyond the cabinets. The smell of her hair and her neck whispered to him of another time and place, reminded him that he had entered the forbidden fruit orchard. He straightened. "There's a back entrance and stairway for them. They have the whole upper floor."

"House sitters?" she prompted.

"A family," he explained. "Jean-Luc and Martine Marivaux and their daughter, Pascale, who's ten. I've been friends with Jean-Luc forever, and they were the ones who threw the Superbowl party. Pascale is also my goddaughter, I think you call it in English."

"It works out for everyone, then."

He nodded again and refrained from laying his family man act on any thicker. "And now," he said, leading her away from the kitchen, "I'd like to show you the painting I bought."

Following him, Alexandra admitted to herself that she enjoyed standing in the special circle that seemed to radiate out from him. She liked the way he seemed to be flirting with her, harmlessly enough, with none of the hot and heavy stuff she had felt on previous occasions.

She was drinking an innocent glass of water with a twist of lime, and her perceptions felt rock-solid dependable. Val was playing the role of charming host and looked—this was no distortion of her vision—handsome as the devil in his sharp navy suit, white shirt, and muted patterned tie. He was showing her around his well-appointed-but-not-out-of-this-world house, and he had told her that he was practically a family man whose nonthreatening existence included a ten-year-old goddaughter.

"Ah, yes, the painting you bought in Dallas," she said, then ventured her own fledgling form of flirtation. "Are you sure you don't have some etchings that you want to show me too?"

As they crossed the dining room, he favored her with his nearly irresistible smile. "My etchings," he said, playing along, "will have to wait for another time, when I'm not host to nearly eighty people." He shook his head with exaggerated regret. "Crowds cramp my style."

She laughed. "So does Jean-Philippe."

He paused. "Do you think so?"

She had no idea why she had said that, and she was aware of a slight rippling of tension in the air around him. This awareness should have warned her that odd things were beginning to happen to her perceptions, but her enjoyment of his company prevented her from questioning her sudden intuition of the way things stood between her host and Jean-Philippe.

She answered with a serene smile, "Why, yes, I do."

"And what makes you think that?"

"The way you were with him when I saw you two together at Seine-Lafitte a few weeks ago."

Dark brows arched in challenge. "Our interactions are nothing if not cordial."

"Oh, I know!"

"And Jean-Philippe is an esteemed colleague."

"But not a friend."

The expression on his face shaded suggestively. "Are you accusing him of underhandedness, or me?"

"Neither," she teased. "I'm only saying that I know about the dynamics of working in a group. In the lab we're always falling over one another's egos."

"I didn't think the dynamics in your lab group had much to do with egos."

He hardly needed to state outright that he believed those lab dynamics had everything to do with bodies—or that that was exactly what was going on between them now.

"I was speaking of ideas," she said. "We're always jealous of one another for coming up with a solution to some problem either by brilliant insight or blind luck."

"So it's not underhandedness you're accusing me of, but jealousy. Is that right?"

She looked down into her glass and saw the bubbles fizzing like so many miniature crystal balls. "I have no idea, really, what goes on at Seine-Lafitte as a whole—what you do or Jean-Philippe does—but maybe it's Jean-Philippe who's jealous of you and of any clever new approach that you might be developing. For drug marketing or whatever."

"Any suggestions about a possible clever new approach I might want to develop?"

It was easy enough for her to sort out the two levels of the conversation. As much as she was enjoying it, she thought it better not to overplay it. "I'll confine my suggestions to interpretations of the painting you're going to show me. Are you committed to it or still thinking about it? What kind of opinion do you want of it exactly?"

"You mean, how tactful do you have to be?" he replied easily, accepting the change in subject. "Let's say that I'm committed to the painting and am interested more in your interpretation than in your opinion."

"Uh-oh. This sounds way beyond my realm of expertise."

"I don't think so, and I'm curious to see how you see it—even more so now than before."

She was curious now too to keep exercising her newfound powers of perception and so took her assignment of art criticism in the spirit of adventure. She followed him into the large room off the dining room, where Scotty was shooting pool, surprise surprise, with the prettiest unattached secretary at Seine-Lafitte. A handful of people were watching the game, and they were more interested in the activity around the pool table than in Val and Alexandra's entrance onto the scene.

The room had a cathedral ceiling, a large arched window at the far end, and a bank of regular-sized windows that gave onto what would be the front of the house. It had almost no furniture beyond the pool table dramatically illuminated with low-hanging halogen mini-lamps. Off the back wall, adjacent to the opening onto the dining room, Alexandra glimpsed another hallway. She didn't peer down it but focused instead on the long interior wall that probably ran alongside some room in what she guessed were Val's personal quarters. The interior wall was massive and blank and apparently the one destined for Val's recent purchase.

She followed him to the midway point in the room where what looked to be a large canvas sat draped in a sheet, leaning against the wall. Val unveiled the canvas with a snap of his wrist and dropped the sheet on the floor.

Alexandra gasped and stepped back, unprepared for the visual assault of tempestuous colors and energy. In astonishment and delight, she murmured, "Good heavens!"

"It makes an effect," Val acknowledged, evidently not displeased by her reaction. "It's called *Primordial Soup.*"

Alexandra moved away from the canvas, attempting to find the right distance from which to take it all in. "You expect me to interpret this? I'm having difficulty *seeing* it." She backed up about five feet. "Ah, it's coming clearer now. What an extraordinary composition! But I'm still not far enough away from it, I think."

Val lifted the canvas up so that Alexandra could have a better idea of the eventual effect of the painting as it would hang on the wall. In so doing, he uncovered a second, smaller painting, which had been hidden behind the larger one.

Alexandra blinked, then walked straight up to the second painting. It was of a woman holding a fan and wearing a mask. The woman was standing on a balcony inside a theater, in the company of two men. "I know this one. I recall having seen others by the same painter. He has a very recognizable style."

Val put the heavy canvas down. "You know Gervex?"

"Is that the painter's name?" she replied. "I had forgotten. This particular one by him must be well known. I can practically see the wall on which I first saw it hanging."

Val paused before he said, "It's never been shown before. It has been in private collections in France for the past hundred years until it was recently sold to the gallery in Dallas."

Alexandra was still looking at the painting, rather fondly. "Well, then I must have seen a reproduction of it in a catalog at some time or another. Not that I come across art catalogs much, but this is the interior of the Opera, isn't it? Or should I attempt to mangle the word *Opéra*?"

Val didn't respond to that, and some quality in his silence caused Alexandra to look at him. She felt a strong force tug at her, curl around her, as if trying to unbalance her. She resisted him and his power by cutting her eyes back at the painting.

She tried to keep her voice light, but it ended up sounding eerie. "I know I've seen this painting because the woman's hat in the foreground, just below the balcony, is very familiar to me. I've always fancied one like that, although I know it's been out of style for a hundred years . . ."

She trailed off. He had taken several steps toward her so that he was standing next to her, looking down at the painting. The special circle of his presence to which she was so responsive moved around her, began to overpower her. She made the mistake of looking at him again, and her mind's eye peeled away the light wool of his suit and the fine linen threads of his shirt in order to see taut skin and feel the strength of his blood and muscle.

He returned her gaze, and she felt stripped down to a stark and startling desire for him. She was swallowed in the undertow of his presence and felt herself following Alice, funneling down the rabbit hole. As she twirled downward, she saw the name of her great-great-grandmother—the name she had been trying to remember just before Jack picked her up—swirl around her, but the letters were nothing more than a dizzy blur, and she couldn't quite make them out.

Before he spoke, she knew what he would say.

"No," he said slowly, "the painting has never appeared in a catalog either."

"Then, I must be mistaken," she said, a little breathlessly.

"Perhaps you are."

"I must be thinking of a different painting," she pursued.

"Surely."

"A different one by Gervex," she said, "which accounts for the familiarity, because his style is so distinctive."

"Very distinctive," he agreed again, "although he is not an artist who is widely known these days, I'm afraid."

"But—" she began in protest, still struggling against the dark current. She followed the line of his gaze when he looked over her shoulder and toward the person who entered the room.

Sophie DuBois was walking toward them, looking perfect and in place. She swept up to them, walked around Alexandra. She slipped her arm through Val's. Gave it a squeeze.

Sophie flicked a pretty smile over Alexandra whom she had briefly met earlier. Her French accent was pronounced. "I see that Valéry, he has you an art exhibition. But can he convince you that he does not throw his money . . . à la fenêtre? *La Soupe primordiale,* it is not so bad, but he choose it from other pieces in the gallery, y compris a Helen Frankenthaler." She heaved an uncomprehending sigh. "You know, then, Frankenthaler, Miss Kaminski?"

Alexandra shook her head. "I've spent more time analyzing lab slides, I'm afraid, than modern art."

Sophie turned to the smaller painting and assumed an attitude of charming bewilderment. "I try to talk him from buying this . . . nothing. By a saloniste, enfin! But my love, he does not listen. Even the gallery owner, he call the painter"—she rolled large dark eyes toward her love—"comment dit-on, alors, Valéry?"

"Schmaltzy."

"C'est ça. He call him a schmaltzy Salonist."

Covering the smaller canvas once again with the larger one, Val said to Alexandra, "I'm thinking of beginning a collection of academic art of the nineteenth-century Salons—you know, the old-fashioned stuff the Impressionists reacted against. But there's not much of it for sale these days."

Alexandra thought it rather kind of Val to let her know, in an offhand, face-saving way, who the Salonists were. "Yes, of course," she said, a little weakly.

Sophie sniffed. "You could 'ave the drawings by Suzanne Valoton. They were there, you know, for purchase, if you want something from the period."

"But I wanted something different, as I told you, ma chère Sophie, now that the Impressionists have become Hallmark cards, calendars, and mousepads."

Sophie's expression was amused. She shook her head, flirtatiously, affectionately. "At least you did not pay too much dollars for your error in judgment, but you will have to wait longtemps before this Gervex gain value."

Alexandra absorbed this exchange, let it sink in that Sophie had been with Val in Dallas. The funneling had stopped. She hit the bleak bottom of the rabbit hole, and the unpleasant thud jolted her heart. She wondered by what magic of time and physics an egg, once cracked open, could be antientropically restored to its shell and made whole again. She wondered by what miracle of molecular biology a cell, once metastasized, could be reversed to its original, uncancerous state. She searched her mind's eye for the name of her great-great-grandmother. She searched around the room for Jack, hoping that he could save her from this painful clarity of perception.

A SIXTH SENSE drew Jack to the pool room. He quickly sized up the situation and saw that it was time for him to take Alexandra home. She was looking politely interested in some god-awful paintings, but he knew that his damsel was in distress.

He walked up to the half-assed tennis player—correction, the hotsy-totsy half-assed tennis player with his fancy house and furnishings—and gave him what he hoped passed as a man-to-man nod. He greeted the foxy DuBois woman, then put an arm around Alexandra's shoulders. When he gave their excuses and led her out of the room and she looked up at him and smiled, he knew his strategy was a good one.

Be there to pick up the pieces, Jack, he told himself, and have patience. You know better what she wants and needs than she does herself. Well, she doesn't really know yet what she wants, but deep down she does know what she needs, and it isn't some rich boy who buys paintings and plays at science. What she needs is a partner who knows science from the inside out. Who is steady and careful and consistent. Whose discipline complements her visions.

Jack stood in awe of Alexandra's visionary approach to her experiments—the way she saw things differently. Now, nine times out of ten, she was way off. But that tenth time usually took her somewhere new . . .

"My great-great-grandmother's name just came to me, Jack," she said as they were leaving the half-ass's house.

Way, way off, this time. "What's this about, Alexandra?"

"The letters were all scrambled at first, but now I've sorted them out. Lisette Wojinski's mother's name was Jeanne Lacombe."

FIFTEEN

ALEXANDRA BEGAN TO invent a story for herself. She fashioned it from scraps of memories and emotions, both real and imagined, much like a bird builds a nest. Or, perhaps, she already knew the story whole and was inspired to tell it to herself only now for the first time. It was a daydreaming story, one she wove in waking moments in the back of her mind.

It began like this:

Jeanne Lacombe had a very particular beauty. Any man who ever saw her recognized hers to be an earthy beauty which could acquire, on occasion, an exquisite refinement. These occasions occurred when she might raise her head (say, to speak to a man superior in height) and present to the viewer the lovely line of her neck, chin, cheek, and brow. But—and here was the essence of her particular beauty—that refinement was, at the same time, firmly tethered to earth by the most intriguing scar she wore on her upper left cheek. The scar was hardly longer or wider or deeper than the size of a clipped fingernail, but it was unique to her and such a part of her that once it was noticed, it could not be ignored. It seemed to define her particular beauty more than did her thick fall of light brown hair or her pleasing young peasant woman's figure.

Jeanne's earthy beauty allied with her alluring line from neck to brow, often glimpsed because men so often spoke to her, made her widely known among the artists who lived in her neighborhood. They desired her, naturally enough, as a model for their paintings; and their desire for her in one role coexisted with their desire for her in another role, the one that linked the artists' new profession to that of the oldest profession. Jeanne resisted, and after a while the artists came to treat her as a friend. Of course, they continued to seek that lovely line. Being artists, they calculated it in the direction from brow to neck so that they could complete, with their well-trained eyes, the even more alluring line that lay beneath her clothing from breast to hip to thigh to calf.

All this Alexandra fantasized about the woman on the postcard of *Le Baiser* without quite knowing why that particular picture had captured her imagination. Alexandra didn't care to think about the man who hovered behind the woman, the one who had seduced her into closing her eyes and who was about to kiss her. Alexandra didn't need to think about him either. It was her story, after all, to piece together as she wished, and she wished to believe (or, simply, she knew) that her Jeanne had escaped the necessity of exercising the usual means by which a working girl raised herself from squalor. Her Jeanne was a talented music hall dancer, and as long as she continued to bring in more paying customers than any other dancer past or present, she was protected from revealing to any man the lovely line of her body below her neck.

This last detail gave the story the flavor of a fairy tale, and somehow the telling of this pleasant tale eased the pain in Alexandra's heart. She had been shaken by what had happened to her in Val's pool room. At the time, the unsettling aspect of the incident had seemed to involve her weird knowledge of an obscure painting by an unknown artist. However, with a few days' perspective, it was clear that what had shaken her was the discovery of Val's relationship with Sophie.

Alexandra had no claim on Val and, therefore, no right to react, one way or the other, to the knowledge that he had a lover. She knew that the strength of her reaction derived, in part, from the fact that Sophie's sophistication and family connections dramatized her own deficiencies in those categories. For the other part, it was obvious that she had been blinded by the sparkle of too-pretty possibilities. Now, if Val had led her on . . ., well then, the two-timing rat wasn't worthy of her. However, this marvelous piece of common sense did nothing to help her escape the ridiculous snare in which her affections were caught.

As for that painting by Gervex, the problem of why it should be so familiar to her was easily solved. She put in a call to Maggy, the reference librarian at the medical school, and asked her to do an online search of the catalogs and exhibitions held by the Art Institute of Chicago in the past twenty-five years. Odd though the request was, Maggy was happy to comply. She promised Alexandra results before midweek, when most people were closing up shop for the long Easter weekend.

Alexandra was sure to discover that she had run across Gervex's work, in one form or another, at the Art Institute, since Marie-Thérèse had been taking her there since she was two years old. Somewhere along the way, then, she had seen his paintings, and although she had forgotten his name, she distinctly remembered having been fascinated by the stories he captured on canvas with the titillating intrigues they implied. She had retained enough from her psychology and neurobiology courses to know that every stimulus, no matter how minimal, made an impression on the brain. Somewhere in her gray matter, then, was a trace of every image she had ever encountered in her twenty-six years. She was not going to start analyzing why certain long-forgotten memories should be surfacing now. She wished only to establish that, during her lifetime, the image of one particular painting had entered her storeroom of sensory impressions.

It was in that well-stocked storeroom (or *arrière boutique*—a word which had been deposited one day in high school French class) that Alexandra made a place for Jeanne Lacombe to live and breathe.

While Alexandra went about her daily task of putting one foot in front of the other, Jeanne was permitted to reorganize that *arrière boutique,* to liberate it from the tyranny of the usual ways of knowing laid down in those twenty-six years of school, science, religion, public displays, high art, low art, and conventional geography.

Then, with one, two, three cancan kicks, she was free.

SIXTEEN

THE MUSIC WAS ending. Jeanne knew her chore-
ography was good, but the execution of the steps
this night had been inspired. The kicks and
swirls of Chérie, Nina, and Louise synchro-
nized with her own had conjured magic and brought the audience to
vibrant attention. Chérie, Nina, and Louise had sensed it too. They
played to the crowd, indulged in final head tosses, voluptuous pouts,
and ruffled tail shaking. Given all the Austrian and Italian officers
present, Jeanne figured the girls would double their prices tonight.

Jeanne wished she could feel for Pierre the kind of affection
Chérie, Nina, and Louise sold for profit. She was receptive to his shy
smiles, but resistant to the silent entreaty in his eyes. She bowed
herself off-stage. Flirty but not seductive. Breathing deeply but not
winded. Happy in exertion. Blood flowing.

She paused in the shadowy wings to hug and kiss Nina and Louise.
Chérie was wasting no time making *la grue* (with one leg bent, low-
heeled foot flat against the backstage wall, like a crane) and licking
her lips for the handsome soldier in the brass-buttoned coat who had
already bared her breast. Jeanne moved past the backstage couple
without a second glance. She let Nina and Louise skip ahead of her.
They ducked through the curtain into the light and smoke of the
hall, giggling with an anticipation Jeanne guessed they practiced but

rarely felt. She was ready to walk through the curtain herself, when Charlotte stopped her.

Charlotte had a cigarette hanging between her lips and was holding a shawl, ready to circle it around Jeanne's shoulders. "Lover Boy's back," she said, attempting to make a joke of it, but any humor was lost in her racking cough and a cloud of blue smoke.

Jeanne put a finger to the velvet curtain and lifted it enough to give her a full view of the hall. She scanned the moving crowd of uniforms and evening coats, respectable bustles interspersed with scandalous *décolletages*. She spotted Lover Boy at the bar, leaning against the edge of the marble slab, speaking with a group of cronies. Maurice hovered behind them.

Tonight the Count d'Albret looked far less correct, far more dangerous than he did that day not too long before she'd run into him at an informal studio open house in the rue de Rome.

It had been her day off, and she met Ellen, an actress and artist's model, who was chumming with the neighborhood painters Auguste and Edouard and Edgar. The day was fine, and the group drifted from Montmartre to the *grands boulevards,* and presently they were at the address of their friend Henri Gervex, who always had his doors and a variety of bottles open.

A painter himself, Henri enjoyed celebrity and notoriety and showed the work of his less-well-off colleagues whose work he was willing to sell straight off his walls. Shortly after Jeanne and her friends had entered the spacious, well-lit studio, another group arrived. They caused a flurry of commotion that drew Jeanne's attention from the painting of the woman at the Opéra holding a fan and wearing a mask and a very stylish hat.

She turned and saw the Count d'Albret for the first time since the day he had bought Le Chat Noir and given her a lesson in manners. She considered her options and knew they were few.

The two groups proceeded in opposite directions around the studio and met in the middle. Jeanne made the introductions. Calling cards were exchanged, along with the niceties. Edgar, a well-born and famous skirt-chaser, found plenty to like in the fashionable ladies who graced the distinguished party.

Soon enough, Jeanne found herself alone with Victor.

"You have promised to tell me what you like," he said pleasantly, "and what you have learned from your friends about the fine art of painting."

The paintings on this section of wall were interiors, all of a traditional sort.

"I like these," Jeanne admitted.

"Yours is a conventional taste, I perceive," he said. "It is for this preference, then, that your friends laugh at you?"

"Yes," she admitted again, half-amused, half-defiant. "I like the stories they tell. They are pretty and easy to understand."

"Is that so?"

She looked up at a painting hung above eye level. She spotted the *étiquette* that bore the title of the painting and the name of the artist. She nearly swooned with pride at being able to read the words. "This one is called *Troubled Conscience,* and so we see the troubled conscience of the young lady portrayed clearly on her face. Why she is troubled we cannot say for sure, but we are able to guess."

"And what is your most interesting guess?"

"I think she has overspent her allowance and fears that her father will find out."

He studied the painting. "Ah yes, I have seen this painting at some Salon or another," he said, "or one quite like it." He glanced down at her with a twinkle in his gray eyes and a slight lift at the corners of his mouth. "I'm not sure, however, that our young lady is suffering from an overdrawn bank account."

He was teasing her, and when she wisely did not reply to his remark, he continued, "Can you tell me why your friends object to such a painting? It is, we can agree, well composed, technically accomplished, and pleasing to view. Quite unobjectionable, in fact."

They began to stroll. They halted before a series of canvases that startled by their subject matter, energy, and use of color. These compositions broke the rules of technical precision but managed to produce controlled effects, and the story lines of their scenes failed to deliver the expected resolutions.

She gave him the answer she knew he expected. "It is the very unobjectionable quality of the Salon paintings that my friends object to."

He regarded the lively café scenes before them. "By contrast, these impressionist paintings are fresh and new. They depict real people in the real life of the city, and not stiff and predictable allegories. Do you not agree that these impressionist paintings define for us the modern and are the ones that we must now like?"

Jeanne looked at one painting of a pretty young woman who was, indeed, individualized rather than idealized as was the beauty of *Troubled Conscience*. This pretty young woman was seated at a busy café and perfectly captured in her boredom. It was true that Jeanne felt the woman's mood and the street scene come alive before her eyes. It was also true that the understated drama of the situation deflected a direct reading of the woman or her purpose. Yet Jeanne saw her only as a prostitute named Nana or Cléopatre waiting for her next client, and she was sure that Victor must see her that way too.

"These paintings do define the modern," she agreed lightly, "but I am not, therefore, compelled to like them."

"You still prefer the dreary interiors?"

Dreary? Those interiors seemed like paradise to her. Her dream was to live the life of the refined beauty whose only promiscuity was financial.

"I do," she said.

"I must ask your advice, then," he said. "Where should I put my money, if I am seeking to buy paintings?"

"On the impressionist paintings, of course."

"Not on the Salon paintings, then?"

She shook her head. "They are dreary, as you say." She added, boldly, "And if I were you, I would look for a woman such as the one in this impressionist painting here with whom to discuss your taste in art. I am afraid that my taste is too conservative to make further discussion with me enjoyable to you."

He registered her answer with a slight bow to his head. They regained their respective parties, and she left Henri's *atelier* satisfied that she had made it clear to Victor that she was not for sale like the woman at the café . . .

Still peering through the curtain, Jeanne asked, "How long has he been here?"

Charlotte answered, "He came just as you went on stage."

Jeanne was pleased that he had seen her most inspired performance. She could permit herself this much measure of professional pride, surely. "But why me, after all?"

"You're pretty, my dear," Charlotte wheezed, "and clean."

In her mind's eye, Jeanne saw the canvases of Edgar's *Bathers* crouched in their tubs and washing themselves in a way that would never make them clean. She heard fearful whispers of "syphilis" flash through the market like a brushfire to be doused by the battle cry of "hygiene!" shouted by the municipal authorities. True cleanliness, for a woman, was next to godliness only when she could afford the godliness. Jeanne had scrimped for that godliness. It had been her fantasy and her pride to be a dancer, not a common whore.

She let the curtain fall such that a bar of light dropped across Charlotte's face, glistening the sheen of fever across her brow. It wasn't the rash of the pox that had Charlotte in its grip, but a black, unseen evil that robbed her dear friend of breath. Jeanne took the cigarette from Charlotte's mouth and crushed it under her heel.

Charlotte didn't say a word, merely held out the shawl.

Jeanne grasped Charlotte's hands. "No, my dear, the night is warm enough for me. You take it." Jeanne put the soft wool around her friend's shoulders. "I'm worried for you."

"My worry," Charlotte replied weakly, "is for you." A cough racked her before she could say, "You're too exposed."

Jeanne looked down at her coquettish costume, thought of Victor on the other side of the curtain. A low moan and a light thumping against the wall behind her brought her head around, and she saw the shadowy movements of Chérie's lascivious acceptance of her uniformed soldier's ardor. Jeanne turned back to Charlotte and saw her own stricken feelings mirrored in her friend's expression.

"I regret ever having let Maurice force you into accepting a drink from the Count. And now he's your employer . . ."

At the unfinished statement, Jeanne's blood ran cold. "As my employer, he intends to fire me if I don't fall into his arms?"

Charlotte coughed. "I believe the Count is wishing to find for you girls protectors from a higher class of gentleman, to improve the custom at Le Chat Noir."

Jeanne's blood ran hot. She doubted that Victor cared about the class of man who frequented Le Chat Noir, and she *knew* he didn't confuse her after-hours activities with those of her dancing partners. She also knew a threat when she heard one. "So he means to fire me if I don't fall into any other man's arms either."

Charlotte didn't answer that.

Jeanne knew the streets of Paris to be unmerciful. Her fall would be swift and hard the moment she could no longer call Le Chat Noir her home. "You think it better for me to go with the devil I know than gamble on the devil I don't know?"

Charlotte said quietly, "You can't have thought you could stay aloof forever, Jeanne. It isn't natural."

"You're saying I have no choice."

Charlotte said sadly, "I've failed you, I'm afraid."

Just as Jeanne had failed Charlotte. Jeanne wished she had insisted earlier that Charlotte get to a doctor. She wished that she herself were a doctor rather than a dancer. She hugged Charlotte fiercely and said, "Go home, my dear. Lie down."

Charlotte coughed against Jeanne's shoulder. She whispered feebly into Jeanne's ear, "You have more of Chérie in you than you realize, my dear. Give him everything he asks for and some things he doesn't, but remember not to give him your heart."

Jeanne left the wings and wove through the crowd, smiling, chatting, turning down offers for drinks. She paused here, stopped there, avoided the bar, but was, finally, unable to avoid him.

Suddenly she found herself standing stock against him. She was so close to him she could see the fine weave of his shirt and trace with her eye the stitching on his well-tailored coat. Through the mingled odors of the hall late at night, she detected his scent, which was dark and held a hint of spice. She was aware that she was wearing black silk and pink taffeta. She forced herself to look up.

The gleam in his eye was assessing. "We will leave now."

"But my shift—"

"Ended ten minutes ago. What took you so long?"

"I was backstage with one of the girls."

"Were you? Doing what?"

As she stood before him, almost against him, she could discern the differences between this man and the one she had met at the Opéra or on the rue de Rome. Victor of the Opéra had been graceful and imperious. Victor of the artist's studio had been genteel and playful. Victor of the music hall knew what he wanted and was through playing games.

"I was discussing modern painting with my fellow dancers."

The gleam in his eye became pronounced. "Indeed."

"Yes," she said, plunging bravely on, "it's my favorite topic, as you must know. Chérie—the one who dances on my left—held to your opinion and was arguing that the impressionist paintings were the only ones a person could truly admire anymore."

It was a puny insult, to tell him that a common music hall girl shared his taste. It apparently amused him more than it offended him. He smiled an irresistible smile. "Really? I will be most interested to continue this discussion sometime, but not now." He put an arm lightly around her shoulders and made as if to lead her to the front door. "But I should mention that I took your suggestion and invested in the paintings by your friends Renoir, Manet, and Degas."

She refused to move. "But you did not take all of my suggestions."

He quirked an amused brow. "You mean, that I turn my attentions to a woman other than yourself? No, I did not take that suggestion." He paused. "When we were at the artist's studio, you told me that you have a preference for paintings that are easy to understand. I can make myself as direct as you like."

She shook her head. He hardly needed to state outright that he was determined to make her his mistress.

"And now I will escort you home."

"I never leave work in these clothes. Ever. I want to change first." She was determined to walk out with her dignity, if nothing else.

"Very well."

Not much later, she had changed and Victor was leading her to the front door. In the street a carriage was waiting, lit by the glittery spill of light and atmosphere from the hall. The night was warm, and the moon was full. Victor handed her up the steps of the carriage, and when she turned to thank him, she thought she caught a glimpse of Pierre coming down the street in her direction.

Perhaps Pierre was coming, as he sometimes did, to walk her home. Her heart caught to imagine that her dear friend saw her now, heading to her disgrace. Her shame rose to realize that, when she settled herself in the seat across from Victor and found herself nestled in the scent and softness of expensive leather, there was indeed enough Chérie in her to wonder how Victor's lips might taste. She had never wondered that about Pierre's.

The carriage made its way through twisting, climbing streets. It was a longer journey by carriage than on foot. The carriage turned a corner and trudged up the steep incline of the street. It came to a halt outside the green door of her apartment building, suggesting that Maurice had divulged her address, for she had not volunteered it. A footman was instantly at the door to open it and to fold down the steps.

Victor helped her out of the carriage. He did not release her hand but drew her to him. With his other hand, he tilted her chin so that her face was bathed in pure moonlight.

He said, "We have yet to discuss the arrangements." He lowered his lips to hers, without quite kissing her. "You will go to your rooms, take what you may need, and together we will go to the apartment I have chosen. My man will accompany you. I will wait here."

She had to ask, "I do not have the power of refusal?"

His brows rose delicately, as if surprised, even impressed by the question. "You are one to fight against circumstances, I am one to take advantage of them, and you made a choice, after all."

"I did? I understood from Charlotte that I would no longer have a job if I did not come with you. That is hardly a choice."

"Do you think I would stoop to such a clumsy strategem?"

When he put his lips to hers, she thought, no, he would not be so crude. She wondered if perhaps Charlotte had misunderstood his intentions and given her the wrong advice.

"And you wound my vanity to suggest," he whispered, "that you have come with me for any reason other than choice."

Was he giving her her first lesson in playing the seductress? Or did he truly think she had made a choice to come with him?

His kiss first surprised her with its sweetness, then thrilled her with its dark promise of passion. When he broke the kiss, she could not resist taunting him, "The streets of Paris are cruel, sir, but your kiss is kind."

His eyes narrowed to luminous gray slits. He turned her toward her door, taunted in return, "And the taste on your lips, mademoiselle, is far better than your taste for dull paintings."

She went to the green door, wondering who was seducing whom. Taking the heavy portal key from inside her embroidered purse, she looked back over her shoulder at him standing in the moonlight. Her attention was caught by a movement to her left.

She saw a man dart out from behind a nearby alley and come running. In the first fraction of a moment, she thought her shy Pierre had been transformed into the hero and had come to rescue her from her fate. Then she noticed that the man was holding high above his head an object like a club. The moon was behind him, so she couldn't see his face, but somehow she knew that he was masked. His figure was big and strong, which was like Pierre, but he seemed intent on doing harm, which was unlike Pierre.

The coachman was sitting idle and inattentive in his perch. The footman beside her was focused on her actions. Victor was standing near the carriage, unaware of the menace that was descending on him.

She did not think, she acted. She moved toward Victor. She might have called out. Victor's head came up, turned slowly, too slowly, toward the attacker who was lowering his club. In another few steps, the club would crack Victor's head with a force that could kill. She had no idea what to do and stupidly moved directly into the assailant's path. The assailant immediately checked his course, and the murderous blow intended for Victor's head landed instead on his lower right back.

Victor crumpled to the ground with a low moan. His attacker kept on running down the street and vanished in another alleyway, the slap of his heavy footsteps diminishing. The coachman leapt down from his perch. The footman sprang into belated action, took off in the direction of the attacker.

"No!" she cried to the footman. "If the villain is from the neighborhood, he'll know the back alleyways better than you. You'll be lost in under a minute, and I need you here to get your master back into his carriage."

She went down on her knees to cradle Victor's battered body. His face was ashen with pain, his eyes half-closed.

"Can you hear me?" she demanded.

He seemed to respond by twitching his eyes.

The blow had not hit his spine, had not paralyzed him, but she feared for other kinds of damage.

The coachman kneeled next to her, took his master's weight.

She said, "Let's get him into the carriage as quickly as possible."

The coachman shook his head. "The trip down these roads is steep and will be rough on a body in pain. Such a ride might make the master's injuries worse."

"Does he have a family doctor?"

The coachman nodded.

"Do you know where he lives?"

He nodded again.

"Then you've got to get him there."

The footman came to bend over his fallen master. "Your place, ma'am," he said. "It's our only choice. Gaston can fetch the doctor and bring him here."

"My rooms are on the fourth floor. We won't be able to get him up there without hurting him more."

"If there's a long board in the courtyard, ma'am," the footman replied, "we can brace him for the four flights. It's a long ride to the Hôtel d'Albret in the rue du Faubourg-Saint-Honoré."

The distance from Montmartre to that luxurious quarter loomed large. She got up off her knees. "I'll look for a board."

She was still clutching her key in her hand. She put it to the lock, but her hand was shaking so badly that she was having difficulty fitting key to hole.

Click, click. Her key tapped the brass plate. Click, click. Hoping to find the fit. Click, click. Finally got it in. Let out her breath in relief when the bolt slid back.

CLICK, CLICK.

Absurd story.

Click, click, whirr.

Too absurd.

Whirr. Beep.

Silence.

"Fax, Alexandra."

Alexandra paused before beginning another experiment. Where was she in the schedule? She checked her notes. Ah, yes . . .

"You have a fax," Jack repeated louder.

"Fax? Oh, fax!" She looked down at the sheet Jack gave her and read the information on the painter Henri Gervex that Maggy from the med school library had sent over to her. She was torn between frank disbelief and creepy understanding.

SEVENTEEN

AFTER A FOLLOW-UP call to Maggy to confirm the worst of her suspicions, Alexandra left the lab. On her way home, she exhausted her disbelief at the fact that no exhibitions of Henri Gervex had ever been held in the United States. No catalogs on him had been printed since his heyday either, apart from a recent one in France. Nevertheless, the feeling that she had seen one painting in particular had been more than just a fleeting déjà vu. She had been bone-deep *sure*. So, if she could not possibly have seen that painting in her lifetime, then she must have seen it in a previous lifetime.

A previous lifetime? She was getting as weird as Erica.

She returned home and relaxed by whipping up a batch of babka. While the babka was baking, she wrote up experimental results on her computer. While the cake was cooling, she took a nap. She woke up, refreshed, well after midnight. She was conscious of the desire to explore an entirely new perspective on the world.

She went first to her clothes closet to conjure an outfit more worthy of her present psychological state, and this consisted of a pair of black leggings she rarely wore and a brown knit tunic that reached midthigh. Her mirror mirror on the wall told her she looked great. Witchy—and not the good witch either. Taking her pan of babka, she returned to the lab, walking under a full moon.

She was delighted by the reaction of Scotty and Hao when she sashayed into the lab. Their eyes bugged out, and one of them ventured to ask her if she knew that it was four o'clock in the morning. She said yes and put her cake pan down in front of them. Then she pushed up her sleeves and took serious stock of the situation.

She realized that her usual way of working in the lab was a poor way of making discoveries about the world. She peered into the crevices formed by the glassy jumble of beakers and test tubes and flasks on the various counters, looking for the Lurking Lab Gnomes who had made their most mischievous appearance in her life a scant three weeks earlier. While waiting for them to crawl out and come to her, she began sorting through the various bottles of chemicals. Uncorking. Sniffing. Considering. She assumed the professional air of a woman at a cosmetics counter, searching for the right tint for her lips and fingertips, tracking down the scent of the subtlest, most irresistible perfume.

She was beginning to think that the lab, even at night, was no proper place to do the kind of work she needed to do. These sterile, distilled chemicals struck her as weak, ineffectual. Where was the eye of newt when one needed it, after all? And now that she was thinking about it, the centrifuge was a waste of space. She imagined a big, black cauldron in its place, bubbling with a noxious and potent brew, its fumes curling up and out a large hole in the roof.

What should she cook up first? She thought of poisoning her plums and sending Sophie some babka, but found she couldn't muster any enthusiasm for that plan. She knew the turns those stories took. The babka wouldn't kill Sophie, it would only put her into a deep sleep from which she would be awakened by the kiss of a charming prince. Now, she certainly didn't want the part of Sleeping Beauty for herself, but there was no reason to cast the Other Woman in the role either.

This was strictly between her and Val—although she didn't yet know what it was between them. In the meantime, she'd pass up the role of wimpy Sleeping Beauty in order to tackle the role of the

Witchy Queen of the Lab. The sorceress who could both cause cancer and cure it. The sorceress who knew just what experiments to perform on OncoMouse, that miracle of genetic engineering developed for cancer research. She wouldn't let her brooms split and march out of control the way that silly mouse Mickey did. She would keep her brooms in control. Why, she would even *ride* one. And that reminded her. The lab needed a cat, preferably a black cat to hunt down Onco-Mouse and Mickey Mouse. A cat who groomed herself with a little tongue.

Now here was an interesting train of thought that led from cats to tongues to . . . French kissing.

Aha! She had hit upon a project worthy of the new powers she wanted to develop. She would mix a magic potion, and upon drinking it the next man she encountered would be driven wild with a desire to kiss her, in the French fashion. What a delightful thought. Knowing that she had to leave the lab to find the charms she needed, she swept toward the swinging door, past Hao and Scotty, and said, "Scotty dear, wipe your chin. You're covered in crumbs. And, Hao, you can close your mouth now."

When the early-morning shift of nurses and janitorial staff began to arrive, she was determined to hunt down a likely person with whom she might apprentice for the day. Say, an old woman from Jamaica who didn't hold the superstitions, held universally among scientists, that history was linear not circular, that reason was superior to emotion, that one event in time "caused" another.

Throughout the morning and afternoon, Alexandra cruised the hospital, perfectly content to do nothing until her pager beeped. She went to the nearest house phone to call her voice mail, whereupon she learned that Erica had left her a message several hours before, and because of an electronic mix-up, Alexandra was receiving it only now. The recording was bad, and Erica's voice sounded odd, but the gist of the message was clear: Alexandra was not to leave the hospital without going to Erica's room, and Erica stressed that this message was urgent.

Alexandra ducked into the hospital restaurant and cadged coins from the cashier to buy herself a Coke Classic (full sugar, full caffeine). She ducked out again, guzzling her Coke. On her way to see Erica, she turned at the next hallway, the one that led to the connecting corridor to Admissions. On the right was the exit to the restaurant. Opposite was the entrance to the cafeteria.

Standing under its green awning were none other than Ron Galway and Val Dorsainville, who was looking straight at her. Even from the distance of a good twenty feet, she saw in the depths of his focused gray eyes his fervent desire to kiss her. In the French fashion. Well, well, well.

She looked at the can of Coke. Who would have thought! She finished off the last drops of the magic potion and tossed it in the Aluminum Cans Only recycling bin outside the restaurant exit. It was nice to know there was more where that came from.

"Dr. Galway," she greeted the Old Goat. "How's the office redecoration going?" She turned to his companion and said, "Hi, Val, how are you?"

WATCHING ALEXANDRA WALK down the hallway, Val felt all his body parts reconnect. In the past few days, they had felt oddly dislocated, but they came back together now. All of them. Bruised back included, and he didn't mind a bit being reminded of it. In fact, he liked the way his old injury made him conscious of a past from which he had been too long removed.

"Lucky that I ran into you, Alexandra," he replied when she greeted him, "because I need you to come to Accounting with me to finalize some tax forms. A few signatures are all that's needed."

She nodded, and Val turned back to Ron to let him finish his comments about the office redecoration.

When Val thought that Ron had drooled over his sexy Slavic cat long enough, he glanced at his watch and said to Alexandra, "We'd better be off before Accounting closes."

Alexandra smiled prettily and said, "I'll have to come around sometime soon to see your new office, Dr. Galway." To Val she said, "Why didn't you ask Larry for the signatures?"

Val fell into step with her as they moved down the hallway toward the main intersection. They were still within earshot of Galway, when he replied, "I just called Larry from the house phone. He said that his hands were full and that I should find you since you were around here somewhere."

They came to the intersection with the Wachovia Bank branch and the connecting corridor to Admissions. Alexandra peered first left, then right. While she was reading the overhead directional signs, Val surveyed her outfit. He thought the chocolate thing she was wearing looked good enough to eat. Her leggings should have been illegal. He began to mutate from man to wolf.

"I have no idea which way it is to Accounting," she said.

He maneuvered her left toward Admissions. "Me neither."

She looked mildly surprised. "Then how are we going to get there before it closes?"

"Maybe we won't."

She gave him a questioning, cat-eyed glance through gold lashes tipped brown.

He was all wolf now. "It's called a pick-up line."

Her glance became skeptical. She echoed, " 'I need you to come to Accounting with me to finalize some tax forms'?"

He smiled. "It worked, didn't it?"

She made a little cat noise in her throat. "Is this your idea of a clever new approach?"

His smile turned confident. "It was clever enough for you not to recognize it as one, which is the reason why it worked."

Her smile turned sweet. "The reason I didn't recognize it is because the last time I heard such a line, I was in high school."

He wasn't going to let her win the point on his serve. "Time tested and ever effective," he replied, "with the charm of youth."

She chuckled and was spared a reply, for at that point, they had to jostle the oncoming traffic from the main lobby. When they had turned the corner, she said, "Nice party Saturday night, by the way."

"Thanks. I'm glad you had a chance to be with the Seine-Lafitte family."

"Yves does have a family-minded approach to his business, doesn't he? I could feel it in the atmosphere, which was not so much one of an employee gathering, but of a family reunion."

"It's his feudal side, I suppose. Lord of the manor."

"Paternalistic, anyway," she agreed. "His daughter works for the company too?"

Not sorry for this turn in conversation, he felt her challenge and met it. "More or less."

"I see. More less than more, I take it?"

He decided to force the issue. "I thought women of your generation no longer automatically assumed another woman in a business setting was mere decoration."

She didn't take the bait. "It was the way you said 'more or less' that drew me to my conclusion." Her smile was very sly. "Now, your tacit refusal to state what she does, coupled with backhandedly accusing me of small-mindedness hardly redirects that conclusion, does it?" Before he had a chance to respond to that piece of counterprovocation, she asked, "How long is she staying?"

He felt Alexandra mutate from pussy cat to lioness. The wolf in him grew sleek and hungry. "Sophie's already gone," he said. "On Sunday, in fact. The day after the reception."

"Ah."

They had arrived at the lobby and the main entrance. He stopped, and she stopped with him. He gestured to the wall of glass with the wide double glass doors.

"My car is in the parking deck."

He meant it as an invitation, and she understood it as such, for she considered him a moment before saying, "I have orders to see someone before I leave the hospital. You may as well see her too." She headed toward a flight of stairs. "Follow me."

A vivid image suddenly filled his thoughts—so real it was like a memory—of a sun-dappled drift of rumpled linen, white thighs wrapped around his, and the scent of a woman's nape mingled with the complex aromatic textures of summer in the city. This fantasy merged with his experience of Alexandra's desire for him when she had stood next to him on Saturday night, surveying his paintings. He had never really thought of art as an aphrodisiac before, but he was willing to reconsider.

He asked, "Where are we going?"

"To the Oncology Unit, or what Erica affectionately calls the 'To Die For Cancer Ward.' "

EIGHTEEN

ERICA WAS IN the commons room, slumped in a chair, wearing a T-shirt that said "No Fear," jeans, and slipper socks. She wore no earrings and no expression, although everyone else in the room was hollering and cheering at the basketball game on TV.

She was vaguely aware that someone had come to stand next to her chair, while someone else was standing behind it. "Erica," the voice said, "what's wrong?"

Erica glanced up at Alexandra, then grudged, "They're winning."

"Who's playing?"

"The Blue Devils."

"Is that so bad?"

"I hate Duke."

"The basketball team?"

Erica looked Alexandra full in the face. "I'm a Carolina fan. A Tar Heel. I figured if Duke lost today, I'd be okay. If they won, well—" She shrugged.

Alexandra kneeled down and whispered, "In the past twenty-four hours, I've altered my notions of science and superstition, but I'm not prepared yet to link basketball scores to cancer prognoses."

Erica blinked her lashless lids and said, "People come to Duke to die. Everyone knows that. The hospital has the worst mortality rate in the state, and you know why? It's not because it's a bad hospital. It's because the incurables are sent here, the hopeless cases. So I told my mother today. She called to ask how I was doing, and I said that I wanted a little dignity at my funeral." She was feeling less like a stone and more like a person. "I told her that I didn't want to be buried in some fucking dress, and I sure as hell wasn't going to let her bury me with a fucking wig."

"What did your mother say?"

"She told me not to say 'fuck.'" Erica returned her attention to the game. "At the free throw line again? Give me a fucking break and miss the fucking basket! I'm too damn young to die!"

The voice of an irritated good ol' boy traveled across the room. "Hey, Monroe! Keep it down! This is a basketball game, not some goddamned cosmic judgment. Jesus!"

Erica was feeling better by the minute. "Mr. Smooth over here," she informed Alexandra, "is visiting us from Orthopedics. You will notice that his lower right leg is in a cast. He had to have his foot reconstructed after it was crushed by a drink machine that he kicked when it ate his quarters and fell over on him. So we can all feel sure that Mr. Smooth has a pretty high spirituality rating and is able to distinguish what's cosmic from what's not."

Stung by the sarcasm, Mr. Smooth retorted, "How was I to know that the machine had just been refilled so that it weighed a ton?"

Erica smiled. "Eleven people a year die in this country from vending machines that exact retribution after being kicked. I learned that last week on *Jeopardy*. The category was Ignominious Deaths, and the answer, 'eleven,' was the Daily Double."

"Jesus, Monroe, could you be a little less morbid?"

"Well, no, actually, I can't. You see, I'm hanging down over the abyss by my feet with a bungee cord wrapped around my ankles, and the experience gives me a very particular view of things."

"There wasn't no *Jeopardy* category Ignorant Deaths."

Erica cocked her head and decided that a reply to the Ignorant of

Ignorant Deaths was beneath her. She chose instead to affect right-
eous disdain. "It was the annual Ig day, didn't you see it?" she said,
flicking a glance at Mr. Smooth. "Another category was Ig Nobel Prizes.
For the answer 'The Southern Baptist Church of Alabama for their
county-by-county estimate of the number of Alabamians who will go
to hell if they don't repent,' the question was, 'Who won the prize in
mathematics?'"

The person standing behind her chuckled. It was a man.

"And to think that I'd ever find a reason to feel lucky that I'd been
born in North Carolina!"

"Any other Ig categories?" the man behind her encouraged.

She recognized Lover Boy's voice, but didn't quite register his
presence. "Yeah. Igloo Art," she said. "Some guy in Anchorage made
a Mona Lisa with sixty-three pieces of toast, and not one of the con-
testants was able to formulate the question to 'A famous painting that
has found edible expression in Alaska.' You'd think they'd screen for
talent a little better than that."

A round of cheering in the room drew Erica's attention back to
the tube. "At the free throw line *again? Fuck!*"

She stood up and faced her visitors. Forget the Blue Devils at the
free throw line. With the reality of the Slavic Queen in company with
Lover Boy before her, she knew she was well and truly fucked.

"You told me to come see you before I left the hospital," Kaminski said. "I met Val on my way and asked him to come along."

Erica ran her eye over Lover Boy's suit, shirt, tie. "I see you followed my advice and found out who she is."

Before Lover Boy could respond, Kaminski said, "I thought you
might like to meet Val under more normal circumstances, and I
came to tell you good-bye."

"Oh, more normal circumstances, certainly." She inquired politely, "You'll come to my funeral, Coach?"

Kaminski put her arm around her shoulder, gave her a shake.
"I'm saying good-bye because I'm leaving for Easter break tomorrow
morning. I'll see you when I get back."

Erica rolled her eyes toward Lover Boy, but didn't waste any politeness on him. "What do you have to say for yourself?"

Val said that he thought the Blue Devils would lose in the next round. "They're playing the number one seed in their region, and their opponents have a better back court and more height. I also think the Tar Heels have a pretty good chance of winning it all. So don't hurry on the funeral plans."

Erica was impressed. "Damn, you're good."

"I follow basketball."

"Like I said. So. What do you two swell kids have planned for this evening?"

In unison, "Dinner" and "I'm going home now."

Erica summed it up. "Dinner at Coach's."

Kaminski shook her head. "I emptied my fridge last night, and I've got to pack."

Lover Boy settled for driving her home. They began to leave the commons room to the raucous cheering of the remaining audience. Erica slowed her step, caught Kaminski's arm. Lover Boy walked on ahead.

"I hope it's all right that I brought Val here," Kaminski said. "You don't seem very happy about it."

Erica laughed. "I was calling to *warn* you, you idiot! Just before the game started, I had the strongest feeling that Lover Boy had entered the hospital, and I *didn't* want you to meet up with him!"

"Why not?"

How much to tell? "Do you know what you're doing?"

"Not really."

"Then I guess it's my job to let you know that you're driving him crazy. I don't know what advice to give you now that you've seen him. I wish I knew what to tell you to do, but I'm afraid it's too late! It's all that bad karma!" She surveyed Coach critically. "I don't think I've ever seen you look so . . . so —"

"Witchy?"

"It's a fine line between witchy and bewitching," Erica said, "so

don't twitch your nose, Samantha, or you'll find Darrin in your bed."
Kaminski drew a total blank. "Elizabeth Montgomery. *Bewitched*." No
change of expression. "You really ought to start watching Nick at
Nite, but you get the idea. Keep it in mind."

"You're saying I shouldn't sleep with him, is that it?"

"Don't have *sex* with him—hey, I need to be clear here. My good
advice might be too little too late, but you never know!"

"Erica, you're going to beat your lymphoma, and I'll see you when
I get back from spring break."

Erica put a hand on Kaminski's shoulder. "I hate like hell to tell
you this, but give Lover Boy the heave-ho, or you won't outlive me by
much."

"Erica." This, repressively, disapprovingly.

"Coach, I just can't shake the feeling that this guy is going to be
the death of you."

"Oh, so, *now* you tell me he's an ax murderer!"

Kaminski thought this was joke. "He's no killer, but—"

"But?"

"But. Period. Leave it at that."

NINETEEN

 ALEXANDRA LEFT THE hospital with Val, thinking less about his killer instincts than Erica's morbid state of mind. As they crossed the parking deck, they kept conversation casual and professional. However, once he handed her into the leather seat of his snazzy sports coupe and shut her in, she felt a twinge of uneasiness. Was this how slasher movies started?

He opened the driver's door, folded and tossed his suit coat behind the seats. Then he slid behind the wheel and brought the electronic wizardry of the dashboard to life by starting the engine. When he threw his right arm over the back of his seat and hers, she nearly cringed, but he was only pulling out of the parking space.

"It's almost the perfect car," he commented, "except that it has an automatic transmission and doesn't give me enough driving to do. I rent a different car every time I come to the States, always thinking that I'll buy the very next one. No luck yet."

"I suppose that's the beauty of coming for so few months at a time," she replied. "No need to make a commitment."

He glanced at her a full second longer than necessary. She held his eyes without blushing or blurting out "a commitment to a car, that is." She looked down to press the button to lower her window. Warm, sweet air wafted in.

They were at the exit when he said, "So, tell me about your relationship to Henri Gervex and his paintings."

His phrasing caused the hairs on her nape to raise and goosebumps to flash over her skin. He stopped the car, handed his ticket and a few bills over to the attendant, then pulled into the line of traffic around the hospital. When he glanced at her again, his eyes teased and demanded an answer.

"I have no relationship to Gervex or his paintings," she said. "I was mistaken to have thought I knew him."

"You seemed very sure on Saturday that you'd seen my painting before, or at least others by the same hand."

"I'm more sure now that I'd never seen it or any others by Gervex. You said yourself that he was obscure, and what I know of the Impressionist period is pretty pedestrian." She repeated what he had said on Saturday night. "Hallmark cards, calendars, and mousepads."

He laughed. "I said that merely to defend my purchase."

"Why did you buy it?"

"I suppose my taste in art is changing along with my taste in women."

"I thought Gervex is considered bad art."

"Bad art? I'm not so sure. He's more like a category to himself."

"How so?"

"In the Dallas gallery I leafed through the catalog of some recent expositions of Gervex's work in France. It seemed to me that although he wasn't quite in the avant-garde, he wasn't an old-guard academic artist either."

"So he wasn't a schmaltzy Salonist."

"Not entirely. He prettied up the Impressionist inventions, making them easy to swallow for the general public, and was loved for it. He's what you might call un bon vulgarisateur—and that, of course, is part of his charm."

"Only part of it?"

"Sure, the other part being his gift for scandalizing that same public with his representations of prostitutes."

143

"Just like Degas and Manet."

He gave his attention to turning a corner. "I thought you said your knowledge of the Impressionists was pedestrian. The suburban mothers who troop their children to the museums don't usually think they're giving them a lesson in the ways of prostitutes."

"Well, when Manet paints a picture of a pretty, bored girl at a café, puts a plump plum in a glass bowl before her, and entitles it *La Prune,* I don't think her profession is in question."

"You know French slang too?"

"Hardly. The association between plums and prostitutes isn't difficult to make."

He turned down Monmouth Avenue without replying. He pulled up in front of her house and switched off the engine. He turned toward her, one hand draped over the steering wheel, and asked, "Did you make the association because you're thinking of offering me some of your plum cake?"

She was shocked by his vulgarity and perversely charmed by it, in the manner of Gervex. She opened her door. "I made babka last night and took it to the lab this morning." She swung her legs toward the curb. "And you are ill mannered, sir."

She stepped out of the car and into the fragrant shadows of evening. The air was warm and wrapped with the scent of forsythia, fresh grass, and early lilac. It hinted that soon azalea bushes would pillow the earth in pink and vermilion, and white dogwood blossoms would float over them, as if dusting them with powdered sugar.

He came around and ushered her up the front walk between thick, yellow-blossomed bushes. As they crossed the porch to her front door, she pulled her keys out of the side pocket of her tunic. He made as if to take them out of her hands, but she wouldn't relinquish them.

He said, "I used to do this for my sister."

"Do what?"

"Go in ahead of her, check behind the furniture, look in the bathtub, and search under the bed. I'd like to revise your opinion of my manners and assure you that you're safe."

She thought his ploy was pretty good, but she wasn't going to let him cross her threshold. "Safe?"

"From bogey men," he clarified.

"Ah, but what if *you're* the bogey man?"

He had backed her up against the door and put one hand on the door frame above her shoulder. She had a curious impulse to raise one leg and put her foot flat against the door frame, but resisted it. She felt herself regressing, not to another lifetime, only back to Schurz High. She fancied that the cutest boy in the senior class had backed her up against her locker, was asking her to the movies on Saturday night, and wouldn't take no for an answer.

"Who knows?" he replied. "But I'll leave you with what you've been asking for."

She returned to the present when the hand above her shoulder went around her and bent her head back so that the line of her neck was exposed to him. His other hand circled her waist and drew her to him. Her arms rose to clasp his neck. He put his lips to her neck, her chin, and when his lips touched hers, she knew she wasn't kissing the senior class stud. This was a full-grown man—or, perhaps, part man and part wolf.

She yielded to the kiss, and when his tongue slipped against hers, exploring his options, she yielded further. She had wanted this since the wee hours of the morning in the lab when her witchy, bewitched self had come out of hiding to fill her sexy leggings and fine knit tunic. He was right. She had been asking for it, and now she was getting it. So the magic potion hadn't worn off, and he was no slasher— only a killer kisser.

He seemed to know just how to move against her, every movement minimal, every separate touch tender. A slight sway, a shift of the foot found the better fit, the more sensitive fit, the more seductive fit. She swayed and shifted in return. Her fingertips moved with the rippling of his shoulder muscles beneath the fine cotton of his shirt. She tasted his lips and skin. She breathed in his scent. She grazed her forehead against the bristles of his short, dark hair. She felt that they were two strands of the double helix curling around one another, attracting and seducing with complementary forces and asymmetrical mysteries.

She felt as if she had been waiting for this French kiss for a hundred years and decided that playing the role of Sleeping Beauty wasn't so far off after all. For someone who had been slumbering for a century and waiting for the kiss of a very sexy prince, she was amazed by how quickly came the desire to be surrounded with nothing but skin and limbs and flowering air. When real heat shot through her, she understood how deeply sensual a character was Sleeping Beauty, how her prince derived his charm from passion, how short was the distance between a French kiss and complete submission.

With his hands on her thighs and his lips at her ear, his thoughts were evidently traveling in the same direction as hers when he asked, "Would you like to give me your keys now?"

She was tempted, definitely tempted, until she recognized the note in his voice as one of triumph. She ducked her head away from him and exerted all her willpower to resist the pull of forces.

"I can open the door myself," she said, dangling her keys before him. "And as for staying safe, I'm sure I'll be very safe inside alone."

She saw him register her no by the change of focus in his eyes. He didn't pressure her, though, and when she moved away, he released her. She opened first the screen door, then unlocked the front door, and pushed it open. Then she stepped back onto the porch and let the screen close behind her. She wasn't through with him yet.

"This is good-bye for a while, then, Val."

"A while?"

She nodded. "I'm taking ten days off—my first real break since last summer." She smiled, thinking how glad she was that there would be plenty of miles separating them for the next few weeks at least. "By the time I return, you'll probably be in France. So . . ."

"Going to the North Carolina beach like everyone else in the state?" he asked, thrusting his hands into his trouser pockets.

She shook her head. "Going home."

146

"To your parents?"

"To my grandmother."

"Where does she live?"

For an answer, she rose on tiptoe and kissed him good-bye. His hands came out of his pockets and gripped her shoulders. She put her heart and desire into the kiss, giving him one he would remember.

Val's memory was selective. When she broke the kiss, he pulled her to him so that his chin rested on the crown of her hair. His gaze traveled through the screen door and stopped at the cellular phone that sat atop a coffee table. He had again that strong fantasy of sex-scented sheets and white thighs, but this time he saw a piece of paper drift onto the linen. In his mind's eye, he picked it up, and his fantasy merged with reality. He was looking at the first month's bill for Alexandra's cellular phone which had crossed his desk this very morning. He recalled that it included one outgoing long-distance call to area code 312. Chicago.

He crooked his fingers in the neck of her tunic, let his hand rest there a moment. "I'll say good-bye for now, Alexandra." Then he withdrew his hand and crossed the porch. When his back was turned away from her, he smiled broadly.

PART II
CHICAGO

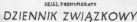

DZIENNIK ZWIĄZKOWY

TWENTY

EIGHTEEN HOURS AND five pit stops after leaving Durham with the Duke students who were giving her a ride, Alexandra saw the overcast skyline of Chicago come into view, a spiky EKG of a city with a frenetic heartbeat—no flatlining here. She breathed in the soot and fumes pouring from the refinery smokestacks in Gary and felt braced by the air of the Rust Belt in hostile springtime. She even welcomed it after her exotic experiences in the too-pretty budding lushness of the silicon-clean Research Triangle.

Soon enough, she was bumping down the potholed pavement on Milwaukee Avenue with its endless stretch of salmon brick and ochered stone two-storied buildings. At last the barrio with its jumble of neon signs in Spanish crowded up against Jackowo Polonia and gave way to storefronts announcing John Bogusz Adwokat, Bobak's Delikatesy, Podlogi/Flooring. Clean lace at dingy windows looked very good to her sore eyes. Once deposited on the broken sidewalk in front of Kolatek's Bakery, she felt she had returned to reality.

In the dim stairway to the second floor, she was surrounded by the familiar smells of yeast and butter and cane syrup and old paneling and all that was dear to her. Then she was in her very own living room, embracing Marie-Thérèse. Over her grandmother's shoulder, she glimpsed the retouched photo of the pope blessing the Warsaw crowds in front of the Palace of Culture which hung over the over-stuffed burgundy brocade sofa, and its solidity was as wonderfully re-assuring as her babcia's sponge-cake breasts. Alexandra's ears were filled with a flow of Polish through which threaded the lilting of a Chopin mazurka drifting out of the kitchen radio set to WPNA and Panorama Polska. She could not have been happier.

She slung her suitcases in her bedroom off the dining room, then installed herself at the formica table in the kitchen to be surrounded by yellow-and-black tiled walls, scrubbed countertops, and spotless linoleum. Marie-Thérèse served her tea and cake and set her to coloring Easter eggs. Within the hour, she was caught up on all the neighborhood gossip, which included the information that Mr. Lukacz had received a shipment of old treasures he was sure would interest Alexandra.

When her granddaughter was relaxed and well fed, Marie-Thérèse laid a crisp one hundred dollar bill on the table and said, "You are to buy yourself a pretty dress for Easter Sunday dinner."

"You don't need to give me money, babciu. In fact—"

Marie-Thérèse waved an imperious hand. "And make it sexy."

"Babciu!" Alexandra chided with mock disapproval. "A sexy dress to wear on Easter Sunday?"

The older woman picked up the bill and pressed it into her granddaughter's hand. "You know what I mean, Alexandra Janina."

Alexandra saw the trend and gasped, "You didn't."

Marie-Thérèse Zelenkovich was a dignified woman. She carried her full figure well, as the daughter of a once-famous ballerina would, and she abhorred American dress-down sport style, which meant that she was wearing a proper satin-look blouse, wool skirt, and gold-trimmed cardigan. She had never dyed her thick, dark blond hair, which was richly streaked with silver and caught back in a bun. Her brown eyes were clear, and her heart-shaped face prettiness was still very much in evidence.

Marie-Thérèse countered, "Didn't what?"

"Didn't invite some man to Easter dinner who is the son or grandson of one of your lady friends at the Copernicus Cultural Club. Tell me you didn't."

Marie-Thérèse sniffed and took Alexandra's plate and cup to the little counter by the sink. She gazed out the window with its view of a sullen alley and the brick wall of the building opposite and said, "I didn't invite the son or grandson of one of the lady friends at the Copernicus Cultural Club."

Alexandra groaned. "That means you invited some other man." She crossed the small space and grasped her babcia by the shoulders, gave her an affectionate shake. Her sweet tone robbed her reprimand of real reproof. "You know I hate it when you fix me up. You do! All I wanted was to come home and be a Polish turnip for ten days. No fuss." She kissed her babcia's hair. "And no matchmaking!"

Marie-Thérèse admitted, "The only reason I invited this young man to dinner was because . . . because . . . well! He says he knows you, Alexandra Janina, and he seems to be an excellent prospect. I wouldn't have invited him, except for the fact that you requested that I send you the family photo album."

"What does that have to do with anything?"

"I thought you were getting ready to settle down."

Alexandra was puzzled. "Settle down?"

"Well, aren't you?"

Alexandra's distinctly unsettling experiences of the past month passed before her eyes. That North Carolina craziness felt as distant now as the far-off warmth and sunshine and oppressive greenness of Durham, and it had dissolved in the sugar-sweet solution of her babcia's incessant matchmaking. The hundred bucks and suggestion for a sexy dress were new, but otherwise everything was back to normal. A god-awful, wonderful normal.

She had to laugh. "You got part of it right, babciu, and as for settling down, I plan to call Elena at Century 21 today and set up some appointments for us to look at houses in Hinsdale. I've got the down payment."

Marie-Thérèse's eyes brightened, but she didn't abandon her

original topic. "Now, let me tell you how I met the young man who will be joining us on Sunday. He happened to—"

Alexandra held up her hand and interrupted with a hasty, "I would much rather be surprised!"

Marie-Thérèse frowned her disapproval. "Do you wish to explain your interest in the photo album, then?"

"I guess being away from Chicago for the first time made me hungry to touch my past." She smiled. "That's all."

IT FELT GOOD to sleep in her very own bed. It felt good to make an appointment the next day with the real estate agent. And it felt good to find the perfect sheath dress the color of old gold that must have been made with her figure and coloring in mind. The dress required some nifty, new underwear, and she bought that too, although she spent much more than a hundred dollars.

Since it felt so good to be back to normal, she decided to get her hands on the family Bible. One of her strangest experiences of the past month had occurred when she was leaving Val's house with Jack, and in her mind's eye had appeared some kind of official document with the name Jeanne Lacombe scrawled by a sputtering pen in an old-fashioned script. Although she couldn't yet account for why she knew the painter Gervex, she was no Mad Hatter scientist who jumped down rabbit holes. She wanted proof that she had not invented the name Jeanne Lacombe but had actually seen her signature in the marriage lines of her very own family Bible.

After asking her babcia for the Bible, she was sent to the third-floor attic where she picked her way to the leather trunks next to which nestled her old ice skates. There she unearthed several diaries and a pack of what looked to be correspondence tied by a disintegrating ribbon which included a disintegrating yellowed newspaper. She began to shuffle through the dusty materials. The topmost items were written in Polish and in several different hands. The bottom-most letters and the newspaper were written in French. She hung on to the correspondence, but she could find no Bible.

She asked her grandmother for it again, and although Marie-Thérèse had to admit she wasn't entirely certain where it might be hiding, she agreed to look for it.

On Easter morning Alexandra wedged herself into the crowd at Saint Hyacinth, surrounded by the crucifix and people carrying baskets filled with eggs, bread, ham, salt, and lambs to be blessed with holy water. She discovered that she liked moving through the rites of a holiday stamped Resurrection Only. Here was one place, at least, where she didn't have to worry about the implications of reincarnation.

Which didn't exist, of course.

She had never before fully appreciated the linear nature of Christianity: birth, life, death, life after death, and that was that. No karma to lug around life after life. No *Wheel of Fortune* quiz shows with prearranged riddles to figure out. No Samsara perfume print ads around which yin and yang turned for eternity. The Christian version was more like a beer commercial. Once around. Irreversible. Give it your best shot.

Strange religion, Catholicism. Elaborately sensual. Darkly masochistic to parade the wounded body of Christ through the church like that. Deeply sexual too. Sexual? Somehow thoughts of blood and wounds had given her impure thoughts, and she realized that she had lapsed into either Budweiser irreverence or the mysteries of that fairy-tale moment when Sleeping Beauty pricks her finger and reclines in Titianesque splendor upon a pillowed couch with a black cat at her feet, awaiting the bigger prick of—no, she must be thinking of a painting by Manet. Or maybe she was having all these erratic, erotic thoughts because of the sexy body slip she was wearing under her new dress.

But what was it about this black cat that kept creeping into her thoughts? And why did she suddenly remember her first conversation with Val when they had been discussing Erica's lymphoma?

Think you're destined to find the cure?

If I live long enough, she'd responded.

Then I wish you a long life.

These weren't the words of a man who intended to harm her, who would be the death of her, according to Erica. As if he had done her harm in a previous lifetime. As if they were destined to do that karma thing and repeat past mistakes . . .

The rabbit hole loomed. She narrowly missed it and was glad when the bells began to ring, signaling that the Resurrection—one life, one death, one rebirth—was complete. She exited to the front steps of the church where she was slapped back to her senses by the early April wind.

TWENTY-ONE

 FOR THE BETTER part of the mass, Bob's mind had been filled with the low-grade static of the blue scrolling accounts receivable files of Dembrowski's Hospital Supply. The office had recently gone paperless, and he'd had to learn about clicks and double clicks and user-friendly icons. He didn't care much about computers one way or the other. They seemed to make everyone else in the office happy, but they hadn't fundamentally changed the nature of the business of moving a particular piece of equipment from one part of the city to another.

His thoughts drifted from last week's date's tits to next week's ass, moved around the crucifix that suddenly blocked his line of vision, and caused him to shift his gaze to a blond head a few rows up and over. Something to look at for a while. The blond head turned toward the older woman sitting next to her. Nice profile. Familiar. Something to think about for a while.

Pretty. Blond. Familiar. Could be almost anybody. But not too familiar. Like someone he hadn't seen in a long time. The field got even wider. Polish, anyway. He hadn't been with any Polish women for a long time now. He hadn't been deliberately avoiding them, but he hadn't been seeking them out either.

Jesus fuck, could it be that dziwka from high school? He hadn't thought about her in years. What was her first name? Sweet thing. Yeah. It was coming back to him in bits and pieces. She had been hot, real hot, in high school. Kind of a tight-ass, though. Dim recollection. Real name? Antonia? No, it might have been Alexandra. That was it. Alexandra.

She reminded him of wilder times. When he had been all muscle and hormones. Still was. But he had it under control now. Hadn't started a barroom brawl in at least five years. Hadn't even thrown a punch in two years, not since that spic delivery man had fucked up royal, given him serious lip about it, and had been too dumb to think a good Polack wouldn't discuss the situation. Some counselor or another had recommended he sign up at the West Side Sports gym for regular workouts—as if it had been his fault the guy ended up in the hospital. But the gym had been good for him. He was in shape, anyway.

Ah, yes, those had been his Bruce Springsteen glory days, high school, when the little man inside his trousers had been up and strutting all day long . . .

Now he remembered. Alexandra Kaminski. Felt it right between his legs. She had been a scrappy thing. Had gotten the better of him. At the time he'd been taken to the razor's edge of anger at her rejection because she'd had the hots for him for weeks, he was sure. But looking at her now, he felt more a kind of a vague nostalgia for the moment. Win some. Lose some.

Try again.

Which was exactly what he intended to do as soon as the religious rigmarole was over, and everyone was milling around outside.

He approached her from behind and heard her answers to the no-brainers she was being asked. "Yes, it's very sunny there." "No, there's no Polish community in North Carolina." "I've begun to understand the Southern accent. At first, I couldn't understand half of what they were saying."

"Alexandra," he said just as the sun broke through thin, tarnished clouds.

She turned, didn't recognize him. She looked good. Really good. "Remember me?" he asked.

He watched the penny drop, and she exclaimed in an undertone, "Bobby? Bobby Dembrowski?"

He looked down, bowing his head to her, then back up. A kind of apology for their last encounter.

"How are you, Bobby?" She hugged her coat around her. The wind was a dervish.

"Bob," he corrected, "if you don't mind. And I'm fine. Yourself?"

She murmured her ditto to his "fine" and tossed her head to get the hair off her face. The wind was a wild comb.

"Home on vacation?"

She nodded.

"For long?"

"Another week or so. And you?"

"I live here. Went into the family business. Hospital supply and home care equipment. We're on Belmont Avenue."

"How's business?"

He nodded slowly. "Thriving."

"You still live in the neighborhood, then?"

He told her his address, said it in a way so she would know he was single. "I overheard you say that you're in North Carolina now."

"I work at Duke University Medical Center."

"And now you've gotten used to the funny way they talk down there."

She laughed. "It's not as funny as they would think we talk up here—especially on Milwaukee Avenue."

"You like it there?"

"It's a job." She shrugged. "Hospital work."

"What can I sell you?"

She smiled. "We have all the bedpans we need, thanks, and I'm in the cancer division."

"A growth industry," he said solemnly.

After a split second, she caught it as a joke and laughed again.

"You were always pretty quick," he said.

That caught her off-guard. The look on her face told him she was remembering her swift teen-age knee to his teen-age groin. Mission accomplished.

Before she replied, he said, "Glad I ran into you, Alexandra. Maybe I'll see you again before you leave town."

OUT OF THE corner of her eye, Alexandra saw Bob speak briefly with Marie-Thérèse before moving on. It came to her, then, that *he* was the mystery man coming to dinner this afternoon. She tested her theory by asking her babcia what she knew of Bob Dembrowski. Her suspicions were confirmed when Marie-Thérèse replied, at her most dignified, "The Dembrowskis have done very well for themselves, Alexandra Janina."

So, bad boy made good. Alexandra was glad Bob had presented himself to her on the church steps, to give her time to readjust to him. He was still handsome in a Marlon Brando as Stanley Kowalski kind of way, broad shouldered and very fit, with the wind molding his suit coat this way and that across his torso. She liked the way he had brought up the old incident in order to dispose of it, and she liked the way he had conveyed his interest in her without being a jerk about it.

TWENTY-TWO

EASTER SUNDAY DINNER, conceived and or-
chestrated by Marie-Thérèse Zelenkovich, was
an event.

On Saturday evening, Alexandra had added
a leaf to the dining table and, upon returning home from mass, set
it for eleven places. The dining room, already crowded by a buffet
and china cabinet, was about to be cramped with conviviality.

Marie-Thérèse had been cooking for a week. The ladies came
early, bearing trays and covered dishes, apparently laboring under
the misapprehension that there wouldn't be enough food, a stately
procession moving up the stairs and through the living room to the
dining room to the kitchen. Lamb. Ham. White sausage. Kielbasa of
many colors and kinds. Nalesniki. Pierogi. Potato pancakes. Fried
mushrooms. Stuffed cabbage. No bite less than a thousand calories
and a hundred grams of fat. Cakes. Torty.

The men came later, carrying bouquets and bottles of wine,
vodka, slivovitz, and boxes of cigars. They sank into the overstuffed
living room furniture, cracked jokes, and called out helpful suggestions as their better halves fussed over the table and the food and circulated trays of appetizers.

Mr. and Mrs. Kolatek, dear neighbors and landlord, had come
with the best their bakery had to offer. Krzysztof and Ludmila Mi-

anowska were there too—her babcia's oldest friends—along with their daughter, Anna, and her husband, Jerzy Tomczyk. Zofia Stevanovic, a widow, had invited Jozef Adamczyk, a well-to-do widower. It needed only Bob Dembrowski's presence to make the party complete.

Alexandra was alone in the kitchen when Jerzy, apparently answering the buzz of arrival at street level, ushered the eleventh guest through the front door of the apartment. Above the general din, Alexandra heard the sound of the new arrival, introductions shouted, hellos hailed. She had stuck her finger in a sour cream sauce and was licking it, her free hand hurriedly tugging off her apron, when the guest was brought back to the kitchen.

Alexandra saw the yellow-and-black tile spin once around her head. In her haste to remove her apron, she had shifted her neckline so that the lace edge of her low-cut body slip peeped out. She extended her hand automatically in welcome.

"Val," she managed, but was shocked out of speech by the touch of his hand when he accepted hers and shook it. The warmth of his touch told her that he was no hallucination.

"Hello, Alexandra," Val replied. "I was pleased to accept your grandmother's invitation for Easter dinner, and she assured me that I would be welcome at your family party."

She withdrew her hand from his. She noticed that his gaze had dropped to the low, scooped neckline of her dress, and she felt her body filling up and spilling out of her slinky slip. In her daring dress of old gold, she felt like a sheaf of ripened wheat. The awareness zinged across her skin that, with his eyes, he husked her of her dress right there in the kitchen, paused at the slip, then stripped that off too.

She twitched her dress back in place and said, "I wasn't expecting to see you." Not a brilliant start, but good enough. She smiled politely. "What brings you to Chicago?"

"A problem at one of our cooperative labs."

"Did you just arrive?"

"I flew in Thursday morning." His smile glinted. "I called Mrs.

Zelenkovich late Thursday afternoon, and she invited me to visit in the evening."

Thursday evening Alexandra had been on the road, imagining that she was putting much-needed distance between them. The small kitchen shrank to teeny proportions. It was warm with cooking, savory with aromas, alive with his presence. She was pleased that her perceptions, although heightened, did not go awry. She was seeing and hearing just fine.

She was thinking just fine too, and she knew which part of his story clunked. "Exactly how were you able to pay my grandmother a visit?"

"Taxi," he explained. "I'm staying downtown."

"I mean," she said, "how did you know where we live? My Chicago phone number and address aren't listed anywhere on my CV on file at Seine-Lafitte, and while there are dozens of Kaminskis in the phone book, I'm not one of them. The phone is listed under Zelenkovich."

His smile was provocative. "You're not the only one with magic powers."

Her eyes widened. She opened her mouth to demand to know what was going on here, but he cut her off by leaning toward her and saying low, "This is the next go-around, Alexandra."

He had promised her another go-around after his first visit to her house on Monmouth Avenue, and she wondered, Mad Hatterish, how many go-arounds they'd had throughout eternity. He was standing close enough to her that she could smell the faint trace of shaving soap on his neck. His lips touched her ear, sending a ripple along her nerves down to her toes.

"And now we're going to play it my way."

She understood. He hadn't liked being turned down on her front porch the week before, and he had crossed the threshold of her grandmother's apartment to let her know it. Her best defense was a good offense. She was happy to be wearing the dress for it.

She moved away from him and struck an alluring little pose.

163

"Think it's your turn to call the shots? We'll see about that!" She spied a bowl of nuts on a nearby counter. "Since you're here at the invitation of my grandmother," she said, picking up the bowl and handing it to him, "I'm sure she'd appreciate it if you made yourself useful."

He accepted the bowl, favored her with a look that reminded her forcibly of the scene they had played in her kitchen in Durham, when she had been down on her knees before him. She thought she had better get out of this kitchen while the getting was good.

She ushered Val out of the kitchen and into the dining room, and caught her babcia's arm as the older woman was returning to the kitchen.

"What possessed you to ask that man to dinner?" Alexandra demanded, dropping her voice to a whisper, even though she was speaking Polish.

Marie-Thérèse looked surprised by the implied censure. "He is a most charming man. Do you not think so?"

"You don't know a thing about him."

"I know that he comes from Paris and that his manners are extremely refined. And he dresses well."

"What is it with this man's clothes?"

Marie-Thérèse was smiling dreamily. "Almost I could think I was back at my mother's apartment in Warsaw, receiving a most proper gentleman caller."

"Speaking of Poland, babciu, have you located the family Bible yet?"

"Alexandra Janina!" Marie-Thérèse chided. "We are in the midst of Easter dinner preparations. Please be more helpful and help Zofia set up the buffet!"

Alexandra did as she was told, and the noisy party in the living room eventually wended its way around the small dining room, each guest carrying an empty plate at one end of the buffet line and a very full one at the other end. To Alexandra's surprise and disgust, Marie-Thérèse encouraged Val to sit next to her and preside at the head of the table.

It was immediately apparent to Alexandra that Val was a big hit with her babcia's guests. Both Zofia Stevanovic and Jozef Adamczyk spoke excellent French and were delighted to have an occasion to use it. The conversation moved in and out of French, English, and Polish, but the rapid shifts neither disconcerted Val nor seemed to make him lose the thread of the conversation. The topics were, in any case, predictable. When the political hanky-panky down at city hall had been thoroughly thrashed out, talk shifted to sports. Everyone at the table, except Val, had a bowling handicap either to boast of or to explain away, after which it was quickly determined that Val's game was not golf, as several men had suggested, but tennis.

Val said only, "I like to keep my arm in shape," and let the conversation drift in another direction.

That direction turned out to be billiards, and a thorough review of the variety of pool halls in the neighborhood was engaged. The men in the group were hard drinkers, and the wine was flowing freely. Alexandra kept her sipping to a minimum, so it was not an excess of alcohol that gave her a Cheshire cat feeling, as if all that was visible of her was the generous smile of her skin above the scoop of her low-cut bodice.

Krzysztof reminded the group of Alexandra's pool hall coup when she had been in high school. "She cleared the table," he said, "on the break ball. It was at Jolly's, remember?"

Alexandra shook her head. "It was at Casay's."

A small argument was engaged by a half-dozen people, only two of whom had witnessed the event, whether Alexandra's feat had been performed at Jolly's or Casay's. Just because Alexandra was the one to do it didn't mean she remembered where she'd done it.

· · ·

THROUGHOUT THE AFTERNOON Val had been feeling comfortable in a way that intrigued him. He liked, for instance, how the exquisite exaggerations of the old-world silverware on the dining table reminded him of another place. He experienced an unusual surge of some force greater than caffeine but less than sexuality to raise a gold-chased wine glass of museum quality to his lips and to taste a harsh, nearly undrinkable wine. He was aware of the small space and of the dignity that expanded it. Amorphous memories came to him that he didn't bother to identify, but they fit together into a pleasant kaleidoscope, reminding him of a time when the world had been arranged to cater to his pleasures.

Val had grown to like Mrs. Zelenkovich. She made him feel tender. Alexandra, on the other hand, did not make him feel tender. He had cornered her, sly cat, and she was mincing around her narrow space, cool and calm one minute, hot and bothered the next, hardly knowing where she should step.

The afternoon became evening, and the theater of action moved from the dining room to the living room. The other women began brandishing pie servers and carrying trays dotted with brandy snifters. His golden cat was stacking up dirty plates. Like a good coach who always knew where the players were on the field, Val had kept track of the positions of the various guests. He calculated Alexandra to be alone in the kitchen.

He strolled into the kitchen, closed the door behind him, and walked toward Alexandra as she fussed at the sink. She was running the faucet and might not have heard him enter. When he was within two feet of her, she said, without turning around, "Don't you dare touch me. I haven't settled all these plates yet, and if I break one, I will blame you."

He walked up and stood behind her but didn't touch her. She looked up and at the window over the sink. The panes were blackened silver and gave back the negative of their reflection, his shadowy form doubling above her and to one side of her. He clasped his hands behind his back and leaned over her shoulder so that he could enjoy the view down her bodice.

She rattled the dishes, then turned off the water. She placed her dampened hands on either side of the sink, palms down on the counter, fingers spread. Her head was bowed. His view was good.

"You are a rat."

"I am not a rat."

"You are a miserable rat who has charmed an old woman into thinking that no traps need be laid for you in her house!"

"I've enjoyed an excellent evening, Alexandra, and I hope I haven't traded badly on your grandmother's hospitality."

He felt her back arching and her soft fur flying.

"My grandmother!" she exclaimed on a knowing note. She grabbed a dishcloth and wiped her hands. She turned around to face him. Her eyes glittered with dawning understanding. "I called my grandmother the day you sent me that . . . that"—she groped for a strong enough word—"that *blasted* cellular phone. You got my grandmother's telephone number off the phone bill!"

"It took you the entire afternoon to figure that out?" He shook his head sadly. "I forget the figure Seine-Lafitte is paying you, but I'm afraid it's too much!"

Her cat eyes had narrowed. "I called you a rat? I was too moderate!"

"I am not a rat," he repeated patiently.

"Then what are you?" she fired back.

"I am a businessman," he said mildly, "competing in a global economy in the volatile market of pharmaceuticals."

"Next you'll be telling me that you're a poor, downtrodden soul with your problem at the cooperative labs and that I'm to feel sorry for you."

"I don't want you to feel sorry for me."

"All right, then, tell me what you're doing here, and *don't* feed me any pablum. Tell me *exactly* what that problem at the cooperative lab is and why it required your urgent presence in Chicago. While you're at it, you can also explain your interest in cancer research. And all this *better* be pretty good!"

"My sister died of leukemia over ten years ago," he said, "which accounts for my interest in cancer research. I'm convinced that if she had been diagnosed with the disease in the early stages she would have lived. The problem that brings me to Chicago involves a diagnostic product I'm developing that has recently encountered patent problems that shouldn't exist. There's a screw up somewhere, and I'm not sure yet where it is, so I'll no doubt be spending many hours with the Abbey Labs patent lawyers this week."

Her jaw had dropped. She recovered, then exclaimed, "I should have *known* you'd have the perfect answer! I'm sorry about your sister, of course, but I'm not yet convinced that what you've said explains *anything* of what's happened lately! And you can wipe that smile off your face, because I'm . . . I'm—"

"Pissed off."

"*Very*," she agreed. Her eyes were darting angrily around the kitchen, as if seeking a target. "I'm beginning to think that all this is very strange and that I'm never going to get to the bottom of it. What a god-awful mess."

She might have been referring to the piles of pots and pans and dishes and utensils that were spread across every surface in the compact kitchen. His gaze followed hers over the cluttered remains of an impressive meal. His attention was caught by a contraption on top of the stove.

"What's that?" he demanded, astonished.

"That's what my grandmother rigs up to marinate the plums," she said and added with a touch of defiance, "for plum babka."

"How does it work?"

"She turns on the stove so that a stick of wax slowly melts, making the little gear turn which holds the hook which skins the plums. The plums fall over into the marinade to soak overnight."

He was looking at an unlikely and ingenious rig which reminded him of so many things at once that he was unable to sort them all out.

"It's remarkable," he said.

"I've always been intrigued by it," she replied, "and fiddled with it forever as a kid, changing the size of the stick of wax and the speed of its melting to see how the adjustments affected the overall efficiency of the gear. I never got it to work better than how my grandmother rigs it."

The kaleidoscopic bits of memories that had shifted so pleasantly throughout the afternoon turned suddenly shardlike and sharp. They pricked him now with suggestions of loss and pain. This plum-marinating contraption was a smaller version of the ball-pitch contraption his grandfather had designed, and its mechanism was central to the TEFS diagnostic product that was giving him so much unexplained patent trouble. He could have sworn, absolutely sworn, that the contraption had been an original invention of his grandfather's. So what was a version of it doing in Alexandra's grandmother's kitchen?

Before he had a chance to ask more about it, the door to the kitchen opened.

In walked Mrs. Zelenkovich, and at her side was a man built for the football field. "Ah, there you two are. I'd like to introduce you to an old friend of Alexandra's from high school," Marie-Thérèse explained. "He ran into Alexandra this morning after mass, and he thought it would be a good idea to drop by after his dinner for coffee and dessert. Valéry Dorsainville, please meet Bob Dembrowski."

Bob stepped forward, his hand extended. "Valéry, is it? Nice to meet you."

Val shook the man's hand, and, as if he didn't have enough on his mind at the moment, he experienced an acute psychosomatic spasm of pain in his lower right back.

TWENTY-THREE

THE NEXT MORNING Alexandra awoke knowing exactly what she needed to do.

Her dream that night had been disturbingly vivid. She was inside a narrow staircase similar to the one that led to her grandmother's apartment, but the staircase smells were very different from the familiar ones of yeast and syrup and Chicago dust. The staircase of her dream had a damper, fresher scent, like that of new plaster, and an airier feel too, as if it opened onto an interior courtyard illuminated by a slice of bright moonlight. And she had not been walking up only one flight of stairs, but several. She'd had the vague sense that Val was behind her. She felt frightened, somehow, by his presence, but not threatened by it. Bob Dembrowski had been in the dream too, but was farther off. Dream knowledge informed her that he was standing outside in the street.

She left a note on the kitchen table and was out of the apartment before Marie-Thérèse had stirred. She traveled to the Northwestern campus in Evanston, went straight to the Kresge Centennial Building, and found the Department of French and Italian. She walked down the main hall on the first floor until she came to a little alcove that housed small offices, probably those occupied by graduate students. She poked her head into one and saw three young women.

Alexandra stepped into the office and announced, "I need help."

The woman at the table didn't look up from her books. The one reading the newspaper turned a page, rustling it with disinterest. Only the woman staring out the window turned. She was an elegant brunette, and her finely arched brows were raised in inquiry.

Alexandra fished in her briefcase, took another step into the room, and held up the pack of correspondence held together by a disintegrating ribbon. "These letters are in French, and I can't read them. I have to know what they say. Can you help me?"

Alexandra wondered if the desperate note she heard in her own voice moved the woman at the window to take pity on her. She said, "I'm a graduate student in French. We all are, but Deirdre is studying for her writtens which begin this week"—she gestured toward the woman at the table—"so she can't help you, and Louise"—she indicated the woman reading the newspaper—"is antisocial so she *won't* help you."

Louise pointedly rustled another page.

"I should be able to help you, though." The friendly one regarded Alexandra speculatively. "You're not in the Slavics Department, are you?"

"I was in Biology here as an undergraduate. Five years ago already. Why do you ask?"

The woman shrugged. "I thought you looked familiar. Sorry. I'm Nancy." She held out her hand for the letters. "Let's take a look. What do you have here?"

Alexandra introduced herself in turn. She handed the letters over to Nancy and said, "Family correspondence. Maybe."

Nancy started to flip through the stack of letters, withdrawing them from their envelopes and sorting through the pages. She hadn't looked at more than two before she stopped, walked over to the table, and said in a voice of suppressed excitement, "Hey, Deirdre. You gotta see this."

Deirdre shuffled through the letters put before her. She whistled softly and asked Alexandra, "Where did you get these?"

"From a trunk in my grandmother's attic."

"Got any anything else from the period?"

"There's an old newspaper at the bottom of the stack," Alexandra offered.

Deirdre touched a corner of the folded newspaper. It broke off and crumbled at her touch. "Better not fiddle with that," she said. "It should be on microfiche anyway. Which newspaper is it, I wonder?" She moved a piece so that she could read the half of the masthead that was visible. "Probably *Le Courrier français.* Hmm. But these letters! Well! They aren't really letters, more like documents. Dated eighteen eighty-something and headlined Montmartre. The stationery and handwriting look authentic. What a find!"

"Deirdre's period is the belle époque," Nancy explained. "Once she passes her qualifying exams, she'll be writing her dissertation on gendered spaces and architecture in *Les Rougon-Macquart.* You know, Zola."

That didn't mean much to Alexandra. "Can you read the letters to me?" she inquired and then apologized for sounding so pathetic about it. "Or maybe Nancy can, if you're too busy?"

Deirdre was an ethereal blond who was pretty when she smiled. She smiled now and gestured Alexandra to be seated at the table. "I need a break, and why should I fight research that falls into my lap?" She studied the pages before her. "I'll begin at the end. The bottom-most document has the earliest date."

Nancy pulled up a chair next to Alexandra, as Deirdre scanned the first paragraph. "A word-for-word translation would be awkward, so I'll gist it." She cleared her throat and read, "'The door opened, and she ushered into her rooms the footman and coachman who were carrying their master between them on a broad board. She motioned them to follow her. The night sky glowed through the generous glass on the roof and lit their way as they moved through the front room into the adjoining bedroom.'"

Deirdre paused. "The woman apparently lives in a top-floor studio with skylights. Is she an artist?"

Alexandra shook her head. "I don't think so. At least, she's not a painter."

"Do you know who 'she' is?"

Alexandra groaned and said, "Maybe."

"She must have been quite a number to be entertaining three men in her bedroom."

"Well, one of them has been injured, no?" Alexandra said, a little weakly, "and the other two are helping to lay the injured man down and get him comfortable."

"He might be drunk," Deirdre countered.

"We'll see what the doctor says when he comes."

Deirdre read further. " 'The coachman went off to fetch his master's physician.' " She put the pages down. "How did you know the doctor would be coming? I thought you couldn't read French."

"I can't," Alexandra croaked. "Lucky guess."

Deirdre continued, " 'She lit the gas lamp at her bedside, turned it low, then tugged the lace at the windows against the bright moonlight. She plumped the bed pillows while the footman rid his master of his outermost clothing. Together they stretched him out on his back on her bed and settled him as comfortably as they could. His breathing was labored, and his pallor was emphasized by the dark hair tousled at his temples and neck. The color of his skin matched the linen of the pillowcase.' "

Deirdre looked up. "Do you know who 'he' is?"

Alexandra's heart was fluttering. Her skin was raised on tiptoe. Her nerves were stretched taut in all directions, like an arabesque. "About as much as I know who 'she' is."

Louise put her newspaper down. She turned a chair backward to the table and straddled it. She had dyed metallic red hair in a graphic cut, shaved at the nape. To Nancy's look of amused satisfaction, Louise snipped, "I've read everything in this week's *Butch and Dyke* and finished salivating over Lucy Lawless in her Xena costume, so I figure this has to be more interesting than grading French 1 papers."

Alexandra was soon drawn into a very different, strangely familiar world that came to fragile life on the thread of Deirdre's soft voice.

TWENTY-FOUR

 "YOU DID WELL, my dear, to bring the Count here," the doctor said as he opened his black bag and began arranging instruments on the bed next to his patient. "Gaston had plenty of time to recount everything that happened, and I must commend you for your quick action."

"Will he be all right?"

The doctor adjusted his stethoscope and opened the man's shirt to listen to his heart and chest cavity. He frowned heavily, as if not liking what he heard. He put a hand across the man's brow and shook his head. "Too warm." He bent to the man's ear and said softly, "Victor, it's Laurent. I've come to tend to you. Can you give me a sign that you can hear me?"

A soft breath escaped Victor's lips. With great effort, he roused himself to murmur, "Get away from me, you old undertaker."

Dr. Dreyfus straightened and said, "Cause for hope." Then he winked at her, and she was reassured by the doctor's calm presence, his shock of white hair, his keen and kindly blue eyes.

The doctor called to the footman and coachman who were standing at attention on either side of the bedroom door. "Help me undress your master and roll him over so that he's not lying on his back. I need to check the extent of the damage where he was hit."

174

She withdrew from the room. Listening at the door, she heard muffled groans from the patient and grunts from the men helping him. The doctor was issuing a series of soft orders, and it seemed that he succeeded in getting a medicinal draught down Victor's throat. When she was called back in, she saw Victor lying on his stomach, his face turned away from the room, his arms hugging the pillow on which his head was resting. A sheet covered him from the waist down. His back was completely exposed. The doctor was methodically covering every inch of it with his stethoscope, listening intently.

As the doctor moved, he crossed the light from the lamp, causing shadows to fall this way and that across the smooth skin of Victor's back. First the line of well-shaped muscles across his shoulders came into relief, then a sensuous rippling of finer muscles harping down the frets of his ribs to the small of his back. The doctor's stethoscope circumscribed a large area at the lower right back, then moved to the upper left chest where it stayed for a full minute.

The doctor withdrew the stethoscope from his ears, stood up, and began putting all his instruments into his black bag. "His heart has stabilized," he said. "I've given him a sedative to calm the pain and keep infectious fever down. He's resting easier now."

"And the extent of the damage?"

"The muscles were badly bruised and ripped in at least one place. His fever and his pain aren't great enough to suggest internal bleeding. However, he can't be moved tonight. He's a strong man in excellent condition, but—"

She anxiously searched the good doctor's face. She completed his thought. "But there's a chance he might not recover?"

He smiled gently. "He'll recover, but it's likely there will be lasting effects of one kind or another. I hate to think what would have happened to him if he had been bumped through the city for an hour in his carriage. Any potential long-term damage was certainly minimized by having brought him here."

"It was their idea," she said, glancing over her shoulder at Victor's henchmen. She would not take credit for it.

"I'll thank you in any case, Mademoiselle Lacombe, and leave you now."

Dr. Dreyfus held out his hand to shake hers. She grasped it and would not release it. "Leave? Why are you leaving?"

"When Gaston drove up, I was on the point of going to attend to a woman who is in labor with her first child. Since there is nothing more I can do for the Count now, I must not stay here any longer. I know he's in your good hands."

"My good hands?" she echoed, bewildered by the implication that she was to tend him.

The doctor's glance slid to his patient, then to her. The shift in his expression told her what he assumed about her relationship to the Count d'Albret. Dr. Dreyfus bowed his head. "I beg your pardon, Mademoiselle Lacombe."

At the moment, she was more alarmed by the turn of events than offended by the doctor's assumption, which was close enough to being accurate under the circumstances. She felt the lines of an invisible trap tangle around her.

She asked with quiet resignation, "What am I supposed to do?"

The doctor withdrew his hand from her clasp. He indicated a brown vial on the bedside table and told her how to mix the sedative. "You can administer it to him every four hours if the Count becomes restless. Gaston will drive me back. I'll take Guy with me, as well, unless you would like him to stay here?"

Much as she didn't want to be left alone, she certainly didn't want to be left in company of the footman whose interested attention had too often darted her way. "I'm sure I'll be fine here without him. I'll set up my bed on the chaise in the sitting room and keep an ear out for any movement. I don't need any help."

The doctor promised to return first thing in the morning.

"I'll look forward to that!" she said softly and with feeling.

The doctor bowed and thanked her with ceremony.

She bobbed a curtsy. "I'm . . . I'm glad to be of service to . . . to

the Count and to you, sir," she said, matching the good doctor's attempt to lend the occasion some dignity.

Then everyone was gone, and she was standing alone next to her
bed. She could hear the uneven rhythms of his breathing, feel the
pulse of his blood, sense the pain that he was sleeping off. She looked
down at herself and thought that it would not be a good idea to
undress.

She turned the lamp to its lowest glow, gathered up cushions and
stray pillows scattered around her bedroom, and went to her sitting
room. She curled herself, catlike, on her chaise longue and made herself comfortable, but not too comfortable, so that her sleep would not
be deep. She gazed at the stars twinkling through the north-facing roof
glass and followed the slow path of the moon as it silvered the tops of her
hothouse plants that grew luxuriously by day in the light of the sun.

In the luminous darkness of her sitting room, she let her gaze
wander over her private space. Her ballet barre ran along one wall,
her plants along another. Her kitchen space was compact and served
her purposes. Her sitting area was furnished with pieces of faded
prettiness that she had salvaged from the discards of grand places.
She felt Victor's presence curling through her rooms, her oasis, possessing it. She didn't resist his presence or his possession. Rather, she
admitted to herself that she liked facing the night with more than
her plants and furniture for company. She relaxed into the gentle
pleasure of this chaste intimacy.

Her lovely respite didn't last. At the sounds of lumbering movement, her head snapped up, and she figured she must have been
dozing for some time, since her neck had become slightly stiff. She
hurried into her bedroom to see him thrashing uncomfortably.

She put a hand to his forehead and was shocked by the sizzle. She
mixed the medicine with shaking hands. To turn him, she had to put
her muscle behind the effort, then drew his head into the crook of
her arm so that she could get the solution into his mouth. He calmed
down a little, lay back against her arm, and cracked his eyes open. In

their depths was a glitter of demand so fierce that her heart jumped into her throat and she thought she had been tricked into bed with him and into holding him in her arms.

His eyes shut again, and she decided that whatever she had seen must have been the play of light. She shifted him out of her arms and lay him back down on his stomach. Still bending over him, she was about to release him when one of his hands came up and covered one of hers. The shock of his touch traveled up her arm, flashed through her breast.

His voice was a whisper of pain. "Is that you?"

"It's me."

"I underestimated you."

She tripped in the snare of the implication. "I didn't hurt you," she said quickly.

After a lengthy pause, he spoke again. He let his hand slip from hers. "You can make it better. In fact, only you can make it better."

He worked his shoulders and shifted uneasily. His movements became increasingly agitated. His brow grew scalding hot. She feared that she had not given him enough medicine or that it did not take effect. She feared giving him another dose, in case it would be too much. He was thrashing, tangling his legs in the sheets, murmuring incoherently. Her alarm increased.

She shoved the armchair that formed part of her dressing area over to the bed and sat down in it. She attempted to straighten the twisted sheet around him. She had to readjust the upper edge of the linen along his waist several times for all of his writhing.

She knew about cramped muscles. She had soothed Chérie's legs any number of times. Her own calves too. Feeling herself swallowed by a force greater than herself, she stretched out her hands and placed her fingertips on his bruised back. At her touch, his writhing lessened immediately. She began to circle her fingers lightly, dancing across skin and wound, feeling for the injured muscles. She was sensitive to the place where the muscle may have been ripped, moved around it. With her fingertips, she could feel the searing heat of the injury at the same time that she could feel the pressure of her fingers soothing it, cooling it, uncramping the cringe of his muscles. He moaned at length, not in pain, but in relief.

She put the strength of her arms and shoulders into her movements. Her hands kneaded, unknotted, sculpted his muscles. She kept up her movements for as long as she was able, hardly conscious when sleep overcame her. She drifted off on the thought that she was connected to him now, for better or worse.

The next thing she knew, the bedroom was flooded with yellow sunshine. She was seated in the armchair and stretched over the edge of the bed. One of her arms lay across the back of his thigh with only the sheet separating his skin and hers. Her other arm cradled her cheek. Her hair was nestled into the curve of his waist, and her nose was pressed against the flesh of his side. She refused to open her eyes. She breathed in heavily and felt a sweet melting suffuse her, like warm butter.

She breathed in again and decided that she felt more like a big bowl of crème fraîche, the kind she might see at the *laiterie,* with a plump red strawberry plopped in the middle. Or, better yet, topped by a juicy plum. She had a hazy memory of standing in an orchard under a plum tree, trading kisses and caresses with her first sweetheart. Bertrand was strong and smelled good, fresh from the fields. She couldn't have been more than sixteen, and it was exceedingly sweet to be touching him and touched by him. She was happy and falling in love and then . . .

The loutish son of the local landowner happened upon them and threw Bertrand off his property. The landowner's son was named Jean-Marc Lafitte, and she would never forget the way that wretch had ripped off her clothes, ripped her open, and left her to bleed beneath the pretty plum tree. Bertrand had returned to the Lafitte property that night and performed a savage surgical procedure on Jean-Marc that ensured he could never produce children. Bertrand had been thrown in prison, of course, where he eventually died.

She had fled to Paris and taken refuge with Maurice and Charlotte. And she had never considered another man's attentions. Until now.

She groaned. She opened her eyes and lifted her head groggily. Her eyes popped open to see the rumple of her day-old clothing. She felt the dishevelment of her coiffure. Dr. Dreyfus could return at any moment. While she was pushing the armchair back where it belonged, she heard a soft knocking at the door.

TWENTY-FIVE

COMING TO THE end of a page, Deirdre decided to give her voice a rest. She put the pages down and asked, "So, what do you think, ladies?"

Nancy sighed with pleasure. "I can picture it perfectly."

Louise pictured it in her particular way. "The Count is a bastard."

"He's an aristocrat."

"Same thing," opined Louise.

Nancy's voice was dreamy. "I think she's really lucky."

"Lucky?" Louise was indignant.

"He's in her bed, and she's nursing him, so that means he'll fall in love with her," Nancy said. "You can tell."

"What you can tell," Louise said, "is that he's going to use her and then dump her."

"On the one hand we have a Romantic," Deirdre said, gesturing to Nancy, "and on the other"—gesturing to Louise—"we have an Unnatural Creature." She noticed that their newfound friend Alexandra had no comment.

"What do you think, Deirdre?" Nancy asked.

"I think she would have made a good massage therapist." To Alexandra she inquired, "You said these are family papers?"

"Something like that," Alexandra replied quietly.

"Well, they can't be classified as correspondence, since the pages aren't addressed to anyone and they're not signed." Deirdre turned the pages front and back, examining the quality of the rag linen. "And they aren't quite a diary either. Although I rather like her descriptions and some of her turns of phrase, the writer was no literary type. Not even particularly well educated. Look at some of these misspellings." She pointed to several lines for Nancy's and Louise's benefit.

"As a specialist in the period," Alexandra said, her voice sounding strained, "would you know anything about this . . . this Victor, the Count d'Albret?"

"D'Albret. D'Albret. Hmm. I may have run across the name, but I don't recall seeing it in a context that suggested he ever did anything noteworthy. I wonder what his family name would be? I might have to look that one up."

"And Jean-Marc Lafitte?"

"I'm not sure."

"Oh, come on, Deirdre," Nancy scoffed, "you know *everything* about this time period, and even I know something about the big nineteenth-century banking Lafittes, even though I can't stand that century."

Deirdre nodded to Nancy and Louise and said to Alexandra, "They think I'm obsessed. I call it professional thoroughness. And what I mean when I say I'm not sure," she explained, "is that I don't think our poor castrated rapist Jean-Marc is in the direct line of the banking Lafittes, since that family is Parisian. From the reference to the plum tree—which seems significant, don't you think?—I'm guessing this story is set in the Southwest. Now, the banking Lafittes had no property there. So our castrated rapist might be from some upstart branch of the family, since it says he was the son of the local landowner."

Alexandra was regarding her with a rather haunted expression in her big, brown eyes. "And Mademoiselle Lacombe?"

"Hey, these are not the highest-profile people of the period, you know." Deirdre waved the pages. "But what we don't know, we can always find out. Want more?"

Three heads nodded emphatically.

DR. DREYFUS, LOOKING haggard, shook her hand in parting at the door that led to the landing. He apologized for having to go so soon, once again. The mother who had delivered the night before had lost much blood, and he was needed by her side.

"The Count is resting comfortably," he said, "and may well sleep through the day." With a nod toward the bedroom, he added with a faint air of puzzlement, "He is doing far better than I might have expected. Although I cannot quite explain it, neither do I wish to question it! Well, I must be off, Mademoiselle Lacombe. I'll return this evening."

She was resolved to look prim and proper for the doctor's return and immediately fetched fresh water to perform her morning toilette. Her arms were so stiff and heavy from her night's work that she didn't have the energy to change her clothes anywhere else but at the corner in her bedroom where her pitcher and basin and cheval glass were set up.

Victor seemed to be sleeping, so she stripped to her chemise and unpinned what was left of her coiffure, letting her hair fall down her back and over her breast. With a glance over her shoulder at the man in her bed, she took her chemise off too and set about washing herself. She was donning her drawers and floating a fresh chemise over her head, when a tingling on her skin warned her that she was being watched. She looked quickly over her shoulder again, but Victor's eyes were closed.

Keeping watch on him, she tied the drawstring of the chemise, then brushed her hair out and tied it at her nape with a ribbon. She left the bedroom to do her stretching exercises in the sitting room. When she returned to the bedroom to put on her dress, she checked her step, startled to see Victor leaning on an elbow, half-propped against the pillows. His eyes were narrowed against the light. His skin had color. His hair was curling back from his temples, as if he had run a hand through it.

He had caught her in a state of charming undress and was regarding her appreciatively. Since he couldn't see much more than he had already seen of her in her dancing costume, she decided to carry the moment off with dignity.

"Good morning," she said. She walked across the bedroom to her armoire positioned beyond the foot of her bed. She was sorry that the armoire door opened toward the side wall and did not shield her from his sight.

"Good morning," he returned. His voice was lazy.

She couldn't tell whether he was still weak or whether he was hiding behind a strength that had partially returned. "You were attacked last night in the street," she said. "Do you remember?"

"A little."

"Dr. Dreyfus came both last night and this morning."

"I remember something of his visit at night but nothing of this morning. I must have been sleeping too soundly."

"He said he'd be back this evening as well, to check up on you."

"And the verdict?"

"You'll live."

"Which was contrary to the intention of my attacker."

"Perhaps." She selected a dress with a wide, white collar and broad green-and-white striped skirt. He watched as she put it on. She was struck by the fact that having a man watch her dress seemed far more intimate than having him watch her undress.

"Do you have any ideas who my attacker might have been?"

She fixed the buttons, straightened the seams, and smoothed the collar, before turning toward him. "No."

"None at all?"

The hairs on her neck rose at the sound of his deep voice, and she guessed that she herself had fallen under suspicion.

"No," she repeated. "The man was wearing a mask."

"So. There was only one man and not a band of ruffians?"

"Only one."

"Who did not, if I recall events correctly, have any intention of robbing me."

"Apparently not. It would have been foolish for him to try, with your coachman and footman standing there."

"Indeed. And so I can only wonder at his motive."

She folded her lips, then said, "It's a disreputable neighborhood I live in, with many uncertain types lurking in the alleyways." She lowered her eyes to avoid sight of his chest. "I suppose you know that you're in my rooms."

He looked at her cozy bed piled with pillows and covers. Over the footboard his clothes were folded. His gaze moved to the side table, the lamp, the frilly curtains at the windows, focused on the furniture grouping at the dressing area, and came to rest on the paintings on her walls.

"Whatever the condition of the neighborhood, your rooms are not at all disreputable," he commented. "I see you followed your own advice and invested in the impressionist paintings."

"They were gifts," she replied with a superior smile, "and I think the water lilies are pretty. The blues and greens are restful. No café scenes for me."

She untied the ribbon at her nape and picked up the brush on her washstand. She would have to dress her hair in front of him, too.

After a couple of minutes, he said, "You have pretty hair." Before she could thank him, he said, "You have other paintings in the corner there that you haven't hung. Why not?"

She placed her hairpins. "They're not paintings, they're posters, and I refuse to have my name and image plastered all over my bedroom, much less all over the neighborhood."

"It's bad for business not to advertise."

She looked him straight in the eye. "Business has never been better, as you well know." She looked at the posters propped in a corner behind her. "These are by a painter—a funny dwarf—who likes to hang around the dance halls. What he hopes to accomplish I have no idea! He carries a cane that conceals, I swear, a tube filled with brandy. As if we couldn't tell that he drinks like a fish!"

"Can I see them?"

She shook her head. "The dwarf didn't ask if he could draw us while we were dancing, so I got angry with him and asked Maurice to make him give me what he'd drawn so far. I haven't had the heart to throw them out."

"Don't throw them out yet, at any rate."

She selected a bonnet from the shelf above her washstand. She crossed to the door. "I'm going out for bread. What would you like me to get you while I'm out? Are you very hungry?"

He shook his head. "I'd like something before you leave."

She wished she could resist the look in his eye and the smile that spread slowly across his face. She felt herself blush like a village maiden.

"I'd like you to massage my back," he said. "I have almost no memory of last night, but I do recall magic fingers making the pain go away. Were those yours?"

Their eyes held, and she felt drawn toward the bed. She perched on the edge of it, placed her bonnet on the floor beside her. He sank down on his stomach. His head was turned away from her. She drew a breath and placed her fingers on his bruised back. As before, she could feel the contours of his injury. She knew just how to coax the muscles, how to press the heel of her hands into his flesh to alleviate the pain. She was aware of his breathing becoming stronger, his blood flowing stronger, his muscles growing stronger. She was aware that this touching was having a strong effect on her, was arousing her in a way she had not known, even when she'd been happy and innocent and standing under the plum tree in the arms of Bertrand.

She felt a strong desire to lean over, to breathe in his scent, to kiss his wound. She caught her breath and stopped her massage. She ſtood, picked up her bonnet, and left her rooms without saying a word.

When she returned an hour later, he was gone.

The realization that she was alone and free on her day off filled her with such a precious happiness that she could not bear to examine it. She ate her bread, exercised at her barre, tended her plants, and polished windows on this perfeɕt early summer's day. A carefree impulse overtook her, and she went to the market for plums. Upon her return, she baked her firſt plum cake in years, then prepared a pot of green tea.

While it was ſteeping, she ſtripped down to her sleeveless chemise that reached midthigh and into a silk Japanese dressing gown that Chérie had given to her. She disposed herself on the chaise in the sitting room, with the tea and cake before her on a low table. The afternoon subsided. The soft blue light of the warm evening crept in to suffuse the room with paſtel luminescence, bringing her plants to eerie life, making the corners myſterious.

Into her world walked Viɕtor. His dark hair was tamed. He was perfeɕtly attired. He carried a hat in his hand and a walking ſtick that he did not seem to need. He bore no hint of having been the viɕtim of a recent attack. He was looking very pleased with himself, with her.

"You were expeɕting me, I see," he said, surveying the pretty domeſtic composition before him. He pocketed the key which had opened her front door. He didn't explain where he had gotten it, and she didn't ask.

Had she been expeɕting him? She considered the possibility, then chose to contradiɕt him. "But you see only one teacup and one plate here, set out for me alone."

"Then set another."

She unfolded herself from the chaise and came toward him. She helped him shed his suit coat of light gray flannel and hung it on the coatrack by the door. She led him to the wide wing of a wicker chair placed next to the chaise. He hitched his trousers to sit, then unbuttoned his veſt and loosened his cravat. She moved to her kitchen area, feeling like a dancer on stage, aware of her kimono fluttering around her bare skin.

"Only one more setting?" she asked provocatively. "I am expecting Dr. Dreyfus this evening."

"Laurent won't be joining us. He sends his regards, however, and credits you with my rapid recovery." He smiled. "He is sure that I will continue to make progress if he leaves us alone."

She fixed him tea and cake, then curled up on the chaise once again. She pulled her legs under her, letting the kimono fall open at her calves.

Charlotte had told her that to entice him was her best protection, that she needed to find more of Chérie within her. She would follow Charlotte's advice, but she wasn't sure anymore that she needed protection. As for Chérie, her spirit was not only pulsing along the silk of the kimono that lay against her skin, it was also within her, in crooks and crevices, in warm and clean places. In her world of few choices, she was happy to be in her own rooms and have the illusion that she was in control. She felt like a delicious bowl of snow-white crème fraîche.

They spoke of this and that and nothing at all. At one point, she said, "I have no idea what you do other than attend the opera and frequent art studios."

He said, "I have stables outside of Paris where I break horses."

"Break?"

"Train."

She had to discard her initial image of the nags she had known in her village to arrive at the kind of horse he was most likely to train. "Is it difficult?"

"It takes a certain skill and experience."

"Are you good at it?"

He smiled. "Are you good at dancing?"

She accepted his answer with an ironic nod. "What do you do with the horses once you've trained them?"

"I ride them."

"Oh! Somehow I inferred that you train more animals than you intend for personal use."

"You're quite right, but I always have to ride them in the process. I regularly break horses for my friends, and I'm always scouting to buy. Although I pride myself on my good eye, it's usually the case that after I train them, I sell them again. Every now and then, however, I come across a creature that I must keep for myself, but that is rare."

"What qualities draw you to a creature that you must keep for yourself?"

"Independence and resistance. The ones who take to me instantly present no challenge."

"Have you ever had a favorite?"

"Well, now," he said, his gray eyes lazy upon her.

She paused, then invited him to tell her more about his hobby. Sometime later a silence fell that he made no effort to break, and she knew what to do. She rose from her lounging position and came to seat herself across his lap. The muscles of his thighs shifted to receive her weight and instantly aroused her.

"I forgot to lay out napkins," she said. She raised her lips to his. "I must correct the lapse." She kissed a cake crumb from the corner of his mouth. She felt his lips turn up and was inspired to kiss the smile lines.

"I apologize, of course," she said and added coquettishly, "You can't expect a common girl like me to know her manners."

He gathered her in his arms with intention. "For such a common girl, you've put me to an uncommon amount of trouble, Jeanne Lacombe."

She trailed her lips to his ear. "Your trouble has just begun, Monsieur le comte."

She felt the faint tremor of his unreleased laugh. Her gown slipped off her shoulder at the touch of his fingers, revealing her chemise. "Let's hope," he said and pressed his lips to hers.

TWENTY-SIX

NANCY PICKED UP a page to fan herself. "God!"

"No kidding," Deirdre agreed. "And think about it. This woman had paintings given to her by the Impressionists. One of Monet's *Water Lilies,* no less! And she was sketched by none other than Toulouse-Lautrec. Since I know of no model the dwarf ever used by the name of Lacombe—and, by the way, I liked that bit about the eau de vie in his cane—she must have succeeded in keeping the posters he did of her concealed. Whoever inherited them—that is, if they still exist—is sitting on a fortune!"

"Yeah, but who's Charlotte?" Louise wanted to know.

"For that matter, who's Chérie?" Deirdre rejoined.

"You're Chérie," responded a male voice at the door to the office in a bad imitation of a French accent. "Ma chérie." He strolled across the room, bent over Deirdre, and embraced her thoroughly and theatrically. His crisp brown hair was close cut, and he was wearing a navy blue officer's uniform. When he finally let Deirdre up for air, her pale skin was pink with pleasure.

Deirdre introduced her beau to Alexandra. "This is Kevin. He's in ROTC." She ran her eye over his trim physique. "I've always loved a man in uniform."

"I've always loved a woman who can speak French," Kevin said.

"My vocabulary is limited to 'chérie,' 'merci,' and 'voulez-vous coucher avec moi ce soir.' "

Deirdre giggled. "The 'merci' comes *after* the 'voulez-vous coucher avec moi,' darling."

With every passing minute, Alexandra was feeling more and more flayed, as if layers of her skin were being peeled away. "How is it," she managed to ask Deirdre over the lump in her throat, "that you've always loved a man in uniform?"

"I was a military brat," Deirdre replied offhandedly. "I grew up with men strutting around in everything from fatigues to full dress, and I guess it grew on me."

"Come on," Kevin said, pulling Deirdre to her feet. "You're already late for your study break. Or did you forget we were meeting everyone at the Hideaway at eleven o'clock?"

"Eleven o'clock!" Nancy squeaked, jumping up. "Already?"

Alexandra stood up too. "You mean, we can't go on now?"

Deirdre checked her watch and unslung her purse strap from the chair. "Not today, hon. But I love this stuff, and you can come back tomorrow, if you want. We have lots of pages left."

Nancy started to go too, and Alexandra felt anxious to detain her. "Where're you going?"

"Dance class. It started fifteen minutes ago. Damn."

Deirdre was already leaving the room with Kevin. Alexandra was following Nancy to the door, desperate to learn more about her. "You like to dance?"

"Love it," she said. "I didn't start until I was a teenager, which is very late, you know, but I discovered that I am something of a natural at it!"

"Where are you from?"

"Kenilworth."

One of the richest suburbs on the North Shore. Alexandra felt a ripple of happiness. "You ended up rich! I'm so glad!"

Nancy paused at the door. "Yes, I did end up rich," she said slowly. "My real father died when I was one, and my mother was working as the hostess of the restaurant at Indian Hill Country Club when one of the club members fell in love with her." She frowned. "How odd that you should put it that way."

Alexandra rushed on. "Do you have a boyfriend?"

Nancy's frown was replaced by a brilliant smile. "I like to play the field." She pirouetted into the hallway. "Look, I gotta go! There's this incredibly cute guy in my class, and you should see his thigh and calf muscles! God! *And* he's straight!" Then she was gone.

Alexandra turned back to the table where Louise was still sitting. "She's a slut," Louise said.

"Excuse me?"

"Nancy's a slut," Louise repeated. "Deirdre's a little better, but not much."

Alexandra folded her arms and leaned against the door frame. She regarded the third woman fondly. "So, tell me about you, Louise."

"Me and men?"

"Anything you want to tell me will do."

"When I was a sophomore in high school, a guy hit on me. He was really persistent. I don't know what it was about him that made me succumb or relent or whatever the word is. Maybe I thought that struggling against him would only make it worse. Well, when it was all over, all I could think was, 'I've had enough men now for a lifetime—for many lifetimes!'"

Alexandra was almost overwhelmed by a huge wave of nostalgia.

Louise pushed her chair away from the table and walked toward the door. "Which is to say that I'm off to attend a Gay and Lesbian Task Force meeting."

Alexandra patted Louise's arm affectionately when she passed by. "I'm glad that you're not completely anti-social."

Louise's smile was lopsided. "For Nancy, anti-men is anti-social." She gave Alexandra a critical once-over. "She's right about one thing, though. You do look familiar." She shrugged. "Well, see you tomorrow."

Alexandra nodded.

When Louise had gone, Alexandra heard faint notes of a music hall band ring in her ears. So. Nina, Chérie, and Louise had returned as Nancy, Deirdre, and Louise.

To the empty room, she said, "It was great to catch up with you girls after so many years."

TWENTY-SEVEN

 VAL TAPPED HIS pen impatiently on the papers littering the lawyer's desk before him and tried to remember what he had liked about this corn-fed Midwestern lawyer as recently as two weeks ago.

"I know that dealing with the U.S. Patent Office isn't a rational activity," Val said, "but the obstacle we've hit now should have been encountered either months ago or not at all."

The lawyer's smile was patronizing. "The problem isn't with the U.S. Patent Office, Val, as I've explained to you—"

"We've had nothing but success since you searched Derwent two years ago for patent titles and got the green light," Val broke in, flat-out disbelieving that there could truly be a problem with the patent clearance in Europe. "I don't understand why we aren't" —he had to pause, uncharacteristically, to search for the right term—"why we aren't test-marketing TEFS right now. I still expect to be first on the global market by the end of the year."

"The restrictions on over-the-counter products seem to be snagging, er, blocking Test Early, Feel Safe right now."

Val was annoyed. Tom Manning had slowed his speech, as if Val was having problems understanding English. Val *never* had problems with English, but he was experiencing big problems with this out-of-shape excuse for a legal eagle. And he was determined to wipe that irritating smile off Manning's face.

"You have yet to explain to me where the . . . the—"

Once again, Val had trouble finding the right word. But that didn't mean he was having trouble with English, only with an incompetent lawyer.

"—the roadblock is. I came to Abbey Labs to benefit from your legal and marketing pipeline, and I'm seeing an all-but-completed project collapse before my eyes. I'd hate to have to pull TEFS and start over somewhere else, but I'd do it if I could find another diagnostics marketer more committed to the project."

"Abbey Labs is behind you all the way," Tom assured him quickly. His smile, patronizing or otherwise, was gone. Good.

"And why wouldn't you be?" Val returned testily. "I came to you with an idea for the first reliable cancer diagnostic that is affordable to manufacture and that any idiot can use in the convenience and privacy of his own home."

"But we can't get the product on the global market, nor even safely penetrate the U.S. market," Tom said mildly, "until we get the full international patent clearing."

"Which is precisely what this discussion is about. We've got the licensing on the polymerase chain reaction process from Hoffmann—La Roche. We've got approval on the reliability of the colormetric test readings from the FDA, *with their compliments!* We have—my God!—the *first and only* test to come on the market that can give a person a reading on cancerous cell activity long before even the smallest tumor can be detected by current technology. And all a person needs is a reasonably priced TEFS kit and an oven, either conventional or microwave!"

Tom said quietly, "I know that, Val."

"So what's the problem? Rear-guard action from knife surgeons who don't want to lose their cutting business?" Val flipped his pen down on the desk. "I've had a pretty good idea all along who would want my heart if I actually got this thing on the market, which is why I've made my alliances with the medical oncologists and the laser surgeons over the years. Everything was on course until about a month ago."

Tom pulled out his handkerchief and mopped his brow. "I'll access LexPat again this afternoon."

"Do that, because I'm about at the end of my patience after spending three full years on this project. Longer, if you count the time I've been thinking about it, at least, since—"

Since his sister died twelve years ago. She might have been saved had she not resisted going to the doctor until it was too late. She might have been saved if their ridiculous mother had been more devoted to her daughter and less to the wine bottle. He had no intention of saying this aloud, but it vexed him to be distracted by thoughts irrelevant to the business at hand, just as it vexed him not to be thinking well in English.

"—since I started at Seine-Lafitte. So my question, of course, is why I don't have the damned patents, international or otherwise!"

Tom shifted uncomfortably in his chair. "Thing is, your patent clearance seemed, well, not exactly clear sailing, because it never is, but at least routine. I still have found nothing in Patents Pending in the U.S. or Europe to compete with TEFS. And your idea for the layered PCR capsule that amplifies the DNA under repeated heating to color-register possible cancerous activity in urine always seemed to me to be unique."

"Not to mention that there's good precedent with a similar technique used in home pregnancy tests. So tell me in plain English precisely where you think the problem is."

"Maybe your idea for skinning the layered PCR capsule *isn't* unique. As quirky as the process seems to me to be, perhaps someone else has a line on it and is somehow blocking you somewhere." Manning held up empty hands. "I really don't know."

Val pictured the plum-marinating contraption on Alexandra's grandmother's stove, felt mild waves of unease course through him.

He pulled himself together and said, "A straight answer to a straight question. Thank you."

"No problem."

It was almost lunchtime, and Val was dying to drain the day's disaster from his body at the nearest sports club. He regarded the lawyer speculatively. "Do you play tennis, Tom?"

Manning laughed. "Not with you I don't."

Back at the office provided him at Abbey Labs, Val tossed the bedeviled project file down on the desk. He stood looking over the Kennedy Expressway, contemplating the pretzels of concrete and the miniature cars twirling around them, going nowhere fast.

Something was wrong, and it wasn't only the international patent treaties. He had no idea what it could be, but his thoughts rolled back to the moment he had seen Alexandra Kaminski walking down the hallway at Seine-Lafitte with Larry Rosenberg, and a bad feeling had come over him—the first truly bad feeling he had ever had about one of his projects. But, no. The first bad feeling had come a few minutes earlier, when Jean-Philippe had shown up to participate in the team-building seminar for no better reason than to keep an eye on Val's love life.

What could Alexandra and Jean-Philippe possibly have to do with one another? The answer to the question was, of course, nothing. Alexandra was involved in therapeutic research, not diagnosis. As for Jean-Philippe, although Val suspected that the wily older man didn't have Val's best interests at heart, there was no reason he would interfere with TEFS. If Seine-Lafitte could be the first on the market with a home cancer test, it would become the highest-grossing pharmaceutical company of all time.

Val glanced at the clock and realized that given the time difference between Chicago and France, he might be able to find some people still at work at Seine-Lafitte-Paris. Maybe Manning was right, and the patent problem was in Europe. He pulled out his calling card, punched in the long series of numbers, and reached the central receptionist who was still on duty.

"Allô, Suzette, c'est Valéry aux Etats-Unis. Comment allez-vous?"

He was surprised by how good it felt to have escaped English and to be speaking French. The last time he had felt that way he must have been fifteen. He chatted briefly with the receptionist before he asked to be connected to his secretary, Marielle.

The next voice to come on the line was a woman's, but it wasn't Marielle's. "Darling!" the woman said. "Marielle left fifteen minutes ago. What luck that I was crossing the lobby after a hard day at my desk and heard Suzette speaking with you."

"A hard day over lunch, you mean, Sophie," Val replied.

"You realize that it is nearly seven o'clock here, darling, and that my business lunch was ages ago. Do I get no credit for being here at this hour?"

"I'll give you all the credit in the world," Val said smoothly, "and then some, if you'll do me a favor."

"Will it take long, my dear?" she asked sweetly. "I'm having my lover over for dinner, and I haven't done my shopping yet."

"Ten minutes, at most."

He heard Sophie's miffed silence through seven thousand kilometers of wire. "Is there something wrong with our connection, Valéry?"

"I don't think so," he said. "Now, I want you to go to the main file room and pull the Institut Pasteur/Abbey Labs dossier. Then give me your lover's phone number so that I can arrange to meet him and put a bullet through his heart."

Her laugh trilled. "Really, Val! So old-fashioned!"

"Just following conventions."

Sophie put him on hold. Some minutes later, she came back on the phone. "I don't see it in Diagnostic's files, my dear." She repeated the title she was looking for, to make sure she had not misheard. "Should I be looking somewhere else?"

"No," he said, irritated by her incompetence. "All right. Get a portable phone and go back into the file room. We'll look together."

With portable phone in hand, Sophie flipped through various

drawers, reading off file headings. *Rien. Trois fois rien.* No file anywhere with the title Val was looking for.

Val's irritation sprouted a puzzlement that flowered into suspicion. This was bad, and to overplay the situation could make it worse. "I obviously made a mistake. Never mind."

"Never mind?" she echoed. "The way you sent me through these files and then 'never mind'?"

"How do you know I wasn't making an outrageous play to keep you on the line by sending you after something I knew wasn't there?"

She paused, at length. The wire crackled with interest. "It's an outrageous line you've given me, that's for sure." She switched tactics and sighed soulfully. "I'm looking out the window now, you know. The Seine is beginning to look so lovely this time of year."

He was sure her view was far lovelier than his view of the Kennedy. "Lucky Sophie."

"You'll be in Paris soon?" she cooed.

"As soon as possible." His voice rang with conviction.

"Hmm," she said.

When they said their good-byes, he could almost see her licking her luscious lips.

He hung up the phone wondering who could have put his hands on the Institut Pasteur/Abbey Labs file other than Jean-Philippe. Wondering too how on earth that simple, unusual plum-marinating contraption came to be on Alexandra's grandmother's stove. The coincidence was extraordinary.

Alexandra again.

Jean-Philippe again.

Any association between the two of them was unlikely in the extreme. And yet—

And yet it was the very unlikeliness of such an association that he was now willing to consider. An important file was missing in the Paris office on a gold mine of a product that was experiencing unexplained patent problems. The central technical gimmick of that product was the multilayered capsule that released polymers into a solution containing a body fluid. That capsule, being heat sensitive, could shed its layers and its polymers in just the right sequenced doses to produce a chain reaction that would amplify stretches of DNA to the point where different kinds of abnormal cell activity would turn the solution different colors.

The innovative dimension of the PCR capsule was that a person could use it easily at home and that it would deliver reliable results. The customary process for cancer detection through PCRs in the lab now took twenty, maybe thirty, individual passes to get enough DNA amplification, with careful supervision of heat levels, to provide a visible result. The PCR capsule made DNA amplification a foolproof, one-step process—which also made it a mass marketer's dream and a product likely to win approval from a wide variety of governmental and nongovernmental health organizations. The crazy thing was, Val's mechanism for repeatedly skinning the PCR capsule was a microscopic version of the plum-marinating thingamajig he had seen in Alexandra's grandmother's kitchen.

So Alexandra and Jean-Philippe—who might have nothing whatsoever to do with one another—might have everything to do with whatever was going wrong with the product that was to be his tribute to his sister and his legacy to the world.

TWENTY-EIGHT

 THE SHADOWS OF the evening had deepened. During the fraction of a moment that her eyes closed to receive another kiss, her lashes separated the dreamy blues into their component creams and pinks and lavenders and violets. The air was warm and seductive, but no more so than the whisper of his lips against hers, the scent of the skin at his neck, the feel of his hand as it moved down her throat and slipped under the woven silk of her kimono to slide down the living silk of her breast, her hip, her thigh.

They had moved through blue shadows into her bedroom and were standing next to the bed that he had claimed the night before as his own. He had shed his cravat and vest. His shirt was open to her touch. She had already become intimate with his back, but touching his chest, with its soft mat of dark hair, was different. His breath took hers and tangled it in his. His heart forced hers to beat faster. His muscles rippled against the flesh of her breasts. Every minimal movement was new and surprising and produced in her a desire for more.

She was used to the soft, safe cheek kisses of Chérie, Nina, and Louise. She knew what it was like to embrace a girlfriend, breast to breast, to feel shifting, unthreatening mounds of flesh press against hers. Laughing at the impediments. Enjoying the comraderie. She often linked arms with her girlfriends, leaned her softness against theirs. She never hesitated to indulge a friendly caress or to accept one. She had always thought of this linking of female bodies—elbows entwined, cheeks touching, breasts touching, hips touching—as a kind of feminine barricade against male invasion.

This was different. In this man's arms, she was aware of muscle instead of softness, angles instead of curves, flutters of excitement and threat instead of feelings of sweetness and comfort. She began to know desire.

But she was still too new to this to react with anything but resistance to a deeper kiss, a stronger embrace, to a more determined and frightening fit of his hips, to the realization that he was going to bring her down on the bed with him.

She pulled back from him and grasped with one hand the kimono that had fallen from her shoulders to her waist. Her chemise sagged open. She drew the silk around her hips and legs as a last vestige of modesty. With her other hand, she pushed him away.

He immediately relaxed his hold on her, but he did not release her. He rested his arms over her shoulders and placed his chin on the top of her head. He drew a breath, then lowered his lips down the side of her head to her ear.

He said, "You can resist me. Or you can submit. Either way, I know what to do, but it's your choice."

"My choice?"

He had given her no choice but to resist him—which could only make him want her more. She pushed harder away from him, turned her head. He broke her hold against him and stripped the chemise over her head. Then he circled the wrist of her hand that had been pushing against him and pulled her back toward him. She did not let go of the silk around her waist.

He strengthened the hold he had on her wrist, making it firmer, possibly bruising her. With his other hand, he trailed a finger down her jaw to her neck, down her breast to its tip where he poised his finger like a question mark. Then he shook his head, minimally, as if deciding that to pursue a caress would not serve his purposes. He lifted his finger from her breast, then bent into her and over her far enough for his hand to slide down her leg and to grasp one of her feet. He lifted it from the floor. He grazed his fingers over her sole.

She gasped. A shiver of involuntary pleasure coursed through her. Her resistance increased. She was outright struggling now.

She could hear the satisfaction in his voice, when he said, his voice muffled in the folds of the kimono at her waist, "You live in your feet and legs, and now your feet and legs will live around me."

He caressed her foot, her ankle, her calf. She discovered that her resistance, coupled with his caress, was arousing her as much as him. She went limp in his exotic embrace, as if she were unaffected by it, imagining passivity to be, perhaps, a different, more effective form of resistance.

He immediately adjusted. The hand caressing her calf moved behind her knee, came up the inside of her thigh and stopped at the apex. He surprised her with a most intimate touch that caused her clutched hand to open and the silk to fall in a pretty puddle around them. Having deliberately lowered her resistance, now naked and completely exposed to him, she found that she was responsive to the soft, secret pressure of his fingers teasing her and tickling her. She moaned in pleasure, in surprise, in defeat. She was a fleshly wave of crème fraîche, inside and out. Her leg was twined around his. She rubbed the sole of the foot he had awakened against the back of his calf, which was still covered in flannel.

He brought his head up to her breast and twirled his tongue over one rose, then over the other. "Either way," he repeated, "I know what to do."

He looked up at her. Their eyes met in the thickening blue-gray darkness. He straightened. He released her wrist and slipped his arm around her waist. He withdrew his hand from between her legs and grasped her thigh to tighten it around his. His smile was an attractive blend of the satisfied and not-yet-satisfied. He put her hands at the buttons of his trousers. He was insisting on her capitulation.

She undid the buttons. She unlooped the tape at his drawers. She slid her hands around his waist and touched the wound at his lower right side. She let her fingertips listen and linger, feeling the heat generated by wounded muscles, pressing the muscles, massaging them, making them obey.

He snapped her chin up, slanted his lips across hers. His tongue found hers. His hands moved around her backside, lifted her, laid her down on the bed. He was within her at once, his thighs pushed up between hers, spreading hers around him, hurting her perhaps more than he intended. Having to hurt her, given her lack of experience.

On her back, she attempted to inch away from his invasion. Her movement did no good, only blended better with his, increased his excitement and his pleasure. She was startled, aroused, disgusted, and filled by a body that was more alien to her than it was repulsive. She was engulfed in male skin and scent, every inch of her covered by opposing muscle and sinew and bone, carried along on the strength of his desire, which was raw but not rough in its utter disregard for her. He pressed her and challenged her to respond with a similar disregard for him.

She felt her body resist, submit, resist, submit, obeying the choices he had given her, and then she realized that those alternating waves came from within her, in response to him, and were building a force of their own. He came to the end of his first claim before she could ride out the limits of her own waves, and she was aware of weight and hot breath and something like a candle inside her. She opened her eyes to a deep-sea-blue world shaped by the curve of his neck and spine and the horizon of his shoulder. She knew that the candle inside her was casting a semicircle of light from her hip bones to the tops of her thighs which still framed his hips, like parentheses. When she shifted, she could feel the candle glow a little brighter and was impelled to shift again. After several long, languorous moments, the candle went out, leaving a faint afterglow.

He withdrew from her, lay on his back. He placed one palm across her belly, at the rim of the afterglow of light inside her. His other arm he folded behind his head. She turned to look at him in the luminescent darkness, which provided no shield for modesty and highlighted no shame. She dared to breathe deeply of the sweet musk wilting sun-dried linen. She dared to let her gaze be drawn into his. She dared to let her lips curve up. She moved her hand so that the backs of her fingers traced a path from his armpit to his groin muscle. His eyes closed slowly, then opened, and she was surprised to be trapped now within his gaze. His palm caressed, claiming his territory.

She curled her gaze contentedly in the trap of his and deepened her smile. She would be able to protect herself, as long as the semicircle of light stayed where it was, low in her belly. He could claim the soles of her feet, her calves, her thighs, even her breasts, but she would be safe as long as the circle of light didn't reach her heart.

Much later, when the color of the room was an impenetrable midnight blue, she was awakened by a hand moving across her. She snuffled to a drowsy awareness of a man's body spooned against hers. She felt the liquid luxury of not being alone. It was nearly worth waking up to appreciate how lovely it was to sleep in a lover's arms. When he pressed his length to her backside, revealing his intention, she was frightened awake to discover who she was with and what he wanted.

She moaned and pushed him away.

His voice held a suggestion of humor when he whispered, "You fancy yourself a wife?"

She turned her head, cautiously, to look at him, wearing a look of inquiry he would have to feel more than he could see.

"Only a wife protests," he explained, "and so soon."

She drew a deep breath and sifted through his meaning. She lay stretched out, seemingly relaxed, but she was tensed, as if ready to scamper away. She asked, "Is that what your wife does, protest your attentions?"

"I'm not married."

She was surprised into a long silence. She asked next, "She died, perhaps?"

"I've never been married."

"You have no family?"

"No immediate family," he said. "I'm the laſt of my line, and it was a thin one to begin with. I have a few cousins, rather diſtant ones, I'm afraid."

"I see. But, then, how can you know about wives and their pro-teſts?"

His lips touched her neck. One hand reſted on her hips. "From their husbands who complain and seek willing miſtresses."

"I'm not willing."

His hand slid down to the closed scissors of her soft thighs. His fingers slipped through her neſt of curls to ſtimulate a moiſt bud and to prove her wrong.

"Convince me."

"I'm not willing," she insiſted and refused to unclamp her thighs. "Wives are the willing ones who have entered into an alliance for reasons that include inclination or preference, or perhaps even love."

His hand remained trapped. "You're a romantic."

She laughed. "No, you are, to imagine miſtresses willing."

His fingers moved enough for her to imagine the candle within her, for her to wish for it within her, glowing.

She swallowed desire. She did not move. "And you're a romantic," she continued, "never to have married."

"And how could that nonaƈt be deemed romantic?"

"Because you fear the fate of being married to an unwilling wife or, at leaſt, to one you don't love."

"Love," he repeated, taſting the word experimentally, as if it were an unknown morsel. "You have ſtrange notions."

"And I'm unwilling."

"Liar," he accused softly. He turned her toward him, her re-siſtance easily overcome by his superior ſtrength. He pulled her un-derneath him and arranged her limbs around him as he liked.

"Romantic," she taunted in turn, but she was unable to think of herself as resisting or submitting because the feelings inside felt more like compliance, even complicity.

He fit himself in her, cradled his hips in hers, reached back and moved her legs to bend at the knee and brace his legs, lady spider—like, the outside of her feet caressing the inside of his thighs. He moved into her slowly, placed his elbows on either side of her shoulders, and put his lips at the hollow of her throat.

"You don't feel unwilling," he murmured.

She fell into the trap. "Oh, but I am," she breathed.

He rolled over, so that she was on top of him, firmly joined with him. He pushed her body up with the heels of his hands at her shoulders and pressed his hands down her front, over her breasts, over her stomach, to the spread intersection of her thighs. He took hold of her hips in a way that made her arch back and grasp his knees, her arms straight, elbows locked.

One hand came down from her hip, circled wet lips, and began to stroke a bead of flesh. He paused, then brought his hand to his mouth and flicked his thumb with his tongue. When he returned to stroke that hidden flesh again, to bring it out of hiding, to make it glisten and pulse and throb for him, she discovered that the candle was burning far brighter than it had before, and she began to worry that she would not be able to keep its power contained within the safe semicircle of her hips.

Fortunately, when she began to move with him, finding the rhythm and the pace that pleased him, he turned her over again so that she was tucked beneath him. The glow was very bright now, but it wasn't moving upward to surround her heart. It was moving downward to pool behind her knees, in her calves, cascading to the soles of her feet, curling her toes.

His possession was lengthy and thorough, and when he was finished he didn't move off her for a long time, nor did he take his weight on his elbows. The blues of the air were so dense they were black, and when he spoke, his voice was thick and intoxicating, like brandy. He said, "I think we understand one another now."

"I think we do," she agreed.

Her eyelashes and limbs were growing heavy, and even with him still within her, she was already looking forward to their next passage. She did not stop to consider that she liked too well the flow of feeling that came from his attempts to lay her low and her narrow escapes that prevented him from succeeding and would keep him coming back to try again.

DEIRDRE CAME TO the bottom of the page and looked up. The three other women took a collective breath in, then breathed out.

"I liked the part about the feminine softness leaning against feminine softness."

"God, Louise!" Nancy swatted her friend's arm with the backs of her fingers. "That's not the point here!"

"Well, I'm entitled to my opinion," Louise said. "What did she say about 'unthreatening mounds of flesh'? It was something about enjoying embracing her girlfriends breast to breast."

Nancy rolled her eyes. "Remind me never to hug you again."

"Oh, yeah, like I'm attracted to *you*."

Alexandra asked Deirdre, "Is there more?"

"There are more pages," Deirdre replied, "but no time at the moment, since I've got my first exam in about fifteen minutes. I should have been cramming for it instead of reading this, but—"

"You know you're not supposed to cram right before a big test," Nancy said. "Not cram for an exam, that is."

"Is there any other kind of cramming?" Louise asked.

Nancy smiled sweetly. "You wouldn't know, would you, my dear?"

"Girls, girls," Alexandra chided softly, "always at it?"

Deirdre liked the way Alexandra had blended into the group. "I've been searching for details on the life and times of the Count d'Albret and put an APB out on the Web," she told Alexandra. "Now, the family name is Dorsainville—"

"Ooh, classy!" Nancy interjected. "Real ancien régime."

"—but beyond that Mr. Victor must have played his cards close to the vest, because I can't figure out what he did with himself beyond train horses. Laurent Dreyfus has been easier. Hey, Alexandra, is anything wrong? Well, it seems our Dr. Dreyfus was well known in his time, an all-around good guy who took benevolent cases and worked at the Institut Pasteur. He was particularly interested in checking the spread of disease among the working class and—"

"Do you mean to say that you've been researching these documents," Nancy interrupted, "when you should have been boning up on your reading lists?"

"You just said I shouldn't cram before an exam."

"I never said that you shouldn't *study* for them!"

Deirdre waved this objection away. "Don't worry, Nance, I'm prepared. So, Alexandra, you'll be back tomorrow afternoon for the next installment?"

Alexandra shook her head and said that she and her grandmother were lined up with a real estate agent for the next day. Since Deirdre had two major exams on the day after that, they settled on early Friday afternoon for their next meeting.

Deirdre thought Alexandra looked pale. "Are you okay? Sure? You know, I'd like to hang on to these papers for the next few days, if you don't mind." She tried a little joke. "Maybe indulge my prurient interests and read them aloud to Kevin."

Alexandra didn't laugh and didn't hurry with her answer. "You can keep them, if they interest you so much."

"Interest?" she echoed wryly. "I admit it, I'm obsessed!"

How to explain to any rational person that researching this time period was like eating a five-star five-course meal that didn't fill you up, so you could eat and eat and eat forever? Alexandra was such a sweetie too. It caused Deirdre a pang to see her looking so love-crossed. But that was absurd! Deirdre decided she must be suffering from a touch of mental heartburn from having just gobbled down so much rich material. But still . . .

"Listen, Alexandra, are you sure you're okay? Really? Now there's a pretty smile for the audience. Good."

TWENTY-NINE

VAL HURRIED DOWN the narrow steps that ran alongside Kolatek's Bakery from the first floor to the street, vaguely aware of the odors of yeast and corn syrup. He opened the door onto Milwaukee Avenue and felt the frustrations of the past few days fall away.

Alexandra stood on the sidewalk before him, and she was fishing in her purse for her keys. The sun had sunk low enough for the street lights to have come on, whitening a gray sky and silvering her golden hair. The air was cool enough for her breath to be wreathing around her. She looked up, met his eyes, and took a step back.

He grasped her by the forearm and began to lead her away from the stairway door.

"Hey, I was going home," she objected, trying to wrench her arm free.

He tightened his hold on her. "Your grandmother's not expecting you."

"Yes, she is. She's probably started dinner and already set the table."

"She knows I'm taking you out to dinner."

"Did you tell her you were planning to meet me in the street like this?"

"I told her I was going out for the evening newspaper and that if I didn't come back it was because I had run into you. She said that you were in Evanston for the afternoon and figured which bus you were taking back, and that gave her a pretty good idea of when she expected you to return—namely about now. And here you are."

He was taking her past brick and stone storefronts still open for business. The sidewalk traffic was heavy. So was the street traffic. Buses were wheezing past, farting on the cars behind them. He could taste exhaust on his tongue. She twitched her arm again, but he didn't let go.

"One question," she said. "Do you like horses?"

He looked at her and realized that she was wary of him, that she had been wary of him from the moment he had set eyes on her in the hallway at Duke Medical Center, before they had even met. He liked her wariness. It satisfied him somehow.

"When they're under the hood of a car. Why?"

She didn't answer that. "Next question. Where are we going?" It was a complaint.

"To dinner." He looked around. "Eventually. Can you recommend a place for afterwards?"

"No. Let me go."

"Why didn't you tell me your great-great grandmother lived in France?"

"Why would I tell you that?"

"I don't know. Your grandmother thought it worth mentioning just now. I noticed she had a French Christian name, of course."

She stopped dead in her tracks and demanded, belatedly, "After *what?*"

They were at an intersection. He knew to turn left. He looked down at her. "I didn't notice it after anything. I noticed it right away."

Her Slavic cat eyes withered him. "I mean," she said evenly, "that you said we were going to dinner eventually and wanted me to recommend a place for afterwards. After what?"

He stopped in front of a green door flanked on either side by large plates of smoked glass, not recently washed. In the corner of one window a Milwaukee Old Style poster was taped from the inside. In the other window a neon sign with most of its letters burned out announced CAS Y BIL RDS. Through the glass, dim dots of lights could be seen.

He dropped her arm, put his hand at her shoulder, and guided her to the door. "After we shoot a game of pool at Casay's."

He ushered her inside before she could utter another protest, and they were surrounded by the scent of stale beer, cigarette smoke, and air cloyed by fried onion ring grease. Two rows of four pool tables each dominated the space. A bar ran along the back of the room. Several pinball machines and a Mortal Kombat game were crowded into the corner next to a door with REST ROOMS THIS WAY above it. Four customers sat on bar stools. Three of the pool tables had games in progress. Mortal Kombat was not in use, so no video guts were currently spattering the screen.

He looked around and pronounced the place to be a step up from the Alhambra in Durham.

"A generous assessment," she said, looking around too. "I haven't been in here in years, and I don't think it's stood the test of time."

The jukebox was playing Tom Petty's "Free Fallin'." Around the guitars and the singers could be heard the clack of balls, the roll across green felt, the clunk and drop at the pockets.

"It's quieter than the bowling alley," she remarked.

He moved to the second table in the row on the right. He regarded the scratched and cigarette-burned surface with disfavor but decided that it would do. "How about this one?"

Next to the table a molded orange plastic chair was shoved against the wall. Alexandra put her purse down on it, unbuttoned the light half-jacket she was wearing, and lay it across her purse. She had on an oversized bottle-green turtleneck sweater, a midcalf brown flared skirt, and low black boots. He was sorry she wasn't wearing her leggings.

He draped his trench coat over her jacket on his way to the bar where he got cue sticks and the rack and a handful of quarters for dollar bills.

When he returned and handed her a cue, she asked, "What are we doing?"

"This is a pool hall, Alexandra."

"I know that, Val. I'm asking why we're doing this."

He crackled his knuckles. "Just a friendly game while we talk things over. I didn't think your grandmother would be fascinated by the finer points of cancer research, and I doubt you're one to lounge in upscale bars, sipping white wine. Besides, I'd like to see you clear the table on the break ball."

"I've been known to lounge in upscale bars, sipping white wine, thank you very much," she said, "and it's not likely I'll clear the table on the break ball, so I can't see you getting any kicks that way. What do you have in mind here?"

"Strip pool."

Her mouth fell open.

He smiled. "To get my kicks, as you say."

THIRTY

 ALEXANDRA CLOSED HER mouth. She narrowed her eyes. "Right. Strip pool. Did you notice that we're in public? Or is that part of the kicks?"

Val fit four quarters into the metal slots built into one end of the table. He pushed the coin holder in, released it, causing a line of balls to roll down into the trough below. He began to flick the balls onto the scarred and faded surface of the pea-green table so that they rolled toward her.

He said, "Fantasy strip pool, I guess you might call it."

She took the wooden triangle and began to rack the balls he was sending her. "What, we undress in our heads?"

"Right. For every ball one of us sinks, the other pretends to take off a piece of clothing. The shooter has to call both the ball and the pocket for the ball to be good."

"And the shooter gets to call which piece of clothing goes?"

Val shook his head. "That won't work in fantasy strip pool. The person taking off the piece of clothing has to name what it is. You see, once we get past the outer layers, I won't know what's underneath what you're wearing, and you won't know what's underneath what I'm wearing."

"You play this a lot?"

He grinned. "No, this is the first time. I'd prefer the real thing, but being a reasonable man, I perceive the difficulties of stripping in public."

"Reasonable," she repeated slowly. "Gee, I wonder how I missed that aspect of your personality?"

"If you do not learn to be more observant, Alexandra, you'll never make a good scientist."

He was determined to be provoking, and he was succeeding. She was provoked. And perplexed. And intrigued. And downright lunatic. She would have been very happy to be *less* observant these days, given the kinds of things she was observing. What she wouldn't give to be restored to the world of plain old experimental science!

While walking together earlier on Milwaukee Avenue, she had told herself, Well okay, the parallels are broken, and I can forget this crazy reincarnation business because Val Dorsainville can't have been that man . . . Victor Dorsainville . . . in some past life because Val isn't interested in horses. Sure, there's the coincidence that Victor is Val's ancestor, but such is the nature of coincidences. They always seem fantastic. The bit with his back is no problem, because any athlete is susceptible to back injuries, especially in a high-intensity sport such as tennis, and who knows what really happened to that man's . . . to Victor's . . . back anyway, because whatever I think might have happened to it is most likely just a product of my fevered imagination.

But now she got to thinking that the horsepower of a car engine was the modern equivalent of horses, as Val himself had suggested, and so the parallels were there, running straight and true. Then again, there was nothing sacred about parallels, which were useful mostly in plane geometry and city planning, so she figured that she must be losing her mind to think that she had been a cancan dancer in a past life or that—come on!—three random students she met in a graduate lounge just happened to be the reincarnations of her dancing partners in Paris.

He must have noticed her hesitation, because he said next, "It's either this or playing footsie at some upscale bar, sipping white wine. Your choice."

"My choice?" Boy, that sounded familiar. Whatever mind-set she was in, she realized she had better get out of it and deal with the problems of the life she was living *now*. "Why should I choose?"

"So you can hear what's on my mind."

Meaning that strip pool wasn't? Or was this an enticement for further enticement? She looked at him, but his expression was unreadable. He was provoking her again. Teasing her. Tantalizing her. She'd be a fool to take him up on this game. She'd die of curiosity if she didn't. While she was considering ways to get him to change his terms and still speak his mind, she saw, out of the corner of her eye, a group enter the pool hall. They began to drift her way. She glanced at the three men and one woman approaching and felt the situation stack up against her. With a wave of fatalism, she realized that the choice she was about to make wasn't really a choice at all.

"Hi, Alexandra," Bob Dembrowski said. He looked down at the racked pyramid of billiard balls on the table. "You two about to shoot some pool?"

Val referred the question to Alexandra with his eyes. His smile was as gentle as a sheep's.

"Looks like it," Alexandra said.

"What's the game?"

Alexandra cleared her throat. "Stripes and solids, I guess."

"We just agreed on the terms," Val interjected mildly.

Wolf in sheep's clothing, Alexandra amended.

Bob introduced his companions. Alexandra remembered Kastas from Schurz High. Stan was made known to her as the assistant manager at Dembrowski's Hospital Supply. Joanna seemed to be Stan's girlfriend. Attention turned to Val. They shook hands with him. Smiled acceptance. Murmured greetings. This was not a crowd inclined to comment on funny first names.

"You need an audience," Bob said.

Like a hole in the head, Alexandra thought, or another past life experience. "Sure," she said.

"Val?" Bob's polite request for confirmation carried an edge of belligerence that had not quite surfaced in that mess of a coffee-and-dessert hour that followed Easter Sunday dinner.

Val smiled gracefully and repeated, "Sure."

Bob and Kastas were carrying their own cues in black zippered cases. They parked these on the adjoining pool table and perched themselves on the edge. Stan stood at the end of the table near the wall and slung his arm over Joanna's shoulder.

Val stepped back from the table and offered Alexandra the break with a gesture of his open palm.

She pushed the sleeves of her baggy sweater up to her elbows and regretted that she wasn't wearing a ring or a bracelet or a watch or even her tortoiseshell combs. She stepped behind the cue ball and shot, scattering balls. One dropped. She looked up, half-surprised and entirely pleased. She smiled.

Val brushed past her, shedding his suit coat as he went. He folded it on top of his trench coat, as if he had intended to take it off anyway. She lined up another shot, called the pocket, and missed the shot. She stepped back.

Val studied the table from several different angles and sank the ball he called in the pocket he called. His next shot took him to the side of the table where Alexandra was standing, which was opposite the peanut gallery. He asked, softly, "Well?"

"Necklace," she said. "It's inside my sweater."

He didn't comment, simply bent over, sank another ball. He stood and slanted her a glance.

"My other necklace," she said.

He turned so that his back was between Alexandra and his audience. With one finger, he pulled the turtleneck of her sweater across her shoulder so that the bare skin of her neck and bra strap were exposed. No jewelry chains were visible.

"You were pushing it with one necklace," he said and pulled her sweater neck back in place. "Try again."

"Boot," she conceded.

He sank another shot. She gave up another boot. He did not have a third good shot available and missed the one he tried, so it was her turn.

She was delighted, and a little relieved, that her shot was perfect. She didn't miss it or the next, which was just as easy. However, then she realized that Val had set her shots up neatly for her. Even before she took the first shot, he had taken one link from his shirt cuff and was folding it back several times from his wrist, and at the same time she was sinking her second shot, he was removing his other cuff link and rolling that sleeve back. When she straightened and looked at him pointedly, he pocketed the links with a very innocent smile. She was so disgusted, she missed her next shot, which was impossible anyway.

Then came a bad run during which she lost both socks and a slip she wasn't wearing. During that episode, Val had made a point of fiddling with his tie, smoothing it down, slipping it over his shoulder, even tucking it in between two lower buttons of his shirt. So when it was her turn and she sank her shot, he took off his tie, as if it had merely been in his way.

He was ahead only by six to four, and the peanut gallery was still offering her encouragement. However, Alexandra began to see that she didn't have a chance, because he still had his watch, his belt, two shoes and two socks to go before he even lost anything worth losing, and she was already having to invent underwear. When he stepped up to the table, his shirt sleeves up and his tie off, he looked ready to shoot pool. It was only then that she remembered he actually owned a damned pool table. Her memory of being in his house and in that room had been overshadowed by her strange experience with an equally damned painting.

He sank his seventh. She relinquished her nonexistent panty hose. He sank the eight ball, and she gave up her sweater.

Val was congratulated. Alexandra was consoled. Stan went to buy a round of beers. Val was challenged by Kastas. Alexandra readily conceded her place at the table.

Val shook his head. "Alexandra was just getting warmed up. I can't stop now without giving her a chance to avenge her loss."

Which Alexandra translated to mean that he hadn't finished undressing her. "It's quite all right," she said. "I'm rusty and not likely to improve in the next few minutes."

"Have a little Polish pride, Alexandra," Bob said. "You don't usually give up so easily."

Alexandra looked at him. His eyes challenged. She felt an odd communication pass between them. He was telling her to—to what? Hang tough? Be true to her people? Her past? Which past?

"Yeah," Joanna said, accepting a lighted cigarette from Stan. "Like, this is fun."

Alexandra laughed. "You want entertainment at my expense?"

Joanna had her inner-city chick persona down. She shrugged elaborately, took a drag on her cigarette. "It's in-neresting," she said, blowing smoke through her nose. "I'm seeing different shots. I'm seeing strategy. I'm seeing, like, the idea that pool would be better as a doubles sport, instead of two guys goin' at each other with their sticks. Whatdayou think, huh, Stan?"

Stan, who had returned to distribute the beers, didn't think anything, but Alexandra was pretty sure that Joanna had picked up on the fact that Val was stripping her naked, and she was turned on by it. For her part, Alexandra was seeing no way out. To Val's unspoken invitation, no, *demand,* for a second game, Alexandra said, "What the hell."

What the hell, indeed. She was outmaneuvered. Again. This time by her fellow Polacks.

Val shoved more quarters in the slots, got the balls, racked them. It was his turn to break, but he sank nothing.

She lined up what she had available and scratched. Total failure.

Val stepped up. Bingo. There went her skirt. She was down to her bra and panties. Somehow, when she bent over the table to take her shot, she was pretty sure that Val saw her in her state of undress. It was hard not to feel wanton as she bent into her shot, knowing that Val's attention was winding around her curves. She felt her brain melting, trickling down into her spine, making her body feel plummy. Traitorously submissive. At least she had a winner lined up and made it.

Val twisted the watch on his wrist several times, then took it off, absentmindedly, as if it had been bothering him. He slipped the watch in his pocket and didn't even look at her to see whether she had registered his action. Instead, his concentration was devoted to the configuration of balls on the table. He circled the table several times, studying the angles, eyeing the lays.

Alexandra was aware that a change had come over him, a kind of focus that seemed to exclude the rest of the world. The peanut gallery seemed to be aware of it too because their commentary on the action and their side conversations had died down. Beer bottles had either been placed on the edges of the unused pool table or were poised midair, waiting for Val's shot. He stopped prowling at a point diametrically opposite where she was standing.

Val crouched to view the table from eye level. When he stood, he said, without taking his eyes off the balls, "What would you say if I told you I was wanting to develop and market a product along the lines of a cancer diagnosis kit for use in the home?"

The question jolted Alexandra out of her body and into her head. A home cancer diagnosis kit. This was, apparently, the project that had brought him to Chicago and that was giving him problems. Patent problems, if she remembered correctly.

She answered, "I'd say that you had a great idea and a lot of problems."

He took his shot, made it. He looked up at her with as much focus as he had just given the pool table. The expression on his face made her swallow a gasp. He couldn't, he really couldn't expect her to announce out loud that she was taking off her bra.

"And I'd say that this is a stupid game," she said, refusing to budge or blush.

He took his next shot, made it too. Looked up at her again, this time with an edge of triumph.

No panties, and nowhere to hide. "A very stupid game."

His slight smile resembled a smirk. He proceeded to his next shot, took his time. "What, in your professional opinion, are the potential problems with the product?"

If he was imagining her naked, so be it. She'd give him something to think about. She planted the rubber tip of her cue between her feet. She put a hand on her hip and leaned against her stick, ever so slightly provocatively. "Cancer is a cover term for a type of cell activity that behaves differently in different parts of the body, no? It's hard to think that you can package a piece of litmus paper or something, have your consumers spit on it, and see blue if they've got cancer, red if they're clear."

"Not spit," he said, "but urine, and a test has been developed that can distinguish colormetrically among colon, breast, lung, prostate and unknown primary."

"Unknown primary? Say, melanoma or lymphoma?"

He nodded and sank his fourth shot. "Yellow, red, blue, green, in that order."

"What about the predictive values of these test colors?" she asked. "Surely there are false positives and false negatives that will cause liability problems for the makers of the kit."

Shot number five. "The tests have a degree of accuracy approved by the FDA, and the American Cancer Society supports the product."

Alexandra's eyes widened. "What's their recommendation for frequency of use?"

Number six. "Once a year for anyone under forty. Twice a year for anyone over forty."

"When's a person supposed to begin?"

"Depends on family history and the individual's personal sense of playing the genetic and environmental odds."

"I doubt such a product would have helped someone as young as Erica."

Seven. "Moot point. It's not on the market."

"Its effectiveness will certainly be determined by the kit's price. If it's out of reach of a certain economic segment of society, well, then—"

"Seventeen ninety-five in the U.S. market. What do you think of its potential to reach a wide audience?"

"Seventeen dollars and ninety-five cents?" Alexandra echoed, disbelieving. "That's cheap." Another thought occurred to her. "And the company that markets it will make a fortune."

He lined up the eight ball.

"But it can't be done," she said.

"You don't think so?"

"There's no cheap and easy process for getting a verifiable reading on cancerous cell activity."

"You know the PCR technique, I suppose."

"I do. Polymerase acts as a zipper to unzip strands of DNA, and it can rezip them into indefinitely larger pieces, but—"

"You can't think of any way a person can use the technique in the convenience of the home."

"That's right. It requires an expensive thermocycler."

He sank the ball and won the game. He stood up and walked over to her side of the table. "No ideas?"

She was puzzled. "Not offhand. I've never performed the PCR technique myself, only worked on DNA amplifications provided me by skilled technicians." She looked down at the slaughter on the table. "You've shut me out on the PCR question, just as you shut me out in pool." She twined her ankle around the bottom of the cue stick. "Regretting that such an unimaginative postdoc is on the research team that Seine-Lafitte has plunked so much money behind?"

For her ears only, Val said, "I'm not regretting it at all. Talking science with naked women is how I get my kicks."

THIRTY-ONE

 BOB NOTICED THE way the fancy asshole had set up Alexandra's shots during the first game, and Bob had encouraged her to play a second game just to see what the Frog really had in him. Having seen it, Bob was ready.

He reached for his cue case, opened it, and began screwing the two ends of his stick together. He flicked the Frog a glance and challenged, "You good for another game?"

The fancy asshole gave him a minimal nod of assent.

Bob hadn't liked him when he'd met him at Alexandra's on Sunday evening, and he didn't like him any better now. "Are there stakes?" he asked. "Or is it only twenty questions?"

"You're in hospital supply, right?" The Frog's accent, almost imperceptible, grated on Bob's ears. "The AMA convention will be in Chicago in August, so I'll stake space for Dembrowski's at the Seine-Lafitte booth against an endorsement from Dembrowski's for Seine-Lafitte's ulcer drug in your local advertising."

Bob could play it just as cool as the asshole. "Fair enough, then. Best two out of three."

Stan, Bob's assistant manager at Dembrowski's, interjected, "Hey, that bet's worth several thousand bucks. Go for it, Bob."

Kastas thought this called for another beer.

"Want a few practice shots to warm up?" the asshole inquired.

"No thanks," Bob said. He put the cue behind his head and across his shoulders, hooked his elbows over it, limbering up. "Why should I want to warm up?"

"So I can see some of your shots, since you've just watched me play two games."

Bob took a step closer to his opponent. The asshole had him by several inches, but Bob had the advantage in weight and muscle. He shook his head and said very quietly, "No, my man, I just watched Alexandra play two games, and that was real nice."

The asshole didn't betray his dislike of that comment by more than a twitch at the corner of his mouth. Such a cool asshole.

They tossed a coin for break. Bob won it. Saw it as an omen. He knew every roll in every pool table at Casay's, and no way was that asshole going to beat him on his home court. And no way was that asshole going to walk off with the hottest dziwka this side of Warsaw. Watching her play pool made him wonder how he had ever let her get away. Made him anticipate the pleasure he would have shoving his cue stick down the asshole's throat. Metaphorically speaking, of course.

Alexandra and Joanna retired to the sidelines. Folding a piece of Black Jack gum into her mouth, Joanna asked, "Where's your boyfriend from?"

"He's not my boyfriend."

Joanna softened the gum audibly, cracked it once. "In—neresting. So, where's he from?"

"I guess you might say he's from North Carolina."

Joanna's jaw halted mid—gum crack. "That's, like, in the South, right?" When Alexandra conveyed to her the finer points of geography, Joanna said slowly, "I thought all those guys down there had long hair, wore overalls, played the banjo and shit."

"I don't know if Val plays the banjo."

Joanna was evidently experiencing a cognitive shift. At the end of several moments of deep reflection, she said, "I hear the weather's good down there too."

"Very good," Alexandra assured her, then whispered, "and in the summer, it's hot and sultry."

"I've been wanting to leave this dump of a town for ages, but never had an idea where to go. North Carolina, huh? And how about that accent? I must be watching the wrong TV shows."

Joanna plainly had something to think about, so Alexandra turned her attention to the first game, which Val lost, but not by much. During the second game, Alexandra noticed that Bob managed to jostle Val several times, either stepping up to the table or stepping back from it. In another age and another setting, Val would have had cause to demand satisfaction and call him out. In this age and this setting, Val retaliated by deliberately missing his own shots— or so it seemed to Alexandra—in order to set up a situation that would thwart Bob's. And so it went, until Val won the second game in a squeaker.

In the third game, everything was at stake. The play was precise and unhurried. The jukebox was playing Cindi Lauper's "Time after Time."

Alexandra moved through the music and the lyrics to become mesmerized by the syncopated rhythms of balls hitting balls and the competing geometries that formed and re-formed until all balls came to rest. She was staring at the rolling balls and the complicated patterns they traced, and soon she wasn't seeing colored round objects with stripes spinning on improbable axes and circled black numbers tumbling. Rather, she was seeing amino acids. Before her eyes, molecules clustered and scattered, producing long, time-elapsed strings of enzymes and proteins that combined and recombined in pathways created by the angles of force applied to them.

At one level, the action looked random. But at another level, if all quantities could be known—force, angle, encounters—the action would be entirely predictable. In her mind's eye, the pool table slid under her microscope, and she was looking at an infinite enlargement of something pea green and soupy and witnessing the origin of organic life. She saw nucleotides, amino acids, and protein chains being formed by the forces bombarding them; and she saw the patterns repeating themselves over and over, with a kind of double vision that made her think those patterns were, at once, both random and inevitable.

Double vision. Last time she had had a double vision she had been cruising the hallways at Duke and revisiting the old neighborhood which came complete with a vivid Bobby D replay. Now, here she was in the old neighborhood, and it seemed as if she was back at the lab at the very moment when her vision had blurred and she had seen her minuscule world of acids and bases produce an enzyme that wasn't there.

The pool table slid out from under her microscope. The room came back into proportion. Her heart was pounding. She wiped her sweaty hands on the skirt that, in Val's mind at least, she was no longer wearing. She looked at the two men before her, the same two who had haunted her in the med center hallway. They were battling it out between them on the pool table, writing and rewriting their age-old script of competition and animosity.

Her double vision rushed together in a way that fused its formerly dissociated parts into coexisting dimensions. Like a fly's vision. Or like everybody's vision, she realized, since we're all products of this billiard ball collection of enzymes and proteins that have bounced off one another in just the right directions to make that certain kind of creature that is us. And we're born again when the right force is applied to reproduce the galactically complicated collection of RNA and DNA that has our name on it. When those ancient enzymes come together randomly, inevitably, they wrap and zap and zip each other to create a new one of us that is sent forth to bounce, yet another time, off others of us in endlessly repeating patterns.

All right, then. She was ready to entertain the question, What if the R of RNA stands for Reincarnation? Well, what if—?

The answer came to her in a blinding flash. She already knew half the pattern, so her purpose must be to discover the nature of the repetitions so she could complete the story.

TWO BALLS WERE left on the table along with the eight ball. Bob had had a run for his money from the asshole, but the lay of the balls was so good, he was starting to get hard. Down, boy. He'd be sure to take his big shaggy dog out for a walk later. The first ball in, the second ball in, and, oh man, yes, sinking the eight ball in the side pocket felt so good. Now came the part where he even got to accept congratulations. Did it get any better than this?

The asshole shook hands like a sport and promised to see through the arrangements for the AMA convention. But the asshole didn't know when to stop. "I'll be in town the rest of the week, at least," he informed the group in general and Bob in particular, "so I expect you'll give me a chance to make up for my loss tonight."

Bob hesitated just long enough to have to cover up the fact that he did not want a second encounter. Jesus fuck. Hoped he didn't overdo his acceptance. He had unscrewed his cue, put it back in his case. "Pool again?"

The asshole went to retrieve his suit coat and trench coat. Bob needed to keep a step ahead, so he moved quickly to pick up Alexandra's jacket and purse. While Bob helped Alexandra with her jacket, the asshole shrugged into his.

Over his shoulder the asshole replied, "Pool? Not necessarily. Your choice."

"If you're here on the weekend," Bob said, "we could play a round of golf."

"Golf, of course. Weather permitting."

"Squash?" Stan suggested. "Bob belongs to a sports club."

"Or tennis." This from Kastas. "Indoors or out."

The asshole was looking down, stashing his folded tie in an inside pocket. "Your call." He withdrew a pen and a business card case from his inside suit coat pocket, took a card, scrawled on the back. He looked up, expression bland. "Here are the numbers for my hotel and the local lab. Let me know."

The group exited. Bob fell into step with Alexandra, figuring his angle for getting her alone with him this evening. Thinking he was a pretty smart Polack to have had the foresight to provide himself with a killer opener next time he saw her. And that on top of beating the asshole two-one.

"I'll be meeting you for lunch tomorrow," he informed her.

She blinked in surprise. "You will?"

"At Staropolska's. Reservations are for twelve-thirty." When she opened her mouth to decline, he said, "Yes, I know you'll be house hunting tomorrow with Elena." He winked. "Elena's my sister-in-law and half her family works at Century 21."

"Elena knows about this lunch?"

"Elena made the reservations." He said this in a way that made him innocent of maneuvers.

He wasn't sorry that the asshole overheard. He should know that the inside was kept in and the outside out of Jackowo Polonia.

The group ambled down the side street away from Milwaukee Avenue. They came to a corner where the streetlights were burned out and the sidewalks not swept. Bob was devising his plan for ditching the asshole when the door of the darkened establishment on the corner closed with a slam followed by the whine of an iron security gate being drawn.

The tall, bent figure of an old man emerged from the shadows. He said, in Polish, "There you are, Alexandra Janina. I was hoping to see you while you were with your babcia. How fortunate that I should run into you now."

Alexandra moved away from Bob to greet the man. She answered in Polish, "Pan Lukacz, is that you?"

"Speak up, Alexandra Janina! My hearing is not what it used to be. My eyes, however, see better than ever."

Alexandra spoke louder. "My babcia told me that you have received a shipment of treasures that is sure to interest me."

"Come," Mr. Lukacz said. He began shuffling back toward the door. "Come now, and bring your friends. I'll open up."

Jesus fuck. Pan Lukacz gave Bob the creeps, and he hated the old man's place with a passion. All that old crap made him sick to his stomach. To the group, he said in English, "I don't like this place. I've never liked this place."

"Like, what is this place?" Joanna wanted to know.

"It's Lucky's Treasure Shop," Alexandra said and directed Joanna's attention to the wooden sign that spanned the two sides of the building on the corner. The paint was so chipped the name was hardly readable, especially in the poor light, and the pattern of the horseshoes and four-leaf clovers was next to invisible.

"Junk?" Joanna said, with amazement and distaste.

"I used to come here when I was in high school," Alexandra said, "and I wanted to make sure and stop by before I left town. This is the perfect time."

Bob felt the keen edge of his satisfaction go blunt.

"If it's not a restaurant, I say we give it a pass." This was Stan's opinion. Kastas, Bob, and Joanna seemed to share it.

With Alexandra chatting happily to Pan Lukacz, Bob saw no way to talk her out of going into that crap hole, and he sure as hell wasn't going in there himself. Before the little man in his trousers shriveled completely, he played his one good card, said in Polish, "See you tomorrow, Alexandra."

Alexandra looked at him as if she'd momentarily forgotten his existence, smiled abstractedly. "Sure thing, Bob."

Mr. Lukacz unlocked the security gate, shoved it open. The very sound of it made Bob's stomach turn.

After brief good-byes were uttered, Stan said, "How about we check out Nicky's? You in the mood for Italian? Hey, Bob!"

"Huh? Yeah, sure. Italian."

Bob saw the fancy asshole follow Alexandra into Lucky's, hoped he'd puke his guts out in there like the cool asshole he was. Then a wave of pure hatred washed over him.

THIRTY-TWO

 THE FIRST THING Val noticed was the scent of her hair. That and the way she filled the dark space around them with womanliness. It was as if he had awakened in the blackest hour of the night, able to see nothing, aware only of her. Or perhaps he was in the deepest cellar of his unconscious, dreaming. In either case, he wanted to roll over and bury himself in her.

When he felt her move away, he followed. Since he wasn't lying in a bed, he had to take a step forward to stay near her, and he proceeded to knock his shin against the corner of some hard object. He groaned and bent to grasp his insulted limb.

He heard her soft chuckle. "Sorry about that," she said. "I should have warned you about this place. There was a time when I imagined I could make my way around here with my eyes closed, but I never thought I'd ever actually have to do it."

He continued to move forward behind her, now more cautiously inching his way.

Her hand reached out and fumbled to find his. "Try this," she said and placed his hand on her shoulder so that she could guide him in the blackness. "There's a slight turn."

A flow of Polish followed. Her voice called out and was answered by the old man's. Then she stopped.

"Okay, we can wait here. Pan Lukacz tells me he has the overhead lights on timers and doesn't want to fool with the mechanism, so he's trying to find a table lamp to turn on. He can't remember exactly which ones are plugged in and have bulbs. It might take him a minute to find—ahh."

A thin, rosy light came on to illuminate an otherworld of clutter and cobwebs. Val looked around to see every conceivable object in the known universe crowded into an inconceivable landscape of dressers, chairs, tables, lamps, dishes, glassware, stacks of old maga-zines, stacks of old newspapers, more chairs, an eclectic cross be-tween tchotchkes and bibelots strewn across every surface, clothing, rags, sofas, cushions, linens, even more chairs, primitive appliances, tassels, garlands, pottery, stained-glass panels, strips of carved mold-ings, banisters, and partial staircases leading nowhere.

"This is Lucky's," she said.

"I don't see anything not to like here," he commented.

She didn't miss the allusion. The look she gave him was complex and provocative. "So, tell me. What do you think it is between you and Bob Dembrowski? I'd like to know."

Call it instant antipathy. And call it mutual. Like the kind he and Jean-Philippe had for one another. He said, "I suppose I object to bad manners. Your Bob did not behave with the greatest decorum on Sunday evening."

"He'd been drinking a little before he came—it's a Polish Easter custom, you know—and Mr. Kolatek's slivovitz can put anyone away. Other than that, Bob was fine or, at least, no worse than Mr. Kolatek or Jerzy."

He said simply, "You are right to defend a guest in your house."

She didn't swallow it. "You know what I think? I think you lost that pool match on purpose."

"Why would I do that?"

"So you could smother him in tennis. But it won't work."

"Probably not," he agreed congenially, "but we have not yet determined what it is about this place that he finds so distasteful. I'm finding it as delightful as you yourself must experience it."

She quirked her brows expressively but wasn't going to pursue the subject. She flapped the lapels of her jacket. "Delightful but hot." She engaged in another discussion with the old man who was turning on several more table lamps, at the end of which she reported, "Mr. Lukacz says that the heater has a mind of its own, coming on in November and shutting off in May. He hasn't paid his heating bill in decades and finds that lighting candles every week for the boiler's soul seems to keep it going. About all I can say is that the darned thing works. Too well."

He helped her off with her jacket. He hung it, along with her purse, on the coatrack standing next to them, then shed his own trench coat and suit coat.

The old man was beckoning them at the end of one narrow pathway that had the potential to be used as an aisle.

"I asked Mr. Lukacz if he had any new old treasures from Paris, and he said he just got in several boxes. Isn't that a coincidence? Let's hunt through them."

She moved forward.

"Looking for more biscuit tins, perhaps?" he asked. "Or will anything do."

"Anything, really." Her skirt was caught by a protruding fire poker. She clucked her tongue, released the fabric. "This is unbelievable. I had forgotten just how junked up this place really is." She turned her head, brows arched. "Did you know that only a small fraction of DNA actually carries the code for making proteins? A whopping *ninety-seven percent* of the DNA in human cells — think about it! — looks like meaningless filler. It's called 'junk DNA.' I'm not kidding. Stanley at BU, Gilbert at Harvard, they all call it junk."

"What do you call it?"

Her eyes glittered with laughter. "I call it junk too, which shouldn't surprise you, but it might surprise you to know what I think is lurking there."

"What's your best guess?"

Her brown cat's eyes narrowed to tiger's-eye slits. "You don't want to know."

"But I do," he said, holding her gaze. "I've already told you that I like it when you talk science."

He saw a wash of color tinge her cheeks and felt the small charge in the air. He intended to nurture it, just as he intended to get lucky at Lucky's and turn fantasy strip pool into the real thing. And having stripped her naked to talk science with her, he was strongly inclined to think that she knew nothing of the PCR technique that was central to TEFS. Now, why her grandmother should have the prototype, he didn't know—and didn't care at the moment, as long as Alexandra wasn't the one mysteriously thwarting his patent.

She lowered her eyes and turned back around. She took a deep breath, and he felt the air around her quivering nicely.

They had picked their way to the other end of the aisle. Val received a critical appraisal from Mr. Lukacz who said something to him, and upon receiving no response, asked in English, "You not speak Polish, young man?"

Val shook his head. "No Polish."

The old man frowned and muttered his disapproval.

Alexandra pointed at the large open crate at the old man's feet. "Can we start looking?"

The old man said, "I have not priced nothing yet here, but you look. Look, please!"

Alexandra knelt down and pulled her sweater away from her, as if it were hot and sticky, which it must have been. She engaged in another conversation with the old man that seemed to center, once again, on the overactive heating system. The old man shuffled away, speaking to her as he went. The words were incomprehensible, but the old man's tone sounded reassuring.

Val squatted next to her, glanced indifferently into the jumble in the boxes in the crate that claimed her attention. When the old man returned, he was holding several lace blouses on hangers which he handed over to her. She got off her knees, accepted the hangers with obvious thanks, but then gestured at the crate. The discussion, in which the word *Paryz* figured highly, was short and to the point.

"You won't believe it," she said. "This stuff comes from Paris, Illinois. I thought it was odd to be going through spattered enamel coffeepots and tin kitchen utensils. I've been looking at prairie life, not Paris life."

"What were you expecting?"

She shrugged. "I'm going to change into one of these blouses. I don't think I can stand the pressure cooker in this sweater." Her brows raised in question. "You don't mind being here?"

"Not at all."

"Oh. Well. I'll be right back." She hesitated. "There's apparently a ton of turn-of-the-century stuff from Paris, France, in one of the side rooms, if that interests you."

It didn't. He didn't like junk—not in the way she did—but he wasn't such a fool to say so. After she left, he let his hand idle through the artifacts of prairie life. Saw nothing of even remote interest. He rose to his feet.

He scanned the cliffs of furniture washed by waves of junk and saw Alexandra halfway across the room, on another shore. She was wearing a lace blouse from the previous century. In his mind's eye, that rich kaleidoscope of colors and feelings and images was churning briskly. He waited for the bits to turn sharp and painful, but they didn't. At sight of her, he felt only pleasure. She was playing with a pair of louvered doors that swung in a self-standing wooden door frame, opening onto nothing but another pile of junk. She let them flap and wobble to rest.

He moved toward her, let his hand graze various objects as he moved down the aisle. A bronzed figure of a horse captured mid-gallop. An art nouveau lamp shade shaped in the sensuous form of a calla lily. The lace of a drape cast around the shoulders of a voluptuous dress mannequin.

When he was almost next to her, she said a little breathlessly, "I had my fairy tales mixed up. I shouldn't have been thinking of Sleeping Beauty at all. It's been Hansel and Gretel the whole time."

He was in the mood to accept whatever turn in conversation she wanted, because no matter what path she took him down, he would determine the ending. "The two children who get lost in the woods?"

"Yes, and of course they try to avoid getting lost by strewing bread crumbs—or was it pebbles?—to make a trail that would lead them back to their house. But they get lost because either the trail they leave disappears or they don't know how to read their own signs. That's what all this junk is. The trail we're supposed to be following back."

"Back where?"

"I don't know."

He stood before her and looked down at her. He smiled. "But there are a lot of people's trails mixed up here. How are you to know what objects pertain to your trail—unless, of course, they come labeled."

"That's what makes it so difficult. Besides which, you have to always keep moving forward at the same time you search backward. You have to keep making decisions about what to do next, based on imperfect knowledge of what came before."

He put his hands out and rested them on her shoulders. "So. You try to get to the end of the story without knowing the beginning?"

She didn't flinch. "Something like that." She was regarding him intently, quizzically. "Every person is supposed to have one favorite fairy tale that is the most accurate projection of their personality. I'd be curious to know what your favorite is."

"Can't you guess?"

She shook her head.

"I think my favorite fairy tale was always"—his English failed him but he wasn't frustrated by the lapse—"Le petit chaperon rouge. I have forgotten what you call it."

"Little and red—ah, Little Red Riding Hood." Her lips turned down. "The little girl who gets eaten by the—?" she began, then understanding dawned. "The Big Bad Wolf."

"That's the one."

She turned from him. He released her. She started to walk away. "I don't think there's anything further of interest here. I want to see the stuff in the back room."

He was enjoying the swish of her hips, enticing him forward, and the way her hair floated around her shoulders. It reminded him of the day he had gone to her house in Durham and she had looked delicious in sweatpants and served him plum cake. It reminded him of the time he had run into her late one afternoon outside an art gallery. He recalled that it was in a street that angled alongside the Opéra, probably the Chaussée d'Antin.

No, that couldn't be right. He had never seen Alexandra in Paris. Nevertheless, the odd scrap of memory persisted.

HE HAD RUN into her outside the art gallery, and they had flirted madly, which was to say she'd been polite, asked all the right questions, then brushed him off.

She had a way of dodging him, dancing around him, and although she never swirled farther away than the length of his arm, she was often able to convince him that she meant to elude him, to escape his grasp. But then he would catch her, come to her, and when he slipped into her, she would slip right under his skin.

That afternoon, when she had nodded her polite good-bye and turned to go, he caught her arm and pulled her to him. She looked up at him, her eyes denying, her lips inviting, and he traced his finger down the line of her chin to her neck to her breast. He far preferred the line from her hip to her toes, but he would get to that later, when the moon ruled the sky.

He bent his head to hers. She closed her eyes against her denial and raised the invitation on her lips. The afternoon was fading to evening, and a delicate blue shadow was trapped below her eyelashes as they fluttered shut. He paused to enjoy the dappling pastels that gave depth to her translucent skin and the enchanting play of light that touched the tiny sickle of a scar on her upper left cheek. Before he completed the kiss, however, his eyes were shocked open by the silver flash and loud pouf of a street photographer's rude bulb. The photographer would probably use this picture to make a vulgar postcard of their kiss.

He blinked, she gasped, and the photographer ran.

VAL BLINKED AGAINST the piercing flash in the darkness ahead, an exterior light glancing off an interior surface. Alexandra gasped and stepped back so that she was molded against his front, arousing him in a way he did not need to be aroused and reminding him of what was to come. He put his hands on her shoulders lightly—no need to insist—and bent his head to her hair. He closed his eyes against the annoying flash ahead and breathed in honey lavender.

"It's just us," she said, relief in her voice, "in that mirror. You see? I thought they were intruders."

She moved away from him again. He let her go.

His lovely, oddly vivid little fantasy had been produced by the gleam of a stray beam of light caught in the corner of a darkened mirror. He figured it had been triggered by all this . . . *brocante*—for want of remembering the English word.

"This is the room Mr. Lukacz told me about with the Paris stuff," she said, disappearing in the darkness. "I'd like to find a lamp for the matches Mr. Lukacz gave me."

He heard sounds of halting movement ahead. A scrape. A flame. Alexandra kneeling on the floor. She placed the glass globe over the lit lamp, brought a soft dim glow to the cluttered little room. He walked over to her to stand above her and look down at her. She looked up. Met his eyes.

He felt strong forces he didn't even try to understand swirl down from him, swirl up from her, invisible yet strong, like two strands wrapping around one another. They had played this scene before, and he was liking it better and better. He bent down on knees that never failed him and balanced the backs of his thighs on his heels. While she watched him, saying nothing, he unlaced her boots, slipped one off, then the other.

She sprang to her feet, away from him. "No."

"Yes." He stood. "Like a cat," he said, commenting on the quickness of her movement. He came toward her, and she backed up. "I've always thought of you as a cat. Do you have nine lives, I wonder?"

"I don't know how many lives I've had." She stumbled backward over a cushion. "Mr. Lukacz," she said, her voice hardly above a whisper, "he's bound to be looking for us soon, you see—"

"My guess is he's snoring away in an old armchair," he said. "He's very tired, and he's very deaf."

With one hand he reached out to the buttons on her lace blouse. They sprang off one by one, yielding to age and his light tug, aided by her backward movement. With the other hand he grasped the hem of her skirt, bunched it up.

"I already knew you weren't wearing any necklaces, Alexandra," he said, "but now I discover you're not wearing panty hose." He moved his hand over the silk of her panties, hooked his fingers over the waistband. "And no slip either." He shook his head in mock disapproval. "At the pool hall, you lied about the clothing you had to take off." He chided softly, "Liar."

"Liar?" she repeated. "Let me see . . . there's a response to that— what could it be?"

"Please, sir. No, sir. I've forgotten the response, sir," he mimicked softly, then added, "Let me remind you."

He backed her up so that she could go no further, propping her against a door off its hinges. The image of her half-undressed and framed by a door reminded him so strongly of the last time they had made violent, satisfying love that with a flick of his wrist he ripped her panties off, hardly realizing the force of his gesture. Then she was matching him force for force, arousing him further.

He moved his open palms over the bare skin of her thighs, put one of her legs around him, pressed her to him. His lips met hers, twirled his tongue to touch hers. Her blouse was open to him. He slid his hands up to cup her breasts and around to unhook her bra. All without effort. Or perhaps with too much effort, because he realized that she was struggling not with him but against him. In earnest. It was as if she was trying to keep him from entering a door he was pushing through to get to her.

He stopped and broke the kiss. There it was again, that strange trick of his imagination. He knew that they had never made love before, and they had never been separated by a door. He was confused by the vividness of yet another nonmemory.

He lodged his chin in the crook of her neck. He brought his hands down to frame her hips lightly, but he did not release her. He paused to monitor his breathing and hers. He wasn't sure whether the tension aching off every inch of her body was excitement or fear or both.

He took a deep breath, and the most logical, most belated question in the world occurred to him.

"Are you a virgin, Alexandra?"

THIRTY-THREE

 HER BACK WAS against the wall. Her breasts were pressed to his chest. Her panties had been ripped off, and her skirt was wrapped around her waist. One of her legs was wrapped around his. The double helix had tightened its grip around her, around them, wrapping her with him. The strands had turned hot and viscous, had twisted themselves into a tight braid that caused the places where their bodies met to cling and want. The heat of those strands turned the flow of emotion within her into syrupy ropes, drizzling them to pool and puddle between her legs. The strands knotted her skin to his where it touched and strained. They gathered strength to form the suggestion of a wave that might edge into violence.

She shrank back but had nowhere to go. His strength increased, and the possibility of violence edged toward a crest. She began to push him away. To resist. Warnings darted through her brain. Watch out for this guy, A.K. Just watch out for him . . . This guy is going to be the death of you . . . He's no killer, but . . . Leave it at that.

She had walked into Lucky's with Val feeling safe and alive with curiosity about what treasures she might find. Even more, she had been happy to escape Bob's presence and the malevolence she had felt emanate from him. Now she was regretting her mistake. It wasn't Bob who would do her harm, it was—

Then he stopped abruptly, sagged against her, and asked an extra-ordinary question.

"Am I a virgin?" she echoed, dazed. She had to think about it, then answered, "Depends on how you look at it."

"How do you look at it?"

"I had a live-in boyfriend once as an undergraduate. It didn't work out."

"I'm glad. On both counts."

"Both?"

"That you only had one and that it didn't work out."

He took her wrists and placed them at his shirt, at his belt, at the buttons of his trousers. He had her where he wanted her and how he wanted her. Her skirt was an irrelevant twist of fabric around her hips. The helix was strong and swirling, binding them together, making them sweat. Nothing was going to stop the force of his entry —or was it a forced entry?

She had a part to play. "You mean to do this against my will?" she breathed, moving her head to one side, away from him.

He wasn't going to answer her question, and he wasn't going to ask permission. He was demanding. He was going to get what he wanted, and her fear—no, it was desire—sharpened as the frightening edge did not crest into violence but curled into strength as he wedged hot and hard desire into her soft entry.

His hand turned her chin back to him. He was part of her and look-ing her straight in the eyes when he asked, "Is this against your will?"

She accepted his penetration, his possession. Had to accept it. Had no choice. Had never had a choice when she was with him. "I don't know."

"Yes, you do. When has it ever been a question of me forcing you against your will?"

She echoed the significant word in his question. "Ever?"

He didn't respond to that. "Forcing you against your will would feel like anger." He let her swallow him. "Like punishment too. Does this feel like punishment?"

She didn't feel anger, not from him, not from her, and there was no room in her to feel punishment, because she was so filled, fulfilled, by his desire braided in her liquid, lacing ropes of slick silk.

"No," she said, wishing she didn't have to agree, finding pleasure in that perverse wish.

"It would be more punishment to stop." He was strong and demanding, but he was also taking his time. "Or never to have started. And after such a long time, I might have been angry if you had put me off any longer, but this—"

He groaned and ceased speaking. Put his lips to hers, his tongue to hers, his hips to hers, his body to hers.

But this—yes, he was right, it would have been more punishment to stop. From the moment she had first seen him and then stepped into an Impressionist painting, her perceptions had been altered, slowly, until the transformation was complete. Seeing. Hearing. Feeling. Understanding. Now touching, such that every individual cell in her body was turned inside out and replaced, but not quite in the same place. The gel plate that existed between her and the world, her protection, her barrier—the one that had begun to crack weeks ago when she was standing next to him in the corridor of some building, or maybe it was in the street outside an art gallery one fine summer's afternoon and the air was soft and blue—opened wide, and the world rushed in, greeting her, exhilarating her. She would forgive him anything, over and over and over again, if this passion she felt around her, within her, from him was real, for her. She would give him anything, everything, forever and ever, if the passion she offered him now in return would be accepted, honored, cherished.

When it came time for him to pour his energy into this lattice of lust so long undone, she no longer felt threatened by the possibility of violence dwelling behind his strength. Instead, she felt the tone and the muscle and the beauty of it. She felt her legs stretch out. She was a ballerina bending over carefully, tenderly to wrap the pink satin ties of her toe shoes around her ankles, just as they were lacing up their bodies and their love. She tied fragile, beautiful bows around her calves, binding together the two ends that were once limp and separated. Finishing them off with fussing, unnecessary gestures, crisping the perfect loops, patting the plump knot.

She breathed in and out with a deep and resonating shudder, and the satin ends of those pretty toe shoes fluttered and extended and began to stream magically in the direction of her heart.

HE HELPED HER make their bed on the cushions. Old linens were at hand, clean and redolent of age and secrets. As they lay entwined, she was casually, almost idly rubbing his lower right back. She had found with her fingers the exact place to knead which gave him the most relief and which was right next to the exact place of his most severe pain. He had only a hazy realization that no one, not even his trainer, had ever found that place before—hadn't even been aware that it existed. As he savored her varying scents, he came to realize that exact place as the most erotically charged spot on his body.

No, not the most, but it communicated directly with that most excellent organ of sexual yearning which yearned again, very soon, for her pouting pinkness, her fresh and abundant well which was right next to him, available to him, at the price of her teasing resistance, whetting his desire and hers and increasing his ability to slice deeper and deeper in her. So he ceased his scented exploration and put his hands on full nipples and hips and buttocks and found again the magnificent surprise that when he lodged himself within her and thought that all of him was there, there was more of him to arrive. Then her hands, womanly hands, grasped him and pressed him and found that spot on his back, and her voice stirred him, whispering, "You aren't supposed to be able to do this again so soon."

His grunt observed that the case was quite the contrary.

"Are you always this . . . rough and ready?"

That got his attention but not his desire to stop. "Complaining?"

He felt the quiver of her laugh along his chest and stomach. "Not at all. It's amazingly effective. But, somehow, I imagined you to be a decorous lover."

"You did?"

"And I'm wondering if you're always this wonderfully indecorous."

"Pas d'habitude," he replied, finding the effort to translate too great, since the distance from his brain to the focus of his attention was also too great.

To close off her words was the easiest thing in the world, and the most pleasant, for he could kiss her and still respond to the moans and cries that came from her and that he heard way down in her throat. And, no, not usually, was he ever indecorous, whatever that might mean in this context of bathing in heat and desire and liquid luxury, because he'd never been with a woman that gripped him ridge and fold so thoroughly or brought him to the tip of himself so completely, so enormously. He was sure that he wanted her under him, perhaps over him as well, no, really and truly under him, or back against the wall, all the time. Rough and ready, yes. She always ready to receive him. He always ready to fill her as he was filling her now, streaming along, rushing free, cutting deeply, sweating, bleeding, spilling, not caring if he healed.

Whatever it was, it was more than he had bargained for. Possibly more than she had bargained for, but she'd bargained for nothing, and when it was over again she was breathing deeply, exhausted, and that was fine with him. At length, she rose to a sitting position, her hair a gentle explosion in the dimming light of the glass-globed lamp.

She said groggily, "Postcards. I came back here to look at old postcards."

Postcards reminded him of something, but he couldn't think what and didn't care. Nor did he care what she came back here to do or what she wanted to do now. So he settled himself comfortably in his stretched out position from which he could admire the swells of her breasts visible above the linen at her waist.

She sorted through several boxes of old French postcards but soon lost the sense of the purpose of this activity. She had come to Lucky's on the trail of her previous life and his, but she had to admit that she was exceedingly happy right now in her present life, which made her wonder why she should bother with past miseries.

And who was to say there were any miseries? No objects spelling doom for her had surfaced in Lucky's as she might have expected, and when Val reached out yet again to pull her to him, she had to laugh. It was impossible to think that she could have been anything less than supremely satisfied in some previous lifetime if Val had been anything like the eager lover he was now.

"You can't be serious!" she said, playfully pushing him away. "I admit that I don't have much experience with men, but good heavens, this seems quite beyond the usual and customary."

With his cheek against her neck, he explained, "I think I've had to be too careful for too long and forgot what it was like to wallow in a woman's lap."

"Oh, sure," she said, trying to pull away, "*you*'ve had to be careful. What about me?"

With a straight face, he said, "I fully appreciate how you've saved yourself, more or less, for me."

"I mean—" she began, struggling in earnest.

He cut her off and brought her down next to him, saying, "I know what you mean. It's because I've been boringly careful that we don't have to be."

"Except for pregnancy."

"Which is the lesser of many evils these days."

"But, still—"

"Well?"

She shook her head. "Don't worry. It's not that time of the month. But more to the point is . . . is . . . all this activity!"

He smoothed his hand from her neck to her hip bone and slid it between her thighs. "I'm in the mood for something decorous now, I think you might say, having worked a few of my rough edges off."

"But not all of them, I hope."

After he had satisfied her that he knew the decorous arts of the practiced lover and they had dozed, they came to their senses knowing they had to get out of Lucky's before daybreak. They sat up, began to grope for bits of clothing.

"I almost forgot to tell you," he said, "that I'll pick you up on Friday evening around six o'clock. We'll be going to a reception at the Art Institute."

"The Art Institute?"

"Abbey Labs is one of the big donors, and there's some benefit or another that night. My presence is required, since the Abbey Labs brass wants me to meet the Art Institute board, which has a strong francophilic streak."

Her reaction might not have been what he expected. She flopped her head back down on the pillow and began to laugh.

"You think the board members are not francophiles?"

She shook her head. "I have no idea. I'm laughing only because I've been avoiding going there all week, and it seems I'm not destined to avoid it entirely."

"Does that mean you're coming?"

"That means it would probably be unwise of me not to come. See you at six."

Increasing her sense of amusement was the fact that she suddenly remembered that the appropriate response to him calling her a liar was her calling him a romantic.

THIRTY-FOUR

ALEXANDRA WALKED INTO the graduate student office on Friday afternoon, took one look at Deirdre's face, and clutched her heart. "Oh my God," she breathed, "someone died."

"Not that bad," Deirdre said, "but bad enough."

"You flunked your writtens" was Alexandra's next guess.

Deirdre flashed a smile. "No, actually, I'm sailing through my exams with distinction, and I'm beginning to think I know more than my professors about the period." Her face fell again. She had Alexandra's documents spread out on the table before her, gestured to some brownish crumbs of paper. "It's your French newspaper. I thought I'd read it over, so I could tell you what was in it, but when I attempted to open it yesterday, the thing crumbled to dust at my touch. I'm sorry!"

Alexandra sat down across from Deirdre and surveyed the ruins of the newspaper.

Deirdre continued, contritely, "I went to the library to get it on microfiche so that I could copy it for you this morning, but I was surprised to discover that our library doesn't have *Le Courrier français*. I'm so sorry!"

Alexandra was sorry too but didn't find it the tragedy Deirdre apparently did. "It's not your fault. The newspaper is over a hundred years old and has not been adequately protected, so I'd hardly expect it to be in good condition now."

"I did salvage the date," Deirdre said. She gave Alexandra a paper onto which she'd taped the bits with the date pieced together. She had included her telephone number on the page as well. "Do you want me to order this issue through interlibrary loan for you? It would only take a couple of days."

"I suppose I can do it myself, if I need it."

"And after my next exam, I'll go out on Frognet to find it and download it for you, if possible."

Nancy walked into the room. "Make sure you do it after that exam, Deirdre, and don't tell me again how you already know much more than your professors."

Louise came in behind Nancy and asked Alexandra, "Any luck with the house hunting the other day?"

"Saw some we liked, but most were out of our price range."

Nancy consoled Alexandra with a pat on the back. "Too bad, but I'm glad we're in time for the next installment."

"The last installment," Deirdre informed them, as Nancy and Louise took their places around the table.

SHE FELT AS happy as she thought she had a right to be. She walked down the street away from the late-morning market, her full basket hooked on her arm, but she wasn't going home.

She might have been smiling to herself. Lately she had noticed giddy-girl feelings inside and guessed that she often wore a betraying expression to match. She hummed a catchy tune, worked out some steps to match it, lined up Chérie, Nina, and Louise next to her. The mental dance turned into an inventive turn on the cancan. True to form, she mused.

Out of the corner of her eye, just ahead, she caught sight of Pierre. He was outside his shop, sweeping a sidewalk she was sure must have been swept several hours before. In the past weeks, she had seen Pierre in the neighborhood here and there, even sometimes at his café, but she had not had a private conversation alone with him. She would have loved to find a way to avoid this encounter, but she couldn't very well cross to the other side of street without openly insulting him. As it was, she guessed that he had seen her coming and had stepped out onto the sidewalk for the very purpose of intercepting her.

Her smile was in place when she came within greeting distance. "Good morning, Pierre."

Pierre looked up. His dark eyes were steady on her long enough to become uncomfortable. "Good morning, Jeanne." He turned his attention to the remaining nonexistent dirt on the *pavé* and swept it into the gutter. He glanced at her basket. "I see you've come from the market."

"Yes," she said, "the season is good for summer fruit, and when I heard that the prices were good as well, I couldn't resist this assortment." She fiddled with the brown wrappers to better display the fruit for his viewing. "You see."

"I see," he said. He returned his gaze to her face. "But you're not going home." He pointed away from the steep street that led to her apartment. "You're headed in this direction."

"Yes," she said, "I have an appointment."

"An appointment?"

She couldn't help a slight blush to tinge her cheeks. Did he imagine she had a rendezvous somewhere in public with Victor? She schooled herself to smile. "Two appointments, in fact. First I am going to my reading and writing lesson, and then I am to see Dr. Dreyfus."

"Ah, Miss High and Mighty with her reading and writing!" he said softly. His attempt at playful irony went awry, for his tone was soured by bitterness.

Now she flushed for a different reason. "You know that I've saved for months to take these lessons." She stressed the word *months* to em-

phasize the fact that her attempts to elevate herself had predated
Victor's interest in her. "You've always encouraged me," she added.
"You've never pinched me for it."

"That was before," he said, emphasizing the word *before*.

She didn't need to be told before what. She also didn't need to
stand here and listen to this. She drew a breath, adjusted her basket,
and proceeded to take a step around him.

He shifted his body and blocked her way. "And Dr. Dreyfus? Why
should you need to see him?"

His question was like a slap in the face, implying as it did that she
was either diseased like the common whores they both knew or pregnant.

She replied, with dignity, "I have ideas about how to improve san-
itary conditions in the neighborhood, and I wish to discuss them
with the doctor. I hope you approve."

His expression turned dark. "Now I am supposed to approve of
what you do?" He held his broom like a club, gestured with suppressed anger. Not at her, but at another man not present.

She saw in this gesture an unmistakable echo of the man in the
moonlight who had held a wicked club high above his head and
brought it down on Victor's back. She took a step back from Pierre.
In surprise, in horror. It couldn't be, could it?

Pierre put his broom down again, thick fingers relaxing. "I wanted
to marry you."

Surprise, again. But no horror, only confusion. Marriage? She
did not dare think of marriage now that she had entered a relationship of another kind with Victor. She circled around the idea. It
made her dizzy. She could hardly think of anything more wonderful
than marriage to Victor. But to Pierre?

"I still do," Pierre told her. He was looking at her sadly, her friendly
Polish bear, so solid, so dependable.

She hoped he wasn't the one who had so viciously hurt Victor, who
had sent Victor to her rooms, to her bed, where she had cared for his
injury and where she now made love with him.

She said, "I can't think of marriage now. Can't speak of it."

"You will, though," he said, half-promising, half-threatening, "and in the meantime, you can write about it." This last was said with a return to bitterness, and he lowered his eyes, as if in apology for the fact that he was deliberately hurting her. His glance fell on some strange objects in her basket, poking out from around the paper cornets of fruit. "What's this?"

"Sticks of wax," she said, pointing at the odd items, "several crochet hooks, wires, a cooling rack, and a miniature—what is it called?—a ratchet wheel. Do you know what that is?"

Pierre had no idea.

Relieved by the change in subject, she explained that she was going to put these oddly assorted items together to make a contraption for marinating plums. She sketched the mechanism with fingers and hands in the air. "You see, if I position the crochet hooks just so on the handle of the ratchet wheel and then rig it up to sit on the stick of wax, I can melt the wax and the hook will slowly unpeel the plums that I stick on the prongs of the cooling rack. You see?"

"Not really."

"Well, it works. First I parboil the plums to soften them up and make them easy to skin. Then as the plums are skinned by the hook, they roll over and fall into the bowl over which the rack is placed and begin to soak in the liqueur. It's auto . . . automatic."

"How it is automatic?" Pierre wondered.

"I put it on top of my oven, stoke the fire and keep it low so that the wax melts slowly, just so."

Pierre was frowning heavily. "Where did you learn this?"

"From an old lady in Sainte-Foy-la-Grande. She made the best plum cake, and it was my favorite when I was a little girl, so I always came around and begged her for some. Then when I was older, she was so good to me after—" she hesitated, "after Monsieur Lafitte's son mistook me for a part of his property. Anyway, the old lady was always so busy in the fields, she had to find a way to skin and macerate the plums in the morning so that she could bake me the cake in the evening."

She stopped short of saying that her present happiness had inspired her to try her hand at her favorite village recipe. She also saw that Pierre was looking even sadder and more disapproving by the minute.

"I . . . I'll bake you some plum cake, Pierre," she said, to close off the encounter.

"Can I come to your rooms and get it?" he asked, with an edge of belligerence. "I've never been to your rooms before, Jeanne."

And he thought he could come now that she was a fallen woman? She suppressed her anger in order to keep her dignity. She would always keep her dignity.

"It wouldn't be proper for me to entertain you alone in my rooms. You know that, Pierre."

THIRTY-FIVE

 "YOU HAVE THE Institut Pasteur/Abbey Labs file in your hands, then, Marielle?" Val repeated.

He was imagining the two possibilities for the fate of the file in the last few days. Either it had been in its place all along and Sophie had missed it. Or Sophie had mentioned to Jean-Philippe that Val knew the file was missing, and Jean-Philippe had restored it.

"Yes, sir," Marielle replied, "and I remember working on it, oh, perhaps the week before you left for Seine-Lafitte-Amérique this last time."

"And you put it back where you found it."

"But of course," Marielle said.

He could hear her pique at having been questioned on the matter, as if she were negligent. "Very good," he said. "Let's go through it, and you can give me all the latest from the Institut Pasteur and the French patent office."

Val quickly discovered that Tom Manning had been right about the patent problems coming from Europe and, ironically, they were in France. Soon he was mired in the judgments of various *conseils juridiques* in Paris District Court and Supreme Appeals Court and working through the problems of infringement, possession-knowledge, licenses, territorial jurisdictions, and acts of good faith, or *bonne foi*.

Mauvaise foi, Val was thinking. All of it. He was infringing on no one and nothing, and he was getting nowhere. No, rather, he was going backward, and he backed right up to the time he had been admitted to the Ecole des Hautes Etudes Commerciales and then been inexplicably denied matriculation. The name Gervais spun around in his head, but it had nowhere to settle since it didn't mean a thing to him other than its association with Jean-Philippe Chevalier's wife, Lucie. He had already determined who the villain of the piece was, but thoughts of Jean-Philippe were not advancing the solution to his present problems.

"Let's go document by document," Val suggested, "and we'll try to put together what you have on file with what I am tracking down through Abbey Labs."

After half an hour of document combing with Marielle, Val was wishing that a version of his crazy grandfather's ball-pitch contraption was not in use as a plum-marinating contraption on Alexandra's grandmother's stove. The web of associations was too threatening— and too weird, for it made no digestible sense.

At one point in the conversation, Val became aware that someone had entered his outer office in Paris and was claiming half of Marielle's attention. After a few moments of side discussion, Marielle said into the phone, "There's someone here who wants to speak to you."

Val assumed it was Yves, but when the voice came on the line, he felt that old itch between his shoulder blades to be greeting Jean-Philippe.

The openers were cordial. Val inquired into the progress of the Barcelona project, and Jean-Philippe clucked and cooed over the excellence of the project. The results for the improved ulcer drug Zolax exceeded expectations, and Jean-Philippe was cautiously optimistic that Seine-Lafitte would soon be cutting into the share of the Swiss and English pharmaceutical companies in this competitive market segment. He was also happy to report that the patent would extend beyond the year 2001.

Val had an inkling what would come next, so he diverted the topic by saying that he would make sure that Zolax would be highly present at the AMA convention in Chicago in August.

Jean-Philippe didn't bite. Instead he said, "And speaking of patents, did I understand Marielle to say that your so remarkable TEFS kit is not yet approved for world marketing?"

"Yes, you did understand that it is—"

Jean-Philippe continued, "And that it is not, therefore, being test-marketed at this time?"

No need to lie. No need to tell the whole truth either. "The American lawyers are working through the details now, and it will take them a little longer than anticipated because the problem, it seems, is not on the American side."

"But, no? Ah, then perhaps it is beyond their capabilities to solve. Have you considered engaging a different company, perhaps one with more international expertise, to work through what must be difficult, though surely not insurmountable, problems?"

He had considered just that. "No, because any further delays now will be costly."

"Costly. Yes." Jean-Philippe sighed meaningfully. "I was working through the second quarter's budget only this morning. It is the end of the day here, already, as I am sure you must know, and I am quite tired, so you will understand if I cannot recall all the figures precisely from memory."

Val knew this script, and he knew that Jean-Philippe knew the figures down to the last centime.

Jean-Philippe recounted, with just the right amount of artful hesitation, the costs already incurred by the TEFS project. He mentioned, with great ceremony, how the debit column would look at the end of the year if TEFS were not on the market and possibly not even ready for the market. Then he expressed his great happiness over the clause in the R-and-D contract with the Rosenberg research team at Duke that would halt funding if Seine-Lafitte experienced a two-quarter downturn.

Every nerve in Val's body jangled. He recalled hearing the suggestion of that same proviso when he had been dancing with Alexandra at Alhambra.

"Is that a new clause, Jean-Philippe?"

"But, no, it was there from the beginning. Of course it was there from the beginning."

Val was sure it hadn't been there from the beginning, since he himself had reviewed the original contract. However, he wasn't going to argue the point or even wonder how Jean-Philippe could have found a way to alter signed contracts. Nor could he stop to think how Alexandra had known about it. He was more concerned about the implications. "Are you truly thinking of pulling the plug on the Rosenberg research project?"

"I must, cher collègue, if Seine-Lafitte cannot afford it."

"Seine-Lafitte must find a way to afford it," Val said. "As important as early detection is—and I fully expect TEFS to be on the market this year to provide an affordable means for that early detection—diagnosis is only the first step. Seine-Lafitte's future should include research to find a cure for cancer that is more reliable and, indeed, less debilitating to the cancer victim than radiation and chemotherapy."

"You are very noble," was Jean-Philippe's response.

Val noted that this was the one and only time Jean-Philippe had ever described him so. Was this a veiled reference to Val's family background?

"In this case, my nobility makes for good business."

Jean-Philippe's soft boff was expressive. "You are thinking of Seine-Lafitte's future, Valéry, and that is good. I, on the other hand, must be responsible to Seine-Lafitte's shareholders not in some imagined and desirable future, but now."

"Yes, but the Rosenberg team is particularly good, and you just can't stop their funding like that. Think about them. What will they do?"

"It is hardly Seine-Lafitte's responsibility to support researchers at Duke. However, I do believe the so talented young woman on the team—Miss Kaminski is her name, as I recall—is pursuing such interesting work that she will surely find funding on her own, if Seine-Lafitte cannot continue to support the whole team."

Alexandra again? Red flags of warning were waving wildly.

"Do you know her work on, let me see . . . telomerase, I believe it is called?" Jean-Philippe asked.

"I don't know her work, but I do know that telomeres are the enzyme structures that cap the chromosomes."

"I'm impressed, dear boy. Now, myself, I know nothing of such things, but Dr. Rosenberg—I keep in contact with him, of course—believes that Miss Kaminski's work is quite unusual and promises to create a breakthrough in cancer therapy. Her work suggests that if telomerase is active, you have sustained cell growth, and if you can find a way to deactivate it, you shut down cancer."

Val considered. "I haven't read anything like that in the literature, and I try to keep up."

"You are so thorough. I admire you. My point, of course, is that Miss Kaminski will do nicely on her own, apart from the team, should their funding collapse."

Was Jean-Philippe implying that Alexandra was in league with him and willing to make a side deal that would cut out the rest of the team? Jean-Philippe might be offering to pay her a little more for her work from the savings he would have from dropping the other four researchers from the payroll. Or was Jean-Philippe simply willing to stop funding a research project from which Seine-Lafitte—not to mention millions of cancer victims—stood to gain so much?

"Are you truly unwilling, Jean-Philippe, to risk a little money to spare the world a lot of suffering?"

"You cannot expect Seine-Lafitte to fund new ventures from old ones whose great promise is not—or never will be—realized."

Since Val had figured that the profits from his innovative diagnostic product would support cancer research through the next century, he knew he was being driven into his trenches. "Yves backed TEFS from the beginning."

Jean-Philippe's voice was as smooth as silk. "Did you know the man who had your position before you?"

The question was rhetorical, and Val didn't answer it.

"Yves had great faith in him too, but his faith could not be sustained. Yves has vision. That is why he leads our company. I have no vision beyond the numbers in my ledgers. That is why I am the general manager." He hardly needed to make his threat more clear or to elaborate on this subject, so he changed it. "I hear from the charming Marielle that you will be coming soon to Paris."

"Very soon."

When Val hung up the phone a few minutes later, he envisioned with relish the tennis match he was to have in a few hours with Bob Dembrowski.

THIRTY-SIX

DEIRDRE PUT THE last page down and said, "She wrote this herself about herself, didn't she?"

"I think so," Alexandra concurred. "Let me see the handwriting. I might recognize it."

"You might recognize her handwriting?" Deirdre cried. "Why haven't you said so?"

Because until Tuesday evening, Alexandra hadn't wanted anyone, beginning with herself, to think she was crazy. However, now that she had entered a world of the scientifically fantastic, she was willing to use any strange knowledge to make sense of this equally strange business. Sure enough, Marie-Thérèse had finally located the family Bible the day before, and none to Alexandra's surprise, it was only about fifty years old, which meant that it didn't have Jeanne Lacombe's signature. Now, Alexandra was sure she had seen Jeanne's signature scrawl across her mind's eye upon leaving Val's house several weeks before. So, the question was no longer how Alexandra had seen that signature, but to what document Jeanne had affixed it.

Deirdre handed the pages over to Alexandra, but when Alexandra peered at them, all she could see was white glare and black spiders. A headache suddenly gripped her temples. It wasn't quite a headache— more like an intense pleasure gone too far. As if the endorphins darting and glittering through her body since Tuesday evening had begun to whorl together. As if what had been a sensuous May breeze was forming into an ominous Oklahoma tornado.

Alexandra shook her head and handed the papers back. "I guess I don't know her handwriting well enough to identify these papers."

"I haven't done justice to the translation," Deirdre said, "but it's clear she was perceptive, and it's lovely to have the results here of all her hard work learning to read and write."

Louise was not impressed. "She was trying to improve herself to secure the affections of her noble lover."

"Didn't you hear what she said to Pierre?" Nancy objected. "She began her reading and writing lessons *before* Victor came into her life. She was doing it for herself." To Alexandra, she said, "So, who is she?"

Me, in a previous lifetime. "My great-great grandmother, I think."

"And she was a dancer in Montmartre?" Nancy pursued. "It must have been exciting!"

"Maybe it wasn't so exciting," Alexandra ventured.

Deirdre entered into the spirit of Nancy's suggestion. "Sure it was! She might have been an actress and a model too, like Ellen An-drée who modeled for Manet, Renoir, and Degas. She's pictured in Degas's *L'Absinthe* and Manet's *La Prune,* among other paintings."

Alexandra groaned. It might have been her headache.

"You know Degas's absinthe painting, don't you?" Deirdre asked, misinterpreting Alexandra's groan. "The one where that woman is drowsing over a glass of nasty absinthe with that other lowlife sitting next to her, but he's drinking coffee, so that makes him already more respectable than her. Now, what are we supposed to make of that?"

"That she's a prostitute," Louise stated. "All those women in those paintings were prostitutes. That's what we're supposed to make of it."

"But it's great art, my dearest Louise!" Nancy objected.

"It was great marketing," Louise countered. "Think about it. All those café scenes, all those dancers, all those laundresses. Easy prey, and pretty prey too. Hey, the guys who sold those paintings to the rich guys back then, they knew that the women, like the paintings themselves, were objects to buy and sell."

To Alexandra, Nancy explained, "Louise is our resident material-ist historian."

"I have my uses," Louise said with a sniff.

Alexandra roused herself to say, "I think Louise is right."

And that was all it took for the four of them to plunge into a dis-cussion of the Impressionists versus the Salonists. They all agreed that, at the turn of the century, it was the young against the old, the alienated avant-garde against the establishment. Alexandra and Louise joined forces to argue that the Impressionists did not produce more authentic art than the Salonists but had only succeeded in sell-ing their work to posterity with the label "authentic art." Deirdre and Nancy expressed shock at such blasphemy.

At the end of the discussion, Deirdre looked at Alexandra and said, "You don't look familiar to me, but I'll be damned if what you say about painting doesn't sound familiar. I can't think who you sound like, but it may well be my mother!"

Alexandra smiled weakly and said, "When I figure out what this is all about, I'll let you know."

Deirdre laughed. "I must say, my darling Alexandra, although I don't agree with all your opinions about art, your presence adds a certain sort of something. A je ne sais quoi that was missing before."

"Like a car with only three wheels," Louise offered.

"Or a square dance without the fourth corner," Nancy said.

"But, you know," Deirdre added with a frown, "I don't think our girl Jeanne ever got together with Dr. Dreyfus."

"What happened to her?" Alexandra asked quickly.

Deirdre laughed again. "I don't mean that she was mugged or anything like that, and she may well have seen the doctor that day. However, I've discovered that at one point le bon Laurent was partic-ularly interested in halting the spread of syphilis in Montmartre, but then—nothing. His interest stopped."

"Do you know why?"

"No, but I can't help but think that if Jeanne had really pur-sued the project with him, she would have persuaded him to set up clinics or at least find a way to distribute to the prostitutes the antibiotics that were being developed at the time by Pasteur and his institute."

Alexandra's headache got worse.

HER HEADACHE RECEDED throughout the afternoon to vanish completely the moment she heard the knock at the door and opened it to see who was standing on the stairway landing.

Val whisked her down the stairs and to the taxi glowing pumpkin orange in the streetlight which was waiting to take them to the reception at the Art Institute. Once seated next to him in the taxi, she noticed a significant aspect of Val's appearance.

"Your hair is still damp at the nape," she said.

"I just showered."

"Where?"

"My shower interests you?"

He said it in a way that made her feel slutty—but then decided that it was her imagination. "No, I'm interested more in the place where you showered than in the shower itself."

"At a club. West Side Sports, I believe."

"Bob's, I take it?"

He nodded. "Might have been."

"Well, what was the game?" she demanded.

No response.

"Tennis," she said a little grimly. "I knew it! I just knew you'd trick him into playing tennis!"

"I didn't trick him. He suggested it."

"When I had lunch with Bob the other day, I tried to talk him out of playing tennis with you!"

"You apparently succeeded only in making him think of nothing else."

Both at the pool hall and at lunch at Staropolska's, she had felt unsympathetic toward Bob, as if he was the bad guy. However, something in Val's manner produced in her a feeling of solidarity with Bob—and a feeling of alienation for Val. Her headache was coming back. Was she getting her good guys and bad guys confused?

"All right, Val," she said, "how bad was it?"

"You don't want to know—"

"I probably don't."

"—but I was generous, considering."

"Considering what?"

He didn't answer that.

Soon they were rambling down Michigan Avenue, a smooth dance paced to the rhythm of the green lights. The Hancock Center, Henri Bendel's, Saks, Nike Town appeared on her horizon to recede just as quickly. She had a sense that this mile, her Chicago mile, was truly magnificent, just like it was supposed to be but how it so often was not for a girl from her side of town. The runway of luxury rolled out ahead of her, red carpeting her way, taking her past the Tribune Towers and the bright, white trapezoid of the Wrigley Building, lifting her over the Chicago River, and carrying her several more blocks where the landscape of Grant Park opened ahead on her left. The waterfront, spangled with lights, came into view. Her cabbie sped through several reds, made his U-turn, and brought the pumpkin cab to the steps of the Art Institute in the shadow of the great lion statues.

She stepped out of the magic carriage thinking dreamily of Cinderella. Fairy tales again, she mused. Always a new one.

But if this was Cinderella, she wondered why she should feel so shabby amidst the elegant women ascending the steps with her, wrapped in their furs. She looked back at Val and wondered why the charming prince suddenly seemed so remote and unattainable.

Perhaps this wasn't a fairy tale, but rather the oldest of old stories. He had gotten what he wanted from her, and that was that for him. But it wasn't enough for her. Having reduced her to a fleshly vessel for his pleasure, he had reduced her to wanting him wanting her that way too. She began to know what it felt like to be a slut.

THIRTY-SEVEN

IN THE LOBBY the lights were glittering. The buzz from the crowd upstairs was drifting down the wide double staircase. The sparkle in the air indicated that the champagne was flowing.

Val helped Alexandra with her coat, checked it for her, and followed her up the grand staircase, majestic and squared. Above them the panes of the double glass ceiling glowed with the smoke blue of evening. For all of his trips to Chicago, he had never been to the Art Institute. He discovered that he liked the space, fresh and open. Perhaps he just liked the way Americans partied, or how the Chicagoans put flesh on society occasions, living as they did in a city whose skin was peeled off and whose intestines could be seen at work.

Once in the upper galleries, Alexandra went one way, and he went another. He got two glasses of champagne from a circulating tray, offered one to a gorgeous brunette, strapless in black. French was the order of the moment, and he relaxed into it.

He had worked out enough frustrations on the tennis court to feel good, although he had had to temper his game after the first few aces against Bob in order to play longer than forty-five minutes. He wound up beating him six-oh, six-one, six-oh, throwing one game at the end of the second set simply to encourage his opponent into a third set. Thrashing that mannerless thug had felt right, like a payback long overdue.

He fell into the habits of another time and place, making it easy for him to skate across the surface of the occasion, skimming off the cream. He moved through the galleries in which hung paintings by every one of the canonical Impressionists and some of their most famous canvases too. They struck him as familiar, even overly familiar in a peculiar sort of way.

He was chatting in a group that had stopped before Seurat's *Sunday Afternoon,* that oversized monument to Pointillism. As the discussion meandered, he happened to glance at the painting. The dots of color seized his gaze and drew his focus into the rounded contours of the oil and canvas in a way that was very peculiar, as if he could see into a dimension inside the painting.

Val blinked away and came face to face with a tall, thin man with intelligent features which were rendered stylish by the latest in wire-rim glasses. Val was introduced to Arthur Huxley, head of Special Collections of the museum and one of the hosts of the evening.

"You like the Seurat?" Arthur asked.

"Best of the lot," he agreed cordially. "A coup."

"It was an early acquisition by one of our biggest early donors, Potter Palmer. He was a leading industrialist in Chicago and made a lot of money in hotel chains. He went to Paris a number of times around the turn of the century and put his money behind modernism almost from the beginning. He and his wife really had an eye for composition and could spot the trends."

Val laughed. "What you mean is that modernism wasn't selling in France. It was the Americans who rescued the Parisian modernists by being among the first to buy their art, and to buy it for high prices and in volume. And, then, most American collectors turned around and gave their collections to the new American museums, like this one. After that came the collapse of the French Salon system and the rise in importance of commercial galleries within the modern art world."

Behind his spectacles, Arthur's eyes twinkled. "We offer the story of the good taste of the Potter Palmers mainly for the consumption of our public in general and our patrons in particular. You certainly know your art history. Or, rather, I should say the economics of art history."

Where had that come from? Val most certainly did *not* know his art history, economic or otherwise. He had snoozed through any class or event remotely educational in that domain. He shrugged it off by saying, "I have my own economic interests in the period now that I've acquired my first Salon canvas. I bought it last month. At a gallery in Dallas, no less."

"What did you buy?"

"An Henri Gervex."

Arthur's eyes grew keen. "What a coincidence! We had an inquiry about him, oh, maybe a week or two ago. The curator in European nineteenth- and twentieth-century art couldn't handle it, and I even took a stab at it myself, but my specialty is Renaissance. We're not strong in the Salonist suit here, needless to say. Is there anything else you'd like to see?"

At random Val said, "Horses, maybe."

"This way," Arthur said, inviting him toward another gallery. "We have a roomful of Degas and his Jockey Club series right now. We got some oils on loan, and I've arranged those with many of the sketches and pastels of both horses and spectators that we have by Degas in our archives. I think you'll like the effect."

Val did like the effect, and suddenly he was surrounded by horses. Arthur's attention was claimed by another group, giving Val a moment alone. This time when his gaze was drawn into a painting entitled *At the Racetrack*, he didn't withdraw it. All at once, he was sucked into a space no thicker than several layers of oil paint but vast in dimensions, turning corners he hadn't known were there.

Then he was standing before an opening. It was dark. Only a tingle across his shoulder indicated to him that the next step he took would be down. He took that next step and was relieved to discover that he hadn't entered a slippery chute but rather a staircase where his footing would be firm.

He was descending a spiral, but the curve didn't flare out like a shell, but remained constant like a helix. After going down several turns, his eyes had adjusted enough to the dark to be able to see dimly. He had the sense that he had forgotten where he was. Then he looked around him and remembered that he was in an old château buried deep in Bergerac, descending one half of a clever double spiral staircase, the delight of Renaissance craftsmen. His father had taken him and his sister to that abandoned château. He had put Christine at the bottom of one stairway entry and Val at the top of the other and told them they would meet in the middle.

The spirits were spooking that day. When he was midway down, he was able to perceive Christine a few meters away, going up. She looked like a wraith in the dimness, and she was crying.

"Valéry! Valéry!" she sobbed when she saw him. "I'm scared."

He realized that the staircases didn't intersect, but turned around one another at a constant distance. Their father had played a cruel joke on them. They weren't going to meet.

He reached his hand to her across the central stairwell. "I'll go down, then come back up to get you, Christine."

"You can't," she said, extending her hand in return.

"Don't worry," he assured her. "I'll hurry." He wasn't able to do more than brush the tips of her fingers with his. He had wanted to grasp her hand and halt her, but he wasn't able to stop her ascent anymore than he was able to stop his descent.

"Good-bye, Valéry," she whispered as she disappeared into the next turn above him.

The yawn of loss gaped within him, as he continued to descend. He was surprised when a small round object came from behind him and bounded past him. He caught a glimpse of it before it bounced around the next curve, and he saw that it was a tennis ball. Sent by his father, no doubt, as a last little torment before that twisted man left the top of the twisting staircase. Maybe he had gone to intercept Christine, to comfort her, but Val doubted it.

He followed the ball bouncing ahead him, just out of his reach. He had no choice. Going ever farther down, he felt his evolution in reverse. Before, he had experienced it as a kind of psychological mutation from man to wolf to lizard to wolf again. This time it felt fibrous and physical. He felt his sinew and muscles relayering themselves along his bones. He was aware that his joints were put together differently, so that he held his head and shoulders differently, walked differently. He forgot the loss of his sister as if he had never known it. He felt good. Never better.

HIS FEET HIT solid earth. He bent down toward a carpet of emerald-green grass. He scooped up the ball. He was unsurprised to see that it wasn't rubbery but rather hard. A polo ball. He straightened, and with his free hand, he pitched it back onto the field toward the other riders. In his other hand he was holding the reins of a horse. He looked up into a beautiful blue sky billowed with clouds. He was in the Bois de Boulogne.

The sport had been good that day. He was refreshed and exhilarated. He was leading his horse away from the polo field and toward his groom when he spotted her. He handed away the reins.

He doffed his hat, stripped off his gloves, and watched her as she approached him. He was intrigued, for she was walking alone, although he didn't think she had come to the Bois de Boulogne alone. She was coming from the direction of the racetrack and the stands, which were erected alongside the track on either side of the emperor's pavilion.

From the angle of her path across the grass, she was making a point of telling him that she was coming from the eastern stands, the ones set aside for members of the Jockey Club with a special compartment reserved for ladies. He didn't know how she had gained entry to that privileged space, for she had refused his several invitations to accompany him. However, he knew she wouldn't have come if she had to display herself in the public enclosure where the proſtitutes profited from the men who liked to follow up one good mount and ride around the course with another.

She wasn't the moſt beautiful woman he had ever seen, but she was ſtill the moſt alluring to him, and he never tired of seeing her move. Her dress was simple but à la mode, and she wore it well. It was brown with blue trim at the wide, squared sailor collar and down the side opening of the overskirt. Her parasol was blue with brown trim, and the hat she wore over her glorious golden brown curls was a frivolous confeſtion of satin bows and flocked netting around an excuse of a brim. He wished she would accept to be dressed by him, but she had refused that privilege along with every other.

She had not, of course, been able to prevent him from buying the building in which she had her rooms. But relieving her of ever again paying rent was a paltry service compared with what he was capable of doing for her financially, not to mention that it fell far short of what a man of his ſtanding would cuſtomarily do for a woman under his proteſtion.

She didn't quite ever let him forget the modeſt terms of their arrangement either. Every now and then, he would offer to buy her jewelry or clothing or paintings. With her arms twined around his neck, she would thank him and refuse him by whispering into his ear, "You saved me from the cruel ſtreets of Paris. Surely that is enough."

"I can do more for you."

"But that is all I choose."

Meaning that she had guessed from the ſtart that he had put her in the impossible position of either entering into a liaison with him or facing the end of her comfort at Le Chat Noir. Of course, he wouldn't have forced her hand in such an ungentlemanly fashion if it hadn't been clear to him that she was going to make him force it; and once it was forced, she enjoyed the game of claiming that she had made a choice in the matter.

Next she would kiss him, caress him, and add, "Why would you imagine that I would want more from you than I already have?"

She had learned her part so fast and so well that he wasn't sure what it was anymore. He knew only that her refusals kept alive his desire to give her what she wouldn't take, which included avoiding all his public advances. But here she was in the Bois de Boulogne, coming up to him now on her own initiative. He could not have been better pleased.

She bobbed him a curtsy of greeting.

"Mademoiselle," he said, taking one of her gloved hands and bowing over it.

She did not let her hand rest in his. "When I wanted to distract myself from the tedium of the races and went to pace behind the stands, I saw you coming off the field, and I was seized by a thought I wanted to share with you."

He teased, in mock-seriousness, "I must tell you, mademoiselle, that the races are not usually described as tedious, but rather the contrary."

She laughed. "I had my program and pencil in hand and was trying my best to question and fuss and choose the right horses, but my heart has never been in betting, and I abandoned the effort! Besides, my companions glued their eyes to their lorgnettes and wouldn't let me look, so I was at a loss to observe the action in detail."

"I'm glad that you chose instead to seek out my company."

"It should be more interesting, in all events, than a race that bores me!"

He bowed. "You flatter me."

She bobbed another curtsy. "I did not mean to, sir. Tell me, did you have a good ride?"

He saw her, then, not as his most delicious mistress, but as a young lady who flirted with reserve and whom he must court. He assured her the riding had been good. "And I propose to tell you all about it over lunch. Will you join me at the Jockey Club? I'm engaged there with the minister of commerce and the prefect of the

Seine, but I can easily bow out of what will be a very dull discussion. They will understand when they see you. And envy me for my charming company."

She shook her head. "Don't disappoint them, for I'm engaged with my friends for lunch, and then I must return to Paris." Her little gesture suggested that she would be at Le Chat Noir by four o'clock. "I only came to tell you that, seeing you now, I was seized by an idea."

"Ah, yes, your idea. By all means, share it."

"Well, I can see that you are a very fine horseman," she said, "and I am sure you enjoy training your animals, but I was thinking about the discussion we had last week at the art gallery where I ran into you, and I don't think your first love is horses."

"It isn't?"

"No, because it occurred to me from the way that you speak with the artists that you take less of an interest in the colors and the subjects and more of an interest in how they mix their paints. A very intense interest, in fact." She was wrapped in the blue shadows of her parasol, and a tint of deeper blue welled in the tiny scar on her cheek. "Now, I have been learning about the study of how materials—like oil paints and such—are composed. It's very specialized and concerns itself with what one can't even see. It has something to do with 'elements,' I think." She frowned in concentration, but was unembarrassed by her ignorance. "No, I can't remember the name of the study. But I am sure that is what you must pursue."

He was listening to this with some astonishment. "Do you mean, the study of chemistry?"

A lovely light came on in her soft brown eyes. She smiled at him, gratefully. "Yes, chemistry. I think you must learn about chemistry."

"So that I can learn to mix paints, perhaps?"

She shook her head, as if she disapproved of the slowness of her pupil. "There are many uses for chemistry, I think. Why, mixing medicines is one of them, no? Or so Dr. Dreyfus was telling me."

Later that night, she had already returned to her rooms from work when he came to her, and after she had fed him cake with her fingers, they were lying together in her bed. His thoughts drifted back to their earlier conversation, and he wondered whether she might not know him better than he knew himself.

The air was warm and fragrant, and her flesh was firm and known to him, but not yet well enough. She still liked to resist him, and he still liked her resistance and the way she would yield to him, but not completely, so that when he took her, he always wanted more. This evening, thoughts of chemistry were unexpectedly erotic, and he was ready before they had settled into kissing and touching and caressing.

He rolled over her and caught the startled look of capture in her eyes that stimulated him further. He pressed himself to her. Her lids fluttered shut, but he wanted to look at her now, having all of her open and available to him.

"Open your eyes," he commanded.

She obeyed. She had her own fashion of obeying, after a fraction of a heartbeat, as if she might choose to deny him.

But her eyes were open. Her gaze was upon him and threaded with his, and he entered her smoothly, with a groan of delight.

"Melt around me," he commanded.

And she did, having no resources of resistance against his sweetly muscular assault.

"YOU LIKE THE Degas?" came a woman's voice at his side. With great effort, Val disentangled his gaze from the painting and returned to his immediate surroundings as if from a very long distance. He felt his joints and muscles conforming themselves to their accustomed patterns, but something inside was different, as if the house he had left was being rearranged even as he was moving back into it.

The woman said, "You were staring at that painting for a full two minutes at least."

Only two minutes? It had felt like hours.

"So, what do you think of Degas?"

An hour ago Val wouldn't have had an opinion. Now he did. "Degas is a fine craftsman," he said, "but on a personal level he was always too much of an anti-Semite for my taste."

The woman laughed. "Does anti-Semitism come in degrees?"

"In France at the end of the last century it did."

The woman held out her hand. "Hello. I'm Ruth Grossman. Tell me more."

When Val began to tell her, his internal kaleidoscope started to churn with painful effect, particularly in his lower back. His out-of-body trip to the Bois de Boulogne made him think, first, that he was losing his mind and, second, that he was losing his game.

Why not face the facts? His beloved sister was long dead and gone, and his miracle diagnostic product could not save her now. Might not ever save anyone, with the patents so bedeviled. He should rather save his sanity and drop the absurd suspicion that Jean-Philippe was behind all his problems and the even more absurd fancy that Alexandra was in some far-fetched league with him.

So why not get off the court and out of the tournament? He could spare himself worlds of pain, lifetimes of pain. Quitting wasn't new to him. He'd quit before, hadn't he? Never won a Grand Slam title. Never honored his sister's memory. Never completed a project. Just quit. Find oblivion and blessed relief from pain.

THIRTY-EIGHT

THE IMPRESSIONIST PAINTINGS had made Alexandra nervous, so she moved restlessly from room to room all evening. At one point she found herself next to a perfectly agreeable-looking man who introduced himself as Arthur Huxley. She had the oddest notion that he regarded her as some kind of female animal in heat, although not on a conscious level. He didn't come on to her in an overt fashion, but he was certainly attentive. Maybe it was her sexy dress of old gold. Or maybe it was the age-old response to her showing interest in his work. The more she listened to him describe his work as head of Special Collections, the more she became truly interested.

"You say your files are strongest in the Impressionist period?" she asked. "What would those files contain exactly?"

"Correspondence mostly. Original letters written by some of the artists themselves. Or the records of the dealers, say, from the most important galleries, such as Paul Durand-Ruel, with the prices particular paintings sold for and who they were sold to. Good stuff, that. Some years ago, at lot sales, we bought boxes of stuff that had been retrieved from old music halls."

"Music halls?" she asked quickly.

"The Folies-Bergère and Le Moulin Rouge, of course. Then La

Cigale. Le Divan Japonais. Le Chat Noir. The buy was a big disappointment, because there weren't any sketches in the stuff, only account ledgers from the establishments and not much more."

She tried for a tone that was halfway between enticing and prim. "What would it take for me to see those records now?"

Arthur bowed gallantly. "Your wish, ma'am . . . and all that."

He led her down the main staircase and across the lobby toward the Ryerson and Burnham Libraries whose doors were open for the evening. Other reception guests were heading toward the libraries just then, and some were already there.

The newly renovated room was spacious and well lit and a beaux-arts jewel with high half-moon windows set in curved, vaulted alcoves. Arthur led her through a door to one side and into a small office. He indicated the set of files against the wall and ran his hand down the drawers. "Will any music hall do, or is there a particular one that interests you?"

"Le Chat Noir, please."

He opened a lower drawer and pulled out the first cluttered file in the row. He started leafing through the documents, shrugged as if it was of no particular value.

"We can find out quite a bit from bills and account ledgers, no?" she inquired, hoping he could cough up some information she could use.

"Yes, but these things are of more interest to sociologists and economic historians than to art historians."

"So, what might interest a sociologist in all of this?"

Arthur was scanning the materials before him. "We know that there was a proprietor, a Maurice somebody or other—what was his last name? I'd have to go to the beginning of this mess to find out—and, among other things . . . oh, his wife must have died."

She was looking over his shoulder and looking at the papers, but since the French made no more sense to her now than it had any other time, she was startled into saying, "What?"

"It seems the former owner's wife died after he sold the music hall to—"

"Was her name Charlotte?" Alexandra demanded.

Her tone was sharp enough to cause Arthur's eyebrows to rise. "It doesn't say. The only facts marked here are the dates, namely the date of sale and the date of his wife's death. That's a bit of bad luck coming so soon after he entered the ranks of the comfortably well-off. He got a good price for Le Chat Noir."

Her heart was beginning a sickening thud. "How soon after he sold it did she die?"

"A little over four weeks."

"What did she die of?"

"It doesn't say, of course, but here are the bills from the funeral which came a few days later and were posted in the next month. You see, here's a doctor's bill. Not much delicacy to send a bill when the quack didn't save her. Well, I'll be! Here's another doctor's bill. No, not a bill because there's no charge, but there's a diagnosis of consomption irrémédiable." He turned to Alexandra and wagged his eyebrows. "I guess so, since she died. We have the bonus of the doctor's signature." He studied it. "Laur . . . ent Drey . . . fus. And that's a big maybe. The medical man's handwriting is always the archivist's worst enemy."

"Consumption? That's tuberculosis, right?" she ventured on a horrified whisper.

"It was very common back then, especially among the working classes. That and syphilis, of course, got the best of them."

Alexandra's blood ran ice cold. Charlotte had died. Of tuberculosis. One month after she had set Alexandra up with Val in the hallway of the Duke Medical Center. No, one month after Charlotte had set Jeanne up with Victor.

Then it dawned on her. Erica was Charlotte.

"Can I use your phone?" she asked, her voice trembling.

"Be my guest."

"It's long distance," she said, "and it's urgent."

He waved her graciously to the phone, and she punched in the numbers to the lab. It rang once, twice.

"Pick up! Pick up!" she muttered into the receiver.

It was Friday evening and an hour later in North Carolina, and she hadn't really expected anyone to be there. Her heart leapt when Scotty answered.

"McCarthy!" she cried. "It's me, Alexandra!"

"A.K.!" he replied. "Great news! You'll never believe it!"

She gave profound thanks to Saint Hyacinth and crossed herself. "I'm so happy!"

"How can you be happy when you haven't even heard what it is yet? Our team was selected at the last minute to go to the International Oncology Conference in Paris in two weeks. We applied last summer, you remember, and were turned down. There must have been a cancellation or something, because Larry just got the call from the organizers this afternoon."

International Oncology Conference? Paris? Alexandra was having difficulty making sense of this conversation. "No, Scotty, I'm trying to get hold of Erica. I need to talk to her. The direct number to her room is penciled on the wall above the phone. It's circled by a skull and crossbones."

"That would be Erica's," Scotty acknowledged. "Yup. Here it is." He gave it to her. "Isn't that great about Par—"

Alexandra had already hung up and was redialing. When the voice of the head nurse came on the line, she knew the worst had happened.

Was happening. Erica was still alive but very weak and not expected to make it through the night. She hung up. Flipped through the phone book at hand, tearing pages. American Airlines, 800 number. Punched all the correct service buttons. Why was technology so slow?

When she had the information she wanted, she slammed the phone down. "I need my coat and a taxi." She hurried out of the room, with Arthur leading the way to the vestibule. "There's an 8:35 flight to Durham. I think I can just make it."

Arthur looked down at the dainty evening bag in her hand. "You might need a ticket."

She shook her head. "I'll beg my way onto the plane."

"You can't beg your way onto a plane, and you can't beg taxi rides," he pointed out. "Not in this town."

She realized he was right. She also realized, from the way he was looking at her, that he must have had a good view down the front of her dress when she had been bending over looking up phone numbers. She smiled with a hint of inquiry.

He pulled out his wallet, withdrew a credit card and two twenty dollar bills. He handed them to her.

She accepted, her smile shifting to one of profound gratitude. "I'll send the credit card back to you tomorrow by overnight mail."

He brought out another twenty, pressed it into her hand as well. "For whatever. You never know."

She thought this was a great way to earn money and wondered why she hadn't gone this route a long time ago. She blew him a kiss, then turned to go.

She turned back around. "Find a man named Val Dorsainville — he's around here somewhere — and tell him I had to leave." Her smile melted him. "Oh! And tell him to call my grandmother to let her know I'll get in touch with her in the morning."

Then she hurried across the lobby and ducked into the first wedge of the revolving door.

FROM THE TOP of the staircase, Val watched Alexandra accept money from the head of Special Collections, run across the lobby, and disappear into the refractions of the revolving door. He waited as Huxley mounted the stairs, heading straight toward him.

"I couldn't be more interested in what you might have to tell me,"

Val said when the man correctly identified him as the Dorsainville he had met earlier.

Huxley gave him the brief and surprising rundown on events, and Val was left to make of it what he could. Then Huxley adjusted his glasses and said, "Say, just a few minutes ago I noticed in the records the name of the person who bought the music hall the woman in the gold dress was interested in. It was Dorsainville."

A fine intuition led Val to the question, "Victor Louis Dorsainville, perhaps?"

"I think so. Want to see the bill of sale?"

Val did. As they descended the stairs and crossed the lobby together, heading toward the library, Val said, "My Great-Uncle Victor had diverse interests, it seems. I knew that he bought a chemical company in the eighties of the last century, but I had no idea he had ever bought a music hall. Wouldn't have even guessed it."

"I seem to recall seeing a title on the bill of sale after his name. Count, perhaps? No, one wouldn't normally guess that a man of his standing would buy a music hall. But, then, those guys back then did what they wanted."

The pain Val had experienced earlier was submerged in a wave of emotions that were thick with strength and appetite. "Yes, Great-Uncle Victor seemed to do what he wanted. From what I can tell, he had a way of arranging things to his satisfaction."

Huxley laughed and said, "Sounds like my kind of guy."

Val smiled. "Exactly."

The competitor in Val roared to life. He wasn't ready to quit. Not yet. Not until he had Alexandra right where he wanted her, and that was under his thumb. Not until he had broken Jean-Philippe's serve and sent him off the court with his tail between his legs. Not until he had regained everything Great-Uncle Victor had possessed.

That's what he wanted—all that and more. Nothing less would do, and no one was going to stand in his way. A taste of the ruthlessness he was sure his Great-Uncle Victor had had in abundance came to his tongue. It tasted great.

THIRTY-NINE

ERICA HEARD SOMEONE enter her room. She opened her eyes, saw on the bedside clock that it was 12:01 A.M. Wondered, idly, why anyone in her condition would ever need to know what time it was. She turned her head with effort from one side of the pillow to the other. She beheld the vision of a lovely golden princess, from the top of her golden hair to the tips of her—well, Erica could see only as far as the generous cleavage and the topmost buttons of a golden sheath dress. Sure beat looking at a clock.

"Nice fashion statement for a deathbed scene, Coach," she greeted her visitor.

"Erica," Kaminski said with a sad rush of emotion and sat down on the bedside chair.

Erica felt her hand being taken and held. She was wrapped in Kaminski's scent, which was mixed either with expensive perfume or cheap shampoo. Either way Kaminski smelled fresh and clean and healthy. One of life's little pleasures.

"I came straight from the airport," Kaminski was telling her. "You cannot imagine the delays! I was so frustrated and anxious I can hardly tell you! But I made it before—" She broke off.

"No need to finish that thought, eh, Coach? But, listen, you're hurting me."

"I'm sorry, Erica! I'm so sorry!"

"My hand, Coach. I'm referring to my hand. You're squeezing it too hard."

"Oh!"

Erica was relieved when the painful pressure on her hand was released. "That's better. No, you don't have to let go completely. Now, you came to tell me a story."

"I did?"

Coach could be such a dumb shit sometimes. "You didn't?"

Kaminski smiled down at her. "You need your rest now. I'll tell you the story tomorrow."

Erica shook her head against the pillow. "Nice try, Coach. So. I take it you've encountered some past lives."

"One, anyway."

"And—?"

"And I began to believe it when the patterns began to repeat themselves around me. Actually, I'm still not sure I believe it completely, but I don't have an alternative, rational explanation for what I've been experiencing."

"Do rational explanations occupy some privileged position in this world?"

"For some people, yes, but I'm not fighting the irrational explanations anymore. Even so, it's confusing. I've been able to identify a number of people from my previous life, but there's one I can't quite figure out. He was a café owner in Paris, and his name was Piotr, that is Pierre, Wojinski. He may have turned up as Bobby Dembrowski in Chicago, but the two don't add up. Although they both have violent streaks, Bobby assaulted me when I was in high school, while Piotr was my unfailing protector in Paris."

"People don't always come back intact from one time to the next. An old self can split into two or three, and a new self can be cobbled together from bits and pieces of other selves."

"But sometimes a self reconfigures itself precisely, no?"

"Of course." Damn, this was tiring, and Erica wasn't interested in discussing the baby basics of reincarnation. "All right, who did you see in Chicago? Besides Lover Boy, of course."

"You knew Val would be in Chicago?"

"Look, I don't have tons of time for small talk, Coach. This is story hour, and it's your turn to entertain me. Make it a good one."

Kaminski laced the fingers of one hand through hers and with the other smoothed each of her fingers in turn. That felt good. Better than the morphine sliding through her system.

Kaminski cleared her throat. "I'll have you know that this week I met three young ladies."

"Do I know them?"

"You employed them once as dancers in a music hall in Paris. This time around they're graduate students in French at Northwestern."

Erica lifted her head from the pillow. "*Grad students?* Oh, Christ, they'll never get jobs. Are they stupid? No, don't answer that. Of course, they're stupid. No doubt, last time around I gave them the bad advice to go into academics!" She sank back again, her strength spent. "So what did you talk about?"

"Mostly the old times," Kaminski told her. "Painting too. It was a lovely discussion." Her voice sounded like she was choking up. "I wish you could have been there." Then she stopped talking.

"You're going to make me guess the rest? I'm not kidding, Coach, this is the end."

Kaminski swallowed audibly and pressed on. "We were talking about how some paintings are considered good art, while others are considered bad art, and the reasons are always so . . . well, they're not arbitrary exactly but historically conditioned, I guess you might say, just like ourselves."

Erica felt an inward smile that took far too much effort to reach her lips. "That sure does bring back the good times. Yeah, now I remember. You girls were always a little flaky about stuff like that, but kinda sweet, each of you in her own way." She was recruiting what little strength she had left. "All that's beside the point. Tell me about you."

"I . . . I don't know what to tell."

Erica scrutinized the golden vision of her Slavic Queen. "In the interests of saving time, let's get right to the point. Was the sex good?"

Kaminski looked away. "Well, we had been playing pool, you see, and it was—"

"What did I tell you before you left Durham?"

"Not to have sex with him."

"That's right, and did I have a reason for telling you that?"

"I don't know—something to do with him being the death of me? But, Erica, that's so far-fetched! We've already determined that he's not an ax murderer, not the violent man in my life. I don't think there's any harm he could or would do me, much less kill me or anything, and so—"

"You've answered my question. The sex was good. Them's hormones talkin', honey. Loud and clear."

"So how do I die, then? Does he have AIDS or something?"

The Slavic Queen sounded indignant, even outraged to have to consider her own death. Funny how people were like that. Been there. Moved on. Moving on.

"News flash, Coach. I go before you. See? I don't know how you die." But, if I felt like telling you, which I don't—too much effort, not right, your karma not mine—your death is quick, and it comes soon. "This much I will say. I wish I could be there for you."

Silence.

Erica became aware of moisture on her hand and arm. She strained to get her golden vision in focus and saw that Kaminski was weeping openly. Not even trying to hide her tears. Such a good kid.

"Just as I should have been there for you." Kaminski sniffed. "I shouldn't have let you—let you get to this point."

"To the point of dying, you mean? You can say it, Coach. It won't hurt you. Or maybe it will, but that's the way it goes. Here's my last bit of advice, for better or worse." She inhaled painfully. "You've got to learn to put your visions to work for you, Coach." She exhaled, just as painfully, and croaked, "Now, lean close."

Kaminski obeyed, looking straight into Erica's eyes through her tears.

"Ask me what the secret to good comedy is."

Kaminski blanked.

Erica recruited the last of her strength. "I asked you to ask me what the secret to good comedy is."

Kaminski still looked blank, but at least she had the sense to sniff, then ask, "What's the secret—"

"Timing," Erica said, feeling a final spurt of satisfaction.

"—to good comedy?"

With the last of the lights in her eyes, Erica saw—one beat, two beats, Coach was such a dumb shit—her register the joke, then smile.

"That's funny, Erica. How do you do it?"

Erica's eyes fluttered. She rattled out of her diseased body, left pain mercifully behind.

Encountered utter darkness. The Void. The Null and Void.

A belated spasm of fear. She hadn't expected nothingness.

First thought, no, last: So the joke's on me!

An astral being appeared before her. Before she disintegrated into a gossamer smear of cells and molecules and proteins and atoms and quarks, she recognized the being as Lucille Ball. Hot damn. Lucy. As in *I Love*—

Lucy laughed and showed her the way.

Then whoosh—a cosmic *Gotcha!*

ERICA CLOSED HER eyes.

"Erica?" Alexandra whispered.

No response.

When she realized that her good friend had breathed her last, Alexandra put her head down on the empty body of skin and bones and cried until she became aware of the two shadowy figures at the foot of the bed, shifting uncomfortably.

She rose to greet them and saw that the man was as fat as the woman was skinny. She guessed they were Erica's parents.

"I'm a friend of your daughter's," she said and introduced herself.

"I'm Maury," the man said, "and this here is my wife, Fran."

"She was my baby," Fran said, the deep wrinkles in her face sagging at sight of the dead body in the bed.

"Smart as a whip," Maury offered, sadly. "The teachers in Shelby, they didn't know what to do with her."

Fran repeated, "Smart as a whip."

"The customers loved her." Maury looked down at his daughter, then looked up at Alexandra as if the wind had been knocked out of him. "Fran and me, we run the Southern Comfort Bar and Grill in Shelby, and Erica"—here his voice broke—"could have the men, mostly truckers, you know, rolling off their chairs, laughing."

At that, Fran began to cough, and it was several minutes before she recovered.

Maury poked his forefinger into Fran's bone of an upperarm. "I always thought Fran here would be the first to go. Smokes like a chimney."

After another extended fit of coughing, Fran said, "I'm gonna have me a coffin nail now." She patted in the purse slung over her shoulder. "I'm gonna light up right here too. None of that second-hand smoke can't hurt my baby now. No, sir."

With tears still streaming down her face, Alexandra said, "I should have saved your daughter, but I wasn't in time." She gulped for air, fought against sadness and defeat. "I haven't found the cure."

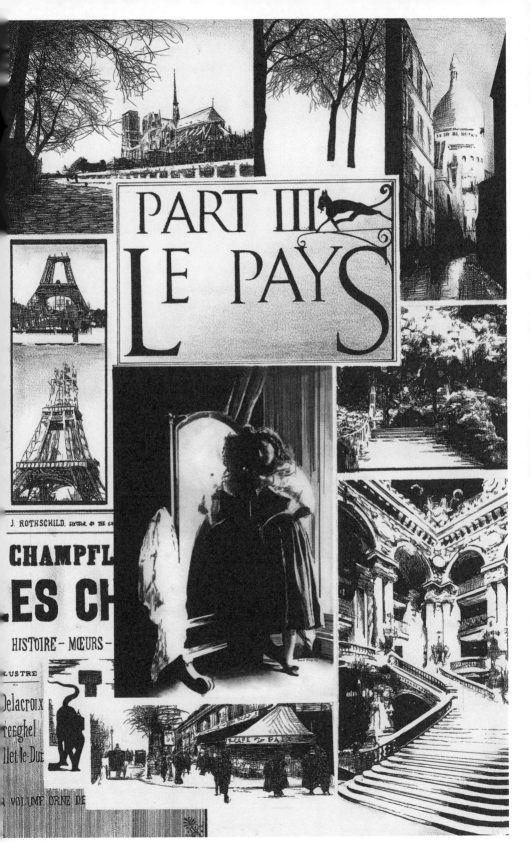

PART III
LE PAYS

FORTY

 THEY STROLLED DOWN the Champs-Elysées. The Arc de Triomphe was behind them. Before them in the distance wavered the Place de la Concorde with its fountains and the obelisk of Louqsor.

Looking at the elegant square ahead, Scotty remarked thoughtfully, "You know, the French like to give the finger from almost every direction. From the air it's the Eiffel Tower. On the ground, well, just look at that thing sticking up."

"It's no different from the Washington Monument," Jack retorted, "and you didn't say Washington was giving us the finger when we were there last year for the molecular biology meeting."

Scotty was unperturbed. "No comparison. The Washington Monument is a Puritan prick. But what could you expect? D.C. has no attitude, only a bunch of bureaucrats. Paris has attitude, and it's giving us the finger all over the place."

They continued on past McDonald's, the Mercedes Benz show room, and Virgin Megastore. Walking beside them, Alexandra wasn't participating in the discussion. She was reacting to every new sight and sound as might a person coming down with a bad cold. Her head was filling with sensory impressions that were putting pressure on her temples.

A part of her hadn't wanted to come to Paris. Another part had been dying to come. Neither part had made the decision. The Tuesday morning she entered the lab at Duke after her return from Chicago, Larry had held up five plane tickets. They were for the team to fly to the International Oncology Conference.

Alexandra had hesitated, shocked at the thought of going to France and still reeling from the loss of Erica, whose funeral had been the day before.

"I thought our application was turned down months ago," she said.

"It was, but the committee's reversed itself, and I'm thinking it's your recent work on telomeres that might have put us over the top."

"But I just began that work," she protested.

"Face it, telomerase is the rising star of enzymes, and we're in on the ground floor. Now, whatever the reason for the last-minute invitation, I'll take it! I got a call from Yves himself today, offering the best wishes of Seine-Lafitte. How he heard the news I'll never know but, damn, this feels good!"

"We'll be in Paris in two weeks!" Scotty and Jack crowed, not quite in unison.

"My passport isn't current," Alexandra said. The part of her that didn't want to go had found the perfect excuse not to go.

Larry waved this away. "Yves anticipated the difficulty, and his connections at the State Department will smooth out any passport problems." He handed her a ticket. "Start packing."

And here she was, walking down the Champs-Elysées, feeling unwell. Maybe it was only jet lag. Maybe it was continuing grief over Erica's death and concern for her spirit which, she imagined, was restlessly traveling the bardo plane. Maybe it was foreign springtime pollens, since the glories of May were almost upon them. Or maybe it was the weather. The late-afternoon clouds billowed above in pillows of whipped cream, but the sky behind hinted at rain.

And nothing looked familiar, but what had she expected?

She had expected a miracle of sorts—not that her recent experiences weren't miraculous enough, but given those experiences, she had thought she would recognize something, anything, or at least feel as if she were returning home. But in the two days since she had been in Paris, her surroundings felt not only unfamiliar but distinctly alien. Added to which, she couldn't understand a word of spoken French and couldn't read it beyond her limited high school level of proficiency. She had imagined, yes, she had truly imagined that she would step off the plane and pass, like Alice, through the looking glass into an altered existence.

So far that hadn't happened. But once or twice, a Parisian smell had stirred her brain like a language she had once been fluent in. As she walked beside Scotty and Jack now, she detected, curling through the urban exhaust fumes, the evocative whiff of distinctive cigarette smoke blending with a bakery aroma that held little in common with Kolatek's. Suddenly she understood every word of the conversation of the couple strolling behind them speaking in a language other than English.

She was so startled that she stopped dead in her tracks, turned, and stared at the couple. They stopped too and regarded her politely a moment. Then the man said, "Vous désirez quelque chose, mademoiselle?"

The illusion was shattered. The man had switched into French, when he had previously been speaking Polish. She mumbled an apology and an excuse in Polish and turned back around. The pressure at her temples increased. She'd had a version of this blasted headache since the day she went to the Art Institute.

Scotty turned off the classy drag and ushered them down a quiet, tony side street before announcing, "Here we are." He gestured proudly at the display window of a small establishment.

Alexandra's eyes popped open, and Jack exclaimed, "This is a porno boutique! Jesus, McCarthy! I thought we were going to the most upscale science bookstore in Paris."

"This *is* a science," Scotty replied, feigning mild surprise at the objection. He peered into the window. "The sheets with the Velcro straps for nights of gentle bondage are a little tame for my taste, but the collection of riding crops is nice." He turned to his companions. "You can't tell me this stuff isn't top shelf."

Jack was disgusted. "How do you do it, McCarthy? We've been here less than forty-eight hours and already you've found the most out-of-the-way sex shop in Paris. Is it an instinct?"

"My excellent research skills," Scotty said. "I got the address from someone at the reception last night."

The opening reception for the International Oncology Conference had been held the evening before at the Hôtel de Ville, a magnificent Renaissance edifice elbowing the Seine on the right bank across from the Ile de la Cité. Alexandra had left the event early, telling Larry that she was feeling stuffed up and wanted to ward off a cold with a good night's sleep. She had been unwilling to admit to herself that she had felt horribly out of place there.

Jack folded his arms across his chest. "I'll stay outside and wait with Alexandra." He had gotten himself a shave and a haircut for the trip. For emphasis he flourished his chin, whose skin was several shades paler than his cheeks.

Although Alexandra's curiosity was piqued, she realized that Jack was embarrassed about the sex shop in a way that she wasn't. She decided that it wasn't so much a question of Jack's staying outside to wait with her but of her staying outside to wait with him.

"You go on in, Scotty, and I'll take Jack up on his offer to stay outside with me. All right, Jack, it's you and me and the street."

Then it came to her, slowly, dimly. Jack was a player in her life. Kind, gentle, overprotective Jack. She hadn't yet considered Jack's role in all of this, but her thoughts were too sluggish at the moment to sort it out now.

FORTY-ONE

VAL LANDED AT Orly, feeling good. He knew he was down a full set if not more, but he had his second wind now and was confident that he could psych out his opponent enough to beat him at his own game.

He went straight to his office and was through the Institut Pasteur/Abbey Labs dossier before noon. He learned nothing new. He hadn't expected to, but he did have to start somewhere. The first item he encountered in the file was a letter of denial from the French National Patent Register that had arrived a few days before. It was a tour de force of ambiguity with a masterful hint of threat that the patent not be pursued at this time and a supercilious suggestion of possible actionable infringement on the part of cher Monsieur Dorsainville.

He interpreted the denial as a delay and figured only that he wasn't scoring points because it wasn't his serve. Yet. He spent the rest of the day catching up on paperwork and company gossip. Toward the end of the afternoon he took a taxi to the apartment he owned in the Sixteenth. He picked up his mail from the *gardienne*, took a quick shower and shave, and upon giving the matter some thought, changed into one of his most formal suits. Then he grabbed an old key ring from a set of hooks in the front hall and called to have his collector's Citroën brought around from the garage across the street. When he pulled away from the curb, he headed toward a part of town where he hadn't been in a long, long time.

He worked his way through the usual jams of the Paris rush hour. Came to the respectable and unremarkable Place Clichy. Found an improbable parking place. Walked up to the door of an apartment building and put the key on the old ring to the lock. He was pleased and a little surprised when the door opened. Once inside the court-yard, he scanned the row of buzzers and pushed the button next to the miniature brass plate inscribed: François-Xavier Dorsainville.

After waiting several interminable minutes, an ancient voice crackled through the speaker. "Oui?"

He identified himself. The door to the lobby buzzed open. He took the stairs two at a time to the second floor where the door was al-ready open on the landing. An old woman was standing there. They kissed on both cheeks.

"You've come," she said, drawing him inside, and closing the door behind him.

"I've come, grand-mère."

"I made tea," she told him. She began to shuffle down the hallway. "Plum cake too."

"Ma foi," he muttered, following her. Aloud he said, "You're still making your plum cake?"

She raised a gnarled hand in dismissal. "Not often. No." She stopped at the first door on her left, the one to the salon. She waved him in. "Sit. I will fetch the tea and cake."

"Can I help you, grand-mère? Let me help you."

She shook her head. "Sit. Sit." She patted his cheek. She blinked at him in a way that made him think her eyes were glazed with glau-coma, but he couldn't say for sure in the dimness of the room which allowed little light from the dying day.

She left him for the kitchen.

He longed to pull the heavy curtains back from the tall windows that overlooked avenue de Clichy. He looked around the room that smelled of wood polish and a widow who had lived alone too long. It was filled with heirloom furniture and memories of the Dorsainville fortune, which had shrunk to this apartment in the Ninth, his in the Sixteenth, and his grandfather's Citroën, which he had restored several years before. He went to one wall and regarded the yellowing photographs on the undusted and melancholy shelves. He had thought of these pictures the moment he had set eyes on Alexandra as she had walked down the hallway at Seine-Lafitte on the other side of the Atlantic. He gazed at them critically, trying to find something he should be looking for. He waited for his internal kaleidoscope to begin churning, pleasantly or not, but nothing came.

He turned away from the shelves. Just as well. He was taking one thing at a time, and he had come here for one purpose only.

His grandmother returned. Her hold on the heavy tray was precarious, so he took it from her and set it on the tea table before the settee. He seated her on the settee, then took his place in an armchair next to her.

"I've come to see how you're getting along, grand-mère," he said, watching her shaking hands at the teapot, ready to retrieve a slip.

She didn't act as if she had heard him. "I made it just the way you like it," she said, cutting the cake and serving it. When she handed him a plate, she said, "You always liked my plum cake, didn't you, Victor?"

An eerie sensation skittered down his spine. He shook it off. He took the plate and gently corrected, "I'm Valéry. I'm your grandson."

She looked at him. After a moment, she smiled, undisturbed by her mistake, and said, "That's right. Victor's hair was almost completely silver in the days when he would come, oh, once a week, it seemed, to have my plum cake. He was so distinguished. His manners were excellent. He dressed well."

He bit into the cake and tasted Alexandra and ambition. He asked, "How do you skin your plums, grand-mère?"

"With a knife," she said.

He pushed aside thoughts of Alexandra to concentrate on the

matter at hand. He could exploit his grandmother's lapse into remi-
niscence. "Great-Uncle Victor and my grandfather were great friends,
so grandfather always told me."

"Who?"

"Grandfa—François-Xavier."

"Ah. Yes." She sighed. "He died, you know."

About twenty-five years ago. "I know, grand-mère. I was at his
funeral. I was there with my mother and my sister and my father."

"Who?"

This was going to be harder than he had thought. "I attended your
husband's funeral with your son, Robert."

"That was nice of you."

"Speaking of François-Xavier, I wonder if you know whether he
left any drawings of his inventions. You remember that he liked to
invent things. Odd mechanical things. Contraptions."

She repeated the word *contraptions* as if trying to conjure a mythic
beast.

"Do you know if he left drawings," he repeated, "or papers of any
kind? Perhaps records of patent applications. Or letters."

A sudden smile dawned, smoothing her fine network of wrinkles.
"Letters. Yes." She rose and inched to the exquisite Louis-Napoléon
desk by the door, shuffled back with a thin pack of letters tied with a
thick ribbon of lavender silk.

He took the pack from her shaking hands, and his own hands
shook slightly to see the topmost letter directed to Victor Louis Dorsainville, Hôtel d'Albret, rue du Faubourg-Saint-Honoré. The
script was beautiful, and the initial *V* was elaborately curlicued. He
tugged off the ribbon and slid the top envelope to the bottom. The
second letter was addressed to a Mademoiselle Odette Someone or
other but the ink of her family name was so faded that he couldn't
make out anything but an initial *C*—or was it a *G*? Her address was
mostly faded as well, but from the letters he was able to put together,
he could probably determine the address if he tried. Her name, however, meant nothing to him.

He looked up at his grandmother who was smiling down on him. He hadn't come here on the trail of Great-Uncle Victor, but then the image of the flirty girl atop the antique biscuit tin Alexandra had given him skidded into his thoughts. It passed by his mind's eye too quickly for him to catch the feeling that went with it, and he didn't try to retrieve the distracting image. He had a vague notion of looking into the matter of the music hall in Montmartre—but only after he had come to terms with other, more important issues.

He was beginning to regret having come to his grandmother's. He hadn't realized that she had slipped this far into senility.

His grandmother sat down, wearing an expression of expectation and encouragement. He shuffled the letters to their original order and obliged his grandmother by opening the first envelope and scanning the letter. It was from Mademoiselle Odette, whose last name he still could not decipher, and it was a love letter, making it highly unlikely that the rest of the correspondence would yield anything of interest to him. He put the thick linen sheet back in the envelope, retied the ribbon. He tried to think of another way to get the information he needed.

His grandmother was plainly pleased with herself. "Take the letters," she said. "They're yours."

He gestured in refusal and tried to hand the letters back to her but she wouldn't take them. She even began to look a little distressed, so he reversed himself and said he'd be delighted to take them. Sliding them into his inside coat pocket, he thanked her.

"You're welcome," she said. "I've been meaning to give them back to you for some time now, and I can't think how I've failed to return them to you week after week! But when you sent your note around this morning, letting me know you would visit this evening, I went straight to the kitchen to make you my plum cake and wouldn't let any of my serving girls help me! I'm so glad you mentioned the letters yourself. Otherwise, I fear the matter would have flown out of my mind again!"

He hadn't sent her any note, and her obvious time-warped confusion encouraged him to switched tactics. "I'm glad I came and mentioned the letters too. But I was hoping to see François-Xavier so that I could ask him about his inventions. I see he's not here, so perhaps you could answer a few of my questions."

She nodded. "He's out riding the horse you broke for him. He'll be back later. I'll be happy to answer your questions as long as you don't ask me about his foolish inventions!"

This strategy wasn't going to work either, so he abandoned the effort of playing into her delusions. "Grand-mère, do you mind if I look around for other papers or records? I'll begin with the desk."

"Be my guest," she said cordially, then chuckled. "It's all yours anyway."

He went to the desk, and while he was opening and shutting drawers that were surprisingly empty, she mused, "We inherited everything from you, you know, but we lost it. François-Xavier just didn't have the head for business that you had, I'm afraid! A pity! I always thought it would have been better if you had had children. Of course, I admired your wife. Oh, yes! But she wouldn't make you the plum cake just the way you had me make it for you. You should have had children. You always seemed a little sad to me. A pity!"

This was getting too creepy for Val. With a touch of impatience, he said, "Great-Uncle Victor died more than sixty years ago, and you're speaking about a time when you were a young woman."

That seemed to snap her out of her reverie. On a happy note, she said, "You're Valéry. I'm so glad you've come. It's been such a long time. How's your dear sister, Christine?"

At that his heart cracked. "She's fine, grand-mère." He heaved a heavy sigh. "Is Magda still coming regularly to see you? I'll call her in the morning to make sure that she's taking good care of you."

"Magda comes every day, just as she is supposed to." She smiled. "But when I told her that I was making plum cake for you today, I wouldn't let her help me. Oh, no."

FORTY-TWO

 THE AFTERNOON OF the second day of the International Oncology Conference was devoted to a tour of the premises of the host institution, namely L'Institut Pasteur. Alexandra had always known that this world-famous facility was synonymous with the science of immunization, which had produced a twentieth century relatively safe from the great plagues of the past: tuberculosis, cholera, typhoid, typhus, pox. She also knew that it was in the forefront of research in the great plague of the present, AIDS.

What she hadn't known was that the ultramodern Pasteur Institute occupied a nice bit of property in the middle of Paris and the Fifteenth arrondissement and that it was built out and around an original building that the French government had dedicated to Louis Pasteur during his lifetime. The original building, which included both Pasteur's labs and the apartment that had been constructed in the building for him and his wife, was now a museum. The conference organizers had planned a plenary session to include a tour of the historic building that the conference-goers from all over the world were eager to see.

From the moment the Eastern European contingent discovered that a young American woman spoke Polish, Alexandra's presence was jealously demanded by them at all of the social occasions and many of the professional ones as well. For the tour of the original building, Alexandra was in company of the Poles who marveled at her fluency and teased her for her American accent. Strangely, she found that when she was in the Polish-speaking environment the perpetual throbbing at her temples eased somewhat, so she didn't mind being kidnapped by the Eastern Europeans.

It struck her as both startling and inevitable that the institute was established in the mid-1880s. The tour, given in Polish by one of the resident researchers, began in what was dubbed "la salle des souvenirs scientifiques," where some of Pasteur's most brilliant experiments had been performed. They went next to his magnificent mosaic-tiled crypt in the basement, then returned to visit the seven rooms of his private living quarters. It was at Pasteur's *cabinet de travail* that Alexandra began to feel clumsy, as if she was losing her balance.

On the walls of Pasteur's *cabinet* were pictures of a wide variety of subjects, including medical ones. Their tour guide said that these pictures were painted by Pasteur himself who was a skilled artist. Alexandra noticed some framed sketches of graphic surgical procedures drawn by a different and distinctive hand—one she recognized instantly—and so she asked about them.

"These sketches look like they were done by Toulouse-Lautrec," the guide confirmed, "because they are by Toulouse-Lautrec. The artist shared an apartment with a well-known doctor of the period and struck up friendship with many other members of the Parisian medical community."

Someone chimed in to say that it was odd to think of Toulouse-Lautrec involved in the medical community because his work was so thoroughly associated with the music hall scene at Montmartre.

Alexandra could practically read the guide's mind to know what he would say next.

The guide smiled and replied, "Ah, but the medical community was hardly divorced from the music hall scene, since it was a breeding ground for many of the microorganisms that so fascinated Pasteur. I'm referring, of course, to sexually transmitted diseases. The hygienists—or the Pasteurians, as they called themselves—were desirous, literally and figuratively, of cleaning up the brothels in the last two decades of the nineteenth century. Toulouse-Lautrec would have had ample occasion to meet his medical friends in Montmartre. And, of course, doctors are people too, and they might have had other, not strictly medical reasons for frequenting the music halls."

This remark got the expected laugh, but Alexandra began to feel woozy. She stepped back from her group and stumbled against the body of a man she had not realized was standing behind her.

"Since we're in a museum dedicated to the master of germ theory," the man said, by way of greeting, "I wonder how one drifts into a discussion of Toulouse-Lautrec?"

Surprised but pleased, she managed, "Hello, Jean-Philippe."

"I don't understand a word of Polish, of course, but I do know a French name when I hear one."

"It's a pleasure to see you again. I wondered whether I might be running into you at the conference."

"Did you? Seine-Lafitte naturally has connections with this institute," he said. "It's part of our job, as you know, to stay current with—how do you say?—cutting-edge cancer research. It is fortunate for me, for all of us at Seine-Lafitte, that the IOC should be held now in Paris."

"Very fortunate," she said. Her group was moving on, but since Jean-Philippe made no move to follow them or to say good-bye to her, she was obliged to stand with him before the *cabinet* in which Pasteur had lived and worked.

"And this good fortune has led me to an exceedingly pleasant surprise. I confess that I had not heard that you were here. When I didn't see you the other evening at the Hôtel de Ville and your name did not come up in conversation, I guessed you had not come, for some reason. Are you enjoying your tour of the facilities?"

She assured him she was enjoying it.

"You know by now, of course, that with the possible exception of Napoléon Bonaparte, no Frenchman is held in higher esteem than

Louis Pasteur. In the 1860s, after his first researches into bacteria, he was credited with saving the French wine industry, and no Frenchman ever performed a more patriotic act than that."

She smiled perfunctorily, wishing her head didn't hurt so much.

Jean-Philippe continued, "But we were speaking of fin de siècle painters—or, rather, your group was—and the mention of the name Toulouse-Lautrec drew my attention as I was walking by. Then I saw you. I suppose you mean to go to the Musée d'Orsay while you are in Paris and take in all the lovely Impressionists."

The Musée d'Orsay was one place she had elected to skip, but didn't think it wise to say so. "I'll try to make time to visit it, yes."

They began to stroll in the wake of the Polish group. Jean-Philippe remarked, "It is very curious. When the program for this conference was circulated about two months ago, I did not see the name of the Rosenberg research team. I cannot think now how I came to overlook it."

"You didn't overlook anything," she said, "because we were invited only within the last month. Larry was delighted since this conference is a very exclusive event, and he imagined that our work on telomerase finally captured the belated attention of the organizing committee."

"Ah, yes, that must be the reason," he agreed, "and allow me to compliment your American efficiency for putting your travel plans together so quickly."

Alexandra shook her head. "Not American efficiency but the French Connection. Yves is in the States right now, as you know, and he helped us work through the last-minute travel difficulties and restrictions."

Jean-Philippe's smile was pleasant. "I'm glad to hear it. You see, then, that Seine-Lafitte is most eager to further the progress of its newest research team. Here you are, my dear," he said when she was even with her group. "I am sure that we will be seeing one another over the next several days."

"I'll look forward to that," she said for the sake of form.

He bowed good-bye. As she watched him make his way down the hall, she was confused by what this encounter had been about.

Her confusion was not lessened when Zbigniew Markowski, a biologist from Warsaw, came up to her. Nodding at Jean-Philippe's back, he said, "That one is *veliky kombinator*. Smooth operator, as they say in Russian."

She lifted her brows in question.

Zbigniew said, "He is Chevalier, no?"

She nodded.

Zbigniew rolled his eyes. "We did not live under Soviets all those years without learning to recognize the *aferist*—the schemer! But Russians could not match this Frenchman's talents, which is why Russians are no longer in power." He shrugged. "Not that I complain."

"You can tell by looking that Jean-Philippe is a schemer?"

"No, no! He looks like least likely man in the world to scheme, which is the secret to his success. It was like this: at the opening reception, I overheard this Chevalier thank the director of the Pasteur Institute for having put an American research team on the program. At last minute, you see! It was clear that Director Schwarz was going to get nice grant in return for favor."

"What?"

Zbigniew misinterpreted the surprise of her question. "I cannot speak English, but my French is good. This Chevalier and Director Schwarz had gone off to be alone near the cheese table. I was at cheese table too, but at just that moment, I was bending over to pick up the napkin I had dropped, so I was not visible to them. If Chevalier had seen me standing there, he never would have referred to the deal he had struck."

Finally absorbing what Zbigniew was telling her, she laughed. "Jean-Philippe Chevalier is a most attentive administrator, and if he schemed to get us here, then he schemed on our behalf. You're right about one thing, though—all those years of Communism have made you mighty suspicious." She was shaking her head, still smiling. "And to think that Jean-Philippe just went out of his way to make me think he had no hand in our last-minute invitation. Why, he doesn't even want our thanks!"

FORTY-THREE

 ALEXANDRA WAS STANDING at the front desk of the small hotel where she was staying. It was on a little street off the Jardins du Luxembourg and a short metro ride from the institute. Because of their late arrangements, the team had not been able to find one hotel with five rooms for the eight days they would be in Paris, and Larry had insisted Alexandra take the one that was most convenient to the conference site. She was grateful for her privacy, and this evening she had decided to screw up her courage and venture on her own into Montmartre and the music halls.

The young man on duty behind the desk was sorting mail, and he gave her a friendly nod when she indicated that she wanted to use the short, wide counter to spread out her *plan de Paris*. She kept one corner of the map flat with her heavy room key, put her purse at another corner, and there she stood, trying to orient herself.

The lobby was small and clean and doubled as an informal bar. The inviting chairs, low tables, and sprays of fresh bouquets were pleasingly arranged to persuade guests to linger with the newspaper or perhaps to take a drink and watch the foot traffic that might pass before the large plate-glass window. The evening sky was spitting, but with not enough energy to cause any of the passersby to open an umbrella. The front door was propped open by a terra-cotta planter crowded with pansies.

Alexandra was aware of the tang of the increasingly wet pavement outside and felt the warm, damp breezes chase each other around her ankle boots as she studied the map. She was wearing a Sunday-best Polish peasant blouse embroidered in green and gold over a flowy, light-weight olive skirt she had bought for the trip. She had rolled back her sleeves and pushed them up to her elbows. In an effort to breathe better, she had undone the collar and several of the top buttons of her side-closure blouse, but it didn't seem to be helping. She had decided to make the trip to Montmartre as a desperate measure to ease the constant pounding in her head that extra-strength aspirin couldn't touch. She figured that if she faced her fears, her head might clear.

Fears? She denied that she had anything to be afraid of and decided that the scary part of recovering parts of a past life had already happened. She supposed she needed to face the rest of it and get it over with, but at the moment she was having difficulty figuring out where she needed to go. The young man on duty pointed out the location of the hotel on the map, but she was lost beyond that point. She stared at the huge cell that was Paris proper, bisected by the Seine, its nucleus defined by the Ile de la Cité and the Ile Saint-Louis, and membraned by the highway that circled around the city, known as the *périphérique*. She knew she would recognize the steep and winding streets and stairways of Montmartre if she ever came across them, but the map told her nothing about relative heights. She traced her finger around the city, hoping to stumble across a street name that looked familiar.

She was so engrossed in making sense of her map that she didn't notice that a man had come into the lobby until he began speaking in French with the man behind the desk. All at once, every tiny hair on her nape and arms stood up, and she knew who was next to her.

She turned slowly to look at him. He broke off his conversation, and when he turned toward her, his gray eyes swept her. That was all it took for the painful pressure inside her head to burst the dam at her neck and for the flood of overloaded sensory impressions to balloon down into her body. The shower coursed through her limbs, sang through her like a river held too long in check, pooled at the bend of her elbows and behind her knees. Her temples tingled with relief.

This is why she had come to Paris. To see him again. And he had come to her, just as she had not even dared hope he would.

He propped an elbow on the counter and leaned against it. He didn't greet her, merely smiled at her faintly, provocatively, with promise. She knew what he was up to, and she was up to playing along.

"American?" he asked first. In English.

"For the most part."

"And the other part?"

"Polish."

He glanced down at the map spread out before her. "First time in Paris?"

"You could say that."

"Looking for an address?"

She leaned her hip against the counter. "Maybe."

"Me, I was looking for a hotel room." He gave a Gallic shrug. "I'm not looking any more. You here for vacation or business?"

"Oncology conference." She paused. "Cancer research."

His "Ahh" was soft. "That makes you a . . . biologist?"

She nodded. "Molecular. My specialty is telomeres."

His expression invited her to elaborate.

"I've always been interested in the fact that in single-cell protozoa telomerase activity continues throughout the life of the cell. This enzyme adds short repetitive DNA sequences onto chromosome ends only, thus solving the problem of why chromosomes don't shorten with each round of cell division."

"Fascinating."

"Isn't it? Now in higher organisms, like mammals, telomerase activity is shut off in most cells after birth, but its reactivation under certain conditions might cause cells to proliferate outside the bounds of healthy growth. Turn off telomerase, and you turn off sustained growth like cancer. Turn on telomerase, and you have—"

She broke off. Out of the corner of her eye, she could see that the man at the desk was all eyes and ears for the hot stuff that was being played out in front of him. He was trying desperately to look busy with the registry book and was failing miserably.

"Unhealthy growth," he finished.

She smiled. "I was going to say 'cell immortality,' but 'unhealthy growth' will do too. In any case, it seems to be a question of timing."

"So. You're into chromosome ends."

She smiled. "That's right. End games."

"Any other kinds of games?"

"Whatever kind you want."

This time his "Ahh" was suggestive. He slid his arm across the counter and grasped her room key. He held it up, dangling it between them. He wasn't asking a question. He was making a statement. She wasn't going to contradict it.

She refolded the map, dropped it in her purse, slung its strap over her shoulder. She began to move in the direction of the stairs. "I thought you looked like the kind of man," she said, sliding him a sultry glance over her shoulder, "who gets his kicks talking science to women."

FORTY-FOUR

THAT MORNING IN the basement of the S-L headquarters, Val had combed the historical files, beginning with those immediately after the merger with Lafitte. Then he went back to the records that still existed from before the merger, when it had been Seine et Companie and his Great-Uncle Victor had held the reins. Through these labors he was able to confirm what he'd always known and what his grandmother had repeated: Victor had a head for business and could be pleasingly ruthless at times; François-Xavier was an idiot. Such an idiot that not a scrap of paper seemed to exist anywhere suggesting that his grandfather had attempted to patent his ball-pitch contraption or any other contraption.

Having turned those stones, Val devoted the rest of his day to telephoning business associates, asking questions, leaving messages, paying visits, shaking hands, asking more questions. Somewhere along the way, he returned Sophie's call and managed to put her off for a day or two.

As determined as he was to get to the bottom of this patent thing, his business activities were apparently not absorbing enough to keep his thoughts from being sucked back, as if by some centripetal force, to the crazy conversation he had had with his grandmother the evening before. Not to mention the double visions that randomly assailed him as he moved through Paris. He had to blink to make the shadow visions go away in order to keep driving. Somewhere between the States and France, his kaleidoscope with the odd bits of memories had been traded up for a big screen that played feature films without sequence or plot, only images to seduce the mind and enthrall. It was like surrealist or dadaist cinema—but he didn't know a damn thing about the history of art.

It wasn't that he minded what he was seeing on this inner screen. And it wasn't that he had minded discovering the day before through office gossip that the Rosenberg team from Duke was at the IOC this week at L'Institut Pasteur. He knew that the participants had been chosen months ago, and needless to say, Alexandra hadn't mentioned it to him. He didn't mind that either, because whatever was between them now, it was a whole new ball game.

By the time the afternoon was over and the dripping sky was slicking the city, he noticed that the journey he had been making through town was tracing an inward-moving spiral that circled ever closer to a side street near the Jardins du Luxembourg. When the journey came to its natural conclusion, he parked Parisian style and entered the hotel where Alexandra was staying.

He saw her at the front desk, puzzling over a map of Paris. It had taken her a moment or two to register his presence, but when she turned toward him, he knew everything he needed about his desire and hers. She shimmered with it. It was aimed at him but radiated and produced a hot force field around her, causing the poor boy behind the desk to gulp audibly. She carried it off just right too. How she responded to his gambits. A second skin of sweat beaded between his shoulder blades and down his sides. On his tongue he tasted the tang of the wet pavement outside and anticipated ways to bring the wet and the tang inside.

She teased and tempted and turned away from him. Beckoned. He pocketed her room key.

He saw that the poor boy behind the desk was torn between gobbling desire and fear of dereliction of duty. The poor boy didn't work at that kind of hotel, *mais non!* Sure, she was everything a man could want, but that man shouldn't want her on his watch!

Val withdrew a five hundred franc note from his *porte-feuille*, put it on the counter. The clerk waved it away, shocked at any suggestion of pimping. Val reassured him with a quick, "You've no part in this, mon vieux, and it's one time only. This is so you treat her real nice tomorrow."

The young man nodded in partial understanding. When he picked up the large bill, Val was confident that he and Alexandra wouldn't be rudely interrupted this evening by the hotel management or other authorities dying for a good show and wanting to enact a high drama of artificial morality. He followed her, reflecting how Americans thought that funny French money lacked the sober seriousness of their greenbacks. They were right. Francs were more playful than dollars, and a man could use them for things dollars couldn't buy.

He caught up with her when she had turned the corner and was at the foot of the narrow snail of a stairway. He clamped one hand at her waist, the other at her shoulder. He turned her, pushed her against the wall, pressed his length against her. He put his lips to her neck, his hand at the hem of her skirt and bunched it up to her thigh.

She bucked away from him. "For heaven's sake!" she breathed. "What do you think you're doing?"

"Just checking," he said. He let his hand roam under her skirt. He clucked his tongue, then ran it around her ear. He chided softly, "You're wearing underwear, Alexandra."

Her breasts quivered against him with her laugh. "Of course I'm wearing underwear, Val."

"A mistake," he said. "Slip and panties. They're in the way." He ran one finger around a silken waistband. His finger hooked inside the silk and ran down her belly, causing more of her flesh to quiver against him.

She said, "Last time we did this, you complained that I wasn't wearing enough underwear."

He shook his head, rubbing his neck against her nape. "No, I complained that you lied about what underwear you *said* you were wearing." He put his lips to hers. He slipped his finger between her legs. "You should learn a lesson from this. Next time, no underwear."

"Really, Val," she protested, moving against the wall. "You don't mean to do this here."

He found what he was searching for, had been looking for all day, and that was a miniature Aladdin's lamp. "I mean to begin here, but not finish here." He rubbed the fleshly side of her secret lamp, desirous of releasing the genie within. He was aware that her genie was already curling sensuously awake and coiling liquid lace around the tip of his finger, tethering him to her in a way he had not quite expected. It was sorcery of the most delicate and powerful sort.

He brought her to a quick point but did not deliver her. He slipped his hand out of her panties, lowered her skirt, and kissed her deeply. He turned her with a little spank to propel her up the stairs.

She stumbled upward, hips swishing, skirts flowing.

He asked, "Why didn't you tell me you were coming to Paris?"

She grasped the handrail and paused to look down at him over her shoulder. The light from the rose-frosted panes of glass in the stairwell backlit her hair into a spray of burning gold. The shadows emphasized her expression, fine and feline.

"What, and spoil your fun in finding me?"

"It was easy. I called Larry for the name of your hotel."

She smiled slightly. "Easy, huh?" She turned around and took the next step up. "I suppose it depends on what you think you're looking for."

At the door to her room, he pulled the key out of his pocket. Opened it, ushered her in ahead of him.

"So," she said, crossing the threshold, plunking her purse down on top of the dresser by the door, "did you find all that you were looking for?"

He stepped into the room. He had found her, hadn't he? "What do you mean?"

311

She pulled her hair combs out, put them beside her purse. She rubbed her temples and breathed deeply. She shook her head. Her hair moved in slow waves, brushing her shoulders. "You said in Chicago that you had encountered problems with a diagnostic product you were developing. Something to do with patent difficulties. I'm wondering if you've found out where the screwup was."

He put the key in the lock. Turned it once. "Not yet."

While she walked to the one tall window, he took stock of the room. An armoire stood against the wall behind him. The small desk was squared to the window and buried by her briefcase and a jumble of papers. A well-stuffed armchair cozied between the door to the bathroom and the bed table. On the table was a dainty lamp with a frilly shade, a travel clock, several blood oranges, the remains of a baguette, and a wedge of camembert. His gaze came to rest on the four-poster bed. The thick blue cover had been drawn back and was folded over the foot of the frame where it trailed flaccidly to the floor. The pillows were plumped up against the long roll of the *traversin*, their cases edged in lace. The sheet was turned back chastely. On one side only.

"Where were you intending to go just now?" he asked.

She opened the window and latched it French fashion so that one pane was caught in the handle of the latch when turned horizontally. Warm, damp air stole into the room. She twitched the sheer curtains across the window. Through their gauze the low wrought-iron grille that barred the window from the outside was smudged, as was the facade of the building opposite. Over the roof of the opposing building huge trees towered, hinting at green. The overcast sky struck steel through the trees, softened to opal through the curtains.

"To Montmartre," she answered, turning toward him.

Val had the peculiar feeling that Victor Louis Dorsainville had just entered the room, as if conjured by a magic word. He had been annoyed by the man's ghostly presence the evening before, when Victor had come back to partial life in his grandmother's addled perceptions. This time, however, his ancestor seemed to have come and gone before Val could decide how he felt about it.

"Curious," he commented. "When I last saw you in Chicago, you were dashing off after learning something about Montmartre, and now I find you in Paris on your way there. It's an odd coincidence."

"You think?" she replied. The response was apparently flippant, but her tone implied a real question. Her figure was outlined in the glow of the opalescent panes. Her stance held wariness, hinted at challenge.

"Let's call it an interesting symmetry. So tell me. What happened after you left Chicago?"

"Erica died."

"I'm sorry," he said, but he wasn't going to dwell on it, not when so many fine sensations were passing through him, along with an awareness of muscle and sinew and a way things were balancing out in the room. Suddenly he realized that Victor hadn't left. Rather, he had spirited himself right under Val's skin.

"Her death was hard."

"I'm sure it was," he said, then changed the subject by asking, "Were you planning to have dinner in Montmartre?"

"No."

He nodded at the bed table. "No gourmet meals in Paris? Only bread and cheese?"

She laughed self-consciously. "I went to a café for lunch today with a group from the conference, which was fine, but last night . . . well, Parisian restaurants intimidate me, so . . ."

He changed the subject again. "I like your room."

She laughed again, this time with pleasure. "Yes, isn't it nice? When I first opened the door, I thought, How perfect!"

"How perfect," he repeated, then let a silence fall. He noticed then that it wasn't the window that glowed. It was Alexandra. He'd laid the groundwork for her pleasure and his earlier at the bottom of the stairs, and now it was her turn.

She understood. She went to him and slipped her hand under his tie near the knot. When he drew his head down to hers, he resisted, ever so slightly. He put a finger at the neck of her blouse, eased open the embroidered flap to the first buttoned closure, exposing her bra strap and the smooth skin of her shoulder. He didn't say a word and hardly changed his expression, but encouraged the idea. She got it. Clever Alexandra.

She caught the focused gray light of desire in his eyes. The air around him was different somehow, yet familiar, even dangerous. She might have felt a thrill of fear, but she couldn't distinguish it from the other sensations rushing through her blood, pounding at her heart. When he resisted her first kiss, she adjusted the hold on his tie, then led him around the side of the bed so that they were between the foot of it and the armchair. She knew what he wanted her to do. She unlaced one boot, toed it off, then the other. She stripped off one sock, then the other. She unbuttoned her blouse, pulled it out of her waistband, slipped it down her arms. She tossed it onto the armchair by the bed.

Her bra was a lacy confection that played peek-a-boo with ivory skin and pink carnation tips. She let him enjoy the sight of the flesh that swelled when she reached around the back to unfasten the hooks. Then she slid the satin straps off her shoulders and floated the formless lace so that it joined the blouse. She added her skirt and slip to the pretty pile on the armchair, then teased him as much as he could stand with the last scrap of lace that covered her. It felt scandalously delicious to be naked before him while he was fully dressed.

She threaded thigh and calf around his trousered leg and rubbed it. She poised her hands on the shoulders of his suit coat, then slid them down so that the pads of her palms joined at the knot of his tie. She loosed the long ribbon of silk, slid it from his collar, and draped it over her panties that topped the delicate heap on the armchair. Suit coat followed. Then shirt. The positions were clear and conventional. Her clothing nestled beneath his on the armchair.

With her palms and breasts pressed against his chest, she whispered, "I know what you want."

He gripped her forearms reflexively. "Show me."

She unthreaded her leg from his. Her heart leapt in panic at possible outrage, leapt again in anticipation of possible pleasure. She moved slowly downward so that she was on her knees before him. She put her hands on her thighs, sat back on her heels. She looked up and saw from his expression etched in twilight that she had not misjudged. She felt the forces come to life, swirl down from him, move up from her, double strands coiling, surrounding her, surrounding him. When she put her hands to his belt, the basic elements of their cells unzipped and rezipped across time and species and kingdoms so that her blood was transformed to sugared minerals, her skin to petals, her body's form to an unopened flower.

From that moment in her kitchen, when she had been searching for an antique biscuit tin with the picture of a tart to tempt him, she had wanted to bare his thighs. She had wanted to caress and kiss them, to feel with her hands and lips the contour of muscle that she had only ever skimmed with her eyes or own thighs. She had wanted to possess the stem to her flower, join it with her lips and tongue, coax it so that it would prod her, unfurl her petals.

She was on her knees before him, facing him, finding a tantalizing connection between her mouth and his body. The sky drained of color, and the shadows deepened. He turned her so that she was on her knees before him, facing away from him. An initial, shy-violet tremble at what might happen. Then he reached out, pulled the bedcover from the footboard, and spread it around her, under her. Comfort in the padding of her knees and now elbows that were down on the ground for him. He was on his knees too, behind her, his hands splayed over her hips. He peeled open her flower with his stem, created it, plowing smoothly. She wasn't humiliated, more intrigued the way the flower of her body gained identity and became an orchid, to be prized and plundered.

She was on her knees before him, just the way he had wanted her for days and weeks now, possibly even year and years. Under his thumb. Under his body. Under his control. He was lord and master. She was his servant. No, he wanted her lower than a servant who merely served the master's desires and who might keep a part of herself to herself. He wanted her to be a slave to her own desire for him, with no part of herself in her own possession.

He reached forward to settle his hand between her thighs, had no difficulty finding the Aladdin's lamp that made her glow. He tantalized it perhaps incautiously. He didn't care what power might be released beyond her own slavish desire for him or what unconscious wishes might be granted when his fingers teased and tormented, slid and possessed. All he knew was that when her rare flower blossomed against him, it felt as if he poured into her everything he had saved for a hundred years.

Afterward, they lay on the floor, entwined with each other and the bedspread. Their sighs were webbed with lingering moans. Their foaming blood beat to the dance of the shadows. The genie was sprung from the lamp, joyous to be released, spreading glitter dust lavishly. Reversible time could play fine tricks when the problems of distance and geography disappeared.

Before his life slipped inside out, he murmured into her ear, "When we recover, I'll take you to dinner. I know just the place."

FORTY-FIVE

HE LIFTED HER up to sit her on the small counter that served as her kitchen. She was *en déshabille*, wearing nothing but her Japanese dressing gown, just the way he liked her. He had slipped on his trousers, put on his shirt, rolled the sleeves up. He was studying the automatic plum-marinating machine on the counter beside her, fiddling with the ratchet and hook. He picked up the column of wax, passed it beneath his nose, pressed it between thumb and forefinger.

The morning sunlight was straining through the gray clouds and trickling through the glassed roof which tinkled atonally with the raindrops. He hadn't yet combed his hair. He was only vaguely aware that it must be sticking up this way and that, roughened from the night's pleasant strife. Even farther back in his awareness was the realization that he rarely spent the entire night with her, and if he did, he never lingered past the dawn. But he had taken a fancy to the automatic machine, and it pleased him to putter with it this morning. It pleased him, as well, to have her next to him, her body full and languorous with the freshness of his lovemaking, delicious in silk with nothing but fragrant skin beneath.

He played with the ratchet. "You say an old woman in Sainte-Foy-la-Grande rigged this contraption?"

"Yes," she replied. "Clever, don't you think?"

"Indeed. I've a mind to draw it. Do you have a pen and paper, perhaps?"

She slid off the counter without letting the closure of her dressing gown sag open and returned a few moments later with pen, ink, and a large notebook whose marbleized covers were held together with three stout ties. She unbound these and opened the book, shuffling some of the top papers to the bottom of the stack so that blank pages were available to him. Evidently the topmost papers contained her work. At a glance he had seen that the pages held columns of words, like spelling exercises. He raised his brows, inviting her to comment on her writing, but she gave her head a tiny shake, declining the conversation, and turned away from him. She crossed the room to her ballet barre.

He applied himself to a first sketch of the machine. After some time, he turned the notebook toward her so that she could see his drawing. "What do you think?"

She left her ballet barre and returned to his side, wrapping the dressing gown around her, tightening the tie belt at her waist. She surveyed the drawing, then observed the machine. "From the angle you chose," she said, "the ratchet and the hook should work together like the fourth position in ballet. You see?" She assumed the fourth position, again without letting her dressing gown fall open, then pointed at the sketch. "Your drawing misses that relationship right here."

He must have been wearing his surprise on his face, because she was prompted to add, "I certainly have knowledge of Beauchamp's five ballet positions, if that is what takes you aback."

He smiled. "I never doubted that you did. If I was surprised, it was only because I didn't see the relationship myself, and I perceive that you're right." He lifted the imperfect sketch from the notebook, crushed the page, and put it aside. He turned to the next fresh sheet.

After observing him a moment, she asked, "Why are you making these sketches?"

"It's an ingenious mechanism, as we've agreed, and someday it will be of use for something other than marinating plums. I'd like to have sketches of it to show to anyone who might find an application for it. A chemist, for instance."

"A chemist?"

He detected a small note of triumph in her voice. "Mais oui, chère mademoiselle! I have taken your suggestion to heart and am considering my options."

"Considering?"

"It is not as if you can say to me one day, 'Victor, mon vieux, you must become involved in chemistry!' and expect that the next day I will be launched down this path. New ventures take time. I'm keeping my eye out, and when the right opportunity comes along, I'll seize it."

"You're thinking of the future, then, and not the present."

"A good businessman must always think about the future."

"But there are pressing needs in the present, particularly with regard to chemistry, as I understand it."

"You ask much, Jeanne, to imagine that I can find the right company to buy all in one day, one week, or even one month—much less make a sketch of a strange contraption and find an application for it on the instant."

"I wasn't speaking of finding a use for this machine—God only knows what that might be!—or even of you buying some company. I had a more modest idea in mind."

"How much more I prefer immodest ideas!" he murmured, running his eye over her curves.

True to form, she didn't tempt him with a glimpse of breast or thigh, for she never responded to him outside certain bounds, never begged for more, never pleaded with him to stay. Never asked him to come to her either.

"I was thinking rather," she said, with a certain dignity, "that you could lend support to some project involving the new medicines I have heard about—not that I have a terribly high opinion of what the medical community might do with those medicines."

He heard the bitterness in that last statement and dropped his teasing. "Charlotte was a very sick woman. She was beyond help when Laurent finally saw her. I hope you don't blame him."

"I blame myself, rather, for not having done something earlier for her," she said, "and Monsieur le docteur Dreyfus was all that was kind and good. It's the other doctors I don't like. The hygienists. The way they poke at the girls."

"The hygienists are simply doing their job. You know as well as anyone how a disease can sweep through a neighborhood and ravage it. Particularly these neighborhoods."

The expression on her face was suddenly very feline. "That was my point, exactly," she said. "Think how wide a field of women you would have to choose from, if all of them were as clean as I am."

She had pinched him, and he had not quite seen it coming. "If you are so interested in giving me a wider choice of women, you should certainly make an appointment with Laurent and talk it over with him."

She smiled innocently. "I have already spoken to Monsieur le docteur on this very subject, and he is quite taken by some of my ideas—my very modest ideas—for improving the health of my fellow dancers throughout Montmartre." She paused, then added, "I think and act in the present, not the future."

"We complement one another, then."

She did not reply to that, merely nodded at the empty cup on the counter next to him. "More coffee?"

He shook his head.

"All right. If you're going to work on your sketches, I'll get dressed so that I can limber up in earnest."

He spent the next half hour sketching, crumpling page after page, while she worked at her ballet barre. At one point, she called over to him, "Why don't I ask Auguste or Edouard to come and sketch the thing for you, if you're having so much trouble?"

He looked down at his latest effort, dissatisfied, and wondered why he hadn't thought of that simple solution himself. He looked

over at her. She was turned toward him with a leg propped over the barre, arms outstretched, torso folded over the leg, fingers touching toes.

"Yes," he said, "why don't you ask either Renoir or Manet to come by some afternoon, or even Toulouse-Lautrec."

She straightened, brought her leg down, and turned away from him to engage in another stretch. "The dwarf does seem to have an eye for technical details. Yes, I think you're right. Toulouse-Lautrec would be best for this kind of sketch."

He watched her move through her exercises, sweep through a series of pliés. Bending, stretching, arching. He liked to watch her move. He liked the way she moved. He liked even more the way she choreographed their relationship, the subtle push and pull of her feelings toward him, her lavish eroticism coupled with her exquisite restraint that continually fanned his ardor. He would not have predicted on the night when the cancan dancer had refused to have a drink with him that she would have been capable of inspiring in him this degree of interest.

She must have been aware of his eyes on her, for she threw her head over her shoulder and said, "You've never told me how you come to know such an unknown corner of the world as Sainte-Foy-la-Grande."

"Did you not know, then, that the Dorsainvilles have estates in Bergerac?"

From the expression on her face, she evidently did not. She turned back around and continued exercising.

"I spent many summers there as a boy, so I know it well," he said, "and you have never told me why you left."

Still turned away from him, she straightened her back and answered him with a name. "Jean-Marc Lafitte."

He was startled. Could it truly be that *she* was the peasant girl whose lover had castrated that Lafitte wretch? He'd heard the stories that had been whispered four or five years before. How Jean-Marc had cast his eye on some young thing and decided to exercise his droit du seigneur. How the girl's lover had returned that night to take vicious revenge on his noble rival. How the lover had died in prison. How the girl had disappeared.

Could it be that she had turned up in Montmartre, under his protection?

He was scandalously amused, even ignominiously satisfied. The Lafittes of Bergerac, a degenerate branch of an otherwise illustrious family, were pretentious upstarts, and they coveted everything within their limited sight, including the Dorsainville estates. Jean-Marc was an ill-mannered boor and had got what was coming to him. However, although he was well known in the neighborhood to be incapable of producing children, he was still capable of making a good match. The Lafittes for all their pretensions—because of their pretensions—had done well for themselves, and Jean-Marc's name was lately linked to that of a young lady from the region whose old, property-rich family was in no position to scorn being allied to Lafitte money.

His worst self relished the thought that he was enjoying the very woman who was the cause of Jean-Marc's masculine disfigurement. His most prideful self realized that he had not been tending to his own backyard in Bergerac. He thought it worth paying a visit to the father of that young lady from the old and well-connected family who now happened to be spending time in Paris.

He said, still to her back, "Then you see how much we have in common. We're both from Bergerac, and we're both enemies of the Lafittes."

She grunted with mirthless humor. "How much we have in common! Do you ever return to your property?"

"Every couple of years."

She stopped her exercises and turned to look at him. "Then that's the difference between us." She shook her head. "I can never return." She stood straight. "I'll never again taste a plum plucked straight from the tree, wade in the waters of the Dordogne, or see the thick rows of grape vines, strung across the *coteaux* like so many perfectly crimped pie crusts or necklaces plump with emeralds."

What a very surprising creature she often revealed herself to be. "Very prettily said, and it is a pity Jean-Marc Lafitte had such a negative effect on your life."

"Yes, noblemen who take advantage of peasant girls are a particularly reprehensible breed."

Another pinch, unforeseen. She was challenging him today with vigor, and he was stimulated enough to determine that he wasn't going to let her get away with it. He left the notebook open on the counter with the pen atop the last sketch he had tried. He went to the bedroom and returned fully dressed to the main room.

When he was next to her, she stopped exercising. A film of healthy perspiration had risen at her collarbone, at her temples. He reached out a hand and brushed a damp curl from her forehead that had escaped its pin. He liked her intake of breath and the deeper flush that colored her skin at his touch. He liked knowing he had that kind of power over her.

"I've a mind to buy you a painting."

"I have more than enough paintings already, thank you."

He shook his head. "I was thinking of the one we saw together that day in Gervex's studio. *Troubled Conscience,* I believe was the title."

"Do I look troubled?"

"No, but it's a conventional composition of a devoutly domestic scene, and I would buy it for you because you admire it."

"However, you won't buy it for me, because I would refuse it."

"You know I can buy you anything."

"I know."

He did not pursue the topic. Instead he bowed, kissed the top of her head, and left.

He had established the custom of coming to her in her rooms at least once or twice a week, and often three times, but he never came two nights in a row. He sometimes came to Le Chat Noir with his cronies, but on those occasions, he never spoke to her, nor would he go to her rooms afterward. This night he chose to come to the music hall with the art dealer Paul, tall and bespectacled, who owned the successful Galerie Durand-Ruel. He also came to her rooms afterward.

He arrived only moments after she did. No lamps had been lit, but he heard her rustling movements in the bedroom. He crossed the main room, and his footsteps brought her to the door frame around which she cautiously peered, whereupon he swept her into his arms and nuzzled her neck.

Resisting him at first, she croaked, "You scared me, Victor. I thought you were an intruder."

He clucked his tongue in mock displeasure. "Not only are you wearing all your underwear, you are also wearing all your clothes."

"I wasn't expecting you."

"Surprise is the essence of attack."

"Attack?"

He was already divesting himself and her of clothing. "Call it what you will."

"Attack, then," she said, still resisting.

He put both her arms behind her back and clamped them at the wrists with one of his hands. With his other hand, he withdrew a small package from his inside coat pocket. Nothing fancy. Wrapped in plain paper, no box. He brought one of her hands around and pressed the package into it, saying, "Don't refuse it."

She opened the paper, and two hair combs of lustrous tortoiseshell winked weakly back at her in the dark room.

"I have always admired your hair," he said, putting his nose to her curls, "and when I saw these in a shop window today, I saw that they would suit you."

She hesitated.

"A modest gift," he said, "for a woman with modest ideas."

Soon enough she was wearing nothing but her hair combs, and he had backed her up to the bed but had not stretched her out on it. He was on his knees before her. She was standing above him, her hands resting on his shoulders. From the soles of her feet to the tops of her thighs he was assaulting her resistance, magnificently mixing their roles. He was on his knees before her, but he remained unbowed. He wanted to melt her flesh and her resistance.

He began boldly and became bolder. When he finished a lavish and extravagant kiss, he smoothed his hand down the inside of her thigh to her knees over her calf then cupped the sole of her foot in his palm. With her leg hinged, she was no longer able to hold her own weight for the trembling pleasure he could feel he had produced in her. Then she was on her back on the bed, his body covering hers.

"Now tell me that you don't want me," he challenged.

She obeyed. "I don't want you."

"Liar," he chided.

"Romantic," she accused.

"But which one of us is the romantic?"

He joined with her then, cutting off her ability to respond, "And which one the liar?"

He gently stormed her defenses, brought them down with purpose and for a purpose. He wanted her to know her master so that he wouldn't worry she would bolt the corral when he wasn't looking. He felt the moment he had been waiting for and working for. Her body's response to him was complete, for he had always known she held a part of herself back from him, secret and clean of sex-drenched desire. More than once had he felt that she kept some lustful light pushed below her belly, refusing to let it rise and turn to love. This night, however, riding wave upon wave of her infinite ocean, he felt her surrender the last of her secret, clean places, as she sank with her whole being into her desire for him. When she emerged from it, water had turned to fire. It blazed up from between her legs in a torch that scorched him too, and it flashed out of her eyes, which opened to midnight light and locked with his. He had her exactly where he wanted her, under him body and soul.

Much later, within the deepest fold of the night, he said, "I won't be able to come to you again, Jeanne, this week or next."

FORTY-SIX

JEAN-PHILIPPE HAD not expected such fine entertainment. Really, it had been grand fun during the past few days to monitor Dorsainville's fruitless searches through the Seine-Lafitte files and to know that he was coming up continually empty-handed.

Empty-handed. *Bredouille*. What a charming expression. How Jean-Philippe loved the poetry of it conjoined to the name Dorsainville. It made his Lafitte heart beat with pride.

Such an old story—sins of the father and all that—but so gratifying to be able to witness the son actually paying for the sins of his father. So gratifying to be the one to make the son pay for the sins of his father.

Jean-Philippe remembered the burning hatred he had felt for Valéry's father, Robert, who had stolen his beautiful sweetheart out from under his nose and married her. Jean-Philippe remembered the bone-deep bitterness he had felt toward the woman who had betrayed him for a nearly penniless Dorsainville—and he had been a rich Lafitte! Over the decades he had consoled himself with the rather tepid satisfaction that his beautiful, betraying sweetheart had paid dearly for her error in judgment, in losing a daughter to leukemia and drinking herself to an early, ugly grave. But he had not imagined that he could ever again feel anything to rival the hatred and bitterness he had experienced as a young man. He was wrong. The saturation of the satisfaction he felt in anticipating Valéry's utter ruin made his emotional experiences of thirty years before pale by comparison. With age came depth.

Pauvre Valéry. He didn't have a chance. Not after the so cordial conversation he had had with him earlier today during which Jean-Philippe had expressed serious concern over the continuing delays on the patent approval. Jean-Philippe would have bet money that, after that conversation, Valéry had run to dance attendance on Sophie. Let him dance all around her. He still didn't have a chance.

And what a difference a few years could make. Ten years before, he had been content merely to block Valéry's entrance to the Ecole des Hautes Etudes Commerciales, but he considered that paltry punishment now. Why, even as recently as four years before, Jean-Philippe thought it right to keep Valéry out of Seine-Lafitte. Now, however, he knew how much better it was to have Valéry working alongside him, how much better it was to be able to destroy him at point-blank range. Jean-Philippe wondered now why he had bothered with these earlier, amateurish acts of vengeance when the one he had before him was so much richer. Well, if there was an explanation for why he had bothered with such petty stuff in the past, it was because those acts had conspired to create the current conditions of Valéry's magnificent undoing.

It was plainly the work of Fate. Fabulous Fate. Jean-Philippe must have done something good to have deserved it. Or else he had earned the opportunity Fate had handed to him by his craft and cunning. And it had been so easy! It seemed as if one day he had reviewed the proposal for Test Early, Feel Safe which contained the ingenious microscopic PCR capsule skinning mechanism, and the next day he had happened, quite by chance (or had it been fabulous Fate guiding his hand?), upon the drawings of such a mechanism that had been deposited in the files of Seine-Lafitte most probably by Valéry's grandfather. Now, what could have been simpler than taking those unsigned drawings and filing them with the National Patent Registry one year ago in the name of his very own wife, Lucie Gervais?

He was with Lucie at the moment, walking into L'Institut Pasteur. He was determined to introduce her to the lovely Polish American woman whom fabulous Fate had handed to him on a silver platter for the perfection of his plan. Lucie could then tell her good friend Sophie DuBois anything she desired about that lovely young woman — that is, if the subject of Valéry's sexual sidelines ever came up, as he guessed such subjects did among friends. He, personally, was always gratified to learn about the hours Lucie spent with her girlfriends hashing over in jealous detail one of his affairs.

With Valéry's frustrations mounting, Jean-Philippe certainly understood why he had gone to the pretty plum's hotel room yesterday evening to relieve his frustrations on her in a most natural way. Jean-Philippe had procured that piece of information for a mere one thousand francs — which was only twice what Valéry had paid to keep the information quiet. Now, Jean-Philippe was not going to divulge this bit to Lucie until after Lucie had met her, so Lucie could give an "unbiased" opinion of her to Sophie.

Oh my, oh my. He could snap Valéry's liaison with the boss's daughter, rid Seine-Lafitte of him forever, and profit exclusively from his brilliant diagnostic product when Seine-Lafitte refiled a new, improved patent application next year. And with no profits from TEFS this year, Seine-Lafitte could cut loose of the Rosenberg research team as well. Yes, the pretty plum would have to be told what junior executive at Seine-Lafitte was to blame for the sudden loss of her funding, and she would dump him too. True, her cancer research was particularly promising, but there were too many people in the world anyway, and those with cancer would just have to be diagnosed first. With the help of TEFS, of course. Ruin upon ruin for Valéry. Profit upon profit for Jean-Philippe. It was better than sex.

There she was now, his quarry, exiting from one of the afternoon seminars. Introductions were made, Alexandra Kaminski to Lucie

Chevalier. Something about the encounter struck Jean-Philippe oddly evil, in a way he enjoyed immensely.

He asked her how the conference was going.

She smiled radiantly, exuding sexuality like the pretty, ripely plucked plum that she was. "It's been marvelous," she said. "This morning I attended a session on retroviruses, and the discussion turned on the question of safe strains because some retroviruses can trigger cancer when they insert their genetic material into the DNA of the host cell they're infecting."

Jean-Philippe professed his fascination.

"And just now," she said, gushing a little, "we were treated to high-color, high-resolution images of cell nuclei that were spreading across the video screen and looking more like fantastic galaxies than nuclear RNAs traveling to the ribosomes." She stopped, then said, "I'm sorry to bore you! But it's been so wonderful to be here and . . . and"—she blushed charmingly—"it seems that I may have you to thank for my being here in Paris."

"I don't know why you should think that, my dear girl, and even if I were responsible, no thanks would be necessary."

"But—"

He held up a hand. "No thanks would be necessary. Bringing a research team in whom I have invested much to the most up-to-date conference on cancer research could not but serve my own best interests. And I believe this talk of science bores my wife."

The pretty plum smiled at him without suspicion. Taking the hint, she turned to his wife and said, "You're not a fan of enzymes, I'm guessing?"

Lucie smiled sweetly. She was perfectly turned out and such a credit to him at all times. He was almost proud of her. In her soft voice and cultured English accent, she said, "I know little of Jean-Philippe's business. My interest is classical music. I play the piano. I am something of a family historian, as my husband well knows." She cast an adoring glance at Jean-Philippe.

He graciously accepted her tribute and, when the pretty plum expressed polite interest in family history, he listened with only half an ear. He was more concerned to wonder how she had come by the information that he had machinated the late-minute Rosenberg appearance on the program. He decided that although she was unsuspecting, she wasn't naive, and it was worth keeping an even closer eye on her. He knew a reliable detective service that could keep tabs on her movements and activities. A precaution, yes. It always paid to be careful with large amounts of money at stake.

"And your family history, Dr. Kaminski?" Lucie asked. "Are you, in fact, American?"

"By citizenship, yes, although I was born in Poland."

"Your name gives something of your history, but with Americans one never knows."

"Americans are a mixed-up lot, myself included. My great-great grandmother was French, actually. She lived in Paris."

"Paris?" Lucie echoed. "Was she Parisian born?"

"No," Alexandra said, "she was from the country, but I'm not sure where, exactly. The southwest, perhaps."

Lucie exclaimed softly, "The Southwest! Did you hear that, my love? Jean-Philippe? Dr. Kaminski's great-great-grandmother is from France, perhaps the southwest. Is that not a coincidence?" To the pretty plum, Lucie explained, "My family has lived in Paris for several generations, but we have had property in Bergerac for many more generations. When my mother died some years ago, I inherited it."

The pretty plum said, "And you will pass it down to your children too, I suppose."

Lucie paused, then said evenly, "Jean-Philippe and I have no children."

Jean-Philippe could hear Lucie add in her head: *The curse of the Lafitte men—the inability to produce heirs.* Jean-Philippe put his arm around Lucie's shoulder, squeezed it sympathetically.

The pretty plum was something of a diplomat. "You're a modern couple, then," she said, "and have freed yourselves to pursue your careers." She inquired more closely into Lucie's music.

Jean-Philippe knew that their childless marriage had been a continuing sorrow to his wife. Lucie had tried for years to get pregnant and had finally submitted to a series of tests, all of which had shown she was capable of conceiving. Which meant that the problem was with him. But he had refused to put himself in the hands of doctors determined to prove to the world his infertility, to cast aspersions on his masculinity. And why should he submit to such degrading tests? He felt no sorrow over his childless state, and there were too many people in the world anyway.

Jean-Philippe looked at Alexandra with new interest. Something about her distant connection to Bergerac reminded him that there were many ways to screw pretty peasant girls. So many ways.

FORTY-SEVEN

 ALL DAY ALEXANDRA had been feeling light and twirly. Just thinking about Val made her feel as if she were wearing a magic beanie cap topped with a battery-powered propeller which lifted her a few inches in the air. After the chance encounter with Jean-Philippe and Lucie Chevalier this afternoon, her magic beanie cap was twirling madly. Now that she had most of the pattern of her life before her—and it was love, always and forever—she decided that she had the power to see into the secret heart of everyone in the universe. She had picked up the vibes that Lucie Chevalier was deeply in love with her husband. And why not? Jean-Philippe was a charming man. Yet Alexandra could have sworn that Lucie loved Jean-Philippe more than he loved her, and so Alexandra decided that Lucie's karma must involve unrequited love.

She could see into secret hearts, but not into such mundane matters as Val's schedule. She had expected him to have contacted her to make arrangements for the evening. However, upon returning to her hotel before dinnertime, she found no word from him. After relaxing awhile in her room, it dawned on her that Val wasn't going to be calling or coming by.

So, she was free for the evening, and although she was disappointed not to be with Val, it was impossible to feel bad when she felt so good. She decided to take a nice Polish couple who had befriended her up on their offer to go out on the town with them. She phoned them, confirmed the plans, then dolled herself up. She left her room looking good and feeling good, and when she swept down the stairway into the lobby, Jack was standing at the front desk, communicating more or less with the young man on duty from the night before.

"Jack!" she greeted him as she crossed the lobby to the desk. She gave him a kiss on each cheek, put her key down on the desk, and winked at the desk clerk whose eyes were popping out.

"I came to see if you wanted to—" Jack began but was not allowed to finish.

"You're coming with me," she said, hooking her hand in the crook of his elbow and wheeling him toward the front door. "I'm on my way to meet Zbigniew and Ewa Markowski. You know, the man who works on cell suicide."

"I heard his talk this afternoon, and it was good, but I didn't like the way he referred to the process of apoptosis as cell suicide. It struck me as morbid, and I was thinking—"

"Don't think, Jack! Look and listen!" Alexandra recommended. "Of course the process of death is morbid, and I think how we describe a process crucially affects our ability to interact with the phenomenon. Cells die in different ways, including accident and old age. Why not imagine certain types of cell death as cell suicide?"

"Because cells aren't people with intentions who can go out and commit suicide."

Alexandra laughed. "Sometimes I think we have it all backwards. We think that *we* are the ones with intentions and motivations and the will to determine our own lives, but who's to say that we aren't at the mercy of the will of the billions of cells that make us who we are?"

"Almost anyone who is rational."

"During Zbigniew's talk, I was imagining a spy-plane pilot who carries a little vial of poison under his seat in case he's captured, and I was thinking that cells carry in their nuclei a genetic program for suicide that can be set in motion if the cell receives orders to self-destruct."

They had stepped outside the hotel and into the pearl gray of the evening and were walking down the street. Jack was frowning. "Sometimes your visions are right on the mark, Alexandra, but this time . . ."

Alexandra laughed again. "Lighten up, Jack! We're in Paris." She scanned his trimmed hair, clean-shaven face, and nearly coordinated shirt, tie, and sport coat. "Allow me to compliment you on your appearance."

Jack grunted his thanks. They had come to a metro entrance. "Where are we going?"

She struck a subdued ballet pose. "Place Diaghilev."

Jack reflected, then said, "Sure. I know the metro line for it." He glanced at the name of the metro stop they were at, reflected again, then began to walk down the stairs. "This one is fine. There's a good correspondence."

Following him down the stairs, Alexandra expressed her surprise. "How can you know the metro system so well already?"

"It's easy. The first day here, I studied the map."

Alexandra had to hurry to keep up with him. She found the metro system confusing and far preferred to be above ground.

When they had found their train and their seats and were tunneling beneath Paris, Jack said, "I was persuaded by Markowski's analysis of the enzyme ICE in triggering inflammation but I'm less convinced about your kamikaze pilot—suicide bomber thing."

"Well, why not?" Alexandra tossed off lightly. "Now, if certain cells in the nervous system are murdered or commit suicide, then the organism suffers neurodegenerative diseases such as Alzheimer's or Parkinson's. On the other hand, if certain cells *don't* die when they should, they may contribute to the abnormal growth of tumors. Programmed cell death—suicide—may be a vital part of a healthy organism."

"I don't disagree with what you're saying, Alexandra. I'm just disagreeing with the way you're saying it."

Alexandra decided that Jack was a grump, and soon they were climbing the stairs back up to street level and tangling themselves in the fray of pedestrians and cars and the elegant congestion of the Opéra. They made their way toward the café that dominated the square where Alexandra had arranged to meet her friends for a drink.

Zbigniew was pleased to shake hands with Jack. Ewa embraced Alexandra with the news that the evening was working out perfectly. At the last minute, a friend of theirs had chosen to do something else, so they had an extra ticket for Jack.

Alexandra accepted that as a matter of course. She hadn't even worried about an extra ticket. She turned to Jack. "I think I should warn you that the ballet is on the agenda for us tonight. It's *Giselle*."

Jack's face paled perceptibly, causing Zbigniew and Ewa, who spoke no English, to laugh. No translation necessary.

"You like ballet, don't you, Jack?" Alexandra teased.

Jack cleared his throat. "I'll find out."

They seated themselves on the caned chairs at a small round table under the awning of the café. The lights on the *place* began to shine then sparkle as the evening sky dimmed. Alexandra and Ewa were carrying on in Polish, while Jack and Zbigniew worked out a conversation in French with the aid of formulae and diagrams sketched out on napkins. Alexandra noticed that Jack's French was pretty good.

At one point Zbigniew said to Alexandra, "Your Jack reminds me of a friend of mine at the University in Warszawa."

Alexandra looked at Jack, struck by whimsy. Was he Polish in a previous lifetime?

Ewa poked Jack playfully in the side. "Not enough meat on his bones for a true Polack."

What a kick! Jack must be the only Pole in the world with a karmic relationship against fat!

The lights from the Opéra beckoned them. As they approached the beautiful beaux-arts edifice, Alexandra searched for any sign of inner discomfort, such as she had experienced at the Hôtel de Ville or on the Champs-Elysées, but felt none. Happily, she was having the opposite experience of feeling as light on her feet as a graceful ballerina. When she entered the magnificent building, she half-expected a feeling of déjà vu, but it didn't come. She crossed the foyer and ascended the wide staircase, swallowed in a voluble crowd distinguished by its perfume and extraordinary range of modern fashions. Nothing looked familiar. Nor did the sight of the grand gallery strike any chords in her memory beyond a rather dreamy feeling that she was where she wanted to be and was supposed to be.

The four of them seated themselves in the first balcony of the beautiful theater. The lights went down. The strains of sweet violins rolled back time. The curtain went up on the dark forest of Silesia. The Wilis were there, the ghostly spirits of maidens who had died in grief before their wedding bells could chime. These were maidens who had been jilted by their lovers, and it was widely known in Silesia that girls with a passion for dancing were more likely to become Wilis should they die young and brokenhearted. Giselle, the lovely peasant girl who loved to dance, made her entrance, laughing with her friends, dancing all the way through the forest to the village. That day a royal hunting party passed through the forest and stopped for refreshment at the village. The moment that Albrecht, the handsome young Duke, saw Giselle, he was smitten.

Although she hadn't seen the ballet in years, Alexandra knew that the story didn't end happily. That was the beauty of it. The ballet would be an occasion to indulge tragic emotion, to wallow in its extravagance, to experience its exquisite dimensions. How beautiful and satisfying was the long catharsis of artistic mourning that was the nineteenth century. Slain heros. Dying swans. La Dame aux Camélias wasting away from consumption. Emma Bovary eating rat poison. Anna Karenina throwing herself beneath the train tracks. Giselle . . .

Giselle's end was for the second half. In the first half, Giselle was still picking flowers, playing love me, love me not, and ignoring the warnings of her friends that her love would play her false. At the intermission the lights came on, and the audience rustled into the late twentieth century. Alexandra rose from her seat, smiled down at Jack who was looking very doubtful about whether or not he could ever learn to like ballet. She cast her eyes around the glittering crowd, the main floor, the upper balcony, the boxes.

Her attention was arrested by the scene in the first box to the right of the stage. From where she stood she had a perfect view of Val Dorsainville standing next to a chair in which was seated Sophie DuBois. His hand was resting on the back of the chair, and he was leaning attentively toward her to hear what she was saying. When Sophie folded her lips into a smile and looked up at him, eyes shining, the look he returned to her caused an ill wind to harp along every nerve in Alexandra's body.

Unable to look away from the tender, affecting scene being played out in the private-public theater box, Alexandra felt that twirly sensation begin to turn inside her again. Only this time, she was not being lifted up by a magic beanie. Instead, she was the little propeller itself, and she was twirling downward, like a miniature helicopter fluttering down from a maple tree.

She made it through the intermission and the second half of the ballet, but somewhere along the way the useful distinction between illusion and reality had collapsed. She saw the poor, dead Wilis and imagined how Giselle would join them in the end by plunging her lover's sword through her heart, but she was unable to distinguish them from the live ballerinas who danced them on stage, for she knew that their graceful limbs and movements had come at the price of suicidal anorexia and hundreds of pairs of bloody toe shoes. When she wasn't thinking of the sufferings of the ballerinas, real or represented, she was torturing herself with glances at the first box to the right of the stage. In this glamorous perch of privilege a more sweetly provocative drama than the one on stage was unfolding.

Her first bite of the story had gone down as denial, and she had choked to see Val in company with Sophie. But once she swallowed seeing him attending to Sophie's whispers, responding to Sophie's caresses, she became fascinated by their dance. Ate it up like a starving woman whose hunger for it was so profound that the suffering taste of it made her appetite grow.

This hungering appetite felt like an illness, one that grew straight out of her bone marrow, weakening her from the inside. At the same time, from the outside, she felt as if she were being skinned, slowly and with precision. Like a bruised plum. Her very bones ached. Every muscle covering them was cramped. Every nerve ending was exposed and screaming. When the pain became too intense to bear any longer, her relief came in the form of a dispersal, and she felt her consciousness scatter like billiard balls across a pool table to funnel down six separate pockets.

The house lights came on. Giselle had been spirited away to the join the Wilis, while Albrecht was left to sob at her grave, a victim of his own faithlessness. Alexandra's six separated selves came back together into one, too-thin skin.

FORTY-EIGHT

JACK LEANED OVER to take Alexandra's arm and lifted her from her seat. He ushered her into the aisle, and when she stood there without moving, blocking the exit, he nudged her gently so that she would move on. She did so, woodenly.

Jack knew his damsel was in distress. He had two key pieces of evidence. First was the contrast between Alexandra's giddy goofiness at the beginning of the ballet and her pale, sullen appearance at the end, and second was the presence of that half-assed tennis player in company of the foxy daughter of Seine-Lafitte's CEO. Jack didn't need program notes to put this story together, but it did shake him up and out of his denial that Alexandra had any kind of physical relationship with the half-ass. The realization that they were lovers put a chill down his spine and murder in his heart, but those hateful emotions were quickly overwhelmed by a more fierce desire to shield his love from further hurt. Jack hadn't really needed either piece of evidence to simply feel the pain she was feeling. Love was like that.

Ewa said something to Alexandra in Polish, and when Alexandra didn't respond, Ewa tried again in English. "You look like you see a ghost, girl!"

Jack tried to make a joke of it. "That's what you get for all that talk about suicide, Alexandra."

"Suicide?" Alexandra echoed, aghast.

Bad joke, Jack, he chastised himself. Maybe a switch to science would revive her spirits. "Cell death anyway," he said. "Apoptosis."

At mention of the word, Zbigniew snagged Jack for further discussion of microscopic cell choreography. Ewa linked arms with Alexandra and was guiding her through the outgoing throng, chatting about the human choreography they had just seen. Jack kept a watchful eye on Alexandra. She wasn't saying much to Ewa, but she wasn't required to. At the bottom of the stairs, the Markowskis invited them for an after-theater drink. Jack declined, inventing excuses, and assumed all the burden of the polite good-byes and assurances that he would take good care of Alexandra.

He led her through the *rez-de-chaussée,* and when they were almost at the doors, she turned away from him abruptly and said in a rather dazed voice, "You know, Jack, I have to go back. Wait for me here."

Jack didn't have a chance to stop her. The best he could do was to watch her wade back through the exiting crowd and climb the stairs with bodies flowing around her, as if she was swimming upstream. When she was almost at the top of the stairs, she stopped and went back down, but then at the bottom, she began to climb the steps again, as if looking for something.

The crowd was jostling her on both side. Her head was down. Jack saw a pair of black wing tips stop on the step directly above her line of vision. She lifted her head, stared at the man while he adjusted a shawl around the bare shoulders of his companion. The woman kissed his cheek in thanks. He smiled in return. The couple continued down the steps.

Jack had never seen the couple, and he guessed that neither had Alexandra. Ewa had been right: Alexandra was communing with ghosts this evening. Jack decided this was his moment for rescue. He took the stairs two by two.

"Come, Alexandra," he said, reaching for her arm.

She turned, blinked at him several times, as if to get his face into focus. "I've left something behind, Jack."

"What is it?"

"I don't know, but I'm sure I dropped something. Or maybe I lost something. I think it might have been a glove."

"You didn't bring any gloves, Alexandra."

"I was at the top of the stairs, Jack, and suddenly I couldn't remember what I was looking for. I was still holding my program, and my purse is with me, but I knew, *just knew* that I had lost something, but I couldn't think of what it was." She shook her head. "The only idea that came to me was that I had dropped a glove."

He took her elbow. "It's all right. Come."

"Do you believe in reincarnation, Jack?"

He led her down the steps. "It's going to be all right."

She looked up and at him. Her eyes seemed to open and shut like a camera lens, and it felt to him as if she was truly seeing him for the first time. As if she had seen into his soul and registered his love for her that was so pure and naked that she must have been amazed she hadn't seen it before. Jack wasn't sorry. It was about time one of her visions focused on him.

She seemed to come back to herself. She even smiled slightly. "Have you ever been to Paris before?"

He shook his head.

"But your French is pretty good."

"My best subject in high school, after Bio."

"It was my worst," she said. "You know, it seems as if I haven't seen you much this week, since I've been with . . . been with the Polish contingent. What have you been doing when you haven't been in the sessions?"

"Mostly hanging out in cafés."

"Well, well, well. And what draws you there?"

Might as well tell her the truth. It was harmless enough. "I like the smells and the feel of the zinc countertops. I like the way the guys bustle behind the counters too, making coffee, drawing beer, pouring wine."

She nodded. "Sure, I can see why you might like that." Then she sighed heavily. "I know you're from Connecticut, but I've never asked you about your family background. What is it?"

"Generic American," he replied. "A mixture of Scottish, Irish, and English. A good WASP. That bit."

"Ewa was right. You don't have enough meat on your bones to be a Polack. It must be all the no-fat yogurt you eat and all the bicycling you do."

"My dad drank, smoked, ate red meat every day, and never exercised a day in his life. He died of a heart attack when he was fifty-two."

Alexandra cracked a half-crazed laugh. "Do you think a person can escape genetics or fate or whatever you want to call it?"

"I think a person can manipulate the genetic lottery up to a certain point," he said gravely, "but other aspects of fate are a lot harder to finesse."

She considered him. "What else should I know about you?"

He thought about it, then said, "I had a twin brother, but he died at birth."

"Oh, I get it," she said, as if awestruck. "You're twenty-nine, and Bob Dembrowski is twenty-eight. Well, I'll be darned. Do you ever have violent impulses?"

Humor her, Jack, he advised himself. "Sometimes, but not often. I've been told that I don't have a mean bone in my body, which is supposed to be a compliment, but there have been times I've regretted not being able to punch some guy's lights out."

She nodded. "It's amazing to think how parts of ourselves get scattered about, here and there." She shook her head. "Isn't life funny?" She smiled, mistily. "We're a pair, Jack."

He didn't ask for explanations of these strange statements. Instead he said, "I'll call a taxi and take you back to your hotel. A full night's sleep will do you good."

FORTY-NINE

A FEW HOURS later the sun pulled itself so wearily over the horizon that Alexandra would not have bet good money that the day would come. She greeted its exhausted arrival wide-eyed and dry-eyed.

She rose from her bed of thorns. Splashed water on her face. Avoided mirror and makeup. Finger-combed her hair. Donned jeans, a Duke T-shirt, and a light jacket. Picked up her purse and *plan de Paris*. In the lobby, she spread the map out on the counter and said to the woman on duty at the desk, "La Bibliothèque Nationale, s'il vous plaît."

When she had the location she wanted, she went out into the dreary dawn, cool and wet. She made her way on foot across the Paris that worked for a living. She took the back streets and side streets jammed with *camionettes* and *triporteurs* and delivery men laden with armloads of baguettes or flowers or crates of vegetables. Harsh cigarette smoke and roasted coffee filled the air with the occasional up-draft from a sidewalk grate or metro exit. She stepped around dog poop and over gutters running with water and the previous day's refuse. This was the Paris she knew.

She drank her coffee standing up at the bar in a café, ate her croissants straight out of the bag as she walked. Her jeans and T-shirt and disheveled hair turned a lot of heads, drew chat from old men and young men alike. Most were wearing overalls. One of the guys was pretty cute. She'd have to think about that.

She studied her map, kept her course, and brought shutters and shops open in her wake. She arrived early at the BN, but not so early that she was the only one milling in the courtyard waiting for the library to open. Scruffy students were already there and equally scruffy professor types, all carrying laptops. Whiny mopeds arrived regularly, a few dogs. It began to rain. Under shelter of the arcade, the smell of wet skin and hair melded with wet cobblestones.

When the doors opened, Alexandra watched as *cartes d'identité* were flashed for entry. When her turn came, she showed her passport, which the young man at the door refused with an impatient shake of his head. She fished in her purse for an envelope and drew out the paper to which were taped the crumbled bits of *Le Courrier français* that Deirdre had pieced together for her that day at Northwestern. She showed this to him and shot misaimed phrases at the idea that she wanted to look at this newspaper — needed desperately to look at this newspaper.

Then she lifted her eyes to his face and spoke to him in the silent language of her past whose perfect syntax and semantics had returned to her in her walk across the city. Her gaze caught him for a moment, held him, pleaded shamelessly. His expression shifted so quickly and so comically that it was all she could do not to laugh when he caught his breath and waved her in. She decided that in another lifetime he must have been an Austrian officer who frequented Le Chat Noir.

Inside, short men with mustaches and blue smocks were scurrying. She stopped one of them long enough to show him the paper with its pasted bits of newsprint. A flow of French ensued from which she plucked the word *journaux*. She followed the direction indicated, which included several turns down a winding hallway. She entered the newspaper archives, half fearing what she might discover about her past, half doubting she would be able to recover anything at all if she was going to have to read an entire newspaper in French.

The woman at the counter was a motherly type. Without Alexandra having to explain too much, the woman peered at Alexandra's pathetic piece of paper and quickly produced a small box whose *étiquette* read *Courrier fr.* for the year that matched the date of Alexandra's bit. The woman opened the box to show a spool of film. Then she led Alexandra to the row of film-reading machines, turned one on, and sat her down. She began threading the film, explaining all the buttons and knobs of the machine in a continuous stream that was both beautiful and bewildering to Alexandra's ear. She was given to understand that she could print any page of the newspaper she wanted with the help of a five-franc coin. Since she didn't know yet what she was looking for, she didn't know if she'd need to print out the entire paper and have someone read it to her. Calculating costs, if she had to print out the whole thing, it would be one expensive newspaper.

She whirled through the issues until she came to the date of the one that had been saved along with Jeanne Lacombe's documents. She moved through the masthead, opening articles slowly, letting her eyes float down the columns of incomprehensible words, looking for any reference she might recognize. She knew how Jeanne felt to be illiterate, and how much it meant to her to have overcome it.

When she came to the *Faits Divers*, then the *Annonces*, she felt afraid. Finally admitted to herself that she thought she might find a notice of Jeanne Lacombe's death. Erica's words came back to her full force. *I just can't shake the feeling that this guy is going to be the death of you.* She kept going, though, because she wanted to know how it had gone for Jeanne in the end. How her end had come.

Her eyes caught at the name Dorsainville.

Her heart caught too.

There it was. Victor Louis Dorsainville. The Count d'Albret.

She adjusted the focus with a shaking hand and saw that the announcement in which his name figured was headed by the word *Mariage*—that much French was certainly not beyond her—and that his name was linked to that of a Mademoiselle Odette Gervais. If Alexandra was any judge of the rows of funny letters swaying before her eyes, the dates and places were given for the civil and religious ceremonies, and descriptions of both illustrious families were supplied. She noted, rather mechanically, that both families had ties to Bergerac. Maybe a *voyage de noces* was specified, but she wasn't sure.

She sat back and let the shock sink in. It crawled up her spine, raised the hairs on her neck and scalp. Victor had married a woman named Odette. And what about Jeanne?

Alexandra didn't yet know the answer to that, but she knew how Jeanne had felt and that was exactly how she had felt seeing Val in company with Sophie. It felt like feminine foolishness in the extreme to have given herself so completely to a man. It felt like abandonment of the cruelest sort.

She turned the film-reading machine off. This is what she had had to learn from the newspaper. This is why Jeanne had saved it for her. She rose from her chair, went to the motherly woman at the counter. She unfolded her map of Paris and said, "Montmartre."

The mother's mouth primmed, her thoughts transparent. The girl who couldn't speak French but wanted to read an old newspaper was curious to visit the fabled mecca of pornography. If it were ten at night, she wouldn't give the girl directions. But what harm could come to her in Montmartre at ten in the morning? The mother's mouth curved up. She pointed here and there on the map, discussed a variety of paths that seemed to include metro, bus, and foot.

Alexandra chose foot. It rained intermittently. She wasn't going to melt, and soon the streets began to climb. Place Blanche. Le Moulin Rouge. Place Pigalle. Live sex shows. Seedy hookers filing their nails, bored with work, bored without work. Boulevard Rochechouart. Everything looked pretty crappy. Might have been nicer a hundred years ago, but probably not. The Tati on the corner of Barbès-Rochechouart made Kmart look classy.

She chose Boulevard Barbès. Went straight up steeply. Left France and entered Little North Africa, brisk with trade. She passed store fronts filled with pastries dripping honey and pistachios. She negotiated sidewalks crowded with bins crammed with wallets and purses, rucksacks, duffles. She had put her map away. She didn't know where she was and had abandoned the notion that she would recognize anything. Instead she relied completely on instinct. How did they feel, these streets? If the trail felt cold, she turned the other way. If the trail felt warm, she kept going.

She wandered. Streets that ventured in one direction had a habit of veering off in another, often making her warm trail go cold until she could get to a likely-looking intersection. She passed in the shadow of the Sacré-Coeur without giving it a second glance and ignored an impressive panorama of Paris. She hit the main square of Montmartre where the schlock-meisters had set up their easels, plastic-wrapped in the rain. She groaned audibly. Just for the hell of it, she decided to take a close look at each of the artists, thinking that perhaps she could detect a Gervex among them, but she ended up not recognizing a soul.

Up steps. Down steps. Le Chat Noir had been closed long ago and turned into something else, she didn't know what. She had no real desire to see it anyway. At one point, she passed a row of buildings that emanated a force that jumped out and grabbed her. The central building was an art gallery, featuring turn-of-the-century poster knockoffs. Above the door was a plaque that stated this to have been the site of the historic café-cabaret Le Mirliton. For all Alexandra knew, Le Chat Noir had become Le Mirliton, and if that was the case, she was not far from where she wanted to go. She'd try the shortcut through the back alleys.

The trail was getting warmer with every step. She turned this way and that, not once hesitating, and then she was there. Knew it by how it felt. By how it looked too. If any view in Paris was going to look familiar to her, it would be this one.

She stood at a haphazard intersection of three streets. In the center of an odd, ill-kempt square was a sapling circled by an iron railing, paint peeling. On the corner opposite her was a café called La

Mazurka. Fair enough. She crossed the street to glance inside, and the sight of the cracked marble floor almost made her cry. She looked resolutely up the street that rose away from the square.

The rain had let up enough for distinctions between light and shadow to emerge. She half-closed her eyes in an effort to dissolve the crummy cars that littered the sidewalk at drunken angles, spoiling her view. Without the cars, the outlines of the buildings were perfect. So were the shadows. She opened her eyes and let her gaze follow the street as it curved up and away to the left just the way she knew it to curve.

Although pain pricked under her skin with a thousand knife points, it was still a relief to be here, walking home, meeting her fate. During the long, sleepless night, she had faced the big question and had arrived at the bottom-line answer. She might not like what she was going to discover next in Jeanne's life, but even if the knowledge should kill her, she couldn't live without knowing it.

She hitched her purse strap higher on her shoulder and began the final climb. She knew the number of steps from the corner to her front door. She paced those out and felt as if she was wading at the ocean's edge, deep sand slowing her down, long fingers of the tide wrapping around her ankles like seaweed, reaching to pull her into the depths. She wished she could discover within herself an emotion other than profound sadness.

Her steps came to an end where an old man was sweeping the sidewalk. She had seen his counterpart all over Paris, on mopeds, on park benches, at bars. He was wearing espadrilles, baggy pants, and an old navy-blue coat over a sweater vest. He was short and bent over. When she was next to him, he looked up, and she saw that he had blue eyes, a Charles de Gaulle nose, and was even older than she had first thought.

He said something long and involved to her.

She replied, "Je ne parle pas français."

He surveyed her hair which was frizzing with the wet and demanded suspiciously, "Allemande?"

Not German! "Polonaise," she replied, "et américaine."

"English, then," he said. "You speak English."

"Yes. English. I can manage in French if I have to, but . . . but I'd rather not have to."

He hadn't taken his eyes off her. "I can speak English. What do you want?"

"I just wanted to look at this building."

"Why?"

"One of my relatives lived in the neighborhood years ago. This building caught my eye, and I wanted to see it. That's all."

"Look, then."

She looked. "It's just that . . . well! Who lives there now, I wonder?"

"I live here," he said and proceeded to name those who lived on the first floor, the second floor, the third floor.

"And the fourth floor?"

"Personne." He shrugged. "No one."

"It's empty?"

He nodded.

"Do you know why the owner of the building doesn't rent it out?"

"I am the owner of the building," he said, "and I don't rent it out because it is in bad condition, dirty. It needs repairs."

"Has it been like that for very long?"

The old man didn't reply. Instead, he asked, "Do you wish that I rent it to you? Is that why you have come?"

She leapt at the possibility. "Well, if I were to rent the rooms, I would have to see them first, no?"

"Every now and then someone comes who hears of my empty rooms." He shook his head. "It is useless. I do not rent the rooms. Not to you, not to nobody. Is that why you have come? Because you have heard of the empty flat?"

"I came because I wanted to see—"

She broke off. She had to look away to compose herself. She blinked away the start of tears, happy to feel fluids flow in her body, sorry that they were so sad. The old man was hassling her for no reason. She didn't need this. She looked back at the building and said the first thing that came to mind.

"The door shouldn't be brown. It should be green." She shifted her purse on her shoulder. "That's why I came. To tell you that your door is the wrong color."

She turned to go.

The man stopped her steps by saying, "Do you want to hear a story?"

"What kind of story?"

"A story of—how you say?—the quartier?"

"Neighborhood."

"Yes, a story of the neighborhood. From before I was born. An old story."

"Is the story pretty?"

His shrug was Gallic. "The story is true. Whether it is also pretty, I cannot say. Notions of beauty are individual."

"I should have asked whether the story is a happy one."

"It is a story of the neighborhood, mademoiselle. How happy can it be?" He reached into his pocket, withdrew a key. He turned to the brown door that should have been green and attempted to fit the key in the lock.

Click, click.

Alexandra's nerves jumped.

Click, click. The door opened.

"Do you wish to hear the story?" the old man asked, standing aside for Alexandra to enter.

She took the fateful step and entered the building, pausing first in the dim of the entry. Ahead of her was a small courtyard, and she checked to see if the stairs turned in the direction she thought they should. They did. There was no construction now in the courtyard. No scaffolding or boards lying about. No smell of fresh plaster. Only a few dried up pots for plants jumbled in a corner and a profusion of wires: thick, thin, black, gray, in coils, on winches, knotted, growing like vines along the paving stones and up the open stairway railing.

The street door shut behind her.

"I was an electrician in my other life," the old man said.

Alexandra turned, mouth open. "You mean—?"

"Before I retired," he explained, gesturing at the snarl of wire. "I began my professional life as an electrician." He gestured her to the door to the left. "I ended it as a director of stage lighting. I worked mostly at small theaters and cabarets. Here in the neighborhood and abroad."

"And now you own and manage this building?"

The old man nodded. "I inherited it from my mother who was given the building by the former owner."

"She didn't buy the building? She was given it?"

"That's right. When the former owner didn't want it anymore, he gave it away. He didn't need the money."

"He didn't?"

The old man ignored her leading question. They had stepped into the front room of the concierge's quarters, a kind of parlor-kitchen. It had two dingy windows both trimmed with lace, one that gave onto the street, the other onto the courtyard. At the courtyard window stood a table covered with a plastic cloth stamped with a French provincial check, now faded, and two wooden chairs. A sway-backed sofa was shoved up against the far wall, which included a door to another room beyond. A sink and a short counter ran along the courtyard wall near the table.

This small, rather humble living room was given an unusual effect by the size and variety of electronic equipment crowding the space. The latest and largest floor model Sony television was positioned for viewing from either the table or the sofa and was topped by not one but two VCRs. A boom box worthy of the toughest street in Harlem sat on the shelf sagging above the sink. A Watchman with its credit-card-sized TV screen shared counter space with an antiquated burner that was hardly worthy of a Girl Scout camp-out. A microwave brooded atop a miniature refrigerator. Remote controls took the place of knickknacks, and the wires from outside seemed to have spread their tendrils inside and slithered all over the floor.

The old man sat her down at the table. She put her purse on the table next to a cellular phone, and the old man began to putter at the sink. He filled a heavily dented kettle with water, lit a burner, and rattled the kettle atop the ring of flames. Back at the sink, he fiddled with cups and saucers and spoons, clattering among the crockery stacked there.

As he prepared the teapot, he began to speak.

FIFTY

 SHE STOOD IN the wings and derived what comfort she could from the dark. She ſtared unseeing onto the ſtage and the hall beyond, hardly aware of the rowdy crowd settling itself in for the evening's performance. She was unable to move. The musicians had scrapèd into their chairs and taken up their inſtruments, but the usually toe-tapping sounds of splintered melodies falling together into familiar rhythms failed to awaken any response in her legs.

She felt like an articulated doll in her skirts and ſtockings and ſtout-heeled dancing shoes. A wooden *pantin,* whose arms and legs moved only when jerked by a ſtring. She winced at memories of an elegant ballet—was it Delibes's *Coppélia?*—in which the heroine was transformed from wooden ſtatue to living being. She, by contraſt, was being transformed from living being to ſtatue. It was a punishment, surely, but what had been her sin? Presumption, perhaps. Giddy girlishness. A foolish heart.

It was bad enough to have turned ſtiff and lifeless. It was wretchedly unfair to continue to feel such pain in a wooden body. It was a cruelty that she should be expeᴄted to go out on ſtage now that her own enchanted ballet had ended, that her glorious world of make-believe had ceased to be. She had refused to acknowledge the illusion of it during those enraptured hours of high passion and life. She could refuse no longer.

She had bought *Le Courrier français* on her way to work, deciphering what she could. She had been so pleased with herself, with the world! Then she turned to the *Annonces,* and her private stage emptied abruptly. The curtain rang down on a pretty, impossible story, and she was returned to the world from which she had come. Where girls born into lowly circumstances found innumerable ways to sink lower. It was an unlovely return. The streets seemed dirtier than she had remembered them, the petty realities of making her living more sordid.

Once upon a time, her life had had a certain dignity, but whatever wicked fairy tale she had just lived through put an end to that. The magic wand had been waved in reverse. Her costumes were humiliatingly cheap, her dancing vulgar.

The overture announced itself as Offenbach, gay and Parisian. Her favorite. A further cruelty. Why shouldn't the pain be enormous and complete?

Chérie, standing behind her, put hands on her shoulders and whispered, "We're on tonight after the jugglers."

"Do they appear before or after the exquisite refinements of the muzzled bear act?"

"After."

"And is the muzzled bear act before or after the excitations of the female wrestlers?"

"The female wrestlers aren't on the program tonight."

"Ah. And the man on stilts who can spin ten plates on a stick strapped to his head? He's scheduled for tonight, no?"

"Jeanne—"

She shook her head. "I'm not going on."

Chérie shook her shoulders gently. "You have to. The house is packed. They've come to see us. They've come to see you."

"If it's the cancan they want, they can go to the Moulin Rouge and see La Goulue."

Nina and Louise were hovering behind Chérie. Nina piped up, "We're much better than she is!"

"Better than Grille d'Egout too and Mademoiselle Patte en l'Air!" Louise chimed in. "Come on, Jeanne. You want to dance. I know you do."

Jeanne didn't want to dance. A deep sigh shuddered through her body, momentarily intensifying her pain. To no one in particular, she said, "You know what *slays* me in all of this?"

Chérie, Nina, and Louise were silent behind her a moment before Nina ventured quietly, "The Count should have told you. He really should have. I can hardly believe he'd do such a thing without telling you. I thought . . . I thought—"

"You thought he really loved her," Louise said on a note of contempt to her companion. To Jeanne, she said, "What should slay you, love, is that you didn't listen to me. *I* knew how he would treat you in the—"

Chérie clapped a hand over Louise's mouth, but since Louise's opinion of the Count d'Albret was well known to Jeanne, she wasn't angry at Louise for having been right.

"No," Jeanne said, "what slays me is that I learned to read—spent hours and hours—only to find that a few words on a page have brought me more pain than I ever before experienced or could even imagine!" She laughed without mirth. "It's an irony, really, don't you think? That my greatest achievement should turn against me—"

This bitter reflection was interrupted by an alarming diversion which, unfortunately, occurred rather frequently at Le Chat Noir.

"Michel!" Louise hissed to the man who was half-in, half-out of a trap door on the stage before the footlights. "You've set your sleeve on fire!"

Michel, who was in charge of the lighting, sprang out of his hole and began a flapping dance on the darkened stage. He had not yet perfected the practice of heating cylindrical blocks of calcium in jets of burning oxygen and hydrogen, but since everyone was pleased with the brilliant light that was thereby produced, his tendency to fiery mishaps was tolerated.

"Cake your nose with calcium next time," Louise recommended to the little man, "and light that! Your snout is big enough."

Michel extinguished his burning sleeve. "That's not the part of me you want burning with love for you, Louise!" he returned, whispering loud enough for everyone in the hall to hear. "I know you have the hots for me!"

In appreciation of the impromptu dance and repartee, scattered applause rose from the audience, along with an assortment of lewd rejoinders. Michel took a bow, then leapt back into his pit to prepare his lime blocks and to set up his reflecting mirrors and rainbow projector.

The lamps came on, drawing an appreciative "Ooh!" from the audience. The bright lights threw monstrous shadows up the walls and bathed the stage in garish green. The acts came out in tawdry, tasteless succession. The motley crew of an orchestra played on. March. Waltz. Polka. Barcarolle.

When the opening notes for the cancan were sounded, Chérie, Nina, and Louise looked to Jeanne for direction, but Jeanne shook her head.

Chérie took charge. "Adjust your garters, mes filles!" She shooed Nina and Louise on stage and motioned for them to take their turns and prance. To Jeanne she said, "You have to dance."

"I can't."

Chérie fussed with the sleeves of Jeanne's peasant blouse. "Do it for Charlotte."

Jeanne groaned in fresh pain at mention of Charlotte. She wanted to die now too. "I miss her more than ever."

"Then dance for your father who was trampled beneath his ox cart and dance for your mother who did not survive her fever. Most of all, dance for the Count's friends who might be here and show them that you are not—not!—affected by the news of his marriage! Dance, Jeanne!"

Chérie rearranged her ample bust for a more provocative effect, winked broadly, then swirled out on stage, a flash of orange skirts, black stockings, and white petticoats. The three dancers strutted their stuff to the opening flourishes, then circled around to the wings where they beckoned to Jeanne, arms outstretched to her and inviting.

"It won't be the quadrille without you, love!"

"You're our fourth! No, you're our *first!*"

"Make the gendarmes arrest us tonight for kicking too high!"

At that moment, an amazing thing happened. When Jeanne did not come out on cue, the men who called themselves musicians knew what to do and began again as one. When they replayed the tempting, opening notes of the cancan for her, the audience caught the spirit and began to clap in unison. Jeanne felt the strings attached to her wooden arms and legs fall slack and her body come momentarily back to life. With the music playing and the audience clapping and the arms of her three friends beckoning, she stepped out on stage and into the limelight.

Chérie assumed the leadership and counted out the steps. One, two, three, four, toe, tap—turn, tease—and one, two, three, four, turn, kick, skirts. Jeanne caught the spirit, let it infect her. Wood became flesh and flushed with the blood and sweat of who she was, and tonight she was one of a foursome. Knowing the steps as well as she knew how to breathe. Performing the repeating patterns. Weaving, reweaving, celebrating the patterns. Defeating routine. Revolting against monotony.

Swirling twirlings of shocking pink, tart-ripe cherry, radiant orange, incandescent yellow. Yards and yards of white cotton trimmed with simple lace. Scandalous puffs for drawers no bigger than the poufs of their sleeves. Catchy kicks of strong, shapely legs in mended and remended black silk. Interlaced arms. Linked elbows. Hand to shoulder, Jeanne to Chérie, Chérie to Nina, Nina to Louise. Over, under, around, once more. Yips of energy. Over, under, around. Yips of enthusiasm. Stamp the steps they had learned as girls dancing in the squares of their villages, dancing to viol and bagpipe, dancing in wooden shoes.

The theme was cancan, the tempo vivace, the kicks con brio. Kick for the men who raped them. Kick for the men who betrayed them. Kick for Charlotte who died an unlovely death. Kick for those who were living. Kick for those who were barely eking a living. Kick, kick. Diſturb the authorities. Diſturb the social order. Kick, kick. Be irreverent. Kick, kick, kick.

Those in the audience, to a French man and woman, knew how to interpret the ſtamping feet, the exuberant patterns, the defiant flashes of fanny. When those four naughty young women on ſtage began to kick, men in blue smocks, holding long pipes, and few sous in their pockets were on their feet. Women wearing plain dresses, old-fashioned aprons, and mob caps were on their feet too. Hoots and hollers of "Vive la révolution!" and "A bas la tyrannie!" began to resound.

The Auſtrian officers joined in, fearing nothing. Four Russian officers fell madly in love, each one with a different dancer. The French police who patrolled the neighborhood ſtood at the back of the hall and watched, fascinated and wary. More than one had lived through the Commune of '71, and it seemed that the Bloody Revolution, not yet a comfortable hundred years away, was caſting its long shadow across Montmartre this night. Behind the bar, Maurice began by wiping away his tears with his apron but ended by weeping openly and setting uncorked bottles on the marble slab before him. The thirſt of the hoarse throats in the room would be slaked tonight at the expense of the wealthy Count d'Albret. The fat cat of the Black Cat was away, and the mice were dancing.

Encores were called for and gratified. The reſt of the evening's variety show was canceled, for what came next were noſtalgic renderings of the songs of the revolution. When those were exhauſted, audience and performers alike sang sentimental songs of the countryside, of all that would always be loved and loſt. Into the choruses even the gendarmes joined.

FIFTY-ONE

 "AND THE CANCAN was never danced more brilliantly." The old man's gesture was definitive. "Jamais. Dans toute la France."

Alexandra gazed into her cup, watched as swirling tea leaves shifted and settled. Her memory, prompted by the old man's story, had embroidered the missing bits.

She put the ending on it. "Then Jeanne went backstage and died."

"Mais, non!" The old man lit the burner to reheat the kettle. "She came back here in the early morning and went up to her rooms. If you want to know who died, it was Michel."

"The man who operated the lights?"

The old man nodded. "He was a careless bastard. Within a year of that memorable night, his sleeve caught in the flame of one of his jets, and there was no one there to tell him to put it out in time." He snapped his fingers. "Whoosh! He was on fire in an instant! But it took him hours of agony to die!"

Alexandra cast a glance at the frayed wires and overloaded sockets and tried to ignore the possibilities for electrical disaster that surrounded her. "What a horrible way to go."

The old man laughed. "I know it! I nearly killed myself once when I was a young man. I didn't know a bad wire from a good one, and my ignorance cost me several months in the hospital. That was almost seventy years ago, so you can say that I learned my lesson. I am ninety."

Alexandra was reassured. If he had made it this many years without going up in flames, she figured he was good for another day, at least. "You were born after the time of the events you have just recounted. How do you know this story?"

"The night of the cancan at Le Chat Noir is famous. Everyone in the neighborhood knows of it. My mother was there with her parents. She was a little girl at the time, and she never forgot that night."

"How did your mother know that Jeanne returned to her rooms?"

"My mother lived here with her parents, grew up in this building. When they died, my mother became the concierge. She knew everything that went on in this building. I have already told you that when the rich owner didn't want it any more, he gave it to my mother."

"So what happened after Jeanne returned to her rooms?"

The kettle whistled. As he refilled Alexandra's cup, the old man said, "She went up to her rooms that morning and didn't come down for days."

SHE CAME TO know her rooms very well indeed.

She knew how many narrow panels were required to cover each wall, how many stripes covered the chaise on which she reclined, how many steps from chaise to bed and back again. She had memorized the arc the sun traced from one wall to the next as it crept across the sky. She had observed the new pattern of cloud cover that signaled the onset of cooler weather, and learned how the rain plinked and plunked on the roof panes and blurred the gray sky. She had come to predict every sound of the street, day and night, every creak and shift of the building. She derived a meager satisfaction from watching the leaves of her plants droop in sympathy with her spirit. Her only true relief came at night when her shattered soul would leave her wooden body and scatter into stars across dark space.

She shunned all social contact. The girls came by, but she refused
to see them. She received several notes from Dr. Dreyfus as well,
shoved under her door. She ignored them. She thought he might
have even come by her rooms once, but she did not respond to the
knocks at the door. As far as she was concerned, all the dancers in
Montmartre could die of the pox and be well quit of the world. In
attempting to save lives, she was doing no one a favor, least of all
herself.

She supposed she should eat but couldn't find a reason to bother.
She hadn't danced in days and figured that not eating was a fine savings, since soon she would no longer have a job. Thanks to Victor,
she hadn't had to pay rent in months, but now that he had a wife, she
wasn't sure that she could depend on that economy anymore. She had
saved her money certainly, but she saw the end to all her comfort, and
it was frighteningly close.

While she lay on her chaise or on her bed, she invented stories to
alter the reality of Victor's betrayal. Devised a dozen different ways to
prove it false. Then, finally able to lie to herself no longer, she admitted that the worst of her situation was her shame and that only
more shame lay in further evasion. Not the shame of having been
Victor's mistress. No, the squalid, intolerable shame of having loved
him so thoroughly, so deeply, so unwisely. Of loving him still. She
had asked so little of him, and yet that little had been far too much.

Her defenses down, she was unable to stem the tide of her fan-
tasies of Victor's domestic bliss with the wife he must love. Simple,
naive, or perhaps only tragically conventional for a woman of her
class, she imagined, after the first week passed and he did not come
to her, that she would never see him again. She had only the haziest
of notions that newly married couples traveled, so she was unable to
imagine Victor anywhere but in Paris, orbiting in a sphere beyond
her reach. She knew that married men had mistresses—it was the
most obvious fact of existence—but loving Victor as she did, she did
not think him able or willing to share his passion and intensity. Her
fantasy was all-encompassing.

At the end of one interminable afternoon, a chill crept into the room that only a lover's embrace could chase. She roused herself to fetch a shawl to wear over her old-fashioned dressing gown of batiste, modestly shirred. The movement exhausted her. When she sank gratefully back down on the chaise, the blues that were seeping in and surrounding her were so thick that her state of pain verged on the mercifully transcendent. At that moment the tiny germ of a thought was born to her, and she was able to entertain the idea that if her ability to read had brought her pain, perhaps her ability to write could ease it. To tell her story. To drain her veins through ink. In her present state of paralysis, she would not be able to undertake such an expressive project, but perhaps a time would come when she could put pen to paper and bleed.

She drew in a labored breath. She shifted on the chaise. Her nerves tingled to sudden awareness. She had heard a noise on the landing outside her door. The softest of footfalls. The most familiar and beloved. Awareness grew to alarm and jangled down her spine. Key at the door.

Fear. No, terror. The lock clicked, and she rose to her feet. Her shawl fell to the floor, and she flew across the room. She had achieved an equilibrium so precarious that she could not risk unbalancing it without also threatening her very existence. She was at the door the moment it cracked open. She shoved against it with all her might, bringing forth an inarticulate grunt of puzzlement from the other side. Before she was able to close the door against his entry and throw the latch, he pushed harder than she, and then the struggle began in earnest.

He was inside. He closed the door with one hand, had to defend himself against her assault with the other. Her rage was pure and fluid and did not allow for tears. Happy to match the strength of her anger to the strength of his will, she was encouraged that he was having to make an effort to fend her off. She was inspired to hear him pant as he tried to bring her under control. She wanted to force him to a choice between releasing her or harming her. Impotence or vio-

lence. Either taste defeat or taste blood and fire the way the men of
her class had learned to relish raw meat and bad cognac.

He met her fury, sustained her onslaught by summoning a
stronger, subtler strength and relaxing into it. He grasped her right
wrist with his left hand and slid his right arm around her waist,
thereby subduing the attack of her left hand against his shoulder. He
adjusted swiftly to the unexpected, unexplained exception she was
taking to his presence. He had long experience breaking revolt. He
knew how to ride the untamed to gentleness. His legs moved swiftly
in response to hers, and with two short steps he backed her up against
the wall next to the door.

The contact of her back against the wall deprived her of breath,
and her resistance momentarily slackened. He took immediate advantage by shedding himself of the constraints of his light overcoat
and suit jacket. Her dressing gown proved a flimsy defense, for in
her furious struggles, the skirt had hiked up her legs to become a
confining twist of fabric around her thighs.

Her back against the wall, his length pressed to hers, she began to
feel forces swirl around her, more powerful than the twirling legs of
cancan dancers. Coiling, binding, knotting, these forces. His strength
increased, hers flagged. He had her where he wanted her and how he
wanted her. It wouldn't take much for the forces that prevailed between them to allow his forced entry.

She moved her head away from him, so that her cheek hugged the
wall. "You mean to do this against my will?"

The question brought a soft chuckle up his throat. "When has it
ever been a question of me forcing you against your will?"

"From the very beginning. I never had a choice."

"And I never gave you one."

"You finally admit it, then."

"I admit nothing. If I had given you a choice, we'd still be standing at the music hall, drinking water."

"You flatter yourself."

"I thought we'd made progress."

"You thought—!"

"That we'd gone beyond the point where you had to deny your desire."

He put his lips to her neck, breathed in. Exhaled as if restraining a sigh, like the kind that a well-bred man, long starved, might make when seated before a savory meal. Then he kissed her neck and shuddered so delicately against her that she could feel but not name his longing for her.

She held the linen of his shirt in her arms, the flannel of his trousers against her legs. Her nose was pressed against his neck, and she was susceptible to the scent of soap blended to warm skin. She felt her resistance melt. She felt his muscles relax.

Mustering strength, she pushed against him.

He countered immediately, matching force with superior force. He grasped her chin and turned it so that she had to look at him. "I didn't come here to do this," he said, his voice edging with the violence she had hoped to incite.

She writhed but did not effect her release. "No?" Her tone was skeptical and provocative.

It was arousing to be gazing into gray eyes that were stained black with desire. It was intoxicating to be grasping the muscles of his forearms and shoulders, to feel him work to subdue her. Her power to command his exertion whetted her appetite for him that she had tried to stifle. It inflamed her desire for him that was lodged in every pore and that had been smoldering in the embers of pain and loss.

"Not primarily." He kept her pinned against the wall and was looking her straight in the eyes when he made himself a part of her. "But I'll take first things first."

He released her chin, put his lips and tongue to hers, moved against her, into her. Her body accepted his and cherished him like a true love lost and found, thirsting for his touch, yawning with the desire of release too long deferred.

He didn't seduce, and she didn't submit. They weren't making love. They were possessing one another. She was consuming him,

giving free rein to her hunger for him. She was scornful of modera-
tion in her desperate happiness to have him with her, in her, desiring
her. She resolutely ignored the funnel of sorrow that surely awaited
her, that would lure her down, down a drain of despair when he was
no longer at her side. She was deaf and blind to the reality that all she
had suffered in the past weeks was only the pale prelude to true pain.

Bathing himself in her heat and liquid, he felt a red carpet unfurl
inside him, stretch endlessly toward her, around her. He didn't care
why she had attacked him or how she knew that he would relish the
astringent sport of setting muscle to muscle. It was enough that he
could apply himself to redressing the irresistible and mysterious balance of forces between them that had gone awry. But, no, it had not
gone awry, it had intensified, and a delightful, dangerous suspicion
germinated in his brain that whatever that balance was, their positions were not, nor never had been, as clear as he had once thought.
He uncurled himself, uncoiled for her, let tendrils of emotions wrap
him, trap her.

When they came to a heaving, satisfied rest, he planted his forearms on the wall on either side of her and propped his chin on her
head, which was bent forward. This most undignified coupling did
not feel to him as undignified, merely necessary. He was entirely
winded.

She said against his shoulder, "If this was first things first, what's
second?"

He laughed at that with what little breath he had. "Death, maybe."

She moaned like a sleeping cat. "Ooh, lovely."

Later, when it was dark and they had settled themselves on her
bed, she indulged every impulse and allowed him every liberty. At
one moment she developed a loving interest in his thighs, moved her
lips along their flex and contours, let her hair spread across his groin
to mingle with his. At another moment, she kneeled beside him. She
put her hands to the wound on his back and brought him to bliss.

"Yes, there," he breathed, stretched out on his stomach, his arms
embracing a swan's down pillow, "and there, yes. Faith, but that feels

good, and what a perfect moment to tell you what I came to tell you."
He didn't want to move off this long horizon of relief from pain that
defined an entire territory of pleasure. "Ma foi. Ma foi. Yes. I bought
a chemical company."

She smoothed his back and drew her fingers away from the area of
his deepest wound. She sat back on her heels, her hands on her
thighs.

"Well?" he inquired.

"Well, what?"

"What do you have to say to what I just told you?"

She considered. "I'm waiting for the rest."

He plumped the pillow, nuzzled it. "I hardly know much more
about it myself. It's called Seine et Companie, and the principal
chemist, a man named Bourges, worked with Pasteur—ah, you know
who he—"

"I've heard of Louis Pasteur."

"Good. Well, Bourges worked with Pasteur over ten years ago on
the destruction of germs in vinegar and wine. While Pasteur has
more recently been applying his knowledge of chemistry to biology,
Bourges has kept on in his researches of agricultural chemistry. He
has a team currently working on stimulants to enhance crop production. I'm encouraging Bourges to continue his researches in
other realms of biology, and I've put him in touch with Laurent
Dreyfus. We'll see the result."

She asked him a few questions about the new project and engaged
him in spinning out his hopes and dreams for his company. She had
not been wrong to think he would find enthusiasm for this line of
work. He was obviously happy to be learning about chemistry and to
be in the position of applying research results to practical outlets. He
concluded some remarks with the observation that she should consult
with Laurent Dreyfus at her earliest convenience about how best to
organize the projects she had in mind for the neighborhood, now
that she had an entire chemical company at her disposal.

She was silent.

He repeated, "You'll wish to see Laurent about all of this, I'm guessing."

She refused to respond to that. Instead, she returned her hands to his back and asked, "That's all you have to tell me about what you have done in the past few weeks?"

He grunted contentedly into the pillow.

She said softly, "I read the newspaper, you know."

She could tell from the slight change in the muscle tension of his back that she had captured his attention.

"Yes, and I read about you. Oh, just the smallest of announcements. Insignificant in size, this announcement, and yet so very significant in effect."

When he moved to shift onto his side, she pressed him back onto his front and straddled him, sitting on his buttocks so that she wouldn't put undue pressure on the small of his back. She stretched her arms out and splayed her hands across his shoulders.

He permitted this gentle subjugation and said, "It doesn't concern you."

"I think it does."

He turned his head to look up at her. It was too dark for her to discern his expression, but she was aware of his focus on her and could feel dark forces gather, entice, and threaten. Quiet and calculating, he said, "A woman who dances in a music hall cannot have certain expectations."

He might as well have driven a stake through her heart. She leaned forward. "A woman who dances in a music hall may, nevertheless, expect undivided loyalty from her lover."

"You have that."

She slid her hands from his shoulders, sculpting skin and muscle, and rested them on either side of his neck. She breathed into his ear, "How little you know of me."

"I know that you approach your dance as a craft. You dress with quiet charm and propriety. Your taste in painting is abominable but endearing. You are observant, particularly with respect to bodily dis-

367

positions. Your strength impresses me and sustains me. You do not bow easily to the inevitable."

"But now you have a wife," she said, conjuring the woman who had come between them, "and must learn to know her and love her."

He grasped one of her hands at his neck. "You imagine that a man must love his wife? Of the two of us, you, my dear"—he levered himself onto his elbow—"are the romantic."

"And you're the liar."

Before she knew it, he had flipped them over, and she was stretched out beneath him flat on her back, legs spread, knees bent. He laced his fingers through hers and pinned her hands on the sheets on either side of her head.

"Which truth do you want?"

Which truth, indeed? The one that would assure her that he had the qualities to be a true and loyal husband? Or the one that would convince her that he loved her and her alone?

"The brutal truth," she answered.

"You want it in words?"

"Yes."

"You are mine, but I am not yours."

Lying beneath him, covered by him, she had never felt so vulnerable or available to him. Time was rolling back, turning itself inside out. She was back in Bergerac, but she wasn't standing under a plum tree about to be raped. She was high above the banks of the Dordogne, and it was eons before she had ever been born a poor peasant girl in Sainte-Foy-la-Grande. She was in a cave, and she was alone. Her man had returned to her. She was excited and happy to receive him, that he had chosen to find his comfort and pleasure at her cave. It made her want to dance and sing and paint and cook and bear children and gossip with friends. It made her want to keep him, to rely on him, to make him hers.

She couldn't keep him, rely on him, or make him hers. When he entered her, she settled for scheming to keep him coming back to

her. When every part of her down to the tip of each finger was satu-
rated with his possession, she decided to scheme no more.

Blue dawn suffused the room. They awoke entwined. He dressed,
and she accompanied him to the front door. She knelt down to pick
up his suit coat and overcoat which had lain crumpled on the floor all
night, just where he had shed them. She shook them out and helped
him put them on. She smoothed the wrinkles, trimmed the shoulders. He slipped his hands into his pockets, fishing for his gloves.
She opened the door for him.

He said, "I'll return the day after tomorrow, Jeanne."

"You will?"

"Yes."

He turned to go, but she stopped him by putting her arms around
his neck. She rose on tiptoe and put all her love into the kiss. His
hands came out of his pockets and gripped her shoulders. She whispered, "I'm fully alive only when I'm with you, Victor."

He accepted the tribute with a smile that was softened by tenderness. He paused, as if debating whether to respond in kind, but let
the opportunity pass. He kissed the top of her head and departed.

FIFTY-TWO

 "SHE DIDN'T COME down, as I say, but then one afternoon he came, and he didn't leave until the next morning."

Alexandra put her head down on her arms crossed atop the table to absorb the impact of that information. From one word to the next, one phrase to the next, the scene unfolded in her mind's eye with such intensity that she was unable to keep her head upright. Nor was she able to raise it when the old man continued.

"He came down the stairs and exchanged a few words with my mother who was in the courtyard. He had excellent manners. He was a Count, you know! In any case, he always spoke to my mother if she was playing outside. She wasn't more than six or seven years old at the time, but she insisted, when recalling the events later in her life, that she had noticed how pleased he had seemed with himself and the world that morning."

"I suppose he would have been," Alexandra said into the crook of her arm.

The old man grunted. "His self-satisfaction didn't last."

Alexandra lifted her head. "No?"

"I will come to that in a moment, but first I must tell you another part of the story. It concerns a man named Pierre who owned the café

370

at the corner. He came from . . . let me see . . . I can't remember which country it was—"

"Poland," she said listlessly. "His name was Piotr Wojinski, and he was my great-great-grandfather."

The old man accepted that piece of information as a matter of course. "Poland. Yes. He was to return to Poland eventually. Well. Pierre loved Jeanne, and he had been biding his time, waiting for the moment to declare himself. He had been following developments in the affair between the Count and Jeanne, and he must have seen his chance in the weeks following the night of the cancan. One day he summoned his courage, put on his best clothes, and bought a bouquet. Unfortunately, he arrived just in time to see the Count enter the building."

"Did the Count see him?"

"If he did, he didn't care. He had no cause to fear the rivalry of a café owner! And if I learned nothing else in my ninety years, it's that timing is all. Do I need to insist that poor Pierre's timing was disastrous?"

Alexandra shook her head. "What did Pierre do?"

"Needless to say, he didn't come to this building or try to see Jeanne that night. It is rumored that he went out and got very drunk. Very, very drunk." The old man wagged a finger. "And he did not have the reputation of being a hard-drinking man."

Alexandra murmured, "Not all Poles are heavy drinkers. So, tell me. Why did the Count's self-satisfaction not last?"

"I'm coming to that," he replied. "Now, our Jeanne came down later that day, in the afternoon. It was the first time she had shown her face in weeks. She looked lovely, but perhaps a little thinner, more fragile. Like a fairy princess, so said my mother who was a little girl at the time! She was nicely dressed too. Hat, gloves, jacket. All that was proper."

He paused dramatically.

"And?" Alexandra prompted.

"She left the building, and never came back."

"You mean, that was the last time your mother ever saw her? Or did she truly never come back?"

"She never came back."

"She left just like that? Her rooms, her clothing, the Count? Everything?"

"When she left the building, she said that she was going out and that she'd return later to fetch some of her things."

"And did she?"

The old man didn't answer her question. Instead, he shuffled out of the room. He returned bearing a small cardboard box. He placed it on the table in front of Alexandra.

He explained, "This is what I picked out of her rooms about fifty years ago. After the Second World War it must have been. The rooms had been unused for over fifty years before that. The furniture was worth nothing, and the clothes were full of holes, eaten by moths. There had been rumors that she owned some valuable paintings, but by the time I went into the rooms, they were long gone—that is, if they had ever been there to begin with."

Alexandra was picking through an odd assortment of ribbons falling to bits, scraps of lace, tissue paper, a long cardboard tube, an old ballet program, a few kitchen utensils, an antique pen, a pot of ink caked dry. The largest item was a notebook with a marbleized cover whose cotton ties had disintegrated, leaving the pages an irregular mess.

She gathered together the pages of the notebook and took it out of the box. As she set the cover aside, she said, "No one, except perhaps thieves, ventured into the rooms until after World War II? That seems odd, especially for the owners of a building with good rooms to rent."

The old man shrugged expressively. "I wouldn't say that my mother considered the rooms sacred, but she always said that it was better not to disturb them. And I never questioned her. It wasn't until she died in 'forty-five that I thought I should do something about the rooms. I went in one day, picked up these things, and closed the door again." He shook his head. "I decided that my mother had been right. It was better to leave whatever was there undisturbed."

Alexandra lifted up the top document in the notebook. She was finally satisfied to see that it was a marriage certificate affixed with the name of Jeanne Lacombe written in an old-fashioned script with a sputtering pen. This, then, was the signature she had seen scrawl across her mind's eye the evening she had left Val's house in North Carolina.

The man's name on the document read Piotr Wojinski.

She said, "All right, then. Jeanne walked out the door that day and married Pierre. But if she never came back, how did her marriage certificate get into this notebook?"

The old man winked. "It makes a good story to say she walked out and never came back." He amended his narrative, unembarrassed. "She came back. Maybe once, maybe twice, I don't know. But it's true that she left everything behind."

"What you mean is, she never saw the Count again."

"Yes, that's what I mean."

Alexandra turned the next page in the notebook and then the next. She hoped she might find the posters of Jeanne Lacombe that had been drawn by Toulouse-Lautrec. She didn't find those posters folded up in these pages but, rather, a strange series of sketches signed by the dwarf. She was puzzled to be looking at drawings of the plum-marinating contraption, the one on her grandmother's stove that Jeanne had described in the last installment of her story.

She said, "This is a very strange subject for an accomplished commercial artist to draw, no?"

"Toulouse-Lautrec," he replied, "had varied taste in subject matter."

"I know, and I've seen his medical sketches. But this—! Although the subject matter is far from captivating, these sketches are surely valuable."

"Yes, and they are now yours."

"But—"

"You said that you are the great-great-granddaughter of Pierre, which means that you are the great-great-granddaughter of Jeanne too. The box is of no use to me."

Alexandra rose, cradling the box in her arms. The old man nodded. She was suddenly so anxious to leave the building that she was out on the sidewalk before she remembered that she forgot to offer her thanks or even to ask whether he knew if Jeanne had accompanied her husband Piotr to Poland.

The door had already shut behind her with a familiar click. She swallowed a gasp to see Piotr Wojinski standing across the street from her, holding a wilted bouquet in hand and wearing an expression of infinite sadness. She didn't question that she had entered a time warp, and she knew it was the day after the last night she had spent with Victor. She went straight to Piotr. She intended to tell him that she would marry him. She also intended to tell him that she thought she was pregnant.

A certain knowledge came to her then. She wasn't Pierre's great-great-granddaughter. She was Victor's. She was a part of him. A very distant part of him.

She was nearly across the street when her vision cleared. She saw that the man wasn't holding a bouquet. He was holding a brightly patterned umbrella that he had collapsed halfway but not yet swirled closed with the snapped tab. He was looking at her in a curious but not offensive way, and then she noticed that he was standing, elbows linked, with a woman. His sister? His wife?

It was too late now for her to change course. The best she could do was to express in wretched French her mistake and back away from the scene.

The man pointed at Alexandra's chest, said "Krzyzewski," then engaged in a discussion with the woman at his side, every word of which Alexandra understood.

Any lingering effects of the time warp were dispelled. The Duke T-shirt she was wearing brought her back to the present. The man was still looking at it when he quoted, in heavily Polish-accented English, " 'I want to be like Mike.' Michael Jordan. Mike Krzyzewski. Coach K. Final Four."

Alexandra felt obliged to speak to the couple about Duke, how the men's basketball team had done this year, her Warsaw-Chicago connection, and the fact that Coach K was also from Chicago. She found it fittingly bizarre to be on this street in Montmartre, talking to two Polish tourists about American college basketball.

The chance encounter came to its natural conclusion. Hugging her box, she hurried down the street, hoping to outrun the rain that was beginning again and the tears that would come when her body fully registered the dreary end to Jeanne's story.

FIFTY-THREE

"IS THAT ALL, then?" Val inquired as he handed the report over to the policeman.

"That's all for now," Officer Surcouf said, exchanging the signed statement for Val's identity papers. "I'll call you as soon as I have some news for you."

"It's the first time this has happened to me in Paris," Val commented. "Or anywhere, really."

"Then you've been lucky."

As they left the back rooms and walked through the prefecture, Surcouf summarized the series of muggings and car thefts that had plagued the Ninth arrondissement and particularly the area around the Opéra in the past few weeks. Val expressed surprise that his car had been stolen from a parking lot known for its tight security. Surcouf speculated that it was precisely the attendants at that lot who had been staging the neighborhood thefts and that when a vintage Citroën had come their way, it had been too much for them to resist. Surcouf hoped that the solving of Val's case would break open the ring.

The police station was alive with activity. Tough-talking, tough-looking *voyous* littered the main hallway and were attended by smartly dressed officers in well-tailored shirts of French blue, crisp even now at one o'clock in the morning.

Val asked, "So you think the ones who held us up at the parking lot exit when we went to inquire about the missing car are the same ones who stole the car?"

"That's my guess," Surcouf said. "Or else there's a rival gang that crossed your paths at the wrong moment. Whoever it was, you were too good a foursome to pass up—just like your car."

Val exhaled gustily. "I wasn't carrying much cash, and my cards won't do them any good. Too many security codes."

Surcouf wagged heavy brows. "It's the loss of the lady's jewelry that poses your biggest problem now, I'm thinking."

Val grunted. It wasn't the loss of the lady's jewelry that was the problem, it was the loss of her composure. Pascale Mabillon, the friend Sophie had brought to the ballet, had suffered a crisis of nerves in the wake of the mugging, and she had blubbered all the way to the prefecture. Her husband, Roger, was good for hand-wringing only. Val wasn't looking forward to the return to the waiting room, for he doubted that Sophie, who had risen to the occasion more or less, would have been able to calm Pascale down during the time it took for Val to file his report.

"If you think of any other information to add later, let me know," Surcouf reminded Val when they arrived at the door to the waiting room.

Val nodded. He cast a jaundiced eye over the scene of Sophie holding a still-blubbering Pascale with a still-hand-wringing Roger hovering behind them.

Surcouf added, "I think I should prepare you for the worst. It's likely that in the next day or two we'll find the Citroën ditched somewhere in Nogent or Boissy, minus a part or two."

Val was philosophical. "It could be no worse than the condition it was in when I inherited it. I have a good mechanic."

"Very well, then." Surcouf extended his hand. "We'll be in touch." He clicked his heels, bowed slightly, and departed.

Val crossed the waiting room. Sophie looked up at him, not bothering to conceal her expression of harassed entreaty. She rose and brought Pascale to her feet.

"All we can do now is go home," Val said, "and wait to hear from the police. I'll call a couple cabs."

Out on the street, with the taxi door open, Pascale would not hear of Sophie leaving her. After several unsuccessful attempts to unpeel Pascale's arms from Sophie's neck, Sophie gave up and got in the taxi with Pascale and Roger. Val leaned in to give the cabbie the Mabillon's address, then closed the door on the threesome.

Sophie rolled the window down. Her disappointment was evident when she said, "I'm sorry, Valéry! I'll call you tomorrow." Then she reached out and grasped Val's tie. Drew him down to her and kissed him. She settled back in her seat, rolled the window up. She turned her head to look at him until the taxi turned the corner.

The way this evening ended was fine with Val, except for the stolen car, and he wasn't sorry to be standing on the curb and watching Sophie speed off without him. The time he had spent with her hadn't been bad. In fact, it had been rather enjoyable. Maybe it was the ballet, but he couldn't recall having ever enjoyed ballet before. He was sure he had never seen *Giselle,* and yet he had known from the beginning how it would end. In seeing the story unfold, he had taken the kind of pleasure he might in watching a good gangster flick, one that both respected its conventions and found new things to say. Maybe he was experiencing a freak of postmugging mellowness. Or maybe it was the knowledge that Alexandra was in Paris, not far from his reach.

Whatever the reason, Val felt liberated to be standing outside the police station, with no Sophie and no car to worry about and no particular place to go. He thrust his hands in his trousers pockets and touched an old key ring. He was wearing his most conservative suit. It wasn't until this moment that he remembered that he hadn't taken the keys to his grandmother's apartment out of his pockets after his visit to her the other day. He looked up and down the street, got his bearings, and realized that he was within walking distance of her apartment.

It had been raining on and off all day. Now it began to mist. The wet air fuzzed the streetlights and glistened the pavement. The distinctive wail of a Paris siren came and went as a paddy wagon screeched around the corner in front of him, heading for the prefecture courtyard. Something about his mood, this moment, and the weather made him decide to stroll to his grandmother's.

Not much later, on the street outside her apartment, he was not surprised, given his mellow mood, to see the lights still burning in her salon. He opened the street door, pressed the *minuterie* for light, and pushed the button by the appropriate name plate.

Hardly a moment later the door to the lobby buzzed open. He went in, took the steps in long strides. When he saw his grandmother standing on the landing with the door open, he couldn't help but say, "What were you thinking, grand-mère, to have opened the lobby door without asking who it was? Do you have any idea what time it is?"

She made an old lady's scoffing noise and gesture and answered his question, "It's two o'clock. Maybe it's the day. Maybe it's the night. It hardly matters at my age, when the next sleep I take may be my last."

Val stepped into the apartment behind her and closed the door. "I spoke to Magda, and she said your health is fine. Nothing to worry about."

She made another scoffing noise and gesture. "Magda, Magda. Elle n'en sait rien, Magda. She tells me to sleep all the time. I don't want to sleep. Especially not tonight. I knew you were coming. You see, I even dressed up for you."

"You look wonderful, grand-mère, and I'm glad you were expecting me." He followed his grandmother into the salon where the floor was fanned with papers. He was surprised into demanding, "What's this?"

His grandmother seemed quite pleased with herself. "After your last visit, I remembered the file box that François-Xavier put in the bedroom closet. I got it down this evening and started to go through it. You seemed so interested in papers."

Had he struck gold? Val knelt and began rapidly flipping through the nearest papers.

"Did you have a chance to reread your letters, then?" she asked him. "The ones you took the other day?"

Somewhat absently he said, "Yes, I read the correspondence between Great-Uncle Victor and Mademoiselle Odette."

His grandmother looked down at him, her brow troubled. "But, Victor, why do you call her Mademoiselle Odette? I thought you married her. Surely you would call her Madame."

With the solution to all his problems possibly at hand, he accepted with equanimity his grandmother's confusion between himself and Victor. However, he was surprised that Victor had married Odette. From his rapid scan of the letters, the lady in question had seemed clingy, weak. Not his type.

Val chuckled. "I did marry her, then?"

"Why, yes. She was a lovely woman, you know. So well bred. She played the piano like an angel. She adored you."

Val picked up the next pile, happy to humor her. "I was quite the devil in my day."

"Oh, you were! You stole her right out from under the nose of a rather strange fellow, Jean-Marc Lafitte."

"Tit for tat, I suppose," Val commented. "I remember your husband ranting and raving about how the Lafittes robbed him blind when he finally sold the last shares of Seine et Companie to them."

"But, you know, the Dorsainvilles have a history of stealing women from the Lafittes. You'll remember that my son Robert married the sweetheart of the only male descendant of the Lafitte line. Now, what was his name? Oh, yes, Jean-Philippe Chevalier."

At that Val looked up, arrested.

"Ah, but you, Victor! You were the best of the Dorsainvilles! You could have married anybody your heart desired, and you chose a most charming woman. However, I always suspected that you married Odette Gervais for her land—although you hardly needed more— and not for herself."

Val's nerves were steady but stretched. "Gervais? Which Gervais?"

"From Bergerac, of course. When you married her, you doubled your land and cut off that horrible Jean-Marc Lafitte's pretensions to grandeur. It always pained François-Xavier to think that, in the end, the Lafitte family finally got what they had been wanting for so long."

Val hadn't been able to read the faded ink of the woman's last name on any of the envelopes, but he hadn't given the matter much thought. Now it caused a shiver to trickle down his spine to realize that Victor's wife was an ancestor of Jean-Philippe's wife, Lucie. Val had always imagined that his grandfather's bad head for business had led to the demise of the Dorsainville fortune, but now he wondered whether the Lafittes hadn't put some kind of curse on the Dorsainvilles. What had remained a kind of nebulous suspicion that Jean-Philippe was working against him suddenly took shape, and Val understood now that Jean-Philippe was actively involved in his patent problem. Which made the sly old fox slick to the point of sleazy.

Just like a Lafitte.

Back to the papers. He was becoming as confused as his grandmother. The pressure of the patent problem was obviously getting to him. It was two o'clock in the morning. He had been mugged earlier in the evening, and now he was kneeling in a pile of papers strewn about by his senile grandmother who thought she was living in the days when her crazy husband had been alive. No wonder he was confused. Nevertheless, it seemed like a good thing to know that Lucie was a Gervais, that Jean-Philippe was a Lafitte, that his father had married Jean-Philippe's sweetheart, and that Victor had stolen Odette from Jean-Marc Lafitte.

He had dug down to a pile of Victor's papers. He was holding the deed to a property in Montmartre. Not the music hall—what was the one Victor had owned, the bill of sale of which Val had seen at the Art Institute in Chicago? Le Chat Noir. Something like that—no, this wasn't the deed to the music hall but to another building, perhaps an apartment building. And the next paper seemed to indicate that Victor had sold the building after the turn of the century to some woman named Hélène Bondieu. Given it to her, rather, for the price of one franc.

Val hardly ever went to Montmartre, didn't like to go there. What Parisian did?

Victor, apparently. Over a hundred years ago.

And now Alexandra.

He pocketed the copy of the deed and the bill of sale. He was about to ask his grandmother if she knew anything about Victor's interests in Montmartre, when an ominous, rattling sound from her throat brought gooseflesh to his skin.

She said, her voice strange, "I must thank you for coming to see me. One doesn't like to be alone at a time like this."

He rose to his feet quickly enough to catch her from falling to the ground.

Cradled in his arms, she smiled up at him and said, "I'm glad I put on my best dress and pearls. I can sleep comfortably now."

FIFTY-FOUR

BY TEN O'CLOCK that morning Val had already seen the doctor, had had his grandmother's body removed, and had spoken to the family lawyer. By midday he had cleaned up the papers on her living room floor and had come up, once and for all, empty-handed. By the end of the afternoon he had finalized the funeral arrangements. Now early evening, he was back at his apartment.

The shower and shave and change of clothing felt good. So did the single-malt scotch on the rocks. He listened to the messages on his machine. A number were from Sophie. Early in the day she was promising steamy sex, later in the day she expressed sympathy at his grandmother's passing. His thoughts veered toward Alexandra, drifted on past her, settled somewhere in Montmartre. Given the complications of the circumstances, he figured Sophie took precedence.

He picked up the receiver, first to call to have his car brought around from the garage, then to call Sophie. He put the receiver down again. What had felt like liberation the night before felt now like acute loss. His car had been stolen, his grandmother had died, and he experienced the pain of Christine's death all over again. What he wouldn't give for his sister to be alive again. To hold his hand. To tell him a funny story. To console him after a defeat. To cheer him after a victory. To seek his advice about her love life. To let him make her comfortable when she became too weak to help herself.

He left his apartment, working on instinct and driven by his demons. It was raining. He hailed a taxi, gave the address. When the honky-tonk of Montmartre came into view, he felt a kind of relief. His muscles began to regroup, as if preparing for more productive effort than that of mere resistance. The taxi turned up a steep street, came to a stop before a nondescript building with a brown door. Deposited him. Drove off.

Val stood on the narrow sidewalk, contemplating the darkened exterior of the building. The rain stopped. Moonlight stabbed through the clouds, splintering them like a silver knife chipping at blocks of ice. He raised his hand to knock on the door, but it opened before his knuckles made contact with wood. A man, short and bent with age, looked up at him. He stood in the shadow of the doorway. Val couldn't see his face, but he could feel a strong and mysterious force emanate from him that curled like a question mark.

Val inquired, "Are you the owner of this building?"

"C'est ça."

Val had always thought that what he didn't know about his past couldn't hurt him. He was coming to rapid terms with the notion that what he did know about it might help him. Strength from knowledge, even at the price of pain. He'd never learned well from pain, except how to avoid more of it, but that could change.

He opened with his most recently acquired piece of knowledge. "Do you know of anyone named Hélène Bondieu?"

"She was my mother."

"I suppose she died some time ago."

"Fifty years. Why do you ask?"

Val looked beyond the old man, into the courtyard illuminated by the moon. He felt the pull of it, wanted to step inside. He felt as if he'd been here before, but if he had, it couldn't have been in this lifetime. Once having made the decision to come here, his body was no longer disposed to resisting anything—not even irrational ideas about a former existence. He relaxed into a strength that he had formerly reserved for a power serve.

His response came from way at the back of his head and halfway down his spine. "Your mother was told that a man might return some day and wish to look around the building for old time's sake. She was told to pass the information along, in the event she died before the man returned."

"Ah?"

"I've come in that man's place."

The old man gestured for Val to enter. "Do you wish me to show you—"

"No need," Val cut him off.

The old man bowed. "Oui, monsieur."

Val stepped inside. He had been rude. He looked down at the man and smiled gently. "My manners were at fault. I should have said that I can manage on my own, Monsieur Bondieu, and have no wish to disturb you further."

The old man bowed again.

Val strode into the courtyard, bathed a moment in the moonlight. The space looked familiar, except for the wires coiling everywhere. He paused at the first step of the exposed staircase that climbed around the sides of the four walls of the courtyard. He took a deep breath, and another world came alive in his head. He looked back at the old man who was hanging by the entryway.

"She's been here recently, hasn't she?"

The old man nodded.

Val took the first step up. He wasn't referring to Alexandra, although she hovered at the edges of his awareness. As he walked up, the regrouping of his muscles accelerated. He felt strong and powerful and in command. He felt the kind of physical evolution he had experienced when he had walked into that painting in Chicago, descended the double staircase, and walked out into the Bois de Boulogne. Only now he was already in Paris, walking up and not down, and the woman he was going to see was the same one who had met him that day on the polo field. Her name was not Odette, and he had not married her.

He ascended the first flight. He winced at the fragment of a memory that the first time he had been in this staircase, he had not been walking. Instead he had been stretched out flat on his back and was being carried up on a board. He ascended the second flight, as if he had just found his legs. He felt the stretch of muscles in his calves as he took one step up, then the next. He was aware of the swing of his arms. He adjusted his new bearing to the set of his shoulders, his neck. This was re-membering: finding the members and putting them back in place. He ascended the third flight and remembered owning estates in Bergerac, the property in Versailles for his horses, the Hôtel d'Albret in rue du Faubourg-Saint-Honoré, his vaults filled with stocks and bonds, this very building. He ascended the fourth flight, anticipating a pleasure rather keener than any other he had ever known.

On the landing he remembered that he had come to see Jeanne. There was only one door. On other occasions he had opened it with a key. Now the lock was long broken. He pushed at the door. It groaned open on rusted hinges. For the very first time he was filled with a sense of foreboding. He doubted that he would find what he was looking for.

He stepped into an eerie, draping forest of cobwebs cleft by swords of moonlight that penetrated the glass roof panes at the far end of the room. A thick layer of moss had buried several large objects, possibly furniture, and had spawned gigantic spores. He proceeded toward the far end of the room, inching his way toward the light, slashing through the cobwebs as an explorer might chop his way through dense underbrush. He looked up and saw that several of the glass roof panes were cracked. Leafy vines, thick as a man's wrist, had climbed through the cracks to trellis the wall and festoon a barre that ran along the wall to the door. Rain had fallen through the cracks over the years, and the row of houseplants below had grown leggy and out of control. Their pots had broken. The dirt had spilled to the floor where the roots from various plants had tangled together in looping coils, like spilled intestines. The dirt and the leaves smelled of seduction and fermentation and death.

He recognized this space and almost wished he hadn't come. This had been a charming room once, but perhaps never again. It had been subject to soft rot for over a hundred years, had bred layers of fungi that had accrued to green yeast, like money well invested. If this were a fairy tale, he might be able to wake the sleeping princess with his kiss and restore the decay to life. But he was no prince pure of heart, Jeanne was long gone, and the room was ruled by a spell that his fortune had no power to break.

He fought his way to the adjacent room, accompanied by furtive moonbeams that played hide-and-seek around the lianas of dust and dirt. The surrealist cinema in his head was running in Technicolor and four dimensions. He saw disjointed scenes play themselves out before his very eyes. He heard quiet sighs of satisfaction. He felt beautiful, sticky sensations course through his veins. The comfort he had always taken in this retreat came to him as a watering in the mouth, and it tasted like plum cake. He blinked in disbelief to see an ethereal plum-marinating contraption float by him and guessed this hallucination to be a trick of moonbeams.

The tricky moonbeams escorted him into the bedroom, darting around the impossible corner of the doorway and scattering throughout the room. They illuminated the bed with its ghostly bridal canopy of cobwebs, the armchair that had disintegrated into an oversized sponge, the armoire whose doors were crippled and useless, the walls whose peeled paper exposed open wounds of raw wood where valuable paintings had once hung. They traveled and twinkled at the corner of the room where stood the washstand and a cheval glass facing the door at a slight angle. They danced around the oblong frame of the glass, glanced off its mirrored surface.

He stepped into the room and swallowed a strangled oath to see an image floating in the silvered depths of the mirror. Whirled to see who was behind him, since he himself was not standing in line with the mirror. Understood in a flash who was in the room with him, but not behind him. When he had ascended the staircase, his bodily transformation had been muscular and skeletal. In the second it took for him to turn his head back around, he felt an electric charge bolt down his spine and transform his nervous system. As he drew nearer to the mirror, the surrealist cinema stopped. In its place was a coherent narrative, known to him but not completely, in every one of his nerve endings.

After several paces he stopped, awestruck. He was looking at an indistinct image of a man several decades older than himself, the face familiar as his own. The man's hair was dark with a silvering at his temples.

He knew who it was and breathed the name aloud. "Victor."

Perhaps the image spoke, perhaps it didn't. In some dimension of perception, the question was asked, "What do you want?"

He laughed in fear and uncertainty. "I don't want this."

The image wavered. "You must want something to have come here."

"I've come"—he cleared his throat, but the words still broke painfully—"to find Jeanne."

The image came into focus. Victor Louis Dorsainville was a distinguished figure of a man. He was dressed with the understated perfection of another era. His bearing was a finely nuanced blend of strength and elegance. His manner reconciled the paradox of the cordial and the aloof.

"You could not have expected to find her," the image said, "so you must have come for a different reason."

He pulled himself together, looked his past in the eye. "I must have come, then, to hear whatever it is you have to tell me."

The image briefly inclined its head. "You wish me to remind you that I have everything you are trying to regain."

He marveled at the self-evident truth of that statement. "That's right. You have everything I'm trying to regain."

"Perhaps you also wish me to tell you how it feels."

"I know how it feels." Vibrant and wolflike. Thick and rich. Sinewy and strong.

"Then I need not belabor the point."

"Instead, tell me how to regain it."

Victor's expression was serene. "You have observed in me what you know as a pleasing ruthlessness. You possess that most useful quality and have only to develop it to a more refined degree. You also already know what you need to do. You do not need me to tell you."

"Is there anything that you do need to tell me?"

"One of your enemies has walked up behind you and has raised his knife to your back."

"What am I to do?"

"You already know what to do," the image repeated.

He did. Marry Sophie and neutralize Jean-Philippe. "What happened to Jeanne?"

The face of the man in the mirror gave away nothing. "She surrendered to me her whole being, then surprised me by leaving me."

"Why?"

The smile in the mirror was graceful. "You are quite right. I should not have been surprised."

"No, I mean, why did she leave you?"

The image paused. "I married elsewhere in order to double my estates in Bergerac and to defeat my rival."

"And how did it go for you after Jeanne left you?"

"I tripled the net worth of my investments."

"How did you do that?"

"By not looking back."

He laughed again, this time wryly. "That is one skill I have perfected."

"Indeed."

"So you didn't marry for love?"

The smile was chilling. "I did not marry until I had first secured love."

"What do you mean?"

The image expressed delicate contempt of the question with the words, softly spoken, "My dear boy . . ."

The image seemed to fade, so he said quickly, "You doubled your estates. You tripled your investments. All that is good. What went badly for you?"

The image returned to consider the question. "Within the first few months of my marriage, a particularly spirited horse threw me, and I am afraid that my back problem worsened over time. Not enough, however, to keep me from riding."

He felt an intensified pain in his own back. "You tried to find her, didn't you?"

The image didn't respond. Instead its presence seeped through the room, saturating it with the deep blue of melancholy and the pitch of penance and regret. Still, he denied the implication of Victor's restless spirit haunting these rooms. "Was it worth it, marrying Odette?"

"Need you ask?"

"Yes."

The smile in the mirror was one of aristocratic hauteur. "Then you are not yet worthy of the answer. You have been avoiding your enemies, and it is almost too late." The smile lingered while the surrounding image dissipated. Then even the smile was gone, and the mirror went blank.

A crackle of electricity jangled through his nerves. His normal senses returned, and he was shocked into the present. Moonbeams no longer defied the laws of physics, and he looked around the room, which had gone completely dark. He was aware of layers of dust and dirt and sadness. He backed out of the room, groped his way around the door frame.

He moved around the gigantic spores in the front room, choked on cobwebs. He arrived on the landing, gasping for air, gulping freshness into his lungs. He shook out his arms, cleared his head, then descended the stairs. With each flight down he felt the loss of love and comfort, then land, then money, then more land, then more money.

In the courtyard, he met the old man. He had lost everything but his dignity. He said politely, "Thank you for letting me have a look around."

The old man bowed. "You laid the ghost to rest?"

Val chuckled, more with skittish nerves than amusement. "You've seen it?"

The old man narrowed his eyes. In the moonlight the shelves of his craggy brows cast deep shadows and hid his expression. "When I went in the rooms, fifty years ago already it was, I thought there might have been a ghost of a man."

"And the woman? Where did she go?"

"Disappeared."

"Did your mother tell you stories of her?"

The old man shrugged. "Many stories she told me, all of them different. Some people said the woman left the country. Others said she stayed in the neighborhood and died. In childbirth, so it was rumored. Still others said she was murdered. What was sure was that she married and had a child before she either left Paris or left this earth."

"Which version of the story do you believe?"

"It doesn't matter, since it was a cruel fate one way or the other that followed her."

"Did the man ever come looking for her?"

"Often at first. Less often as the months went by. Then, at last, he gave the building to my mother, as I have said, and when he died"— he glanced upward—"he returned, perhaps for eternity."

A few moments later Val was standing once again in the street outside the building. Victor had chided, chastened, and dismissed him. The old man had refused to tell him the end of the story.

He knew what to do.

FIFTY-FIVE

 JEAN-PHILIPPE WAS aware that someone had come to the threshold of his inner office, but he continued to give his attention to the papers before him, making notes in the margins. He let the seconds slip calmly past, twenty or thirty of them perhaps, just for that special touch, before he looked up. He smiled slightly, put down his pen, and invited his visitor into his office. He didn't rise from his own seat at his desk or offer his hand.

Jean-Philippe did, however, offer his visitor his condolences at the passing of Madame Dorsainville. The fine young man from such an excellent old family accepted them, then took a seat in the leather chair Jean-Philippe indicated in front of the marble-topped desk behind which he sat.

Jean-Philippe proceeded immediately to the point. "You've come to give me good news."

The fine young man who looked so grave this afternoon shook his head. "I've come to discuss my patent difficulties."

"You have not resolved them, then."

"They are currently unresolvable, I think you might say."

"I am distressed to hear it."

"But not surprised to hear it."

Jean-Philippe cocked his head. "What do you mean?"

"My patent difficulties begin and end in France."

"Ah?"

"Yes. The French National Patent Registry has suggested on several occasions that I drop my patent application because of possible infringement."

"Infringement is a serious and often expensive matter," Jean-Philippe said. "I am not sure that Seine-Lafitte could withstand the loss of a patent infringement case. It could run into millions of francs—that is, if you were determined to persist in marketing your product outside of France."

"And if I were so determined?"

Jean-Philippe said seriously, "I would be compelled to advise against it."

"Would you?"

"I must give advice that is best for the company." Jean-Philippe sighed. "It is a pity that advice could so adversely affect your career here." His eyes rested on the fine young man who once had such a promising career on the international tennis circuit, such a promising career at Seine-Lafitte. "I am sorry to say that I have, in fact, already felt compelled to mention to Yves the mounting losses attributable to the interminable—and now to hear you say it, unresolvable—delays on TEFS."

"I'm sure it pained you to do so, Jean-Philippe, but I must tell you that I suspect the National Patent Registry of either incompetence or malfeasance."

Jean-Philippe appreciated the fact that the fine young man was willing to play this out in the grand manner. Jean-Philippe could do no less than play his part, and so he affected proper shock.

"You see, I believe that the microscopic mechanism I developed for skinning the PCR capsule was entirely original."

"So it seemed. Quite original, in fact, when I first took a look at it." Jean-Philippe smiled apologetically. "But, as a mere accountant, I am hardly a judge of such things."

"Perhaps you know that the mechanism was not an original invention but rather an original application."

"I am in no more position to know that than I was to have guessed that your difficulties were unresolvable. You seem to think me unusually prescient, Valéry. I am flattered, of course, but I am afraid that you overrate me."

The fine young man paused a moment before understanding dawned on his unmistakably Dorsainville features. "You and I have been playing different games, Jean-Philippe. Mine is tennis. You like cloaks and daggers."

Jean-Philippe frowned with concern. "I begin to wonder, cher Valéry, whether the stress of your recent difficulties hasn't caused you to become, perhaps, mildly delusional."

"It's no delusion of mine that when I was growing up my grandfather had built a ball-pitch contraption. One that worked with a ratchet and a hook and columns of melting wax that could be regulated to pitch tennis balls at a variety of intervals." The fine young man leveled him an impressive gaze. "I suppose you met my grandfather when you were younger. Perhaps on the estates in Bergerac. Although the Dorsainvilles and the Lafittes were never best of friends, they had more than enough contact with one another over the years."

Jean-Philippe did not deny his family connection. "I may have met your grandfather. And so?"

"Then you may know that he fancied himself something of an inventor. My PCR capsule skinning mechanism is a microscopic version of my grandfather's ball-pitch contraption, and that contraption was based on an even older plum-marinating mechanism. Thus, the National Patent Registry is mistaken, for one reason or another, in its suggestion of infringement on my part. If there is a prior or pending claim on the mechanism it would be in the name of Dorsainville."

"You would need proof of your family's right to the mechanism, no?"

"I have told you the origin of the idea. Since I do not believe that such a mechanism would be invented twice independently, it is my belief that you found drawings of such a mechanism in the files of Seine et Companie."

Jean-Philippe permitted himself an unkind laugh. "Et alors, mon cher Valéry, you *are* delusional! You think that I would hand your grandfather's drawings over to you just like that?" He snapped his fingers. "Because you ask for them? Or are you threatening me in a way that I am too dull to have perceived?"

The fine young man echoed, "My grandfather's drawings?"

Jean-Philippe perceived his mistake, attempted a cover-up. "You did say that your grandfather developed the ball-pitch contraption, did you not?"

"But I didn't say that he had ever made any drawings of it." The fine young man looked almost satisfied. "I had thought him too crazy to have had such a wise business idea. It is a comfort to me to know that he was not stupid, but rather trusting. It seems that the Lafittes have a habit of stealing from us."

Jean-Philippe decided that he had made no mistake. Let the fine young man writhe in the knowledge that he had been bested. "You may think whatever you wish about the competence of the National Patent Registry—or about the Lafitte family, for that matter—since I have no need to defend my family's honor to you. As for you making any personal claim to the patent on your so excellent cancer diagnostic product, you will need proof."

The fine young man rose from his chair. "You're right, Jean-Philippe," he said pleasantly, "in order to initiate any personal legal claim, I will need proof."

The fine young man stretched out his hand, as if over the net, to congratulate the winner. Jean-Philippe recalled that Valéry had always been portrayed in the press as a graceful loser. So many qualities he had, Jean-Philippe mused, including the ability to bring a radiant glow to a pretty plum's cheeks. Too bad he had no more business sense than his crazy grandfather who had whistled away Seine et Companie to Jean-Philippe's uncle for a song.

Jean-Philippe accepted his hand.

"I may never get that proof," the fine young man continued, "but I want you to know that I know what you are."

It was an insult, and Jean-Philippe bridled minimally, withdrew his hand. "You are angry, certainly, over the loss of such a promising product, so I will overlook your comment." Jean-Philippe fixed his mask firmly in place. "And to show you that I hold no hard feelings, I will ask you, please, to let me know if there is anything I can do for you in the future . . . ?"

"Thank you for your kind offer, and I will ask you not to withdraw funding from the Rosenberg team."

Jean-Philippe smiled indulgently. "I have not yet reviewed the profit projections for this year, but it is possible that Seine-Lafitte may well not be able to afford them any longer."

"Seine-Lafitte cannot afford not to afford them. Their research is verging on a breakthrough in cancer therapy, as you yourself know."

Jean-Philippe held up his hands, shrugged helplessly. "But, my dear boy, what do expect me to do?"

"I expect you to have TEFS on the market within the next eighteen months."

Jean-Philippe clucked his tongue. "Have you forgotten the patent difficulties? You have called them unresolvable, and I cannot work miracles." He smiled as if he were twisting a knife into the gut of his worst enemy. "I shall try, of course."

The fine young man turned to leave the office, then turned back around to ask, "So what is it, in your opinion, Jean-Philippe, between you and me? Beyond the fact that you didn't like my father, of course. Any ideas?"

Jean-Philippe found that he was rather charmed by the question. "I have never given the matter much thought, and why should I? Let us say simply that I do not like you any better than I liked your father."

The fine young man left his office. Jean-Philippe returned to his papers, reflecting that it was true he had hated Robert Dorsainville. However, upon further reflection, he acknowledged that there was something more to the dislike he felt for Robert's son, Valéry. Something deeper and purer, more like loathing.

Yes, loathing, complete and total. And from the request the fine young man had made about funding for the Rosenberg team, it seemed that he meant to be wearily noble—despite Jean-Philippe's best efforts to set doubts in his mind about his pretty plum. Now, it seemed unlikely to Jean-Philippe that sex could turn to love—or that anything could turn to love—but with such a noble fool as a Dorsainville, anything was possible.

Which was why Jean-Philippe was so pleased with himself to have prepared for any and all possibilities. No matter which way Valéry turned now, Jean-Philippe already had it covered.

FIFTY-SIX

"THAT'S A WICKED case of the flu you got there, A.K.," Larry said. He put the back of his hand to Alexandra's forehead. "No fever. But no color either. You're as pale as a ghost, and you look as weak as a kitten."

Jack was standing at Alexandra's bedside, not saying a word.

Larry exhaled. "I wish I'd paid attention to you earlier in the week! Already the first night at the opening reception, you were coming down with it. At least we can rule out something you ate here, because you obviously came with the bug already in you."

"If I could just get some sleep," she said, her voice thin and lacking energy, "I'll be a lot better."

"You'd be even better if you saw a doctor," was Larry's opinion.

Jack still said nothing, but he didn't think a conventional doctor would cure this unconventional illness.

She shook her head. "No doctor."

"Food, maybe," Larry suggested.

She held up her hand in an expression of horror. "No food, really! I couldn't stomach it right now."

"Well, it's the flu, for sure," Larry pronounced. "I don't think there's anything you can do, A.K., but to sleep it off and then get on the plane tomorrow."

When neither Larry, Scotty, nor Hao had run into Alexandra at the meeting on the fifth day of the conference, they figured that she was hanging out with her Polish friends. Jack wasn't sure where she was, but he was giving her breathing room away from him. When she didn't show up on the last day for their very own team presentation, all four were understandably concerned, especially Jack. As soon as their presentation had ended that afternoon, they hightailed it over to her hotel. Larry and Jack had found Alexandra lying on top of her bed, wearing jeans and a Duke T-shirt, looking as if she had worn them a day or two and slept in them overnight.

"Call me if you need anything," Larry said. "You've got my number."

Jack left the room with Larry, and together they went down to the lobby where Scotty and Hao were waiting. Larry was expressing his various medical interpretations of Alexandra's physical state, while Jack kept his very unscientific explanations to himself.

"I guess she'll be all right," Larry said somewhat dubiously to Scotty and Hao who wanted to know how their team member was faring. "Although I've never seen her look quite that . . ." The appropriate adjective failed him. "Well, now that we've assured ourselves that she's alive, what's up for our last night in Paris?"

Scotty had plans with a stylish gene therapist from Paris. Hao had other cats to whip, as the French saying went. Jack decided to settle himself right there in the lobby of Alexandra's hotel. Larry sat down with him, to chew a little fat before moving on for the evening.

They installed themselves in the cozy seating area. Another man was already there, reading a newspaper. Jack had noticed him over the past several days when he had stopped by on irregular occasion to see whether Alexandra was around. She never was. It wasn't until Larry insisted on getting into Alexandra's room that Jack realized she had been in bed the whole time. Anyway, this man in the lobby was still there, still reading his newspaper, still minding his own business. But what the hell was this guy's business? If he was a businessman, he should at least be doing business, and if he was a tourist, he should be out and about. But he didn't seem to have any job other than sitting there reading his newspaper. Looking nondescript. So nondescript that Jack wasn't sure if it was every time the same guy sitting there.

Jack was suspicious of him. But, then, he had begun to be suspicious of every French man in Paris—and there were plenty of them.

Larry was discussing how their team presentation had been received and the lively interest in A.K.'s innovative work on telomeres—too bad she hadn't been there to answer the many questions that arose. Larry was now convinced that her quirky reinterpretation of the enzyme process in cell life and death might be the real breakthrough that would arrest the cancer plague of the late twentieth century.

Jack was listening, even participating in the discussion after a fashion, but he was more involved in his own thoughts.

He was remembering a story. One he must have read when he was a little boy, although he couldn't think how he might have come across such a story, since it didn't fit the usual lines of a legend or a myth or a fairy tale or a Hardy Boys adventure. It was a dislocated story about a young woman who was French—or was she Polish?—he couldn't quite remember her nationality. Or was it that he couldn't remember the nationality of the hero? French? Polish? Despite his hazy recollection of the particulars, he had a vivid image in his mind of the events and the main elements of the story. As he recalled it—and this was the part that had struck him so forcefully as a little boy when he had first heard (read? dreamt?) it—there was no hero. So, actually, what he didn't know was whether the nonhero was French or Polish. Or both. Or neither. But there was a villain, and the villain was unmistakably French.

Jack had identified with the nonhero, of course, and the nonhero had been in love with the young woman. As a little boy, Jack had always pictured her as a "damsel in this dress," and that dress had consisted of—again, the specifics were out of place for a children's story—a pink-lined black silk–laced bodice and puffy pink taffeta skirts gathered in front to the knees and dropping like a swallow's tail in back, completed with black silk stockings. In later years, he had re-examined that image for latent cross-dressing impulses on his part, but since he'd never had any homoerotic urges, he figured that such was the dress of the woman in the version of the story he knew. As for the young woman, his adult mind knew that he had confused her completely with Alexandra. Fine with him.

The story went like this: A young woman had been seduced and betrayed by a noble lover who had gotten her pregnant. The nonhero had watched the seduction, had tried to stop it, but had not been successful (as befit the role of a nonhero). When the noble lover betrayed her, the young woman left him. She wanted to hide from her noble betrayer and sought the nonhero's protection. But the nonhero (again, as befit the role of a nonhero) did not protect her. No, in the end he had been careless with his treasure, and he had underestimated the villainy in the French villain's heart.

The nonhero had an errand to run, some foolish, insignificant errand that he could have accomplished at any time — or never. His timing had always been bad, but this time it was disastrous. The villain came when the nonhero was away from the apartment, found the young woman heavy with child, started slapping her around — so it seemed from the way the furniture was displaced. She fell on her back. It must have been a hard fall, for when the nonhero returned, he found her dead in a pool of blood, and an infant crying, still attached to the umbilical cord.

Neighbors later reported having seen a nasty, wicked French nobleman leave the apartment. They had heard the noises, the shifting of heavy furniture. No one could describe the villain's face or which way he had come from or which way he went. It made no difference to the nonhero who could not prosecute a nobleman and win. The nonhero raised the baby as his own, as a living product of his dead love. Sometime later the nonhero went back to where he came from — wherever that was.

It was a strange story for a little boy to have come in contact with, much less remember in such painful detail. Jack didn't care how he had heard it, he only knew that it was guiding his actions now and that no way was he going to move from Alexandra's hotel until he left with her the next day to go to the airport. He wished he could get her the hell out of this country tonight.

Presently, Larry stood up to leave. Jack rose with him, and at that moment who but the half-ass Dorsainville should walk in. It felt to Jack as if he had waited a long, long time to be in the right place at the right time. To be the hero. Who would get the girl.

VAL WALKED INTO the hotel to hear Larry exclaim, "This is a lucky encounter!"

Val had certainly not expected to meet Larry in the lobby of Alexandra's hotel, and he needed only one glance at the suspicion that registered on Sandifer's face to realize that this was not a lucky encounter at all.

Val greeted Larry with apparent pleasure, shook his hand, extended it to Sandifer. "I've come to see Alexandra," he said easily. "I can guess that you have too."

Sandifer took his hand but didn't return his greeting. Instead, he said baldly, "She's not here."

Val thought that Larry was going to say something, but whatever it was, he swallowed it and began to cough.

Val asked, "She isn't?"

"Nope," Jack said.

"Do you know where she is?"

"Out."

Val could hardly miss the open hostility. "Do you know if she happens to have plans for the evening?" he asked next, glancing to Larry and scanning his studiously blank face.

Sandifer wasn't relinquishing control of the conversation. He said, "She's coming back shortly, which is why I'm waiting here in the lobby for her to return. She and I are going to a movie later."

Wherever Alexandra was, Sandifer wasn't going to let Val get near her. Val had no choice but to retreat. He was getting a lot of practice at being the gracious loser this evening. "Well, then, I'm happy to have run into the both of you, so you can brief me on the progress of the oncology conference."

Larry saved the situation from complete awkwardness by dutifully recapping the week's activities. As he spoke, Val's newly sharpened perceptions began to pick up peculiar signals. One moment Val was looking at Lawrence Rosenberg, Ph.D., a good, honest man at the head of a cutting-edge cancer research team. The next moment he was seeing another good and honest doctor, Laurent Dreyfus, who had been a friend of Victor's over a hundred years before. Laurent had kept abreast of the latest developments in medical research. He had been compassionate. Val guessed that Laurent had always been kind to Jeanne. And now Larry was helping Sandifer shield Alexandra from Val.

And Jack? Val had a strong impression of Sandifer as a guard dog. Or a hydra who grew another head for every one Val cut off. Hadn't he already slain this guy—or some version of him, anyway—on the tennis field of battle back in Chicago?

Jack sat back down. Val had no choice but to leave the hotel with Larry. They said their good-byes. When he was standing alone in the street, Val felt patterns weave and reweave inside him, around him. Larry, Jack, Alexandra. Jean-Philippe. Lucie.

His thoughts turned to Sophie. He tried to place her in the context of his past life and came up with nothing. A total blank. Toward her he felt—what?

He felt hungry. He went to the nearest telephone booth and punched Sophie's numbers. Yes, he was hungry. For a win, and Sophie was his ticket to the Grand Slam title that had never been his. Wouldn't Chevalier be surprised? Val could almost see the look on Jean-Philippe's face when Val would be holding the victory trophy in his hands. In his mind's eye, he held the trophy above his head for all to see, kissed it.

Victor had told him that he had not yet confronted all his enemies. Plural. He had confronted one enemy in Jean-Philippe, but he had a sense that he still had one more enemy to defeat.

Sophie answered. "Allô?"

He heard her voice and knew that his last enemy was himself. Would he be strong enough to resist temptation and the desires of his own worst self?

"Sophie."

After a long pause she said, "Valéry," and her voice rang with all the hot anger of a woman scorned.

"You've been talking to Jean-Philippe, I take it."

"Lucie too," she snipped.

"We have some things to talk over, you and I, Sophie."

"You do. I don't."

"I'll accept that distinction and, yes, I have things I'd like to talk over with you."

"Your low-class philandering?" she demanded scornfully. "Spare me!"

"I'd rather not."

"You already know I am against infidelity, but I don't think you have heard my thoughts on your little choice."

Val saw the fork in the road. He could develop his capacity for ruthlessness. He could, for instance, marry Sophie. Or he could end the cycle. Walk away. Let Jean-Philippe carry off the prize.

He thought of Victor's riches and felt that appetizing strength flow through blood and muscle. He thought of regaining his family's fortune and rightful part of Seine et Companie. He thought of the wealth that would be his, if he did indeed marry Sophie and become a permanent part of the Seine-Lafitte hierarchy. However, he also knew that none of that wealth would come from the profits from TEFS, for Jean-Philippe was capable of withholding the patent application indefinitely, and all of Val's efforts to produce an effective, low-cost cancer diagnostic that could save millions of lives would go down the drain. If he walked away, however, TEFS would be out on the market in the next calendar year.

So was it going to be the drain? Or his dream? To turn his back on everything and let Jean-Philippe take it all would require an enormous amount of personal integrity. And integrity, Victor would have said with a charming smile, was a damnably inconvenient bother.

He said, "I'll be over in fifteen minutes."

"You won't."

"I will."

A pause, a passionate sigh, then the capitulation Jean-Philippe had worked so hard to prevent. "All right. You can come over, but I'll give you only a half hour to explain yourself."

He experienced again that evolution in reverse, from man to wolf. As the reverse evolution continued, he figured he could have Seine-Lafitte and Alexandra too. He could have the world arranged to his satisfaction. The way it had been before. The way it was supposed to be. Victor would have been proud.

But Victor had paid a price for his ruthlessness, although not in terms of money or possessions, and in the end he had had nothing.

At the thought, the reverse evolution halted. When Val considered the end of his association with Seine-Lafitte, when he released his grasp on his dream of regaining his family's fortune at whatever cost, he experienced a curious new sensation. He felt as if he were taking up less space and more space in the world, both at the same time. He felt the patterns weave and reweave into an internal fabric, something durable and dependable. This, then, must be integrity. He guessed that integrity held a more true and abiding strength than ruthlessness.

And, yes, cultivating that integrity was going to be a damnably inconvenient bother. Beginning now.

"That's all I need, Sophie dear."

FIFTY-SEVEN

 ALEXANDRA CLOSED HER eyes and let her head fall back. She had just shot a blue tracer dye into the gel with the enzymes and proteins she had grown overnight in her yeast culture. All of a sudden, she was seeing the sequencing results before her very eyes, which was impossible, but she didn't want to clear her head of the vision. She wanted to tap into the powers of the Lurking Lab Gnomes that scurried around and chattered at her from the cracks and crevices.

She was seeing flower chains floating on a sun-dappled pond. She was seeing an impressionist painting of thymine and guanine spread in shimmering TTGGGG patterns across the canvas of her mind's eye. She was seeing uninhibited cell division brought about by telomerase.

Turn telomerase off, and turn off cell division. Turn telomerase on, and cancer grows unchecked. The chorus line of TTGGGGs was dancing wildly in her head, meaning that telomerase was present and active, but she had no idea how to turn it off, how to make the cancan cancer stop. And if she couldn't stop it, Jeanne would dance herself to death.

Jeanne was dying.

Alexandra opened her eyes. She was losing her mind. No, she

was experiencing a scientific breakthrough. Same difference. Breakthrough. Heartbreak. Both verged on death.

She snapped off her gloves and announced, "I'm going out."

Jack, working steadily at his station, looked over at her, brow fur-
rowed. Scotty and Hao stopped fussing at the thermocycler long
enough to exchange glances of concern. Larry walked through the
door at that moment and asked, "Feeling better, Alexandra?"

No, I'm dying. "I'm fine," she said. "I just need a breath of fresh air."

"Good idea," Larry said. "You haven't regained your color since
Paris. By the way, have you been to a doctor yet?"

She shook her head.

"We're standing in the middle of one of the world's best medical
facilities, and it's foolish for you not to see one of the specialists at
Duke."

"Too late now, since I'm over the worst of it," she said, "only a little down."

"Aren't we all?" Larry said glumly. "I always knew that funding
wasn't secure until everyone had signed on the dotted line, but I
never before considered the possibility that such a rich company
would actually invoke an escape clause." He shook his head. "Or even
write one in. Guess I overlooked it."

Bad news had hit the lab on the day after their return from Paris.
Seine-Lafitte was withdrawing funding from the Rosenberg research
team. What had taken two years to negotiate had fallen apart in less
than two months. Although no one spoke his name just then, it had
been reported that Val Dorsainville was to blame for the mess. He
might have plumped up profit projections for his diagnostic product
or mucked up the legal matters concerned with it or misrepresented
the test results for it. Whatever the case, Alexandra was left not only
unloved but also unfunded, and when the call came from the real estate agent in Chicago, saying she'd found the perfect house in the
suburbs, Alexandra no longer had the down payment and became
too depressed to work.

Still, she was gripped by the idea that if she didn't focus on her work, she would die, and she'd known all along, deep down, that her life depended on a choice between love and work. Jeanne had abandoned her work with Dr. Dreyfus, and Jeanne was dying . . .

"Yeah, escape clauses are the pits," she said, looking at Larry, "and that's what I'm going to do now. Escape. I need a little air."

"Going for a walk?" Jack asked. "Want company?"

An eerie feeling spirited over her. This was how it had begun. Two months ago she had been hallucinating telomerase and had intended to take a walk in the gardens. Instead, she had cruised the hospital hallways and had seen Val.

Break the pattern. Make it all come to an end.

Jean-Philippe had called on her at her hotel in Paris when she had been at her sickest. He had told her that she needed to take time off from having worked so hard for so long. He suggested a resort in Colorado often used by the executives at Seine-Lafitte where he was sure he could secure a room for her free of charge.

"Take a holiday," Jean-Philippe had said. "Go to Colorado."

She was sorry now that she hadn't taken him up on the offer while the Rosenberg team still had a connection to Seine-Lafitte. The idea was growing more attractive by the hour.

Break the pattern. Or die. "No, not the gardens," she told Jack, "and yes, I'd like company."

Jack shed his white coat. "What do you have in mind?"

"I'd like you to help me buy a car, Jack."

"A car? Now? Have you thought about this?"

"Do you want to help me, or do you want to ask irrelevant questions?"

"Either you're cured," Larry commented, "or you're coming down with something else."

Leaving the lab with Jack gave her a sense of change, but no accompanying sense of happiness. That would have to come later. When she learned to love him, if she could learn to love him, and it wasn't as if he wasn't trying to win her love. He dutifully drove her to a half-dozen used car lots, kept his disapproval of her final choice to himself, and helped her through all the paperwork, although it made him fifteen minutes late for a dentist appointment he had made months earlier.

Before he drove off, she said, "I'm going to write up my latest lab results and send them to you to give to Larry. I don't think I'll come in for the next few days."

Jack looked unhappy with this news, but accepting of it. "What will you be doing, Alexandra?"

"Recuperating, I suppose. From my recent illness."

Val's name hung unspoken in the air between them. "You know I'm there for you."

Dependable Jack. Patient Jack. He'd wait forever. And he might just have to. "I know."

"Will you be going anywhere?"

She had no plans, didn't want to tell him even if she did, since she preferred her own company in her misery. She shrugged. "Depends on how far my car can take me."

BECAUSE IT WAS old and she was a brand-new driver, her car didn't take her farther than next door to Lauri Hopper's house. She tried to do anything that would break old patterns, but it wasn't easy. Whenever she thought of Val or Victor—which wasn't more than fifty times a day—she felt like the butt of the joke of a cosmic sitcom that Erica might have wanted to write. Erica might have said that Alexandra wasn't a love object, she was a love abject, and it took every particle of her strength to overcome the sense of death that hovered.

During his sympathy visit to her in Paris, Jean-Philippe had casually conveyed the news—so apparently happy to him, so heartbreaking to her—that Val and Sophie were getting married. She decided that she couldn't worry at length about the specifics of Val marrying Sophie. She was engaged in a more rigorous, life-and-death struggle to understand what it might mean to acknowledge a man's power in her life without either submitting to him and dying, or resisting him and retaliating. That was the old pattern she knew she must break—Jeanne's relationship to Victor. It was a shameful, delicious sense Jeanne had had of utter enslavement, body and soul, to a man she acknowledged as her master. Alexandra had learned that there was only one position worse for a woman than being a slave to a master, and that was being a slave to a master who divided his mastery, who was not hers exclusively.

Alexandra could not give up on her research. She could not give up her life because her love had abandoned her. She had to buck up. Get on with it. Cure cancer. Let others live, even though she wanted to die.

It was June, and the American Dance Festival, which summered in Durham, was in full season. Alexandra had been dying to see a dance performance, but she honestly thought that she might die if she did see one. She saw that this night was a performance by the Japanese dance pair Eiko and Koma, and they sounded safely and healthily removed from anything in her experience, past or present.

Alexandra considered asking Jack to accompany her but decided that next week was soon enough to learn to love him. She would have given almost anything to have gone to the performance with Deirdre, Nancy, and Louise. She still had Deirdre's Northwestern phone number in her wallet and was tempted to call her just to say hello, but didn't really have the energy for it. She'd call her in a few days when she might feel a little better.

She drove over to campus alone in her new-old car, bought a ticket at the box office in the Bryan Center outside of Reynolds Auditorium, then entered the comfortable theater from the top row at the back which looked down on the stage. In reading through her program, she was somewhat alarmed to discover that *Eiko* meant female and *Koma* meant male. She feared the pain of witnessing the representation of the wrenching twists in the heterosexual divide. Fear of pain turned to puzzlement when the performance started, and the elemental forces of Eiko and Koma appeared. And then appeared not to move at all. Puzzlement gave way to a strange peace, and she was soothed to move herself into the apparent nonaction. She found that her pain dispersed in the infinite dissection of each movement of male and female on the stage, opposed and exposed and gliding in the slowest of slow motion. "Wind" moved across the stage. "Rust" climbed over chain-link fencing.

The house lights came on.

Alexandra joined the crowd going up the stairs and out of the auditorium. Halfway up, she noticed that she didn't have her program. Since she wanted to reread the information on Eiko and Koma, she moved around the people going in the opposite direction to return to her seat. Her program wasn't there, so she climbed the stairs again, eyes on the steps, watching for an abandoned program. The flow of the exiting audience had diminished to a trickle, but a few remaining people were obliged to move around her slower pace. Then, at eye level, her gaze stumbled against a pair of men's shoes.

She raised her eyes slowly, scanned trousers, suit coat. Her heart was thumping painfully, happily. The pattern was repeating itself. The same, hideous, wonderful, enslaving pattern. She marveled to realize how little she had learned, how dazzlingly quick she was to repeat an eternal mistake, for here she was, dying with pleasure to think that she was going to look up and see—

"Alexandra."

"Hello, Jean-Philippe. What a surprise to see you here. I didn't know you were in the States."

"I arrived this afternoon."

"And you weren't too tired to come to a dance tonight?"

"I see Eiko and Koma wherever they perform and no matter how tired I am. Japan, Germany, New York. And now Durham."

Alexandra was impressed.

"Are you alone?" he asked.

She nodded.

"So am I. Would you like to join me for a drink, and we can rehash"—charming smile of apology—"bad company politics?"

She summoned a smile. "All right."

She consoled herself with the thought that here at least was an altered pattern, something new. Somehow, it didn't help her feel less like Val's love abject, didn't make her less drenched with a desire to submit to him utterly if he would only leave Sophie and love her as wrenchingly as she loved him.

FIFTY-EIGHT

JEAN-PHILIPPE HAD determined that most peo-
ple in this world were unlovely patchworks of
conflicting aims and desires. These poor slobs
muddled along in the middle, were content with
a little of this, a little of that, and a whole lot of nothing in particular. They lacked the ability to sort out what they really wanted from
what was before them and within easy reach. They lacked the motiva-
tion and the vision to move in a clear direction and follow the course
to the end. They lacked purity.

Jean-Philippe did not lack purity. And the older he got, the purer
he became. Now, he had always been focused, even as a young man,
but what had been mere ambition early on had sifted, in the full
flowering of his career, into a fine resolve. As a young man, he might
have settled for half-measures, but no longer, and his present position was beautiful in the degree to which it allowed him to remain
immaculate of compromise. His recent conversation with his soon-
to-be-former colleague had clarified the progress he had made on
his personal quest for purity, for during it he had become aware that
the hatred he had once felt for Robert Dorsainville had been but a
motley ore from which he had mined the pure, unalloyed loathing he
now felt for Robert's son.

Jean-Philippe felt as if some essential, previously missing part of himself had been returned to him. But no, it wasn't the missing part that had been returned, but rather the missing motive. Jean-Philippe felt, quite simply, that in engineering the absolute destruction of Valéry and all that was associated with him, he was redressing some elemental, intimate wrong. Something on the order of an eye for an eye.

But what part could he be missing, after all?

Not the biblical eye or tooth, certainly. However, the context of the consideration satisfied him that even his pursuit of petty revenge had been purified over the years into a force that resembled divine retribution. Yes, divine. He embraced the thought, for he would not affect the vulgar hypocrisy of those who routinely condemned the possibility of playing God, all the while killing one minute and conceiving the next. For what was taking a person out of this world or bringing a person into it other than playing God?

Of course, these were the same poor hypocrites who muddled in the nondescript middle, had no vision, lacked resolve, and knew nothing of purity of purpose. Their names might as well be Lawrence Rosenberg or Jack Sandifer, for when Jean-Philippe telephoned the lab that afternoon looking for Alexandra, neither one knew where she was or even if she was in town at the moment. But they were happy to speak to him and to accept his apologies for the demise of what had been such a promising project. No, they didn't know when Alexandra would be back. As if they, top research specialists, had no idea how to go about discovering such arcane information.

Jean-Philippe knew. It wasn't difficult, and Sandifer had shown him the way. (This poorly dressed bench scientist had always ranked low in Jean-Philippe's estimation, but he sank beneath contempt when it became clear to Jean-Philippe that he truly knew nothing of the whereabouts of a woman with whom he was obviously and appallingly in love.) First, Sandifer had told him that Alexandra was taking a break from the lab. (Poor dear! Jean-Philippe's heart bled for her!) Second, Sandifer had told him that Alexandra had bought a car and suggested that she might be anywhere on the North American continent. Now, Jean-Philippe, who already knew much of Alexandra's history, did not need special powers to guess that a low-income city girl who was a very new driver had not traveled very far from Durham.

Where to start looking for such a pretty plum? Why, at her rooms on Monmouth Avenue, of course, and with an innocent question posed to her landlady, to one neighbor, to the other neighbor, the deed was done. The second neighbor, eager to be helpful to the inquisitive gentleman with the French accent, informed him that Alexandra was staying with her, intimating that Alexandra was resting up in the wake of the loss of her team funding (the regret over which Jean-Philippe could not express profoundly enough!)—and perhaps Alexandra had another reason for seeking refuge at her next-door neighbor's, one that might be too personal to mention to a stranger on the doorstep. But this so helpful neighbor was more than happy to tell him that Alexandra had gone to the dance festival this evening and that, no, no one else had come around looking for her in the past several days.

He found her after the performance alone—how fortunate— walking up the stairs of the theater, scanning the ground as if she had lost something.

"Alexandra."

She looked up at him, her expression delicately shading from disappointment to relief.

"Hello, Jean-Philippe. What a surprise to see you here."

Only a naive thing who deserved whatever was coming to her (and Jean-Philippe had not yet decided what it was that was coming to her in the end) could be surprised. Only a naive thing would agree to have a drink with him, to follow him to his car, which, he informed her, was parked in the lot on the other side of the gardens.

They stepped out of the Bryan Center into a warm summer night that was heavy with the scent of magnolias and pulsing with crickets. They skirted the floodlit Duke Chapel, its gothic spires thrown high into the dark blue sky. Passed under a quaint stone arch or two. Discussed Eiko and Koma. Crossed the main campus. Found a meandering trail. Came to the wrought-iron gate, nestled in dense shadows, that opened onto the gardens.

There she hesitated. "I've never been here at night," she told him. "It's a hangout for tough townies, I hear, and maybe even drug dealers. Those are the rumors, anyway, supported by an occasional report of evil doing in the newspapers."

He took her hand, tucked it into the crook of his arm, patted it reassuringly. "You doubt my ability to protect you?"

She cautioned, "Everyone has a gun nowadays, it seems."

"Such a violent country you have," he murmured.

They went in the gate, and the gardens closed around them, humid and extravagant. Beneath their feet was a slate-flagged pathway. Above was a canopy of trees and moonlight. The whole was backlit by the gothic wonderland campus behind them.

Strolling through the luxurious dark, he mentioned the financial problems that had arisen at Seine-Lafitte. He didn't dwell on the unpleasantness, but instead moved on to what he would pass off as a more cheerful topic and that was the date of Valéry's wedding.

"It's set?" she asked. Her voice wavered bravely.

He looked down at her. She was such a pretty plum in the moonlight. Such a pretty, pretty plum.

"Deferred," he told her, truthfully.

Why should he lie? The fine young man had apparently fallen prey to the common virus of second thoughts. In any case, he was one of those who evidently lacked resolve and had put off setting the date with Sophie. Now, it hardly mattered to Jean-Philippe when the fine young man married the boss's daughter. The plan was already set for his eventual professional ruin, which would necessitate the complete collapse of Seine-Lafitte. Why, Jean-Philippe might even hasten the day, so that he could produce TEFS entirely on his own. In the meantime, however, the fine young man was determined to be tedious. He had left Paris for North Carolina, and Jean-Philippe guessed he meant to indulge a noble qualm for the way he had treated the poor, suffering Alexandra.

Jean-Philippe had no intention of letting him get near the pretty plum, no intention of letting him hedge his bets between corporate love and cream-pot love. Monsieur le comte could not always have everything he wanted, could he? Women, land—Bergerac land and women, no less—and let's not forget his companies. Or his money. His piles and piles of money. What else? Oh, yes, his horses.

"That's too bad," the pretty plum said. On a hopeful note.

What was too bad? And why was she hopeful about it? Jean-Philippe pulled himself back to the conversation. "Is it, my dear?"

"Usually when a couple decide to marry, they're eager to set a date. A deferral sounds as if one or the other is not quite committed."

"It is a delay, only. Sophie is no doubt making her beloved pay for having strayed recently. Or so it was rumored! But it was also rumored that his little affair was nothing. A peccadillo."

It felt good to punish the pretty plum like this. As if it would make her more vulnerable to him. He savored the word. *Vulnerable*. He decided this should be the moment he renewed his offer to send her to Colorado. To relax. To regroup. To vanish.

"Oh, I see," she said. Pain in every breath.

Everything was perfect. The setting, the mood. He looked about him. They had passed the murky fish pond where fat old goldfish slumbered. They were treading shallow steps flanked by tier upon tier of begonias, thickly planted, and heading toward a gazebo covered in wisteria at the head of the steps. There was no one else around. The field was wide open to him. Or was it more of an overgrown tennis court? How Jean-Philippe relished demolishing Monsieur le comte at his own game. What was the score now? Six-oh, six-oh, and edging toward another six-oh. They were almost at the gazebo. They were passing under a tree. The air was fresh and fragrant.

When he looked down at her again, thoughts of Colorado evaporated, as if he had never heard of such a place. He'd never heard of a place called North Carolina either. They were in a garden, yes, where it had all started, but it wasn't Eden. It was a plum orchard in Bergerac, and he owned it. He *owned* it. Which meant that he had a right to whatever was on that land, and what was there now before him was a most delectable plum of a peasant girl, ripe for the plucking. About to be plucked, in fact, by some young peasant boy who was kissing her, fondling her under her blouse, lifting her skirts. She was responding, all passion.

Banish the peasant boy from the garden. God's divine riding crop helped. Get on top of the girl. Peel away her skirts, peel away her skin. A virgin, yes, yes, yes. So plump and plummy. Feast on her juice. Or was it her blood? More blood. Whose?

She was telling him to let her go. She was looking afraid. She was saying his name. "Jean-Philippe." That was the wrong name. His name was Jean-Marc, and she should be addressing him as Monsieur Lafitte. With courtesy. Respect. Submission. She should not be upright. How could she still be on her feet if he had just screwed his pretty plum under the plum tree? How could she still be resisting him?

He was confused. Tricks of moonlight. His eyes ran red with blood. His legs ran with blood. His blood, not hers. Then it was as if scalding water poured through his brain. Cleansing him of confusion. Purifying him with knowledge. Filling him with purpose as potent and concentrated as the drops of semen he would never again be able to produce.

Hot rage. He remembered the parts that were missing. Saw to it the peasant boy died a cruel death in prison. Never meted out justice to the peasant girl because she disappeared. Quelled the snickers of the neighbors by contracting an illustrious alliance with Odette Gervais. He could still get it up after all. And children? Who needed children? But then Monsieur le comte snatched Odette and all her land out from under his nose, and in him was born a cold desire to destroy everything that belonged to Victor Dorsainville. He would start with the women. Begin by stealing one of Victor's mistresses.

It could only have been divine justice that sent him to Paris, to Montmartre, to the apartment house where lived a little girl named Hélène Bondieu, who sent him to another apartment where lived some no-account café owner. It could only have been divine justice when, on the trail of the mistress to whom Victor was reportedly attached, the door cracked open to reveal a pretty plum of a peasant girl, the very one who had been the cause of his humiliation years before.

"Why, it's Jeanne Lacombe," he said. "From Sainte-Foy-la-Grande. To think that I should find you after all this time."

"My husband is returning home presently, sir," she said formally, as if she didn't know who he was. She began to shut the door. "Perhaps you'd prefer to wait for him outside."

He pushed his way in, slammed the door behind him. "Your husband?" He laughed in her face. She had been Victor's most beguiling mistress, this one!

"Yes, sir, I'm married, sir."

Then looked at her, truly looked at her. And stopped laughing.

She was big with child. Enormous. And she was reported to have been Victor's mistress within the last several months. Divine retribution was his. He could not bring a child into this world, but he could certainly take one out of it. How perfect that it should be Victor's. But why was she still standing? Why was she still struggling?

He smelled her fear, was aroused by it. Derived strength from the perfection of this revenge. The purity of it. Wanted to watch her fall flat on her back. Wanted to see her thudding pain. Wanted to witness the death of Victor's mistress and spawn in a spreading pool of blood.

FIFTY-NINE

ALEXANDRA WAS FEELING more nervous by the second. She didn't like walking through the gardens at night, and she was imagining bogey men everywhere. She had an unpleasant memory of Bob Dembrowski attacking her at Edison Park, but, then, after Jean-Philippe mentioned that Val's marriage to Sophie has been deferred, she had to remind herself that Val was the real bogey man, not Bob. She had never been good at sorting out the good guys from the bad.

It was disheartening to hear herself referred to as a "peccadillo." It was debilitating to be dismissed as a "little affair," a "nothing." She peered into the shifting shadows of the garden. She fancied that she could see the thick, braided branches of the spreading magnolias snarl into wicked knots. When Jean-Philippe patted her hands, her nerves jumped. She forced herself to settle down. She didn't want him to feel her nervousness, because that would make her vulnerable to him . . .

No. The only reason to hide her nervousness from him would be if she had something to fear from him. They were speaking of the glories of the Sarah P. Duke Gardens in lush summertime. Nothing threatening in that. Her escort was completely calm, evidently fearing nothing, not even the possibility of encountering punks with guns. They were mounting the shallow steps that led to the charming gazebo above, mysterious in shadows. They were strolling slowly, slowly.

Too slowly. Alexandra would have liked to move more swiftly toward their destination of the parking lot that lay at the end of the wide graveled path that ran behind the gazebo.

"The blooming of the flowering Japanese cherry trees was extraordinary this year," Jean-Philippe informed her as he looked about him, admiring the beauty of the quiet dark. "Did you come here when they were in bloom?"

Alexandra had not come to the gardens. She shook her head.

"I came several times this spring," Jean-Philippe said. "Once for the flowering of the cherry trees and the dogwoods, and a second time to see to blooming of the"—he paused—"why, my English seems to have failed me. *Glycine* is the word I am looking for. Large bunches of lavender flowers, like grapes. The gazebo was draped in these flowers." He smiled down at her and repeated, "Glycine."

She searched for the word. "Wisteria? Yes, wisteria." She felt a little frantic. "I—we—could we hurry?"

At that Jean-Philippe stopped. They were at the top step, just below the dark entrance to the gazebo. They were standing under a tree thick with foliage.

"It's a pity there are no fruit-bearing trees in the gardens, is it not?" Jean-Philippe remarked. He sighed, wistfully. "Of all the fruit trees in the world, I am sure that my most favorite is the plum tree." He shifted his position so that he was facing her. He moved his hands so that he held her forearms in a light grip. He looked up briefly into the branches above them. "You are fond of plum trees, aren't you, my dear?" He brought his gaze down, looked at her again.

She took a step back. He tightened his grip. Fear burst through every pore, flashed through every nerve ending. Her double visions rushed together so that she perceived the whole cloth of her neverending pattern. She saw her mistake.

"I don't like plum trees, no," she said shaking her head, denying it even while the dimensions of time and space wobbled and warped around her, turning the visible world inside out.

This was the eternal moment of her violation, and they were in the garden of his original sin. The landowner wanted her. She knew desire, but it wasn't for him. That was her gift for another man. But the landowner would always rob her of it. Destroy her gift. Bring her down. Make her a slut. As long as she was weaker than he was. As long as she had no protector.

Where was Jack when she needed him most? Where was Pierre? Where was Bertrand, the one she had been with under the plum tree?

Stay upright. Stay upright. Be strong. Be stronger than you have ever been before. Don't be a fallen woman. Don't fall flat on your back. If no man is there to protect you, do it yourself. Resist. Use force. Use words.

"He should be here any moment," she said. "He is coming home. He's coming back."

Who was coming back? Her husband? It was a flimsy defense. She had no man she could count on.

He laughed in her face. He was stronger than she was.

Erica had said, *This guy is going to be the death of you.*

But Val wasn't the immediate cause of her death. He was the mediate cause. He was the man Jean-Philippe hated so passionately that he would destroy anything that Val-Victor might want or have. But only if what he destroyed was weaker than he was. So that he could be sure of winning. So that he could be sure of destroying. Jean-Philippe—Jean-Marc. The taker. The stealer. The rapist.

He deserved what had come to him. The body-ripping horror of it.

If she could only stay upright. Not fall down. Not let him push her down. There was more at stake now than avoiding a rape. It was her life and her death. She was finally—too late, far too late!—able to sort out the good guys from the bad guys. The bad guy had knocked on her door, and she had opened it, because she was destined to make that eternal mistake.

Think you're destined to find the cure? Val had asked her.

If I live long enough.

Then I wish you a long life.

Val could wish her a long life, but he couldn't give it to her. Only she could ensure her own long life. Only she could desire to live long enough to do her work. To find a way to distribute antibiotics to the prostitutes in Montmartre. She had found a way, but then she threw it away. She had let her love of a man suffocate her love of life, her own and others'. She had let herself die.

The killer's hands wrapped more tightly around her forearms, shaking her violently now. She pushed. Resisted. She feared for her neck. To save her life, she had to get free of her clinging for Val. To unwrap the tendrils that wrenched and choked. To continue to live—here was the paradox—she needed to stop cell immortality. She needed to stop endless cancer. She needed to turn telomerase off in order to bring things to an end. The end. Telos. Create a new ending, one that came to an end once and for all. Smooth out the pattern. Uncling. Unwrap. Unwrench. Live for herself. Not someone else.

She heard her name being called. From a distance. Her breath was coming shorter. Her muscles were failing. Her will to live was flagging. Was it Erica-Charlotte calling to her from another dimension?

You've got to learn to put your visions to work for you, Coach.

If I live long enough!

What's the secret to good—

Jab your knee into the place where he's weakest. Where he deserves to be missing a part or two. Where he lost a part or two a few lifetimes back. You did it to Bob. You can do it again. Or kick him. Hard. Jeanne knew how to kick. Too bad Chérie-Deirdre, Nina-Nancy, and Louise-Louise can't step out of the chorus line and help you to kick. Ohmygod, that's *it!* The best way to turn telomerase off is not to bombard it with radiation but to break the chorus-line pattern of thymine and guanine TTGGGGs. No, not break the pattern. Alter it. It's a matter of life and death. But Jeanne must have wanted to die, which is why she was alone at the head of the line and didn't have her friends with her to kick, kick, kick herself free of her killer. Oh, so you want to live? You want to bring your research to its rightful conclusion? Well, that's something new. But a little late. You know that it's always and forever a matter of—

Timing.

SIXTY

"ALEXANDRA! ALEXANDRA!" VAL was calling louder now, walking faster too. The gravel crunched underfoot, announcing his approach, for better or worse. Probably worse, since this was Duke Gardens after sundown. On a fine summer night, no less.

Definitely worse, when two, three, no, four strapping young men stepped out from the shadows. They were looking for trouble and found him. Damn. He didn't have time for a mugging. He unclasped his watch, withdrew his wallet from an inside coat pocket, handed these items to the punks as he passed by them. He didn't have to tell them he carried his passport and credit cards in a different inside coat pocket. He hoped the cash he had in his wallet would keep them counting for a while.

No such luck. Even punks had their pride.

"You think you the man, huh?"

"You sweatin' us, man?"

"Word."

A fist into his shoulder.

Stopped cold, he had an idea. Looking at each one in turn, he said, "I'm going after a guy in the gardens. He wears a Rolex. See that piece of crap?" He gestured to his watch that one of the punks was now holding. "It's fake," he lied. "Now, the Rolex, it's genuine. So is the BMW 535 in the parking lot behind you, in case you hadn't noticed it. The guy with the Rolex, he owns it, and I wouldn't mind you helping me get his key ring with the automatic opener."

Murmurs appreciative of the 535 were uttered, but the idea was scorned that any of the brothers would have to bother with a key ring in order to steal a car.

"But what I really want," Val said, "is his blood."

They were up for cars and money this night but not for blood, so while they engaged in a professional discussion of the various methods for defeating the security systems of expensive German cars, Val crunched on. Without pausing, he called out over his shoulder, "I hope I'll soon be sending the guy with the Rolex your way. An older gentleman. Silver hair. French accent. Carrying lots of credit cards and no doubt plenty of cash. Don't let him con you into letting him go without taking him for all he's worth."

The idea they would have to be told such a thing was even more laughable than the idea about needing the key ring.

"You have no idea," Val said and left it at that. He walked on, bellowing, "Alexandra! Alexandra!"

He had recognized Jean-Philippe's car in the parking lot, which had elated him but it had worried him too, since he was receiving no response from her. He had learned from Alexandra's next-door neighbor that Alexandra had gone to the dance festival this evening and that Jean-Philippe had come looking for her. Val had been tearing through every parking lot for the past hour and had finally hit on the gardens as a last resort. Spotted la belle BMW. Unmistakably Jean-Philippe's. Hoped he wasn't too late.

Too late for what? Chilling question, because he knew Jean-Philippe was capable of almost anything. Takes one to know one! He himself had been capable of almost anything until not too many minutes before walking into Sophie's Paris apartment, and she had wrapped her arms around him and sighed, "We're going to be together forever, you and me. Forever."

Toujours. Forever. The word had struck him less like destiny and more like doom.

He knew more about forever than most men, and as he unwrapped her arms and told her what he had come to tell her, he noticed that the constant, dull pain in his lower back was easing up. At that moment he had dared to ask himself, What if? What if he was to start over on his patent? What if there was another way to skin a PCR capsule? What if he was to ask someone who might be able to help him think of another way? What if he was to ask Alexandra?

The what ifs had carried him from Paris to Raleigh-Durham to Monmouth Avenue to West Campus to the American Dance Festival to Duke Gardens. His prospects were looking worse by the minute. Victor had been a fool not to have known where to look for Jeanne when she had been right under his nose in her own neighborhood. Val was ten times the fool, because he had been told that Jeanne had suffered a cruel fate but had done nothing to prevent Alexandra's possibly equally cruel fate.

He was running now, his feet spitting gravel. He rounded onto the gazebo, thought it worth a quick look through the shadows and down the terraced steps. He heard a muffled groan come from under a nearby tree. He peered into the darkness and made out the shape of a body of a woman. On her back. A man above her. His hands around her neck. They were not making love.

Too late!

"No!" His feet flew down the few steps from the gazebo to the tree. "Mon dieu, non!"

He didn't know anymore what garden he was in, but it was one that was entirely new to him. Or infinitely old. He grasped the man by the scruff of his neck, lashed him to his feet with the force of one brutal upward yank. Nose to nose with a man he still recognized as Jean-Philippe, he wasn't sure whether his own transfigured emotions or Jean-Philippe's caused his shock at sight of his enemy's distorted features. Either way, he was looking at evil unbound. No restraints.

437

Desires that would fill all available space. Would take the space, make it available. At whatever cost.

His enemy was strong. Arms and legs ageless, already engaged with him, his new prey. Countering him. Maneuvering. Motivated. Aroused from the kill. Ready to kill and kill again.

If Jean-Philippe was going to kill him, Val wanted it to be face to face. No more smiles and handshakes and knives between the shoulder blades. God, it felt good not to have his enemy breathing down his neck anymore. Somewhere at the edges of his consciousness he was aware that the dull pain in his back—his constant companion for the past ten years—was finally and truly disappearing. His movements should have rendered him a useless mass of pain by now, but instead he was feeling more whole by the moment.

His newfound wholeness gave him the decisive edge. He delivered a knockout punch that caused his enemy to stagger back, to stumble up against the steps to the gazebo. Val had the opening he needed to strangle his old enemy, but the look on Jean-Philippe's face stopped him from lurching forward to finish him off. In that fraction of a heartbeat, Jean-Philippe—or whatever manner of creature he was—saw his opening. Turned tail and ran up the steps. Disappeared in the shadows of the gazebo.

Val heard the soft spray of gravel and retreating footsteps. Didn't go after him. Decided to let the four punks roll him. He had more important things to do. He squatted down on his heels beside the motionless body of his lost love. He propped his elbows on his knees and buried his head in his hands. Let the emptiness wash over him. It would take time for the regret and self-loathing to catch up. Head still hanging, he lay a hand on her still-warm brow.

Under his hand he felt her stir. He brought his head up and saw her open her eyes. She blinked once at the ink blue sky above, but didn't otherwise move. Then she said, "Nina shouldn't dance between Chérie and Louise. The sequence would work better if Louise danced between Chérie and Nina. It's a question of timing. Always has been."

A miracle, surely. He was startled, hopeful, but not fully reassured. He bent closer to her. "Alexandra," he whispered, "are you all right?"

"To alter the pattern at just the right time, Jeanne begins at the end of the line, then weaves her way toward the front, just like we used to do in our best numbers. That way, Jeanne will be there at just the right time to turn telomerase off. That's it. Not break the Ts and Gs, but get them to repattern themselves."

Was this some strange postmortem reflex? "Alexandra?"

She rolled over, propped herself on an elbow, looked up at him, shook her head clear. He took her hands in his and pulled her up, taking her entire weight in his shoulders, back, and thighs. Moving upward he was aware again of the strange absence of pain in his back. However, now came as well a more positive feeling of blessed relief.

"There has *got* to be a better way to do science," she said, lumbering to her feet. "The lab has been a dangerous enough place for me in the past few months, but this . . . this is too much."

He didn't think it worth asking her what she was talking about, since it was obviously complete nonsense.

"And by the way," she said, "when are you marrying Sophie?"

Not complete nonsense, but nearly. "Alexandra. You have just had a life-threatening experience. Isn't there something more to the point we can talk about just now? Like how glad I am that I arrived here when I did?"

"Nick of time. Not a moment too late. Not a moment too soon either. So, when are you marrying her?"

"I'm not."

She nodded wisely. "Jean-Philippe told me Sophie had delayed setting the date."

"You have reason to continue to believe anything Jean-Philippe has told you?"

She looked doubtful. "Well . . ."

"I was willing to do a lot to get what I wanted, Alexandra. Almost as much as our good friend, Jean-Philippe"—Val cocked an ear and picked up faint sounds of squealing tires coming from the direction of the gardens parking lot—"who is experiencing car trouble at the moment, if I'm not mistaken." He looked back at Alexandra. She was still ghostly pale. "But I finally drew the line at marrying Sophie."

She paused. "Are you saying that you broke it off with her?"

He placed his hands lightly on her shoulders. "It is a time-honored custom in such situations for the woman to discover that the man does not suit her and to cry off."

"So officially Sophie broke it off, but you refused to marry her. Is that it?"

"More or less."

"Do you also mean to say," she asked, "that you didn't consider it?"

"Only for a minute."

"I don't believe you."

"All right. I seriously considered it for half an hour."

"But—?"

"But it wasn't worth it."

"Why not?"

"You know why not."

"I don't! You're going to have to tell me."

"I will, but not here."

He saw a new life stretch out before him. He experienced internal patterns weave and reweave into a new and different fabric, one that was durable and dependable. This, then, must be integrity. He suspected that integrity might hold a more true and abiding strength than ruthlessness. And his back felt wonderful.

He continued, "Since this isn't the time or place, I suggest we get out of here as quickly as possible. Campus police patrol here regularly, and Jean-Philippe will surely be flagging one down soon. Come to think of it, he looks like the perfect victim of a mugging, and I really don't want to be around to answer any questions."

Alexandra felt herself coming back to herself. Slowly. Piece by fragmented piece. It wasn't easy going to the brink and looking over the edge. The perspective was dizzying. But she still had some of her wits about her.

She asked, "Is your car parked near Jean-Philippe's?"

He affirmed that it was.

"Then we had better leave it there—"

"If it's still there."

"—and go this way." She led him down the steps away from the gazebo. She indicated a side path, one that would angle toward the back of the hospital complex. "Will breaking off with Sophie cause you problems at Seine-Lafitte?"

His response was calm, matter-of-fact. "I believe my career at Seine-Lafitte is over. And if it wasn't before tonight, it is now. God only knows what Jean-Philippe will tell Yves about what happened here—if anything. My unemployment won't be official until tomorrow morning, however. That's when I have my appointment with Yves."

"What will you do?"

"I'm considering my options. Maybe apply to Abbey Labs because I want to stay in diagnostics. But I'd like to determine . . . to what degree I can begin again."

She drew a deep breath and took the plunge. "Sounds like you're a man who has wiped the slate clean."

His laugh was a grunt. "Yes, my slate is pretty clean."

"How clean is it?"

"In material terms, I own an apartment in Paris and one vintage Citroën which is currently in an intensive care unit at my mechanic's."

"And your house in Cary."

"Ah, yes, the house in Cary. Well, the market's good, and it will sell easily, if need be. I've got a buyer for my grandmother's apartment in Paris, by the way, and the proceeds will more or less cover my mechanic's bill. I exaggerate only slightly. Did you know that my grandmother died last week?"

"I'm sorry!"

"That makes my personal slate pretty clean, as well, since there's no one left in my immediate family. You see, then, that I'm free to begin again. Or, at least, to try to do it right. This time around."

Her heart began to thud. "This time around?" She glanced at him quickly, aware that the air was thick and vibrating with that past and all that remained unspoken. "Val, about—"

He didn't let her continue. Instead, he inquired politely, "And how has it gone for you since I last saw you in Paris? What's the state of your slate?"

She realized that what stood between them could not be repaired all at once or even easily. He was right to take it slow. She would do herself and him a favor to be considerate.

"On the personal side," she said, "I'm glad to say that *my* grandmother didn't die. On the material side, I'm not as plump as I was a few weeks ago, but I did scrape enough together to buy a car, which you'll be seeing shortly." They emerged from the darkness of the gardens and came into the sulphurous light of the back of the hospital. "And in Paris I came into an inheritance of sorts."

"An inheritance?"

"Yes! Some ribbons falling to bits, several old ballet programs— very appropriate, don't you think?—let's see . . . a beautiful pen, a marriage certificate—oh!—and a notebook full of sketches by none other than Toulouse-Lautrec."

"*The* Toulouse-Lautrec?"

"The very one, but the subject matter is so unusual that I'm not sure the sketches would fetch much money. I really don't want to sell them, anyway. But guess what they're of!"

"A music hall? A dancer?"

"*Unusual* subject matter I said. Guess again." She pointed the way again. "My car is over there. In the next lot beyond this one. What, no clues to what the sketches could be of? Not a one?" She looked up at him and smiled. "They're of the plum-marinating contraption that you saw in my grandmother's kitchen!"

Val's expression was arrested. "Are the sketches dated?"

"Yes," she said, "signed and dated. Isn't that funny?"

Val's face remained immobile for one more frozen second. Then he started laughing.

She frowned. "I meant funny-strange, not funny-ha-ha."

"It's funny-ha-ha. Believe me." He couldn't stop laughing.

"What is this all about, Val?"

"To think that I have Jean-Philippe exactly where I want him. And to think I was not exactly looking forward to my meeting tomorrow with Yves!"

"I don't understand!"

He controlled his laughter. "You'll get a full explanation. Eventually." Looking down at her, and his expression was an irresistible mixture of wonderment and tenderness. "Perhaps the most amazing thing is that the sketches are not the highest item on my list of things to discuss with you."

Since she was more interested to hear his list of priorities than an explanation of his amusement, she was happy to change the subject. They had arrived at the correct parking lot. She pointed to the second row. "There she is," she announced with a grand gesture.

The lot was nearly empty, so Val had no difficulty determining which car was hers. His expression was of such exaggerated disbelief that it was her turn to burst out laughing.

"It's a '67 Malibu," she said.

"I can see that."

"Well, what did you expect?"

"Not a teenage hot rod." His voice still held a trace of shock when he murmured, "C'est une vraie bagnole." He demanded, "What possessed you to buy it?"

"It's my first car. I had to start somewhere, and I liked the color. You can't tell in this light, but it's sky blue."

He circled the junk heap curiously. "Does it run?"

"Of course it runs," she said haughtily.

He kicked the tires, tested the body with his fist. "How much did you get taken for it?"

"Fifteen hundred dollars. NADA list price. No rip-off. I bought it from an old guy in the neighborhood. It's only on its second engine."

"Ah! Only the second engine!"

She jangled her keys. "Get in."

"Must I?"

"If you want to get anywhere in the next few minutes." She pried open the driver's side door and crowed with pleasure when a beautiful realization sank in. "Our slates are wiped clean, and I'm in the driver's seat! This is certainly a refreshing change for the better."

Val slid into the passenger side. "You sound happy about what you perceive as my newfound poverty."

She revved the engine. "Let's say I'm not unhappy about it." Seeing him eye with distaste the state of the vinyl seats, she accused, "You old snob."

"Old habits die hard."

"I know all about the low life, by the way, and can teach you a thing or two. First lesson: Get used to it."

"I have my limits."

"They're about to be tested."

He grunted noncommittally.

She backed out and hit the opposing curb.

"You have your license?"

She didn't dignify the question with a response.

He cranked down the window, stuck his elbow out. "You're safe enough in this tank, I suppose. It's the safety of everyone else on the road that we have to worry about. You took that corner too wide, Alexandra. Now, tell me about those Toulouse-Lautrec sketches."

"What do you want to know?"

"Where they are, to begin with."

"At home."

"Is that where we're headed?"

"That's what I had in mind. Or would you rather drive around to the other parking lot and see if your car is still there?"

"Your place is fine," he said. "For now, I'll simply have to hope that my friends in the gardens preferred a BMW to a Cadillac."

"Still driving it?" she asked.

"I have a week left on the lease."

"And then you turn it back in?"

He considered. "I might buy it, provided it's still all in one piece." He glanced at her. "It's about time I made a commitment to a car. I think you pointed that out to me not too long ago."

"Did I?" she replied. "Well, Mr. Cool, you missed the point of my first lesson. You're still thinking like a big shot."

He didn't respond. They fell silent to enjoy the companionship, the warm velvety air, the rumbling of the old Chevy around them. She pulled up in front of her rooms on Monmouth Avenue. They strolled up the front walk together, side by side, not touching.

When they were on her porch, she had her keys in hand, but before she could open the door, he took her in his arms. He placed a light kiss of peace and respect on her forehead. It felt so good to be held by him that she raised her lips to his. He didn't deny himself what she was offering him, and what began as a sweet embrace shot roots deeper down into what they had both feared and desired most. He was surrendering the old perception of himself that had been altered through her, and she was giving him the part of herself that had been a part of him all along. The kiss threatened to overpower them both.

He released her and managed a shaky, "I think we had better wait for that." Then he took her keys from her unresisting hands, opened her front door, and held it for her to precede him. Once inside, he left the front door open and latched the screen.

She crossed the dark room. "It feels good to be back. I haven't been here lately in the evenings." She switched on a low lamp, bringing into soft focus aged wood, faded wallpaper, luxurious plants, and plump furniture.

"Much better," he said, looking around. "Much, much better."

"Did you go up to—?" she began but couldn't finish.

He nodded and moved into the room. In her presence, in her rooms, he felt his age-old, marrow-deep desire to possess and dominate. When he reined in that part of himself, he was able to let the comfort of her personal space surround him. He was able to recognize that an entire individual separate from himself existed. It was a pleasure to discover that he hadn't destroyed her, that Jean-Philippe hadn't either. She had survived, just barely, on her own. Good girl. The more he relaxed the grip of his desire to possess and dominate, the more he let her survive on her own, the more she was present for him.

"I couldn't bear to," she admitted.

"It's just as well you didn't. I'll tell you about it sometime. But not now."

She gestured to the coffee table atop which sat an ancient notebook with a mildewed cover crossed by an antique pen. "There are the sketches."

"I don't need to see them now."

She said slowly, "There is one signed with the name Victor Louis Dorsainville and dated, if that tempts you."

"Not at the moment. Please remember that the sketches are your property, even though one is signed by Victor, and given that, I'm hoping you'll let me put them to good use." To her look of inquiry, he said, "They clear up some of the patent problems I've been having in the past several months, but in those same months I've also changed my notions of ownership and possession. Of belongings and belonging."

She couldn't resist saying, "You betrayed me."

"You wanted more than I had to give."

"I asked for nothing."

"Except my entire self."

"You never would have married me."

"You pushed and prodded and possessed me in a way I had not known was possible. Why me, after all, Alexandra? I lost a part of myself to you, and I was a man who possessed, never one who was possessed."

"I—I wanted—" she began and stopped when she knew he was right. I wanted the whole of you and more.

She choked on the realization that he was really here in her parlor, the whole man whose integrity had been hard won. She read his expression and needed no further words from him to know that he had crossed painful time and distance to drop his heart at her feet. Now was not the time to lash out and accuse him of having abused her generosity. Now was the time to comfort him as she had always comforted him, but not to cling to him, knowing that their future would be different. That they would finally have a future together, entwined but not twisted.

"I wanted," she said, "to offer you some tea."

He smiled and nodded. He was shaken once with gratitude to be the recipient of her unbounded love. He was shaken twice with profound relief that he had not lost this treasure a second time.

"It's a miracle," he replied, with feeling. She turned away from him. He followed her down the short hallway. "I have a choice between Darjeeling and decaf peach, I believe."

She glanced over her shoulder and caught him at the moment he slid a speculative glance toward her bedroom. She smiled nostalgically. "We've done this before, haven't we?"

"It's a gift to be able to finally do it right."

"And Jean-Philippe?"

"I don't think he'll be coming between us again."

She had her hand on the kitchen switch, but he covered her hand with his.

"Let me turn the light on," she said. "I haven't been here in days, so the kitchen is as clean as it's ever been, and I want you to see it. Last time you were here, it was a mess."

"Last time I was here, you had just baked a plum cake."

She looked at him. He looked at her.

He took a step toward her. She took a step back.

"I'd like plum cake now," he said, moving her out into the hallway.

The funnel of forces started to turn around them, less haunting, more life giving, always mysterious.

"Val!" she chided on a note that was half-shocked, half-seductive. "You said we should wait until—until we've sorted things out a bit."

"I now realize that the stories we have to tell one other are so involved that they'll delay the inevitable beyond the humanly possible."

He backed her up against the door, which opened onto a bower of pillows and fringe, cozy curtains, soft moonlight, and a bed neatly made. The whirlwind picked up, gusted and swirled.

"What if I say no," she said. "Is that the end of it?"

His hand was at the scooped neckline of her dress. " 'The end of it?' " he quoted back to her. "You must be joking."

"No, really, I mean it."

"So do I."

She threatened, "I know the exact spot to attack on your back that will bring you great pain."

"Try me," he challenged.

"Don't tempt me," she said, as she began to fight him off.

"Ah, so you're the ruthless one now," he accused.

"I think I can be, on occasion."

"Normally I'd be glad to hear it, but not at the moment." As if weakened by the mere thought of his poor back, he pleaded, "You wouldn't strike me at my weakest spot."

"I would."

She went for his weakest spot. At the contact he didn't even flinch. Instead he grasped her wrists, thrust them behind her back, and circled them both with one of his hands. With his other, he pulled her to him. When he had her at his mercy, he whispered into her ear, "I forgot to mention that my back never felt better."

"Tough guy," she returned. "Here I thought the terms had been equalized."

He laughed. Tonight he would let her enjoy the fact that his personal fortune had been wiped as clean as his spiritual slate. Tomorrow he wanted her to enjoy the extraordinary fruits of her own great foresight in having preserved the sketches. He wanted to share that good fortune with her.

He kissed her with promise. "The terms have most certainly been equalized."

ABOUT THE AUTHOR

IF YOU WANT to know what lives Jeanne-Alexandra lived after Jeanne Lacombe's death and before Alexandra Kaminski's birth, you'll have to ask their alter-soul, Julie Tetel Andresen, because Julie's earliest infant-toddler dreams were of those interim lives. As a child growing up in a suburb of Chicago, Julie bridged Jeanne-Alexandra's karmically critical worlds by constantly roaming the city's Polish neighborhood and by dressing up as a cancan dancer at Halloween. In college she wrote poems to Jane Avril (Jeanne Lacombe's rival at the Moulin Rouge) and made a pilgrimage to Montmartre, where she confronted all her ghosts for the first time. They are less frightening to her now, and she visits them regularly.

Always one to take a perfectly reasonable idea and push it to its absurd conclusion, Julie perceived the implications of the fully digitized and webbed world we now inhabit and accordingly abandoned her path as a mass-market romance writer in order to set up her own publishing studio. The current incarnation of Johannes Gutenberg, whom Julie has known since her days as a manuscript illuminator in medieval Germany, wants nothing more to do with the latest advances in print technology, since it was only in his previous life that he finally paid off the publishing debt that ruined him financially five hundred years ago. At present, he is an extreme skiboarder in Colorado.

In addition to her career as a romance writer, Julie holds a position as a linguist at a major private university. She describes this double life in her article, "Post-modern Identity (Crisis): Confessions of a Linguistic Historiographer and Romance Writer" in *Romantic Conventions* (Popular Press, Bowling Green State University, 1999). She has recently opened another cosmic suitcase and is sorting through it to write *The Crimson Hour*.